PENGUIN BOOK
NEWS FROM THE CITY

G000167102

Isabel Colegate's novels are *The Blackmailer* (1958), *A Man of Power* (1960), *The Great Occasion* (1962), *Statues in a Garden* (1964), the Orlando trilogy comprising *Orlando King* (1968), *Orlando at the Brazen Threshold* (1971) and *Agatha* (1973), *News from the City of the Sun* (1979), *The Shooting Party* (1980), which won the 1981 W. H. Smith Annual Literary Award, *A Glimpse of Sion's Glory* (1985), *Deceits of Time* (1988) and *The Summer of the Royal Visit* (1992). All of her books are published by Penguin.

Isabel Colegate is married with three grown-up children and lives near Bath.

ISABEL COLEGATE

NEWS FROM
THE CITY OF THE SUN

For here we have no continuing city;
but we seek one to come.   Heb. 13:xiv

PENGUIN BOOKS

PENGUIN BOOKS

Published by the Penguin Group
Penguin Books Ltd, 27 Wrights Lane, London W8 5TZ, England
Penguin Books USA Inc., 375 Hudson Street, New York, New York 10014, USA
Penguin Books Australia Ltd, Ringwood, Victoria, Australia
Penguin Books Canada Ltd, 10 Alcorn Avenue, Toronto, Ontario, Canada M4V 3B2
Penguin Books (NZ) Ltd, 182–190 Wairau Road, Auckland 10, New Zealand

Penguin Books Ltd, Registered Offices: Harmondsworth, Middlesex, England

First published by Hamish Hamilton 1979
Published in Penguin Books 1993
1 3 5 7 9 10 8 6 4 2

Printed in England by Clays Ltd, St Ives plc

In middle age Dorothy Grant was faced with a choice. Two paths were equally open to her. At the same time she felt her good fortune in having alternatives and did not plan to hurry her decision.

These two were not her only possibilities. She might, instead of choosing either, stay at home and look after her mother; she might go back to her job in Florence, which she liked, and her flat there, which she had let on a short lease to an American art historian and could soon recover. She could no doubt, if she wanted to and if she thought it her duty to stay in the same country as her ageing though not so fragile mother, use her by now considerable experience to secure herself a job in London, as an archivist, librarian, researcher, something of that kind; and perhaps live with her half-brother Hector, a bachelor solicitor much older than herself of whom she was fond in spite of their temperamental differences. They might divide his comfortable house in St John's Wood between them; he'd be glad of the company and the diminished expenses. But the other possibilities, the two she felt she ought to consider seriously, both held out the prospect of a closer and more likely to be continuing relationship with a man, and would therefore be more of a commitment, and to that extent, she supposed, more constructive.

She thought about it walking on Salisbury Plain, having climbed the steep path behind her mother's house through a wood of now leafless beech trees to reach the winter sunlight and the open grassland, where all her life she had been accustomed to walk in the clear air under a sky whose immensity invariably induced in her a sense both of harmony and of expectation.

Telling herself that she was lucky to have any choice at her age did not help. She did not believe it, for one thing, for though in some ways—most of them, she considered, quite good ways—she did feel middle-aged, she never felt in the least old, and for another thing consciousness of being lucky to have either did not help her to choose one rather than the other.

She could marry Peter Ridley, who had one leg shorter than the other and ran a printing press. He was younger than she was. She liked him but sometimes found him rather humourless. He had a twelve-year-old son whom it would be no exaggeration to say that Dorothy, who despite her cool exterior had strong affections, adored.

Alternatively, she could accept Guy Thornton's invitation to go and live near him in Wales and become a partner in his farming enterprise. This would, she imagined, involve becoming on some basis or other a partner also in his life, but it was, like so much with Guy, left vague.

She thought that perhaps if one had once been deeply in love with someone one never could see him plain. Guy baffled her. He always had; but he had a kind of charm for her which seemed nothing to do with his qualities, such as they were, and everything to do with his presence. She had loved him passionately once, years ago, right back at the beginning of the war. He had married since and divorced, and no doubt had had affairs since his divorce; she had had affairs too. Everyone knew that people didn't go back to old lovers; but everyone, besides being often wrong, saw things, Dorothy thought, according to too brief a time scale. Five years maybe, ten, but what about twenty years later, thirty, a lifetime? The feelings one would have in that event would be different, not the old obsessional ones; those were for younger people. Or was she fooling herself? Was she pretending to have achieved a quite impossible condition of invulnerability as a prelude to exposing herself once again to a pain whose intensity she had only half forgotten? How cross her father would have been with her.

She smiled, walking briskly in her gumboots along the familiar path towards the distant though clearly defined Marlborough Downs, to think how deeply her father would have disapproved of her, if he had been alive. In his view women hardly had independent existences; they had husbands instead. Neither

2

Peter Ridley nor Guy Thornton could possibly have met with his approval—a bolshie printer without a penny to his name and a ne'er-do-well with a prison record who was probably after her money—how could any daughter of his have come to such a pass? How, stranger still, could she be glad of it?

She had reached a part of the steep northern escarpment of Salisbury Plain from which she could look down over the flat distance of Wiltshire below her. The path she had by habit been following was the one she had always taken when she wanted to walk back to the Abbey by way of the Plain. The road was quicker, but when she was not in a hurry or it was a lovely day or she had the dogs with her she went that way because she liked walking on the Plain. From the point she had now reached she could see below her, emerging from the trees which grew between the small field behind Hamilton's workshop and the beginning of the slope up to the Plain, the conglomeration of roofs and the short tower of the place whose inhabitants—and as much as its inhabitants its own atmosphere, as indefinable and familiar and personal to her as Guy Thornton's atmosphere—were as much as anything surely responsible for her not being everything that her father would have liked her to be. For really most of her education had come from the Abbey; and education, as her father had always said and he was right according to his lights, was a doubtful blessing, especially for women. It was not just a little learning that was a dangerous thing. A lot of learning was dangerous too, and not just book-learning, in the sense of scholarship and fact-finding, but that other sort of learning, that awakening to awareness of more than was good for you, those priorities, values, moral sensibilities, that openness to the possibilities of things; her father was quite right, it was all thoroughly dangerous.

She was too much involved in the Abbey, too much subject to that atmosphere, to be able quite to say what it was—or had been, for it was more or less over now. But though her connection with it had been intermittent and the times when she had been completely a part of it infrequent, she felt—and it was this which she had been trying to explain to Guy the day before—that it was to the Abbey that she owed, not her existence obviously for that was the responsibility of Charles and Nora Grant, but what she would probably have called her real life.

She was nine when she first saw it. She thought it was a ruin. The low winter sun had put everything immediately below the escarpment into shadow and the brightness above and behind made the shadow particularly deep, so that what she was walking towards was at first vague, merging into the field and the trees (she was still half a mile or so away). She could distinguish the broad squat tower whose castellations were outlined against the sky, and as she approached and her view of the buildings became clearer the sun shone through the top windows of the tower from behind, and then through the four big windows of the room which was Fisher's library, so that the building looked like a skeleton or a sham castle. There might be no one there, or someone very strange, or a wounded prince.

She had started out at dawn. It was her latest habit. No one had so far made any objection to these early morning expeditions or expressed any curiosity about them. They did not seem to mind her missing breakfast, but she was always back in time for lunch. Being late for lunch ranked high in her father's list of serious crimes. Her older half-brothers had sometimes offended in this way in their irresponsible teens; severe unpleasantness had always ensued. She was afraid that if once she were to be late for lunch her whole new freedom would be jeopardised, so she was always back punctually even when it meant running the last half-mile.

That winter, the winter of 1931, she often left the house when it was still dark outside. She would have checked her knapsack the night before. It had been one of the boys'. They used to go to Boy Scout Camp in their last years at prep school. She packed and re-packed it many times—candle, matches, string, notebook and pencil, first aid kit, penknife, provisions.

She would have liked a dog to take with her on those expeditions, but her father had said that if she did she would have to keep it in a kennel, and since she felt that that was an impossible condition there was no dog and the new fitted

4

carpets retained their pastel shades unblemished. They had only just moved into the house and there were new carpets everywhere and new paint and quite a lot of new furniture from Maples and Heals and new chintzes from Harrods. Dorothy liked all this newness very much in spite of not being allowed to have a dog.

Her expeditions usually took her up on to the Plain. It pleased her to reach the top of the hill and see the huge expanse of this quite different world in the shadow of which she lived. From the shadow you could not guess, unless you knew, how high and wide and light it was up there, how huge the sky was sometimes when it was summer and all the larks were singing, or what unexpected indentations and small valleys there were, their grassy sides looking from a distance so soft you wanted to brush the back of your hand against them, or how across the intervening lowland you could see as far as the Marlborough Downs, humped up like a smooth beige bolster with creased hollows as if two giant heads had rested there, or how the ancient pathways criss-crossed the expanse of the Plain like memories. Sometimes it was too windy to stay up there for long and in the winter it could be icy cold. Sometimes too if the wind was in the wrong direction the firing from the Army ranges could sound uncomfortably close. Generally speaking, though, it was a good place to walk.

The day she first knocked at the door of the Abbey was one of the days when it was too windy to stay long on the Plain. She turned back, and instead of going down the path by which she had come, she took an earlier path, thinking she would walk home along the road at the bottom of the escarpment, which might be sheltered from the wind. She had not been that way before, and following the path down one of the steep recesses of the land where the narrow inlets of greensand infiltrate the chalk down, making all the northern face of it like a coastline worn by the sea, she found herself on an unfamiliar road. After walking along it for some way without seeing any familiar landmark, she began to look around for someone of whom she could ask the way to Winterstoke. She was very thirsty and her watch had stopped at half-past ten. The horror of the possibility of being late for lunch made her walk faster,

A*

and it was then, as she approached the deep shadow at the bottom of the hill, that she made out the shape of the group of buildings which constituted the Abbey, and walked towards it.

As she came nearer and saw that it was not a ruin, her next thought was that it must be a church, but then she came nearer still and saw that there were several other buildings, less ecclesiastical in appearance. The tower had in fact belonged to a church, but the nave had fallen down, and at this time there were still heaps of stone lying about, and occasional broken pillars and tops of gothic windows and tiny pieces of stained glass. All that changed over the years. The slow labours of the inhabitants smoothed the rubble, rescued such remnants of architectural ornament as remained, spread soil, grew grass, and fostered creeping plants and musk roses and a form of purple flowered potato that grew to a tremendous height on the north-facing wall. Hamilton Whitehead fitted together some of the many hundreds of pieces of coloured glass which lay among the stones. For years the pieces lay in his workshop, spread out on yellowing newspaper among the other oddments he collected, stones of strange shapes or colours, broken pottery, flints from the prehistoric encampments on the Plain, bunches of dried herbs, rusted carpenters' tools and stiff unusable paintbrushes. The sun through the window of the little stone building which, before it became Hamilton's workshop, was Father Augustine's cell for solitary meditation glinted sometimes on the half-finished puzzles and made them look precious, which they were not, being weakly executed pieces of sentimentality, memorials to the appalling taste of Father Augustine, the fraudulent 'monk' who lived in the Abbey around the turn of the century.

Every least relic or piece of evidence about Father Augustine was lovingly sought out and cherished by Hamilton, the youngest of the three Whitehead brothers. His book *Father Augustine and the Order of the White Rose of Winterstoke, a Memorial*, was published at the beginning of the war and sank without trace. Not many of its few readers were able to appreciate its subtlety.

There were several separate living places within the group

of buildings. Already by the time of Dorothy's first visit those that were habitable were lived in by contributing individuals or families, on a basis which varied according to whether Fisher's anarchistic principles, Arnold's co-operative socialism, or Hamilton's Epicurean despair, was in the ascendant at the time of the inception of the tenancy. This, together with the fact that the three were referred to locally as 'the Whitehead brothers' which was not always understood by those who did not know them to be a simple statement of consanguinity, meant that, at any rate during the early years there, the general impression in the district was that they were running some kind of religious community, and when young girls were seen to be coming and going, which happened not infrequently, this was taken as evidence of orgiastic goings-on, and only to be expected.

Dorothy knew nothing of local rumour, but the house looked forbidding to her that morning all the same, and the neglected grounds struck her as strange, used as she was to the immaculate gravel and clipped grass edges of the drive at home. She decided to go round to the back, since in her experience servants were kinder at the back door than at the front. She walked rather quickly past the front of the house and followed the drive round to the back, but before she reached the door it was opened, and a number of dogs came out who, surprised to see her there—since they had been let out only in the ordinary course of events and not as guard dogs, in which capacity they were anyway erratic—began to bark with extra enthusiasm to make up for not having known she was there. In the next few minutes an awful lot of people seemed to be shouting and Dorothy would probably have run for it if a firm hand (Fisher's) had not seized her by the arm and pulled her into the kitchen. Once she was inside at least the dogs stopped barking.

The kitchen was big, but even so seemed crowded with people and things. Dorothy, embarrassed already to have caused such a stir by her arrival, was further embarrassed to find that she could not tell which were servants and which were not. She was afraid she might reveal this lack of perspicacity by some inappropriate action which would expose her to ridicule, or to the sort of comment she had heard her mother make about people who had visited them and not behaved properly—'rather an odd sort of person, she seemed to have no idea . . .'—which meant of course that the person she was talking about was common, and that was not so much a bad thing to be as just an agonising thing to be, a condition of eternal embarrassment, a condemnation to a lifetime in a terrible unfamiliar world where nothing was done as it should be done.

So she stood stolidly in the middle of the kitchen with her knapsack and her boots and a rather red face and hoped they would not think her common and wished they would not all talk at once.

Having got her inside and silenced the dogs—a motley collection of mongrels—they seemed to have forgotten her. There was baking going on; a delicious smell filled the warm kitchen, and one end of the long table was covered with loaves of varying shapes waiting to go into the oven.

Fisher was saying that his liver was a filter. He obviously was not a servant. There could hardly have been imagined a person whose demeanour was more lacking in deference.

'Every poison you put into my food is arrested by my liver and there causes me the most violent distress in the short term and in the long term a hideous death. I hesitate to believe that this is your conscious aim.' He had a light-toned but resonant voice which could carry far without apparent effort and was one of the reasons for his popularity as a lecturer. He claimed to have inherited it from his Welsh ancestors but his brothers denied that he had any. 'The currants,' he now interrupted himself. 'The blackcurrants. Have we done anything about them?'

A pale young man said he had ordered them and Fisher went back to his complaint about being poisoned, which had arisen because he had come across some little bottles of artificial flavouring on the big oak dresser which covered most of one wall of the kitchen.

One of the women in white aprons at the kitchen table said in a gentle voice, 'We never use them, you know,' and the other said, 'They ought to go in,' meaning the blackcurrant bushes. These two were Mrs Trew, the wife of the cowman, and

8

Marjorie, Arnold's wife, an expert cook. The pale young man, who was keeping as close as possible to the stove because he was always cold, was Timothy Moore, Fisher's secretary and somewhat confused disciple. The girl who was crouching at his feet was Hilda, a short story writer who as well as being always cold was always tired, but she had an inferiority complex which made her feel unworthy of sitting on a chair, and so her most usual position was a squatting one on the floor. She was a source of endless irritation to Marjorie who was never either cold or tired and certainly did not suffer from an inferiority complex.

Arnold had smelt the baking and had come into the kitchen too, feeling hungry. One of the things he loved about Marjorie, and there were many of them, was her cooking. Arnold looked less distinguished than Fisher his elder brother; though handsome too, he struck a note of reliability rather than romanticism. Hamilton the third brother was not there. He was in his workshop, still muttering crossly about the noise the dogs had made.

'I thought it was ulcers,' said Hilda dreamily from the floor.

'It is ulcers,' said Fisher. 'I have duodenal ulcers and I have a bad liver. How my temperament remains so consistently sunny is a matter for wonder. Have I told you my theory about the liver and the creative process?'

'Yes,' said Arnold.

Marjorie had gone out of the room, wiping her floury hands on her big white butcher's apron and now came back with a glass of lemonade which she gave to Dorothy.

'My own special recipe,' she said, smiling at her. 'It's very thirst-quenching.'

'Thank you,' said Dorothy, taking the glass from Marjorie's clean reddish hand. It was a working hand, but was she the cook? Her cheeks were red too, her hair light brown, with wisps at the side which had escaped from her bun. She had a snub nose and a friendly expression.

'Is this a school?' asked Dorothy. She thought Marjorie might have been cooking for a school, which would be not quite the same as being an ordinary servant.

'My brother would like to make it one,' said Fisher.

9

'Not really,' said Arnold.

'We are all didacts,' said Fisher.

'Where do you go to school?' asked Marjorie.

'I have lessons at home.'

'With a governess?' asked Fisher.

'Yes.'

'And with other children? Brothers and sisters?'

'No, just me. My brothers are older. They're my half-brothers.'

'Who do you play with?' asked Fisher.

Dorothy went red in the face. 'I like being by myself,' she said. She hated admitting she had no friends.

'So do I,' said Fisher. 'But not as much as my brother. Not this brother but another one. He likes being by himself so much that sometimes we don't see him for days on end.'

'We only know he's still here because food disappears from the larder,' said Marjorie.

Dorothy smiled at her. She thought they all seemed very friendly, although Fisher was alarming: so much feeling seemed to come from him it was as if there must be more than one person there. He was very tall, for one thing, and had a lot of dark hair, greying at the sides, and big dark eyes.

'Where have you come from?' he asked.

'We used to live in London.'

'No, but today?'

'Oh. Winterstoke. I was going for a walk but it was very windy so I came down to go home along the road, but I wasn't sure which way to go when I got to the bottom of the hill.'

'You like walking on the Plain, do you? So do I,' said Fisher. 'What did you see today? Hares?'

'Nothing much, it was too windy.'

'Do you often go up there?'

'Yes.'

'I shall lend you a book. Wait.'

He went out of the room, and then Dorothy remembered to ask the time. When she was told it was half past twelve she was horrified.

'I'll have to go. I'll be late for lunch.' She made for the door without waiting for the book.

'One of us will take you back in the car,' said Arnold. 'Don't worry.'

'Oh no, really, if I go now it'll be all right.'

But Fisher had come back with the book, *A Shepherd's Life* by W. H. Hudson. She could not listen while he told her about it because she was so anxious about being late.

'Timothy will drive you back,' he said. 'Don't worry.'

'It's very kind of you.' But she was unhappy. Would it be all right to be driven home in a car by a stranger? What if they saw her arriving? Would they be cross?

'When you've finished it bring it back and if you've liked it I'll lend you another,' said Fisher. As he had said, they were all didacts.

'Thank you,' she said politely. 'Thank you very much.'

Timothy drove her home. He was not interested in children. He told her he hoped to go to Russia soon. He said Russia was the best country in the world. When he had dropped her at the back door she ran in as quickly as possible and went to wash her hands for lunch, but at lunch her father said, 'What was that car that drove up, just before lunch?' and she had to tell her story.

'How kind of them to send you back in the car,' said her mother. 'You mustn't wander too far away though.'

'I don't usually,' said Dorothy.

She thought that was going to be all, but then she saw her father's face. He was going up to London that afternoon and he was wearing his City suit, which was dark grey with a pin-stripe, double-breasted. He looked authoritative in his City suit, and prosperous, which he was. After twenty years of hard work in a company manufacturing chemical products in Elstree, he had found himself on the losing side in a boardroom power struggle; after a takeover he found himself without a job but with a reasonable sum of money in compensation. This sum together with the profits he had made through having always been a shrewd investor on the Stock Exchange, meant that he could afford to buy a nice house in the country and only spend three days a week in his London office—he had set up a small firm of investment consultants. At this time he was wondering whether living in the country might become a bore. He did not hunt, although he did shoot, and he had rather expected that his wife, who was better connected socially than he was, would have done more about getting them accepted into local county life. In fact as it turned out he need not have worried; in due course the county accepted them and they took what seemed to him their rightful places in society, but in these first years he was impatient and found that he looked forward each week to the return to London, to getting a few things done in the office and hearing what the chaps were saying in the Club; with his City suit he put on an extra briskness, an extra certainty of the rightness of his own opinions.

He had an opinion about the Whitehead brothers. He had heard talk of them at one of the few local dinner parties to which they had been invited. When he realised where it was that Dorothy had been that morning he assumed a very serious expression and said, 'You are never to go there again.'

'Why?' Dorothy asked, in a curious rather than a rebellious spirit.

'I'd rather not say.'

'Oh Charles . . .'

Nora Grant was nearly twenty years younger than her husband, and his second wife. She had soon come to believe that the first, who had died, had really done it all much better than she herself could ever hope to do—three sons, a bit of money, embroidered chair seats—Nora Grant could never match all that. The nervous only child of a father who had died when she was a baby, she had been kept firmly under her handsome mother's thumb until her rescue by Charles Grant, the self-confident widower. 'A business man,' her mother had said scornfully. 'His people were nobodies.' That was because of the Dorset relations in the shadow of whose propertied wings Nora had grown up, though she had only met them once before they came to her wedding. 'I suppose he's better than nothing,' her mother had said, lashing out unkindly in her distress at losing her docile daughter. She had not shaken Nora's determination—Charles Grant was Nora's ideal of a mature masculine man, an ideal not so much attractive as absolutely necessary—but she did give her a feeling of guilt which she never got over at having left her mother alone in the little house in Kensington with only the succession of cross maids and crosser Pekingeses and the visiting Major and the bridge evenings. Guilt came very easily to Nora Grant. She was afraid she might have to feel guilty about Dorothy's expedition, which was why she looked flustered.

'Do tell us why she shouldn't go there, Charles?'

'I happen to have heard a thing or two about that establishment, that's all.'

'What sort of thing?' asked Nora, duly alarmed.

He frowned at her and shook his head, not wanting to say too much in front of Dorothy.

'Undesirable,' he said.

Dorothy was sorry to hear it, because they had seemed nice though a bit odd; but she had no doubt that her father was right, because he always was. She did not want to know in what way they were undesirable because this might make her feel sorry for them: she hoped not to have to hear anything more about them.

But her mother was still looking puzzled, and her father, feeling obliged to make himself a little clearer and searching for something that would make his wife understand most easily how absolutely out of the question these people were, shook his head again and said quietly, 'Free love.'

Dorothy did not know what free love was, but apart from anything else it sounded horribly embarrassing. How on earth was she going to return the book without meeting any of them? Perhaps she had better post it.

That night Marjorie told Arnold she was going to have a child. The wind was still strong outside. It seemed to blow straight through the windows of their little unheated room at the top of the house, but in the big bed under the duvet which they had brought by car all the way from Switzerland they were warm as toast. It was in Switzerland that their love had first been consummated, under another such vast duvet, and since sex was to them an act of worship, of each other's bodies and of the life that informed them, the bringing home of such a reminder had seemed, for all that it was lightly undertaken, a sacred duty. Marjorie had been working in a Rudolf Steiner school for mentally retarded children and Arnold had spent

13

some weeks there studying the school's methods for a book he was writing on educational theory. He was nearly forty and had never met anyone as spontaneously loving as Marjorie; it was a surprise which he never quite got over.

Now he lay with his head on her stomach, which in its softness and smoothness and warm smell was like an egg fresh from the straw under one of the Rhode Island Reds in the farmyard.

'A child. What a responsibility.'

'Not really. I'll look after it.'

Some of her long brown hair, which she let loose at bedtime, was on his face, because they were curled round each other like interlocking embryos, her legs being round his waist and his knees touching her buttocks. He blew the hair away, and pushed his face more firmly against her flesh. They both thought of the child. They thought it should grow untrammelled, only protected from the encroaching undergrowth of superstition and convention. They thought of the fresh vegetables and wholemeal bread they would give it, and of how they would let it make its own mind up about God. They did not need to voice their thoughts, because each knew the other's, and that they were the same.

Fisher and Hamilton, theoretical libertine and actual celibate respectively, thought the relationship between Arnold and Marjorie faintly ridiculous.

Timothy Moore had written to Fisher after one of the latter's lectures. Timothy had just come down from Cambridge and was looking for a job: he was interested in politics and journalism. He went to one of Fisher's University Extension lectures in London.

At this time Fisher was having a good deal of success as a lecturer. His reputation had been founded in America, where he had done two highly successful lecture tours in the late twenties, but even in England he was becoming quite well-known, although the established seats of learning still looked at him askance, because he did not fit into any of their known categories, and there were some people among those in authority at such places who thought him either dangerous, or a char-

14

latan, or both. His choice of subjects for his lectures was eclectic. He could do Dostoievsky, Machiavelli, Cooking, Kropotkin, Godwin and Shelley, Marx or Bakunin, the English Novel, Lost Causes or Happiness. As a matter of fact he could do anything. He had such a fund of ideas, not to say passionate convictions, that any subject could easily become a focus for them, and the underlying song was the song of freedom, of the natural human heart, morality without obligation or sanction, mutual aid without government interference; it was a song which had much appeal for the young and optimistic.

Timothy Moore was young but he was not really optimistic. He thought that huge changes were about to take place in the world. He believed these changes to be inevitable and he thought of himself as being on the side of history; but at the same time he was afraid of the coming revolution, and afraid that under the new scheme of things he himself would not manage any better—would not, for perhaps that was what it really came down to, be any better liked—than under the old. He was a member of the Communist Party; and had thought when he wrote to Fisher and asked him whether he needed any secretarial help that Fisher too would probably be a Party Member; it had been rather disturbing to find out that the Left to which Fisher's politics apparently belonged did not seem to be the Communist Left.

Another thing which bothered him about Fisher was the latter's earthiness. The morning after Dorothy's first visit, for instance, he was working in the kitchen garden with Hilda. Everybody was supposed to contribute a certain amount of manual labour towards the maintenance of life at the Abbey, but Timothy had so far managed to do his share of work indoors because of feeling the cold so acutely. Today, however, he and Hilda had been detailed by Arnold to spread manure on the cabbage patch, and wrapped in jerseys and overcoats, college scarves and woolly gloves, they were somewhat half-heartedly doing so. Overlooking the cabbage patch, surrounded but by no means concealed by thyme and lemon-scented balm, stood a misshapen little stone figure with perfectly enormous genitalia.

'It's Fisher's god,' said Hilda, seeing him looking at it.

'Priapus. A scarecrow and a guardian and a god. That's how they used it in ancient Greece, he says. I don't know where he got it from.'

Timothy laughed shortly through the scarf that covered his mouth. Fisher would, he thought. But why did Hilda know so much about it? Hilda came and went from the Abbey in rather a mysterious way: her presence or absence seemed so much taken for granted as to be unworthy of comment, and she herself was uncommunicative about her personal affairs though friendly enough otherwise in a dispirited kind of way. He found her attractive, and was annoyed at the thought of possible connections between her and Fisher and Priapus. He could not help wondering what intimacies were implied. Was Fisher similarly endowed, did Hilda know it? It was not the sort of thing you wanted to think about, particularly if, in spite of being twenty-two and having come down from Cambridge, you still had spots.

Arnold meanwhile was complaining of Fisher too but on different grounds.

'He can't organise,' he was saying to Hamilton. 'That we knew. But what we underestimated was his capacity totally to disrupt other people's attempts at organisation.'

Father Augustine's cell was a castellated pillbox with lancet windows and a gothic doorway, more like an eighteenth-century garden folly than anything so serious as a monk's cell. Hamilton spent a great deal of time there sorting through Father Augustine's papers, sheaves of which had been found in the Abbey when the brothers bought it. He was interested not only in Father Augustine's religious community, which had never been officially recognised by the Church of England to which he claimed to belong, but in the Father's researches into the much older community which had built the Abbey.

There was a chance—and it was one which Hamilton cherished—that these original founders might have been not quite orthodox either. The record of the foundations of the order was obscure. Some time in the late thirteenth century, a local grandee (but it was said that the Black Prince himself was involved) made provision for a college of twenty brethren

16

and a rector. Of the original buildings there remained the tower, the ruins of the church and some parts of the house which adjoined the tower and which was substantially altered when it was turned into a farmhouse after the dissolution of the monasteries. The remainder of the buildings round the big courtyard at the back of the house were built over the years to accommodate the needs of the farm, which at one time would appear to have been large and prosperous. In the late nineteenth century it was bought by a rich American lady as a gift to Father Augustine, her spiritual leader.

One of the garden walls bore evidence of having once been a cloister wall, and Hamilton claimed that certain just discernible relics of old frescoes which he had found there bore out his contention, based on his other researches, that the original founders of the Abbey had belonged to the order of Bonshommes and came from South-West France. The likelihood then was that they were heretics, of the sect of the Albigensians or Cathars, possibly supported by some figure of influence in their own country who, when the persecutions in France became too intense, arranged for an English sympathiser to offer them patronage. Hamilton was temperamentally drawn to any faith which ascribed equal if not superior powers to the spirit of evil as opposed to the spirit of good; the idea that the harsh faith to which the Father's more illustrious namesake St Augustine had in his youth adhered might have endured in this quiet countryside in the shadow of the Plain seemed to him a satisfying one. His brothers, while not sharing his enthusiasm for that particular heresy, agreed with him in finding it appropriate that they should be living where heretics had been before them. It was their rejection of current orthodoxy—political, social, moral, rather than specifically religious—which had brought them there, and it pleased them to think that they were not the first of their kind.

Hamilton, listening to Arnold's complaints about Fisher, had turned from his notebook to the assortment of tiny pieces of coloured glass which were spread on old newspapers on the workbench under the window. His short fleshy fingers moved gently among the pieces as he listened. The blue sleeve of a Madonna was slowly materialising. Her head, inclining at an angle suggestive of a dislocated neck, was already in place. Hamilton's fingers moved ceaselessly as if he were reading Braille.

Only his fingers were short: like his brothers he was a big man, less tall than Fisher but more solidly built. Since the age of twenty-five he had been white-haired. His face was more fleshy than either of his brothers.' It could just possibly have been a woman's face, some matriarch of an old gypsy line, with deepset dark eyes, a big mouth and an aquiline nose. It could look tragic, but more often bore, as it did now, an expression of deep kindliness.

'I thought I knew what I was in for,' Arnold was saying. He sat on a stumpy stool leaning against the wall. There was only just room for both of them in the little building. 'I hadn't counted on the effect he has on other people.'

Hamilton smiled. 'The new Christ boys?' he said.

'Or whatever they are,' said Arnold. After a pause he said, 'And girls.'

'Don't we depend a bit on Fisher's disciples? Their labours of love?'

'Labours! If only they would!'

Hamilton continued to smile. There was only the sound of the little pieces of glass being pushed slowly across the newspaper. Arnold felt a lightening of his burdens, as he always did when he came into Hamilton's workshop. It made it easier to talk about them.

'When I said I'd come and run the farming side, I didn't expect to be landed with all the financial organisation of the whole project. Let alone everyone's personal problems. Marjorie's wonderful at sorting those out but it's very exhausting for her. People can be so demanding, and now that she's pregnant I don't want her to have too much to worry about. I sometimes feel that if only they'd work a bit harder one could feel more sympathetic about their emotional tangles.'

'They come from the wrong social class,' said Hamilton. 'Can't you get hold of some simple sons of the soil?'

'Sons of the soil, like other sons, can't wait to get away from father,' said Arnold. 'I've a feeling one has to wait for
18

the grandsons. Trew has found a village boy who wants to come here when he leaves school. He sounds hopeful. Trew and Mrs Trew are both great standbys of course, but I'm rather pinning my hopes on the couple who are coming next month. I think they might stay. The young people just pass through, pass on; that's as it should be I think, unless one should happen on the odd one who wants to make a life work of it. Even then he ought to go elsewhere, start his own place. But a few more middle-aged people will give stability. And this man Maiden, who's coming, should be able to give me a hand with the accounts.'

'She had a wild look in her eye.'

'Oh no, do you really think so? I thought she was going to take an interest in the poultry.'

'It may have been poultry she was thinking of,' said Hamilton. 'But I doubt it.'

'What then?'

'Young men,' said Hamilton in a doleful tone.

'Blast! You're always right about that sort of thing, too.'

'It may work out all right even so.'

'No, it won't. The husband won't like it.'

'He might. You never know. He might have been waiting for years for someone to take her off his hands. And I tell you another thing, which I quite forgot until this moment. I met a very nice man the other day, a local schoolmaster. We got into conversation in the Public Library—we were both looking for the same thing. Apparently he does quite a lot of local history with the children—that inclined me in his favour of course. Anyway he asked me if I'd go and talk to them about the prehistoric things on the Plain, and then, what with one thing and another, by the time we'd got that arranged I'd told him a bit about this place, and I had a sort of feeling, though I may be wrong, that he might like to come and live here with his wife and two children, keeping on his job of course but contributing in his spare time. You might like to meet him some time.'

'You didn't see the wife?'

'No, but the children are a good age, not so young as to prevent her from being any use for anything else and not old enough to be as tiresome as adults. Eight and ten I think he said, the best sort of age really.'

Arnold smiled. 'It would be you, who are supposed to be a recluse, who make the first proper link with the local community. It sounds an excellent idea. I've always liked the thought of some people going outside to work so that we don't become too inward-gazing. That's the thing that worried me from the start. When Fisher first began to talk about it I said, I don't want to retreat from the world, I want to be in the world.'

'He likes the idea of the illuminati, the little groups setting the example.'

'Yes, but where are the other little groups? We ought to be in touch with them, however differently they may be run. We ought to meet, have conferences.'

'Yes, you'd like that. A proper conference, with an agenda and all that. You'll have to keep Fisher out of it, though, or he'll take it over and turn it into a Revivalist meeting about something quite different.'

'Fisher has his own life in the outside world, through his lecturing and his literary life and all that. He doesn't feel any need for the community to be more in the world.'

'One thing I can tell you. If we get more in the world I'm off.'

'Oh Hamilton, you know you don't mean that. You couldn't go back to that water-logged shack.'

'I was very fond of my little house.'

'You'd have died of rheumatic fever if you'd stayed there much longer. I don't know why you'd never let anyone look after you there. I wish you'd get a woman, Ham. I know it's boring when people think the solution for everyone is the same as it is for them, but it is so nice having your person, you know, of the opposite sex. It completes you, fulfills so much. I don't believe you've even been to bed with a woman have you?'

'I have not,' said Hamilton, his fingers moving gently over the glass fragments. 'Most decidedly not.'

'I don't know how you can say decidedly not when you've never done it,' said Arnold.

'If I did,' said Hamilton calmly, 'I should certainly kill her.'

'My dear old thing!' Arnold slid off his stool, and putting an arm around Hamilton's shoulders gave them an affectionate hug before with his other hand picking out a piece of blue glass and trying to add it to the half-finished sleeve: it did not fit.

'No good,' said Arnold. 'You've got a life's work here you know.'

That his brother might be a potential murderer should have been inconceivable, but it was not—not quite. Hamilton's periodic moods of impenetrable blackness were perhaps better left unexamined.

Dorothy read *A Shepherd's Life* quite quickly so as to be able to return it and get the whole thing over. She was a conscientious child, and it would have seemed to her wrong to return the book without having read it, even had the idea occurred to her; but she found some parts of it rather boring and thought perhaps it was too old for her. She did like the stories about sheep dogs. She thought she would like very much to have a sheep dog one day.

Lessons had started again, with Miss Gamage. She quite liked Miss Gamage, now that she had got over the ghastly embarrassment of having to call her Gammy.

'Miss Gamage sounds so formal,' she had said. 'The Maconochie girls used to call me Gammy.'

Dorothy knew she could never be on such terms with Gammy as the Maconochie girls had been; friends, it seemed, rather than pupils. Elspeth, Jo and Kate they were, they'd been terrible tomboys and now they were all doing awfully well at Cheltenham Ladies College. Dorothy never really quite liked the sound of the Maconochie girls, but she did not say so because she could see that they meant a lot to Gammy, who talked about them often, their high spirits, their brains, the fact that they belonged to a 'very wealthy family'.

Gammy often had headaches and sighed a lot. This was really because she was terribly bored, but both she and Dorothy put it down to the fact that she had been engaged to someone who had been killed in the Great War. His photograph was by her bed, standing to attention with his cap under his arm, his hair, centrally parted, slicked down as if with black boot polish, his face completely round. She had heard him calling her name in the night and when the telegram came she was prepared for the blow. She and Dorothy both thought that her tragedy made her more interesting than she would have been otherwise, and gave her every excuse to have headaches and sigh. The fact that she disliked arithmetic almost as much as Dorothy did was another point in her favour.

Many a time when Charles Grant came back from London his wife would say to him, 'What *shall* I do? Nanny and Gammy are at daggers drawn again' and Charles Grant would say, 'They'll just have to put up with it. If we get rid of Nanny, who's going to look after Dorothy in the holidays?'

'She almost looks after herself now.'

'What if we want to pop down to the Riviera for a few days? We can't leave her alone with the servants.'

So Nanny and Gammy remained at daggers drawn (and without enough to do). Their attempts to conceal their mutual hostility from Dorothy meant that she became accustomed to pursed lips and cross looks, sniffs and innuendoes and doors being shut with significance. None of it bothered her particularly. Only when she saw tears in Gammy's already slightly watery eyes did she feel uncomfortable, and then she would lead the conversation round to the Maconochie girls, which usually worked. Nanny never cried.

One day when both her parents had gone to London, to go to a party, Dorothy had a free morning. Gammy had stayed in bed with a headache. Nanny was so fully engaged in sniffing and muttering and generally registering disapproval and disbelief that she made no objection to Dorothy's leaving the house with her boots and her knapsack and the book in her pocket, although she had been given strict instructions never to let Dorothy go out without first finding out where she was going and telling her what time she must be back.

Dorothy walked to the Abbey by road, which was the quickest way, and kept to the grass verge as she went up the drive, in the hope that no one would hear her coming. There did not seem to be anyone about, but the difficult bit was to open the front door and put the book inside without the dogs hearing. She achieved it, but as she put the book on the table just inside the door, she noticed that there was another book on which lay a note in writing much too large and clear to be ignored. The note said THIS BOOK IS FOR THE LITTLE GIRL WHO BRINGS BACK A SHEPHERDS LIFE AND WHO I HOPE WILL RING THE BELL AND COME TO TEA WITH ME.

Scarlet in the face, she grabbed the note and the book, shut the door as silently as possible and walked quickly down the drive, keeping to the grass again. As soon as she was out of sight of the house she began to run. Ring the bell and go to tea! What a terrifying idea. If he ever asked her about it, she'd have to say she'd rung and no one had answered.

When she was out of breath she stopped running and sat down on the grassy bank beside the road to look at the book. It was bigger than the last one and had rather nice pictures. It was called *Bevis, The Story of a Boy*, by Richard Jefferies. Warm from running and with her feet in the dry ditch, she leant back against the bank and began to read.

Fisher had seen her half-running down the drive, keeping to the grass. Poor little thing, he had thought, what are they doing to her in that rather pretty house? He had had such a happy childhood. He sometimes thought that all they were doing now was to try and recapture it. That it should have been so happy was hard to account for: a mad father and a melancholy mother hardly seemed ideal as parents. It was true that the madness and the melancholy had deepened with the years and perhaps by the time they were severe enough seriously to impinge on the self-contained life of the children, everything had been spoiled anyway, by school.

They were children of the Vicarage. Their father, Frederick Whitehead, came of a family of Trowbridge solicitors. His own father, a tyrant in the home, had decreed that he should go into the Church, being too stupid for the family firm (he was of nervous disposition and read poetry). The alternative to taking orders had been to lose his inheritance, which though not large

23

was worth having. Poor Frederick Whitehead, though a religious man, came to have an absolute loathing for his profession, or rather not so much for his profession as for his parishioners. He had a poor opinion of humanity. The lower orders in his experience were drunk or illicitly pregnant according to age and sex, the upper simply thieves. He was extremely intelligent, though not in such a way as to appeal to his father, for he was not only appreciative of poetry but given to speculative philosophising of a sort which his father was probably right in thinking inappropriate in a country solicitor. Frederick's sense of wasted ability and deep distaste for his work encouraged in him a morbid hatred for his father; he drank too much, he could not sleep, he suffered from periods of intense irritability, and in early middle age there began those occasional attacks of actual mania which continued throughout his life.

During these attacks two male nurses from the local asylum would move into the Vicarage to look after him, this privilege at least being secured by the private income he had hung on to by obeying his father's wishes in his choice of profession. Often before the nurses arrived, and if their mother had been inaccurate in her reading of his symptoms, the children and their mother would have to hold him down on the bedroom floor. Fisher could remember several such occasions, sitting on his father's chest on the faded Turkey carpet with the neatly packed suitcases open all round them (he always packed when he was going mad, day after day sorting, tidying, rolling his socks into neat little balls, shining his shoes before wrapping them in their special cloth covers with red tags to tie them up with, stowing them neatly in rows in the bottom of a suitcase). It was lucky they were all such big strong boys. They took after their mother. Their sister Mary (there were four children altogether) was more like their father, fair-skinned and small-boned.

Their mother Mildred came from a huge family of clergymen, huge both in the extent of the family ramifications and in the size of its individual members. In the downstairs lavatory at the Vicarage were two framed photographs: one was of Mildred's father and his eleven brothers, all of them clergymen or dons and several of them both, and one was of Mildred herself with her sister Faith, who had died as a missionary in Kenya, and their six brothers, of whom four had gone into the Church, one had been a tea-planter in Borneo and the other had been killed taking part in a cavalry charge in the Zulu Wars. The uniformly melancholy intensity of gaze of these twenty enormous people made a visit to the downstairs lavatory in the Vicarage an alarming experience for the unsuspecting visitor. To the children it was just at it should be: both photographs hung in the downstairs lavatory at the Abbey.

It is to be assumed that Mildred Whitehead, like her husband, had her disappointments, but she never mentioned them. When her depression became acute, which it did sometimes (never during her husband's attacks of insanity: she was at her best then) she only became increasingly silent, and though this made her at times rather distant as a mother she never even at her most sorrowful allowed her children a moment's doubt as to the total reliability of her love for them, whether they were good children or naughty children (although they knew that it caused her real grief if they did not read a page of the Bible every night before going to sleep). This was while they were still children: in Mary's case at least, it was different when she began to grow up.

Like her husband, Mildred Whitehead had an unexploited talent. In her case it was for drawing. She had an intense love of nature, and would sit for hours on end in the Vicarage field in front of a cowslip, her board and sketchbook on her knees and her long dark skirts completely covering the low camp stool on which she sat. Her drawings were mainly botanical, extraordinarily accurate both in line and colour. Sometimes when the children were small she would illustrate stories about animals and birds for them. At first it was Fisher who would make up the stories, and then Hamilton; Arnold was never any good at it. Years later, after the Second World War, Arnold's wife Marjorie came across some of the manuscripts of the later stories, dictated by Hamilton to his mother and written out in her beautiful clear writing, interleaved with her illustrations and tied together with faded ribbon. Marjorie suggested that they should be published, and three of them were printed by the Abbey's own press in the early fifties. After that they were reprinted many times, and brought money into the Abbey at a time when it was badly needed. Mildred Whitehead of course had been dead for years by then.

The success of the books would probably have left her indifferent: she had little respect for the opinions of the world in general. That was one of the reasons why she dressed so badly (the other was that she thought herself ugly). She wore always the same immense outfits in thick dark serge, with voluminous long skirts and pockets stuffed with useful things like handkerchiefs and string, sketch pads, pencils, rubbers and razor blades (for sharpening the pencils). She was a good gardener and her hands were not always clean. Mary was a fastidious little girl who grew up to be very pretty indeed. From an early age she was made uncomfortable by those strong, competent, earthy hands of her mother's.

The boys liked earth. To each of them the thought of childhood brought back the smell of leaf mould. The parents, wrestling each with their own difficulties, were in the background. The children's world was the space of the big Georgian rectory, the attics and back passages which their parents hardly ever visited, the wild garden where everything grew in such profusion under their mother's care and where only the vegetable patch was seriously weeded; the orchard, meadow, stream and beechwood, the paths made by the badgers, the dark corner between orchard wall and ancient yew where vows were made, secret societies instituted, discoveries reported on, hard green apples consumed. That was their childhood, knees perpetually grazed and green from sliding down trees, old grey flannel shorts, much mended, faded aertex shirts, in summer the hairs bleached white on sunburnt arms, in winter the thick polo-necked jerseys their mother knitted smelling faintly of woodsmoke, tree-bark and earth. School, as long as it was the village school, hardly impinged: they dreamed their way through, accepted as oddities but respected as physically tough, and drew into their circle Morgan the blacksmith's son who taught them to fish and Bob the publican's son who taught them about sex—five boys on a summer evening under the yew tree measuring their erections with a ruler—but that was after Fisher had gone away to school. He was with them on that particular occasion because it was in the holidays, but he carried with him his burden, the burden of the knowledge of exile.

Mary, their sister, must have always wanted exile. She found it mentally in music and as soon as she was old enough physically in America. She went to study the piano in London and without finishing her course married an American fellow-student and went with him to live in New Hampshire. Fisher visited them there, and met the agent who arranged his American lecture tours: there also were sown in his mind the seeds of the idea which later became the community at the Abbey.

The Maidens too had visited Mary and her philanthropic husband Edwin in New Hampshire. That was how they came to be more or less founder members of the Abbey community. Mary had said to them, sitting at the end of the refectory table surrounded by admiring music students, the sun shining through the big windows of the long white room on to her neat fair hair and impeccable English complexion, 'Oh if you're going back you must go and see my brothers, you'd be so interested in what they're doing.'

'Are they also musical?' Gerda Maiden had asked.

And Edwin, whose motives, for all the widely acknowledged philanthropy, were sometimes mysterious, said, 'You really should go. They may not be musical in the generally accepted sense, but if ever there was anyone who could hear the music of the spheres I'd say it was Fisher. Yes, you should go. I really think Fisher would find a lot in common with Gerda, don't you agree, Mary?'

Mary had looked a little surprised. She had a great capacity for not seeing anything she did not want to see, but even she had noticed Fisher's partiality for pretty girls, especially thin ones. Gerda Maiden hardly came into this category.

'Why yes, I suppose so,' she had said. 'Anyway you'd be interested I'm sure. We'll write you a letter of introduction.'

And then because she felt she might have been guilty of uncharitable thoughts about Gerda, she had written a letter of such warmth to Fisher that he had suggested to the Maidens, with Arnold's agreement, that they should come straight to the Abbey on their arrival in England and stay there as long as they liked.

It was Philip Maiden who had been more cautious and had suggested that they should go down there for the day before committing themselves, but although that day (on which Hamilton decided Gerda had 'wild eyes') left doubts on both sides, Fisher's letter had amounted to an offer which was difficult to retract (he could hardly say, 'Mary should have told me you were fat—she knows I like thin girls', and it was hard to find anything to criticise in her enthusiastic acceptance of the idea of the community) nor did the Maidens want to do anything to offend Edwin and Mary, who had been so kind to them in so many ways.

'What can we lose by spending a few months there?' Philip argued, persuading himself. 'We can say we can't commit ourselves beyond that, because when I've finished my book I may have to do something else to earn a living—something that might mean we had to live in London, for instance.'

They were in bed, in the little hotel in Bloomsbury where they always stayed when they were in London. Gerda would be paying the bill because Philip had given up his job as music critic of the *New Statesman* so as to be able to concentrate on his book about Corelli. Gerda had a small private income because her father had been shrewder than many of his fellow Baltic aristocrats (Gerda was a Baroness) and had invested some money in London years before his exile. Her income had made it possible for them to go to America, so that Philip could spend some time working on his book at the Edwin Price Foundation in New Hampshire. Gerda herself was engaged on her life's work, the complete translation of Kafka. They worked in bed, side by side, surrounded by books and papers. Philip smoked incessantly, Gerda drank herb tea.

'They are not as intellectual as I had hoped,' said Gerda.

'Fisher is very well-read.'

'But he does not want to meet people, to discuss.'

'He says he dislikes London literary life.'

'It is a pity. I could introduce him to everybody who is anybody in that world.'

28

'I don't think that's what he wants. Probably he knows all those people anyway.'

'Not at all, he is completely on the fringes. I could give him the entrée to the inner circle.'

'I know you could. But he despises all that. He wants to be right away from it.'

'I never saw anyone less suited to be a monk. He is sexually attracted to me by the way.'

'Attracted or attractive?' asked Philip coldly.

'Attracted.'

There they sat in bed, with pillows and books and papers strewn all over the place, the stuffy little room full of cigarette smoke, he balding on top, such hair as he had longish, with his glasses, musicological expertise, Cambridge background, low vitality, she fleshy, coarse, overbearing, snobbish, hard-working —he saw it all so clearly it made him feel sick, like certain surrealist paintings which are clearer than clear, or the first sight of home after long absence, when the familiar is seen as strange but endowed with overwhelming significance, a trick of consciousness, not very agreeable. He felt that he was seeing the prison of existence; and that he must wait until his pity for his fellow prisoner broke through his hatred for her.

'It may be necessary for me to surrender myself to him,' said Gerda. 'As you know, my libido is at present unsatisfied.'

'And prowleth up and down,' said Philip softly. 'Seeking whom it may devour.'

The pity had not broken through. He lowered his face onto the rough blanket, which was held up in the middle of the bed by his bent knees, and tried again.

'I have made an appointment for you with Doctor Wiseman,' she said.

'I shall not go,' he said, without raising his head. But he had an awful feeling he would go, would expose himself to humiliation, would possibly cry. How could he do that sort of thing unless somehow he liked it, and if he liked it how could he think of himself as anything but despicable?

'I don't think it's Doctor Wiseman I need,' he said into the blanket, so that he felt his hot breath on his knees. 'I don't think it's Fisher Whitehead either. But it's certainly something.'

Fisher thought it was important that the Abbey should have a guest house. He had in mind something quite spartan, rather like a Youth Hostel perhaps, where visitors could be offered bed and breakfast and would otherwise be expected to cater for themselves, or else they might join the communal midday meal, for even at its most extended the community always took one meal of the day together. It was agreed that the part of the quadrangle of farm buildings which had been stables should be adapted to provide the necessary accommodation. The part which had been stalls was to be turned into a big living-room and kitchen and the hayloft above was to provide two small bedrooms and two dormitories, each with four beds in it.

Fisher hoped that Philip would help with the actual building work and that Gerda, as well as her duties with the poultry, would take on the housekeeping side of the guest house when it was finished. He had no particular reason to suppose that either of them was in the least suited to these functions, but his optimism was at any rate partially justified.

'Maiden will be able to do the drawings,' he said before they arrived. 'The calculations and that sort of thing. Music and maths always go together.'

Philip was at first horrified to find out what was expected of him. He had thought that he was going to spend his time getting on with his book while Gerda made their joint contri-bution to the community, preferably in the form of heavy manual labour which would tire her out and distract her thoughts from her unsatisfied libido; but Fisher's love of building was infectious and Philip began to share his vision of the dark old stable transformed. As it happened, music and maths in his case did go together, and with a good deal of hard work Philip found that he could provide such calculations and drawings as were necessary. By the time the actual building work began he was as keen as anyone to share in it. Fisher said to him once, 'You're over-educated, that's your trouble. You cerebrate too much. Just stop thinking for a bit, especially about yourself.' Philip was still doubtful about Fisher—indeed there was some-thing about him he never did learn to trust—but this piece of advice he took to heart. The building of the guest house took him away from his book, which made very slow progress as a result, but it gave him extraordinary satisfaction and mindful of Fisher's advice he did his best not to examine this sense of satisfaction but simply to accept it. He felt it could not last: for one thing he expected that at any moment Gerda would precipitate some kind of explosion which would mean that they would have to leave.

Gerda took longer to settle down at the Abbey than Philip did. In the first place it soon became clear that she was not a suitable person to look after the poultry because she was a vegan, which meant that she did not approve of eating eggs, let alone the chickens themselves. No one had asked her whether she would like to look after the poultry, but when it appeared that she would not, there was a general feeling that she had failed. She was helpful in the house, but there did not seem to be much else for her to do at first and it was she rather than Philip who spent most of the day working in her room. Her translation of Kafka progressed, but this was not how she had envisaged spending her time. She found the brothers elusive. Hamilton never spoke to her at all and both Arnold and Fisher had a disconcerting habit of walking away in the middle of a conversation. She began to think, rightly, that they were avoiding her. She found this hard to understand. She had envisaged long talks with Fisher, up there in the library with a pot of herb tea between them, talks about love and death and alienation, possibly followed by her surrendering herself to his demands on the nice big sofa that had come from the Vicarage drawing room. The only conclusion she could come to was that he was nervous of the strength of his own desires, and that therefore her best course of action was to be very gentle and calm and win his confidence.

For the first week or two of their stay at the Abbey Gerda was accordingly quieter and less obtrusive than Philip had ever known her, and as a result the brothers, who had thought she was going to be a frightful nuisance, began to revise their opinion. Arnold and Fisher did anyway—Hamilton never really spoke to Gerda all the time he knew her, but then there were quite a few people Hamilton never really spoke to—and when eventually Gerda decided that the time had come to carry her relationship with Fisher a stage further, and presented herself at the library door one morning carrying a tray, he did not react unfavourably.

'How very kind,' he said, getting up from his desk and taking the tray from her. 'Tea?'

'Herb tea,' she said, following him into the room and settling herself down in an armchair. 'Behind your god in the garden I am hoping to grow some more herbs of medicinal value. I don't disturb you I hope?'

'No no,' he said politely, sitting down opposite her and holding out his hand for the cup which she had filled for him. 'I'd nearly always rather talk than work.'

'I too. But I will not keep you long from your work. I have been here long enough now to have one or two questions in my mind which I should like to ask you, and when we meet at meals there are so many other people, and so many practical matters demanding your attention. Tell me, if you please, what is it that you hope to do here?'

'I don't know that I hope to do anything. I think I hope to let things happen.'

'What things?'

He smiled.

'Anything. Absolutely anything.'

He had an attractive smile, which made his rather heavy features look humorous and kindly instead of saturnine.

She smiled back.

'Then this is the Abbey Theleme? Faites comme vous voulez?'

'In a way perhaps. But I shouldn't like to be tied down to a Rabelaisian any more than to any other vision. People must bring their own visions.'

'It was Mary and Edwin who gave you the idea I think. But their's is a simpler thing, because it is a place for music. They can have summer schools, seminars, offer sanctuary to composers who need somewhere to work. Besides, America has a tradition of that sort of community, it has always existed there.'

'Quite. Also it is all based on Edwin's money and here we have no benevolent despot. I think their influence on me was only to show me some of the practical day-to-day possibilities. I had been living, in so far as I had been living anywhere, in London, and I loathed it. I wanted a different sort of life.'

'You could have bought a cottage in a village.'

'In a village you are stuck with the traditional hierarchy of class. I wanted something without a past.'

'But you are mad about the past, all of you.'

'Yes, but not the immediate past,' he said, becoming interested. 'It's the distant past we are all obsessed with. The distant and possibly largely imaginary past.'

'You mean, a lost golden age?'

'Perhaps past, perhaps to come. But not the way we are going. You could say the idea of this place is purely negative. It's just no to England in the 1930s.'

'But then why are you not in politics?'

'Because the change we need is much more than just a change of political structure. The structure doesn't really matter all that much. All that matters is that it should not be totally inflexible; therefore, if you like, it should be complex because complexity leads to flexibility leads to stability. This is as true in physics as it is in human affairs. That's what that poor ass Timothy can't grasp, clinging to the monolith of Marxism as he does. But the real point is that no form of government is any use among bad men, and good men can make use of forms which are far from perfect. And we haven't got good men.' He got up and began to walk up and down in front of her. 'You ask how this place came about. It was like this. I came from nowhere. My parents for sufficient reasons of their own were recluses. We grew up in a vacuum, socially speaking. We went to a bad school, we saw nothing but naked competition there, and this was encouraged. We were encouraged to do each other down by fair means or foul so long as the privileges we were fighting for were the conventional ones. We were taught to stifle the sound of our hearts, despise women and prepare ourselves for a lifetime of bullying the blacks, whether as proconsuls or as missionaries, it didn't matter which. In this system my brothers and I were failures. I went to University. There I found the better minds given over to uselessly brilliant intellectual exercises and to drink and sex. The sex was mainly

33

homosexual because this was still a world almost entirely without women. How clever some of those public schoolboys were! All those classical authors they could quote, those dotty extravaganzas on the meaning of the verb to be, those desperate introspections. All those first novels written to shock Father and cock a snook at school—but how many of them managed to free themselves of Father, forget about school, how many of them grew up? On they went in their little inward-turned mutual admiration society, so sophisticated, so unbalanced, so far from the realities of human existence on this earth. And they were the cultured élite, mind, the favoured ones. Think of the others, think of the dark night of the soul of the conformist others.'

'Well, but the intellectual life of a nation does not depend only on its undergraduate population.'

'Ah, but I haven't finished. I am telling you the story of my life. I became a journalist, in order that I might learn about the society about which I knew so little and in which I felt myself a stranger. I travelled the length and breadth of the land interviewing people, unbeknownst to my editor who was often startled by the articles I sent him and who as soon as he was able to trace my whereabouts gave me the sack. Not before I had made several interesting discoveries.'

'This I like,' said Gerda, nodding vigorously.

Pleased by her appreciation, Fisher resumed his walking up and down.

'What did I find?' he asked rhetorically. 'I'll tell you what I found. Everywhere this divorce from reality. Everywhere people trapped, by economic circumstances and by the inhibitions imposed on them in their youth, trapped in situations which made it quite impossible for them to live a proper life, a natural life, with body, mind and heart working to capacity, trapped and unable to see any way out of the trap. Of course I met individuals who were free, communities too, but so few. And yet the answers are there. We can free ourselves from the burden of the past, economically, morally, emotionally, socially. Economically, we need to make ourselves less dependent on the outside world, free ourselves from the desperate struggle to keep competitive in world markets. We can consume in

34

England what we produce in England if we distribute wealth in such a way as to put purchasing power where it is needed.'

'Yes, yes,' said Gerda, nodding again but this time rather dismissively. She was bored by economics and wanted to get on to the moral bit.

'This means re-organisation,' Fisher went on. 'Decentralisation, a better use of land, new forms of work unit. You will find no one thinking about these things. The Socialists want nationalisation and bureaucracy, the extreme Left labours under a gigantic illusion about Russia, the Conservatives want Imperialism and unrestricted competition and the survival of the fittest. But even Darwin, you know, has the story of the blind pelican who is brought food by his fellows—that's not the survival of the fittest. Only one or two cranks concern themselves with the real needs of the situation. Cranks, that's all. We are cranks.'

'I would not say so,' said Gerda. 'Arnold, for instance, is a very practical man.'

'Practical yes, but he wants to manure his fields with human excrement. That is cranky.'

'But this crankiness then is something in which you glory perhaps?'

'No, I don't glory in it. I particularly do not want us to glory in it because there is of course that temptation. That is why I don't like to be pinned down too much as to motives. I want things to happen by themselves, because everything changes as it goes along, everything develops in action. Like Robinson Crusoe I want the day to invent itself, I want this community to invent itself. All I ask is that its common life should be on a level somewhat above the sum of our individual lives. Thus we shall reap the spiritual harvest.'

He sat down again and poured himself out some more tea.

'I don't like this tea much,' he said, drinking it.

'It is of great benefit to the bowels,' said Gerda. 'So on the practical side it is your agriculture, this shit upon the fields and so on, which is to support you?'

'Anything. There again anything. This place lends itself to agriculture. The land you know we got for virtually nothing— the waste of good agricultural land at the moment is quite mad

—and what can be more satisfying, more romantic really, than reclaiming neglected land? Agriculture, art, writing, all that is obvious, but Arnold wants to get some industry going, timber works, a foundry, workshops, he has many plans. And then there is the propaganda side—that is where the guest house comes in—so that people may learn by example. But first there is the building work to be finished. And so many sums to be done. The sums are terrible, who is to contribute what, what they are to get back, the sums will be the death of us, in the end they'll be the death of us. But like all sensible women you are not interested in sums.'

'No, I am not interested in sums. I am interested in all the other things you mentioned, the search for a full life, the freedom from inhibition. Especially of course in my case I am so shocked by your English attitudes to sex. Freedom from guilt, yes. Shit upon the fields I do not so much care about, but I am in favour of more sex and less meat. I also am a crank then?'

Fisher shouted with laughter.

'You certainly are, my dear. More sex and less meat. Oh yes, you certainly are a crank. But why less meat? I like meat. How shall I get my protein if I give up meat?'

'Pulses,' said Gerda.

'Pulses?'

'Beans, peas, lentils.'

'They'd give me flatulence.'

'No, no, not if properly prepared. May I prepare you some? You could try for a day or two sharing my diet.'

'I didn't like the look of your breakfast this morning.'

'That is my own special version of muesli. It is very good, cooked or raw, which you prefer. It is the answer for the great intestinal canal.'

'Ah, now you're talking. Anything that might make that particular passage a less turbulent one deserves my fullest attention. Let us try the diet. Roll the oats and prepare the pulses. That shall be our meeting ground, the great intestinal canal.'

It was not the meeting ground Gerda had had in mind, but she was nothing if not game.

'It shall be so,' she said with solemnity. 'We start today.'

36

'Bear in mind also,' said Fisher, 'that the well-intentioned can be very boring. I know that. I don't want only serious seekers after truth here. The frivolous are free to visit us, the hostile too. You may ask your worldly friends, when we get the guest house going, as long as they don't stay too long, or sponge, or gossip, or annoy me. Everything is possible here, and of course democratic, completely democratic.'

'Ah,' said Gerda, smiling. 'Now you are fooling me. For everything else I am a sucker, as they say in America. But for this no, democratic it is not.'

He was annoyed. 'I really don't see how you can say that. The whole basis of the thing. . . .'

But she held up her hand, still smiling.

'Don't worry,' she said. 'This way I like it.' And she began to gather up the tea things.

After that conversation Fisher decided that although first impressions were against her, Gerda was really rather a good sort.

Dorothy went to the Abbey to return the book about Bevis.

She had liked it so much that she had traced the map from the frontispiece and coloured it in and pinned it on to her bedroom wall, where it became over the next few years the prototype for many imitative invented regions of her own. Obviously a man who would lend her such a book was not a bad sort of man, though it was not hard to recognise that he was a very different sort of man from her father. Dorothy accepted absolutely that the sort of people her father approved of were the right sort of people. All she felt now in view of the book was that though obviously the people at the Abbey were the wrong sort of people, probably for them, from their own point of view, that was all right. In other words while not doubting for a moment their wrongness she was not going to hold it against them.

At home her reading had consisted mainly of the adventure stories which had been given at various times to her brothers, and which were about life in different parts of the British Empire and dangerous encounters with wild animals and savages. She enjoyed these well enough but by now she had read most

B*

of them several times and would have welcomed some variety (or even some more of the same). The thought that Fisher might have shelves and shelves of books like Bevis was what made her walk quite boldly on the gravel as she approached the Abbey and look about her hopefully even if still with some apprehension.

There was no one about. She opened the front door, but there was nothing on the little table inside, no book, no note. Dust danced in the rays of sunlight in the hall. There was no sound. She hesitated with her hand poised over the doorbell, but she could not bring herself to ring it. It would sound so loud in that sunny quiet. Perhaps if she went round to the back she might find that friendly looking person.

As she went round the corner of the house, she heard in front of her the scratching of a hoe, and paused for a moment, wondering whether to go on round to the back of the house or to turn into the kitchen garden and see who it was who was working there. The sound of a woman's voice from that direction decided her; obviously Marjorie must be in the kitchen garden. She walked towards it, came round the wall and the box hedge and was immediately assaulted by a visual impression which was startling in the extreme. An enormous woman whom she had never seen before was looking at her from among the raspberry canes, apparently absolutely naked. Further away but approaching along a path between the beds of vegetables was Fisher, holding by their hands two girls of about her own age. As she took in these two facts, adding her own interpretation, which was that in the first place something disgusting was happening and that in the second place Fisher, having these other children with him, would not be in the least interested to see her, Dorothy noticed that there was someone else in the kitchen garden—Timothy Moore, with his back towards her and a hoe in his hand. It was towards him in fact that Gerda was looking across the raspberry canes.

Dorothy would have fled, but by the time she had recovered from her shocked surprise enough to be able to move, Fisher had seen her and had shouted out, 'Hallo there. Have you finished the book? Come and meet Jane and Caroline,' and it was too late.

She walked slowly towards him, blushing because she would

38

have to pass Gerda who was standing there making no effort to cover what seemed to Dorothy to be quite unnaturally enormous bosoms. She caught a glimpse of huge extended purple nipples. Oh God, she thought, please make her put some clothes on before I get any nearer. But Fisher was giving his shouting laugh.

'No inhibitions here, my darlings, you can see what you're in for now. Aha, yes, splendid. Well, Timothy, how's the hoeing coming along?'

The truth was that Dorothy was not the only one who was embarrassed. They all were, even Gerda. Alone in the sunny sheltered garden with Timothy, she had meant only in thus exposing herself to his gaze and to the unexpectedly beneficent sun to cheer him up a bit, cheer him on. Her relationship with Fisher having settled down in a manner really quite satisfactory though not what she had anticipated (she had also come to suspect that he might have some kind of liaison with Hilda, though she was not yet sure about this), her freed attentions had wandered towards Timothy, whom she thought she might help to liberate from his inhibitions. Inhibitions he certainly had, and though he had not thought of Gerda as a temptress, still vaguely yearning after Hilda in this respect, her gesture in removing her shirt (she seldom wore underclothes) had had the intended effect. His desires, wayward as he often found them, were in fact aroused by the very features so appalling to Dorothy. Thus the sudden arrival on the scene of Fisher and three children was even more embarrassing than it would have been had her nakedness left him (as it was beginning to leave her) cold.

Gerda's dilemma was that though she would have liked to put her shirt on again, she did not want to appear in any way ashamed in front of the children. She believed strongly—and was indeed in this respect as unlike Dorothy's parents, Nanny and governess as possible—that children should be brought up in clear and simple knowledge of everything there was to be known about nakedness and about sex, and that anything shamefaced or furtive in the behaviour of adults was a betrayal of their obligations towards the young. Thus with the best of intentions she forebore to cover herself and, slightly goosefleshed, greeted Dorothy as she approached with a friendly 'Hallo!'

Redder than ever Dorothy muttered an answer and gazed firmly at the spring cabbages.

'Well, it's a little chilly in spite of the sun,' said Gerda carelessly, and picking up her embroidered Austrian shirt from the raspberry cane where she had left it, she put it on and slowly buttoned it up.

'Yes, well,' said Fisher, feeling sorry for everybody. 'Now this is Dorothy. And this is Jane, and this is Caroline. Jane and Caroline are going to come and live here soon and I've just been showing them round.'

Of course after this episode Dorothy might never have gone to the Abbey again, might have believed her father had been proved right in a rather final and convincing manner. The only thing was that looking in a sideways awkward sort of way at Jane and Caroline, who looked back at her in much the same sort of way from beneath their whitish-fair fringes, she thought she would very much like to get to know them. She had always rather wanted a fringe herself.

Charles Grant, seated at his desk some weeks later, was thinking that he ought to go into politics, if only he could afford it. The trouble was that his financial affairs, through no fault of his own, were not what they might have been. Share values were down, taxation was going up. He had to give allowances to his sons by his first marriage, Hector and Rory, who shared a flat in London, and who, though they seemed both to be doing reasonably well at the jobs he'd found for them—one in the City and one as a solicitor—earned as yet very little and needed something for their expenses as young men about town, in which capacity he was very much hoping that one of them at least would capture an heiress. Decorating the new house had been expensive, running it was not going to be cheap, with six servants plus Nanny and Miss Gamage.

These worries and perplexities being on his mind, he was not specially well-disposed towards the Mr Whitehead with whom he had an appointment, he was not quite sure why. It seemed to be something arranged by Dorothy, but when he wanted to ask her about it, Nanny said she was doing her lessons with Miss Gamage and what with all she'd missed lately through Miss Gamage's headaches she'd think herself it would be better to let her finish. As to this Mr Whitehead, Nanny knew about that, it was all to do with piano lessons. There were these two girls, Nanny said, whose mother was a piano teacher and they wanted Dorothy to have lessons with them and Dorothy had quite rightly said they'd have to speak to her father about it and she, Nanny, would think herself that it would be a good idea, that poor Miss Gamage being so completely unmusical, tone-deaf she understood, and if he didn't want her to walk, Rogers could take her along in the car and fetch her again, he didn't have all that much to do in the week and spent too much time hanging round Mary the housemaid, who was a nice girl but did encourage him.

Thus briefed, and having found out from his wife, who was going shopping in the car with Rogers, that she had discussed the matter with Dorothy and was in favour of it, Charles Grant took up his position behind his desk and waited for Mr Whitehead—the apostle, he believed, of Free Love.

The visitor who was soon shown into his presence was not what he had expected. For one thing he was wearing perfectly decent shoes. In fact a great deal of thought had gone into Arnold's appearance. It had been unanimously decided that he should be the one to confront Dorothy's father. In spite of the inauspicious beginning of their relationship, Jane and Caroline, who were the daughters of Hamilton's new friend Mr Arkwright, the local schoolmaster, had asked Dorothy to come and see them again. After that Dorothy had, with Gammy's connivance, asked them to tea with her one day when both her parents were away in London. The Arkwright family was moving into the cottage on the opposite side of the courtyard from the guest house. Mrs Arkwright was indeed a piano teacher, though it was many years since she had functioned as such. The idea of the piano lessons had been suggested one evening after supper at the Abbey when she had repeated her children's account of their visit to Dorothy.

'It's no wonder she's shy, poor little thing,' said Mrs Arkwright, who was small and freckled and Scottish. 'Anyone

41

would be, living like that. I don't believe she sees another child from one month to the next.'

A plot to open an avenue of escape for Dorothy was something into which they could all enter. Of the various alternatives it was decided that piano lessons sounded the most respectable and twice a week was the most to be aimed at: the delegate entrusted with the request was to be Arnold.

'You're far the most respectable,' said Fisher. 'What we must do is dress you for the part. He will be expecting a left-wing intellectual in sandals and grey flannel bags. You must take him by surprise with a dark suit and a short hair-cut.'

'I absolutely draw the line at a hair-cut.'

'Then Marjorie must trim it over the ears. The rest can be done with hair-oil.'

'Not a dark suit in the country, surely? Why not tweeds? I've got a tweed suit somewhere.'

'Shoes. Who's got some good shoes?'

So there he was in Charles Grant's study, a picture of respectability, asking on Dorothy's behalf whether she might go to the Abbey twice a week to have piano lessons with Mrs Arkwright, wife of the schoolmaster. It was hard to think of any reason for refusing, but in spite of Arnold's reassuring appearance, Charles Grant remembered the rumours he had heard and remained suspicious.

'Schoolmaster, is he? Not a Socialist I hope?' He laughed, to show he meant no offence.

'I don't think he's interested in politics.'

'Because that I can't have, you know. Joking apart, a man has a right to bring up his children as he thinks best. And if I thought that any child of mine was being exposed to any of that kind of nonsense. . .

'I'm sure she wouldn't be exposed to anything. Except the friendship of two nice little creatures of her own age.'

'Because it's all cant, that sort of talk. Dangerous cant.' He had a capacity for very quickly achieving a state of self-righteous indignation, especially when he felt himself criticised. There was something he did not quite like in the very mildness of Arnold's tone as he referred to the other girls. 'We do what we can to arrange for her to see other children. It's not easy with an only child. There are not many people of our own sort round here. I'd rather she had no friends at all than the wrong sort. I tell you that quite frankly. I've seen what can happen. I've two older children you know, boys, both in their twenties, the children of my first marriage. I know the dangers. I've seen it happen. Children of friends of mine, friends of my sons. There was a boy they were at school with, got into the wrong set at University, communism, unnatural vice, the whole caboodle. Of course they never see him now, thank God. They're all right. But I've seen it happen, the young are very easily influenced, you know.'

'Yes, of course,' said Arnold.

'You can't afford to mess about with human nature,' said Charles Grant. 'You can't trust it, that's why. I'm a Christian, Mr Whitehead. I believe in original sin.'

'And the piano lessons?' said Arnold, smiling pacifically.

'You think it ridiculous, no doubt. You come to talk about piano lessons and we end up discussing original sin. But that's the sort of person I am. I like to think things out thoroughly, Mr Whitehead.'

'I'm sure you're right.'

'There's too much sloppy thinking in this country. I believe in discipline, mental, physical, emotional discipline. Without discipline, Mr Whitehead,' he said, leaning forward urgently across his desk, 'Believe you me, without discipline there is nothing but the abyss.'

Arnold stood up and walked towards the window.

'What a lovely garden you have here,' he said as if suddenly struck by it. 'No, really, I'm sure we don't disagree. It just seemed a nice idea for Dorothy to come along for some music lessons with Jane and Caroline and she asked me to speak to you about it, but if you'd rather not, or if you think it would be better to wait a bit, of course that's absolutely up to you.'

'What are your fees?'

'I think Mrs Arkwright has some standard sum she charges —two or three guineas a term sort of thing—would you like me to ask her to let you know exactly?'

'No, no, I'm sure it's reasonable. Dorothy can start when she likes. You make the arrangements and let Miss Gamage know.

Miss Gamage can arrange transport and so on.' Suddenly he was all bluff friendliness. After all, he was thinking, looking at the shoes again, the fellow appears to be a gent. 'Yes, the garden's beginning to look nice, isn't it? We had an awful lot to do when we came but it's beginning to take shape a bit now. Are you a gardener, Mr Whitehead?'

Half an hour later, after a quick tour of the improvements in the garden, Charles Grant saw Arnold into his car, waved a genial goodbye, and returned to his study, confident that he had impressed the other by his authority and seriousness as well as by his geniality. Nora would be pleased, he thought, when she came back from her shopping, to find that he had arranged it all.

Arnold drove slowly away in the old Morris. At the end of the drive a gesticulating figure dashed out from the bushes. He stopped and wound down the window.

'What happened? What did he say?'

He smiled. 'It's all right. You can start when you like.'

Dorothy flushed scarlet and her eyes filled with tears.

'Oh *thank* you!' She disappeared again into the bushes.

Later, in bed, Arnold said to Marjorie, 'It meant so much to her. I felt awfully depressed by the whole thing. What an odd man—so uneasy, so strange—and yet I think there may be a lot of people like that. You'd think something awful must have happened to him and yet I don't suppose it did. Just an ordinary conventional sort of man. And yet someone must have told him all that stuff at some time or other, when he was a child I suppose. About original sin and all that. I don't think I believe in original sin, do you?'

'Of course not.'

'All the people here—I don't really agree with everything they say—but I don't think any of us believe in original sin, do we? I mean, not like the Colonel.'

Marjorie laughed. 'Then we are heretics. Hamilton would like that, you must remember to tell him. We really are heretics. He'll be so pleased.'

After that came the good years, the best years of all.

The guest house was finished and work began on restoring

44

the roof of the barn, which was to be turned into a woollen mill. The farm began almost to meet its own expenses: it might have done better had Arnold been willing to slow down the rate of expansion. Mrs Arkwright took over the vegetable garden and as a result of her re-organisation it became the one part of the whole enterprise which never failed to show a small profit, even in the worst years.

Timothy was in the grip of his physical obsession with Gerda, and secretly rather shocked by the strength of his own desires. Gerda on the other hand was secure in her conviction that she was doing him a world of good. At each of their sexual encounters she felt that she engulfed him, swallowed him up like the little minnow he was. She would let him go when the time came. A woman of her experience knew how to gauge these things: he would be amazed by the ease, the absolute lack of fuss, with which she would release him when she had taught him to be a poet and introduced him to the people who mattered in the literary world. In the meantime, one result of their affair was to make her less dissatisfied with Philip.

Philip, having finished his manual labour on the guest house, felt much less personally about the barn, and finding that in the meantime he had completely lost all interest in his book on Corelli, had a few days of acute anxiety before it became clear what his next assignment was going to be. Fortunately Arnold had entered into communication with a number of other communal undertakings in different parts of the country, and had been so gratified by his discoveries that he had decided to organise a conference in a year or two's time, so that people involved in all these different projects could meet together to share their experiences, clarify and confirm their purposes, and further the spreading of the message to the outside world. These were the optimistic years for Arnold, the years in which he felt sure that there was a movement slowly gathering strength which was going to change the world by example. He wanted Philip to help him with the considerable correspondence and organisation in which his attempt to widen the relevance of the Abbey community was increasingly to involve him.

Fisher meanwhile came and went about his purposes. He was planning another tour of America; there was talk of a trip to India. He was also at work on his book *What to do now*, in which he described his investigations into the state of the country and his proposals for the future, and in which he wandered blithely through many disputed fields, ignoring all artificial barriers and touching upon politics, anthropology, literature, religion, universities, cities, labour, international relations, education, planning, social history, economic theory—the polymath in person at the height of his powers. At least that was what he felt like some of the time. He had never been so busy, nor felt that so much was within his reach. He was going to have an effect, that was what he felt during these years, he was going to make a difference to things.

Much later, in one of his moods of depression, he said to Dorothy, 'We were so arrogant in those days. There we were, thinking we knew all the answers, despising the people running things as poor benighted creatures who'd never seen the light, thinking we could have done it all so much better ourselves—and we were no more right than they were. We'd have made just as many mistakes. Not the same mistakes but just as many. And all we did was talk, and build a few walls, and leave nothing behind us, nothing at all. Except the walls.'

'And the books and the ideas and the example.'

'All forgotten, all gone,' he intoned.

'What about the effect you had on other people's lives? You've no idea what the Abbey was to me when I was a child. Every time I crossed the threshold it was as if I'd woken up out of a dream of being half alive. It was so funny, for one thing. The way you all talked so much, and so fast—much faster than anyone at home—and the way you argued, with everyone talking at once and Gerda's English getting more and more extraordinary and no one agreeing with anyone else. And the way you were all so polite to children and listened to what we said and never told us not to be impertinent like my father—and all that building and planting and cooking and planning things. I remember a stuffy friend of my father's asking me about you, because you know everyone was always very nosey about you in those early days—they thought you were in league with the Bolsheviks or doing filthy sexual practices or something—and he said, 'Why are they living there all together like that? What's the point of it?' and I said, 'I think it's because they enjoy it so much,' and they looked at me scornfully thinking what a stupid child I was. But it was what I really thought.'

'I was bored to tears half the time,' said Fisher. But his expression had lightened a little all the same.

As her father and mother were often in London in the middle of the week, Dorothy found it not too difficult to extend the amount of time she spent at the Abbey, especially in the summer. Miss Gamage, finding herself with less and less to do, though they kept regularly enough to the morning timetable of lessons, in the afternoons took to her bed with increasing frequency and wondered, though she was barely forty, if her headaches could be anything to do with The Change.

Dorothy gave total trust and loyalty to Jane and Caroline. They never ceased to seem much freer than she was herself, though in what way she would have found it hard to say— perhaps she meant it in the sense of freedom from anxiety. She realised that though they accepted her companionship readily enough, they did not feel about her in the same way as she felt about them. They were self-contained, efficient children. Jane was better at climbing trees and tying knots, Caroline at thinking of things to do and remembering what she had read in books. They were both tall for their ages—taller than Dorothy—and had long brown legs. Dorothy admired them both enormously, and they filled the foreground of her life at this time, together with the youngest of the mongrels, who was called Mat, not so much as an abbreviation of Matthew as because someone had said he looked like a doormat. She loved her anxious mother, but did not see a great deal of her. She knew that her father was always right but avoided him, without asking herself why. The Abbey's visitors, whether their visits were short or long, passed in a vague talkative procession. Only much later, in other places, did she sometimes hear or read the name of a writer or politician and remember a lady with trailing skirts and a hat and a drawling voice, or a man with floppy trousers in a deck chair arguing with Fisher. They had not seemed important at the time.

About this time there was an influx of Germans. Only one of them stayed for any length of time; the others moved on, usually to Universities. They were friends of Gerda's or friends of friends. The one who stayed was Sophie Goldblaum, a gentle creature of whom Dorothy once thought she saw a picture in a book, only it turned out to be George Eliot; she spent a lot of time with the children. She tried to teach them German from a book called *Ich Kann Deutsch Lesen* which had pictures of a family of rats in it, and they sang German songs while she played the piano. Dorothy forgot most of the German but went on singing such fragments of the songs as she remembered all her life—'Sah ein Knab'ein Röslein steh'n,' 'Der Kukkuck und der Esel,' 'Weisst du wieviel Sternlein stehen'—once in the middle of that one, about how many stars there are, Sophie broke down and wept. She leant her arms on the top of the piano and put her head down on them and cried and cried. Her parents were in prison in Germany. She was afraid—rightly as it turned out—that she would never see them again. That was later; Marjorie's son Joe was walking by then.

The only person at the Abbey at that time whom Dorothy did not really like was Hamilton: she did not like him because she was afraid of him. He came so silently in and out of the house at mealtimes; she thought someone so big had no right to be so quiet. Mostly he sat in his workshop. Nobody really knew what he did there all the time. Once Dorothy was walking slowly through that part of the garden on the way to take some message of quite minor importance from Marjorie to Arnold, who was working on the roof of the barn, when she saw Hamilton crouched over his workbench with his head in his hands. The door of his little cell was open—it was a hot day—and his massive figure was framed in the gothic doorway, dark against the window behind him. He was so still and so hunched that she stopped some way away and stared at him across the grass, which was full of daisies because he had not mowed it, and wondered if he were ill and if she ought to go back and fetch Marjorie. Then he spoke, still with his head in his hands. He spoke in a slow, thick, heavy voice, which seemed to Dorothy the most awful voice she had ever heard.

'See,' he said. 'See where Christ's blood . . .' Here he lifted his head and put it back as if he were going to howl, and raised his arms in front of him with the elbows bent and both fists clenched, and said loudly, making the first word last an almost unbearable length of time, 'STREAMS in the firmament.'

Then he put his head in his hands again.

As soon as she could move—terror made it difficult—Dorothy ran back the way she had come. She went to the barn the other way, through the kitchen garden.

He sat on his father's chest, holding him down. He was fifteen, a strong boy whose big hands held his father's arms pinned to the floor, to the faded orange and green rug of the dressing-room floor, between the packed but open suitcases. His father's strong frame writhed and strained beneath him, between his thighs, and his father's wildly questioning eyes searched the air, the ceiling, the window, and his mouth opened wide showing discoloured teeth and fillings and a string or two of saliva depending from this thick retracted tongue. Hamilton looked down his father's gullet as his father shouted those words and heaved his strong torso under the restraining boy. 'See,' he bellowed. 'See where Christ's blood STREAMS in the firmament.'

Once when Fisher was at Cambridge Hamilton spent a weekend with him and they went to see a much-praised production of Marlow's *Faustus*. Hamilton had had no idea that the phrase his father had shouted in his madness came from the play, and when the actor reached that speech—and it was indeed a splendid performance—and said those words, Hamilton had to leave his seat and stumble out of the theatre. He walked up and down outside for a long time until he realised that he was more or less alone in a quiet street and that the figure waiting patiently some way away was his brother.

When he joined him, Fisher said, 'Let's go and find something to eat.'

His brothers did not ask Hamilton questions they knew he could not answer.

'Hilda, Hilda, weedy little Hilda.'

Fisher in his bedroom (which was much the nicest) looked at Hilda who was lying naked on his bed.

'Skinny you are, a skinny girl, with a skinny body and a skinny soul. What shall we do with you, skinny Hilda?'

She reached out for the eiderdown and said, 'Don't look at me.'

He was wearing a silk dressing-gown, and looking handsome. He did not always look handsome: sometimes his intensity was alarming and made him look older than he was. Now he was relaxed, had had a bath, brushed his hair. He felt serene and kind.

'Why don't you like yourself better, Hilda, just a little better?'

'Because I'm not very nice,' said Hilda, holding the eiderdown over her mouth.

'I like you,' said Fisher.

'I tried to kill myself once,' said Hilda. 'Quite a long time ago, in Purley. I swallowed a whole bottle of aspirin.'

'That was a very silly thing to do.'

'My mother used to do it every time she had a row with my father.'

'Then you were being unoriginal as well as silly.'

'Yes. But it was a lovely feeling.'

'Rubbish. You're not to start annoying me just when I'm in a good mood. You're very tiresome about not being happy, you know.'

'If I were happy I might not write so well.'

'Who cares? Being a writer is only important in the sense that somebody has to do it, somebody has to be keeping the pool up to the watermark as it were. But that's all. If one person stops, do you think it matters? There'll be someone else to do it. They won't do it in exactly the same way, but that doesn't matter in the least. So let's have no self-importance on that score.'

'But it's all I have, it's all I am,' she wailed, clutching the eiderdown more tightly than ever.

'There are plenty of clever girls with catty pens. Another of Miss Hilda Bolding's needle-sharp characterisations. She impales her victims with unerring skill. Miss Hilda Bolding, the darling of the reviewers.'

She laughed.

'I must be someone's darling,' she said.

'Why?'

'Otherwise I won't be here. I'll disappear into thin air.'

He shook his head. 'Very bad. A very bad case. I suppose it's all Daddy's fault. Dreadful Daddy with his pinched suburban attitudes and all those guilty love affairs and no time for his clever little girl.'

She looked hurt. 'He wasn't dreadful. At least, not exactly. Although I hate him.'

'Forget all that. I will be a father to you. You can rely on me. Not too much because that's not good for you. But I'll always be ready to remind you that you're not thin air when you need reminding. And in return you can whack me a bit, just every now and then. You don't mind that do you?'

She shook her head.

'Because we must have a clear understanding. I want to give you strength not take it away from you. I want you to feel able to go from me to the real mature love between man and woman which you deserve.'

'Can't I have that with you?'

'It doesn't work for me, I don't know why. I've tried and it's a mess every time. I don't mind, to tell you the truth, I haven't really the time for it. The sort of friendly arrangement you and I have is just right for me. But I want it to be right for you too. You can be just a little bit happier, you know. It really won't do you any harm.'

She closed her eyes.

'I am happy,' she said. 'Nearly, anyway.'

Some time in the mid-thirties the brothers offered one of the cottages free to an unemployed miner and his family in return for their labour in cultivating their own plot of land and helping Trew the cowman with the growing dairy herd.

Dorothy and Jane and Caroline helped to get the house ready for them. Mr Arkwright, who was a kind man and a conscientious father, had told them about the work of a coal-miner, and about the severe unemployment in the North Somerset Coalfield, and about the dole, and the means test and other sad things of that kind. The children responded with vigorous concern. They thought it would be awful if their fathers were coal miners. Their easily aroused sympathies found an outlet in helping, rather sporadically but with a most satisfying sense of doing good, with the work on the cottage.

There were two cottages, of which the Trews had one and the other was almost a ruin. They were some distance from the house, facing onto the back drive, with small gardens back and front. The work on the miner's cottage took many months: everything had to be done, plumbing, electricity, new floors, new roof beams. Towards the end Arnold decided that the damp course was inadequate and would always give trouble unless it was attended to; that meant a good deal more delay.

Fisher was glad of it. He knew it must be right to make the offer, but he was nervous of the consequences. Everyone was so enthusiastic, the adults almost as naïvely so as the children, and he was afraid they might be in for disillusionment. They were thinking in terms of the Trews, but the Trews had always lived in the country and worked for the gentry. Their attitude, a pleasing mixture of independence and deference, was that of the self-respecting servant, happy in his work. Trew was a good cowman, Mrs Trew a good cook: Trew worked under Arnold, Mrs Trew under Marjorie. The only difference between their situation and that of any other similar couple was that they sat down for the midday meal with everyone else at the big kitchen table. They did this with dignity, to humour their employers, but would just as soon have eaten in peace in their own cottage, as they did in the evenings. Fisher knew that there was no particular reason to suppose that an unknown miner and his family would necessarily settle down so easily; nor did he over-estimate the true tolerance of the Abbey community. It was Stanley Arkwright and Arnold who were the keenest on the project, which they looked on as no more than a beginning. Fisher was therefore privately amused to think that Arnold's last-minute insistence on the damp course might have been something to do with cold (rather than damp) feet. He did not say so. These were the good days. He wanted everyone to have their heart's desire in the way of the Abbey's undertakings.

The damp course anyway prolonged the pleasant days of preparation. The children fetched and carried, mixed cement, sloshed whitewash on the walls, and messed up their clothes. When she could, Dorothy slipped away to gaze at little Joe.

Jane and Caroline thought nothing at all of the baby. Dorothy was rather ashamed of her feeling for him. She wanted to be as tough and competent as Jane and Caroline; but when she had first seen Joe as a tiny baby of only a few days old she had been overwhelmed by love for him. Her feeling was so intense she hardly knew what to do with it. At first she only stared, from a distance. Then she leant a little closer (but it was days before she dared) and whispered, and then at last Marjorie said, 'Would you like to hold him?' and had the sense to look away while she did.

After that she often wheeled him round the garden in his pram, or held him while Marjorie mixed some food for him; later she watched him kicking on his rug and received the benefit of his marvellous smiles. Jane and Caroline found him boring, if not positively disgusting; Dorothy was helpless with love. When she held him she sometimes trembled, or squeezed him too tight so that he cried. She put him down then, and talked to him in the way she knew he liked until he smiled again : she had to put him down because of the temptation to go on squeezing him in spite of his crying. When he was old enough to enjoy quite rough games on his rug, games in which Dorothy butted him in the stomach with her head and he pulled her hair until it really hurt and they both screamed and laughed quite loudly and his heels thumped vigorously on the floor in his excitement and sometimes he arched his back, with his eyes shining and his face pink, at such times she occasionally felt an admixture of something puzzling, a physical longing which could not be appeased. She could squeeze, tickle, kiss, but still something more was needed to express her absolute delight in his softness and smoothness and milk and honey smell. Agonies of love, transports of love, these were what she felt; and sometimes she wished they were not so strong. It was

53

her first intimation that love might not be an unmixed blessing, whether for lover or beloved.

When the cottage was nearly ready Arnold put an advertisement in the *Western Daily Press*. There was a flood of answers. Bewildered, the brothers offered the cottage to one of the first applicants, Ivor Hedges, who was married and had two children. A week or so later Hamilton, in the course of his researches into local history, happened to come across a reference in the journal of a man who had been a vicar in those parts in the early nineteenth century. He had written 'Ivor Hedges, a collier, died this morning of a consumption, brought on in a great measure by excessive drinking. I besought him to think that he was on the brink of eternity and to repent of his mis-spent life, but his mind was not to be worked on and he died impenitent. His second wife—the first having drowned herself in the canal in despair at his excessive drinking and violent behaviour—was at his bedside, a poor helpless creature near her confinement. She did not seem much afflicted by grief, any more than did the two daughters, one in the same condition as her mother though neither are wed —both are known strumpets. The boy is in Shepton Mallet jail after beating half to death another collier in a drunken brawl.

It might have been a different family but it did not seem to Hamilton a good omen. He thought it best not to mention it to anyone for the time being.

Fisher stood in Marcella Maysey-Smith's drawing room, feeling —and looking—out of place.

'Divine of you to come,' she said. 'Do turn the gramophone off, someone, we can't hear ourselves think. I adore hot jazz, don't you?'

Ralph Blatchford had told Fisher it was going to be a quiet lunch. Ralph was an old Cambridge friend and had introduced Fisher to Marcella with an end in view. 'It would be nice for both of you,' he had said, 'if she were to take an interest in your concerns.'

Fisher looked about him in some surprise. The room was enormous. Long as it was it was still too high for its length:

the proportions were not harmonious. Outside the many windows, some of which constituted a large bay and opened onto the terrace, could be seen smooth lawns, formal flower beds, and a distant balustrade, interrupted by steps leading down to a tall wrought-iron gate between columns. Beyond the gate lay the park, with clumps of rich green trees and a tree fringed lake curving away into deeper woods, with promise of laid-out walks, Chinese bridges, and rustic boat-houses.

The house had been built in 1901 by an architect whose instructions had been simply to build something of a decent size. The client, Marcella's late father-in-law, had been pleased enough with the result, and had liked it better than the more modest Georgian building which it had replaced and which had been accidentally destroyed by fire.

The drawing room walls were painted pink. There were pinkish chintz curtains with fringed pelmets, sofas and armchairs covered with the same chintz, an immense Audubon carpet worth certainly several thousand pounds, and many groups of smaller chairs, in twos and threes, of an imitation French design, with upholstered backs and seats and white-painted woodwork. Many of these groups had small tables beside them, mostly ormolu, on which were bowls of roses and framed photographs. The walls, quite incongruously, were hung with Cubist paintings. A huge radiogram in one corner had been playing the latest Bix Biederbeck record, while half a dozen or so people stood about looking embarrassed and holding cocktail glasses. Fisher had not expected so many people.

The brothers were running short of money. Even though most of the labour at the Abbey was unpaid, only the Trews being on a wage basis, there was the cost of the building materials to be met, as well as the endless bills in connection with the farm, at this time only just beginning to pay its expenses. Old Mrs Whitehead had been rich—a fact which had come as a surprise to her sons after her death—but the capital which had not been exhausted in the buying and restoring of the Abbey was in shares whose value in these years was much reduced. The Maidens had contributed all the small capital they had and Mary had given loyal support from her husband's charitable trust; but this too, limitless though it had

55

once appeared, was suffering from the economic situation in America. The Arkwrights had nothing to contribute but their labour and nor had the various younger people who came and went, some of these indeed having views about property which made it wiser to avoid discussion of such matters. The fact that the community could not have existed without the Whiteheads' considerable inherited capital fitted in with no one's ideals and was as far as possible ignored by everyone, including the brothers.

Most of Fisher's income from his books and lectures went straight into the Abbey funds, and might possibly have sufficed as an explanation, had one been needed, for the fact that he lived so much more comfortably there than anyone else (the question, perhaps oddly, never seemed to arise). A new benefactor, however, would certainly be a help.

Ralph Blatchford had met Marcella in her capacity as a patron of modern art, in which he was passionately interested. She was enormously rich, mainly through her marriage to Noel Maysey-Smith, who was heir to one of the great banking fortunes. Noel himself was an explorer and an amateur aviator, but even after the aeroplanes and the expeditions up the Amazon had been paid for, there was plenty left for Marcella to invest in pictures.

She was the daughter of a sporting Earl. Her mother, Kitty Carlington, had been one of the great beauties of the Edwardian age, adored by many distinguished men. Marcella's two brothers had both been killed in the Great War. Most of their friends, the dashing young men Marcella had admired so hugely from her schoolgirl seclusion, seemed to have been killed as well. Her sisters, Cynthia and Diana, had inherited something of their mother's looks. Spirited girls, they had been Bright Young Things in the Twenties, a little scandalous and terribly smart. Cynthia had married an ambitious and well-connected young politician, Diana a bridge-playing Guards officer who was a friend of the Prince of Wales. They were both London hostesses, their progress still closely followed in the gossip columns. Marcella was the plain one. Her mother used to look at her and sigh and say, 'Marcella is so artistic', which even she must have known was quite untrue.

Following the hint as best she could—for her mother's hints were not to be ignored—Marcella traipsed round art galleries in London, Paris, Florence, Rome and Madrid, and finding that with the best will in the world (and she did have that) she still could hardly tell one painter's work from another, she decided to go in for Modern Art, where it seemed that one could get by on nothing more than enthusiasm. She became a familiar sight in the more avant-garde of London galleries, a short stocky person standing with her legs apart—she always seemed to be bracing herself against a moderate gale—tossing back the straight brown bobbed hair which tended to fall over her face and saying loudly, 'Divine. Too divine. I adore it, don't you?' and probably then going on to ask the painter, the gallery owner and anyone else who happened to be around to come to cocktails the next day, for she was nothing if not generous.

The fact that her purchases turned out to have been so judicious and that the collection which she left in the end to the Tate Gallery was such a considerable one was due almost entirely to Ralph Blatchford, who at that time had no particular qualification for the task of adviser other than absolute faith in his own judgement. Later he became well-known not only as an expert on modern art but as a writer on rather obscure metaphysical subjects, but at the time it was brave of Marcella to trust him to the extent that she did. He was a man of strong convictions, despite his outward gentleness, and lived a simple, even ascetic life, devoted to the furthering of the ideas in which he believed. His discernment in visual matters was not matched by his intellectual capacity. He had a gullibility, a sentimentality even, where ideas were concerned which led him later to be scorned when he took to philosophy. At the same time he was a nice man.

Marcella, having battled her way towards the new arrival in the teeth of her own private gale, seized onto his arm as though to steady herself (Fisher wondered, not realising that the whole performance was no more than the equivalent of a nervous tic, whether she might be drunk) and said breathlessly, 'Now let me introduce you.'

Ralph had said, 'She's got a very quiet weekend because she's just been packing Noel off to South America, and that's always a great strain for the household. It's just the time for you to come and meet her quietly. Then she'll be able to listen to what you say. She gets so jumpy if there are a lot of people there.'

She had only her cousin and the cousin's husband and Ralph staying in the house, but against the latter's advice had insisted on asking some local neighbours to lunch. 'One couldn't expect him to lunch with just us, *en ménage*, when one hardly knows him. What would he think of one?' So she had asked Colonel Sir Giles and Lady Lambert and the Dowager Duchess of Towcester and Mrs Lea, widow of the late George Lea of Cookham Park; and then, still feeling that that really would hardly do for dear Ralph's interesting friend, she had asked Mr and Mrs Hancock from Bradford-on-Avon whom she particularly disliked and whose views she knew perfectly well to be violently opposed to all that she had heard of the views of Fisher Whitehead. There again, it was nerves.

They all looked relieved when Marcella's cousin's husband turned off the gramophone: unlike their hostess, they did not adore hot jazz. Marcella's cousin's husband, Edward Rowse, was a banker. Through the family connection he had taken what might well have been Noel's job, had Noel not decided to diverge from the accepted pattern; he felt an uncomfortable mixture of jealousy and guilt towards Noel and was happier staying with Marcella when, as was most often the case, her husband was away. His wife Penelope, Marcella's cousin, was much obsessed by her family, which was large and in some of its ramifications impressive. Her obsession and her assumption that it was widely shared made her conversation almost incomprehensible to outsiders.

'Virgin would scream,' she now said, shaking hands with Fisher. 'As for Cyn and Di. . . .'

Cyn and Di were Marcella's sisters, Virgin another cousin, beautiful Virginia who had recently made a brilliant marriage, and the reference was to the turning off, or not, of the gramophone. It was all as obscure to the country neighbours as it was to Fisher.

Penelope settled herself on one of the pink sofas and accepted the refilled glass which the butler brought her on a silver salver.

'Bliss,' she said. 'Such comfort staying here. Stuffy's got rid of half the servants at Dorley. Too boring.'

'Why?' asked Marcella.

'Cutting down, tightening his belt, Mr Baldwin said one should.'

'Surely it would be better if he employed more people rather than less?' said Ralph Blatchford mildly. 'Then he'd be creating jobs.'

'Oh don't let's bewilder him,' said Penelope. 'It took him such ages to make up his mind and now he's feeling so patriotic without a second footman.'

'Funny old Stuffy,' said Marcella. 'What fun.'

Having been born with a quite unusual lack of discrimination, which the indifferent education in those days considered adequate for a girl of her background had done nothing to ameliorate, born also with an inheritance, through the families of both her parents and the fame and multiple connections of her mother, which meant that inevitably she knew most of the notabilities of her time, together with an enormous number of well-connected non-notabilities, Marcella had come to rely on certain catch phrases which recurred frequently and sometimes rather mechanically in her conversation. People were often referred to as 'Funny old . . .' or 'Poor old . . .' and almost everything elicited the comment: 'What fun!' By these means she conveyed her familiarity and fellow feeling with the Establishment, and her flustered faith that everything would turn out for the best if only she kept cheerful.

Fisher, not yet as familiar with Marcella's character as he was later to become, thought that funny old Stuffy sounded the opposite of fun. Indeed certain reactions aroused in him by Penelope and Marcella, unfamiliar through disuse but remembered, made him wish he had not come: he should have remembered earlier how much he hated that sort of person.

Lunch was announced; there was no getting out of it now. At least he was not sitting next to Penelope; but she was opposite, which was bad enough.

'Colin's too funny about his asparagus,' she said, helping herself to the first course and looking across at him. 'Do you have much Todcombe life?'

'Todcombe?' he repeated.

'Tara's mad about hunting now. She's Joint Master or something. Too funny.'

'I don't think I know them,' said Fisher.

'I thought you'd be bound to, being so close. You'll soon meet them if you're living down here. They're our cousins.'

'Mr Whitehead doesn't want to meet people like that,' said the Dowager Duchess severely. 'He's an anarchist. He thinks people like Colin and Tara should be blown up.'

'Oh how ghastly,' said Penelope, quite unperturbed. 'Trust me to get it all wrong. You are marvellous, Marcie, Cyn and Di will shriek when I tell them. An anarchist, how thrilling.'

'I'm glad you think so.' Mrs Hancock, reddish complexioned at the best of times, had turned much redder now. 'I'm afraid I can't see it that way.'

Fortunately she was at the other end of the table.

'What I want to ask Mr Whitehead about,' said the Duchess, 'is Mrs Arkwright our great botanist. Isn't she living in your stables now?'

The Duchess was a straight-backed seventy-five-year-old with the sunburnt hawk-like face of an old Spanish peasant; whose preoccupations indeed she would most probably have shared, had they been the family and the land. She had been the second wife of a much married Duke. When he left her she moved into a smaller house, choosing a not particularly attractive one on the grounds that she could walk the cows there. She had brought up her three children according to such a strict interpretation of maternal duty that none of them had been able to live a normal adult life. Now in their fifties, all three were still dependent on her for everything, nor could any of them, least of all her eldest son the present Duke, handle their own finances, marriages, children, or over-active imaginations. Bank managers, estate offices, schools, brain specialists and nursing homes had all trembled at the visits of the formidable and frequently grieving matriarch. In the intervals between family crises, she won prizes at cattle shows and made her garden the wonder of the experts. Mrs Arkwright, it appeared, had addressed the Women's Institute of which she was a member on the subject of local wild flowers.

60

'I want to ask her about Spiked Star of Bethlehem. Bath Asparagus it's sometimes called, do you know about it? It grows in the woods round Bath and is perfectly delicious to eat, and when I dug some up and planted it in a shady place in my garden it all died. Now why, I want to know? My soil's the same, clay, lime, why does it not transplant?'

He did not know, but he knew the flower though he had never eaten it, and knew the legend that it had been brought by the Romans; and so the conversation diffused and separated and the danger of an explosion from Mrs Hancock was for the time being averted.

'I don't suppose you heard my name,' Fisher's next-door neighbour said in a gentle voice. 'It's Lucy Lambert.' She inclined her long neck a little way towards him and smiled faintly. She was beautiful, in a delicate sort of way, neat and controlled, as if she might have been a ballet dancer.

'Do you think there will be great changes?' she asked in the same quiet tones, as if she did not want anyone else to hear.

He said he thought there might be.

'I do hope so,' she said. She hesitated, then went on. 'It seems so terrible that after the War we didn't have a better world.'

'Perhaps not enough people wanted it.'

'Oh, but I believe they did really. Or would have found out that they did, if there'd been the leadership. I really do believe that.'

Her perfectly oval smooth face looked into his hazel eyes full of concern.

'Giles wanted to go into politics, you know, after the War. My husband, that is.'

'But he didn't?'

'He found . . . he said he found too big a difference between the people who'd fought in the War and the people who hadn't. And it was the people who hadn't who were going into politics. He said it seemed an unbridgeable gap.'

Fisher looked across at her husband. He was as elegant, as delicately made, as she was, tall and thin, dark-haired, with a neat drooping moustache and a gentle melancholy expression. Fisher felt an immediate conviction that he would find nothing in common with him.

'Did he enjoy the War?'

'Oh no. But he said there were feelings of comradeship and so on between the different ranks which he really believed would go on afterwards. He thought that that would make life quite different.'

'He was a good soldier then.'

She looked surprised. 'Of course.'

'Won medals and so on?'

'Yes. But he doesn't like to talk about it. He was quite badly wounded, twice. But tell me,' she seemed to want to change the subject. 'When you say you are an anarchist, what does that mean?'

'I don't say I am an anarchist. Someone else said that. But I suppose the anarchist principle is the one which I should want to support more than any other. It's too complicated to explain now what I mean. One would like a society which better enabled people to live in harmony with natural law. I could send you some literature if you're really interested.'

He wanted to be friendly, and felt he had been too dry in his questions about her husband. He had been a conscientious objector himself, and though he had worked as a stretcher-bearer—well, there was no need to tell her all that—neither she nor her husband would have the faintest idea what he was talking about.

'Oh I should be so pleased,' she said, looking at him indeed with disconcerting gratitude. 'We do worry. I think one does, don't you, when one's quite outside things? Well, you're not outside things perhaps but we are, and if you're on the outside everything seems worse than if you're at the centre of things, because then at least you can feel you might be able to do something even if that's really an illusion. Just sitting and reading the newspaper is enough to make anyone worry themselves to death, don't you agree?'

She was smiling, but he could see that she meant it.

'What is it that you worry about? Abyssinia? Unemployment?'

'All the quarrelling and conflict and bitterness. If socialism proper comes, they won't want people like us, will they? Perhaps we'll be put in prison or something.'

62

'My dear, I feel quite sure you won't,' he said, shocked.

'One wouldn't mind if one had no children. Well yes, I would mind. I'd like things to change for the better and I would make sacrifices of course, if I thought it would help. But when socialists talk of class warfare I feel so sorry. The people in our village are my friends, I've known them all my life : we share so many interests. But if it's class warfare they'll have to come and burn our house down, won't they, and we should all hate that; I really don't know who would hate it most.'

'I do think it's tremendously unlikely that it will come to that,' said Fisher.

'And then all this talk of war, and taking a strong line in Abyssinia and so on, surely anything would be better than another war? But let's not think about it, let's talk of something else.'

'What does your husband do, since he didn't go into politics?'

'He looks after the estate but it's not very big, only a very small home farm and a couple of tenant farms and some woodland. He shoots, of course, in the winter. But he hasn't really quite enough to do and we can't afford to entertain much. Land is such a bad investment these days. He does a lot of needlework. I think he ought to sell it commercially but he won't. Petit point, you know, he does it quite beautifully. He's done so much for our house, there's hardly room for any more. Cushions and chair seats and two hangings for four-poster beds and even curtains. It suits our house very well you see because it's very old, early Tudor mostly, with a lot of panelling, you know the sort of thing, little dark secret rooms, the needlework goes well with that.'

'How charming it sounds. Is the garden as old as the house?'

'Yes, it's divided into secret rooms too in a way, with very old yew hedges and paths that lead nowhere. People get lost in it and then they're afraid of the ghosts.'

'And you love the ghosts. Almost as much as the village people.'

He was afraid he had been rude again, but she laughed.

'They are the village people, I suppose,' she said. 'Or their ancestors, or Giles's. We live right in the middle of the village, you see.'

'Now do tell me—' Marcella turned to him suddenly. 'Do tell me about your wonderful settlement.' At the same time she let her glance wander disconcertingly round the empty plates on the table and over to the hovering butler as if in anxiety lest he might delay in removing them, or drop them, eventualities each as unlikely as the other. 'Is it too divine?' she asked, looking at Fisher now with, it seemed, some other and much more desperate query on her mind.

'I don't know about that exactly,' he said deprecatingly.

'Oh but Ralph says it is,' she said. 'I know the house of course. I went to look at it when it was for sale. I'm so nosey about houses, aren't you? Such a heavenly position. Too lovely. I wanted to buy it and sell this but of course it was out of the question really.' Her eyes were still searching the room. 'Let's see now. Yes, what fun. So it's communism really?'

He said that no, it wasn't communism only co-operation and tried to explain what that meant, but Marcella appeared only half to listen, her questioning eyes sometimes focussing on his face and sometimes searching the room as before. On her other side, opposite Fisher, Sir Giles Lambert listened with close attention, nodding slowly from time to time. Fisher found this disconcerting: he could not make out which side the man was on.

'The family of course . . .' Sir Giles said hesitantly. 'I suppose. . . .' He fixed his melancholy gaze on Fisher. 'I suppose you would think that very old-fashioned, the family? With its standards?'

Fisher began cautiously to explain that he had nothing particular against the family, but Marcella, who was not even half listening now, suddenly interrupted him, put one hand on his arm and said, 'Look here, if you can offer places for artists to work, for a short time, to get away and really work, I'm on. I mean it. I'm absolutely on. I mean I happen to think art is the only thing in the world that matters, that's all. Just the only thing.'

She let go of his arm and pushed back her chair.

'Coffee,' she said in quite a different tone of voice. 'Coffee in the drawing room.'

64

Later Fisher walked on the terrace with his friend Ralph Blatchford.

'It would help her as well as you if she could take an interest in your concern,' Ralph said. 'She wants to come over next weekend and have a look round. Unfortunately, she's got a pretty awful crowd of hangers-on staying, she's no idea about people, you know. I'll try and be here too if I can.'

The scrunch of gravel on the path along the terrace made them turn. Mr and Mrs Hancock were marching side by side towards them.

'Sorry we didn't have a chance to talk,' said Mrs Hancock with robust good humour. 'I expect we should have had a good knock-up.'

'She'd have put you through it all right,' cried Major Hancock with a jovial laugh. 'Put you right on a few points, what?'

'Perhaps some other time . . .' murmured Fisher.

'Rather,' said Mrs Hancock. 'We've got to dash now though. Poor Musso will be getting so bored, sitting in the car.'

She shook hands firmly with each of them and turned away.

'Our bull terrier,' the Major explained. Pointing at her receding back he whispered loudly, 'Her hero!' then hurried after her, smiling happily.

Dorothy took the message from Marjorie to Mrs Trew. It seemed there were to be a lot of people for lunch on Sunday, and Marjorie felt that Mrs Trew should be forewarned of the necessity for a conference. Dorothy held Joe's fat hand in hers. He liked walking with her, conversing volubly if not always quite comprehensibly about the many marvels they came across on the way. At least he welcomed them all as marvels, but he was willing to change his mind at the slightest indication: his enthusiastic commendation of the prettiness of a cow-pat could change at a hint to the most heartfelt expressions of disgust. He was not inflexible in his views; it was the conversational exchange he enjoyed.

Dorothy, who usually enjoyed it too, tried to hush him as they approached the Trew's cottage. She was afraid Rena and Janet would come out of the cottage next door and pick him up and kiss him and when they did this she could hardly bear it; but Joe would not be hushed and chattered on loudly, unaware of the danger. As she had feared the door opened, the dreaded smell of boiling washing wafted towards them and fat Rena and thin Janet slowly emerged, looking shifty but determined.

When Marjorie had once asked Mrs Trew if she had any idea why Mrs Hedges found it necessary to be perpetually boiling washing, Mrs Trew had said that as she understood it both the girls wet their beds, adding that she shouldn't wonder if Mr Hedges didn't do the same, seeing how drunk he was most nights by the time he got to bed. Marjorie had asked herself yet again how any of them could have been so idiotic as to have entered into an agreement with the Hedges without far closer consultation with the Trews, the only ones who were to be immediate next-door neighbours, and the only ones who had expressed apprehension after meeting them for a moment while they were being shown the house. It was the Trews who were suffering most, thus adding a burden of guilt to the unhappiness felt in varying degrees by everyone at the Abbey as a result of the presence there of the Hedges. The most cunning malignity of an ill-wisher towards their project—Mrs Hancock herself endowed with superhuman powers—could hardly have chosen a more disastrous family.

It was Jane and Caroline with their lack of the usual inhibitions who first said it. 'The Hedges are horrid,' they said after the first day. Dorothy thought they were horrid too but would certainly not have liked to say so. Mr Hedges was huge and dark and brought with him an atmosphere of suppressed violence. In the evenings it appeared that the violence was not suppressed and that Mrs Hedges and Rena and Janet suffered accordingly. He drank. The gentle conversational probings of Marjorie elicited from Mrs Hedges only the fatalistic, possibly even proud, reply, 'It's in the family.' She did not seem to wish to discuss it further. Mrs Hedges was thin to the extent of being more or less concave, and quite white. This, together with her lank hair, hopeless expression and nasally shrill voice made Fisher liken her to Olive Oil, the innamorata of Popeye the Sailor Man. Dorothy had never been to the cinema (her parents were certain there would be some sort of contamination, whether physical or moral or more probably both) but the name sounded suitably disagreeable. Why the mania for cleanliness which must have been responsible for all that boiling never induced in her a desire to wash her own hair remained a mystery. Perhaps that was in the family too; certainly it had been passed on to Rena and Janet. Both had inherited their mother's complexion, though only one—Janet—her build. 'Rena', as her mother put it, 'is a big girl. Needs her liquids, like her father. She's always at the tap, is Rena.'

This information was vouchsafed to Mrs Trew, to whom Mrs Hedges would from time to time make observations of a similar nature; beyond these she would not go. She told Mrs Trew that the other people at the Abbey were not her class, that she knew her place and besides had always kept herself to herself. The friendly overtures which were made to her by Marjorie and Mrs Arkwright were firmly—even brusquely—rejected. It seemed that the talk about community spirit which Fisher had given her and her husband when they came to see the cottage had left them unmoved.

Mr Hedges—or Ivor as those who were bold enough called him—whose strength and size had been points in his favour at the time of his first visit to the Abbey, seemed in spite of them to have little inclination for physical labour, unless the hearty laying about his wife and daughters with a big stick in the evenings could come under that heading. He showed no signs of serious intentions towards the bit of land which was supposed to be his own responsibility and when Arnold offered to spend a day with him digging it over, Ivor complained of backache after an hour or two and went indoors to lie down. Had he had backache down the mine? Arnold asked him. Never missed a day's work, was the answer. Depressed, Arnold dug on alone.

'It's the demoralising experiences he's had in the last year,' Stanley Arkwright said. 'The dole and so on. It's been a shock to his system. We can't expect him to get over it in a moment. We must give him time.'

They gave him time. Their forbearance, their carefully thought out moves in the direction of co-operation, seemed to have no effect on him at all, whereas his heavy silences, his

67

inactivity, his evening drunkenness had an increasingly depressing effect on everyone else.

Gerda minded least, partly because she was preoccupied by her self-imposed task of making a poet out of Timothy, and partly because though she was all in favour of a new world she did not care too much about its being a classless one. An intellectual élite at the very least being obviously inevitable, just as she herself was inevitably destined to be part of it, she was not unduly shocked at the thought that one of the workers might be of low calibre. Everyone else minded a lot, the children because of the uncomfortable atmosphere in that part of the Abbey grounds which meant that they avoided going there as much as possible, and the adults because they felt in varying degrees that the Hedges family constituted an affront to everything in which they believed, and they were baffled by the failure of their goodwill to make any difference at all. Arnold most of all, who could not believe that honest work and an interest in a piece of land, pastoral beauty and the welcome of a friendly community, would not cure all of anyone's ills, was deeply upset, could not sleep, sat with Hamilton in his workshop saying, 'Why, Hamilton, why? Marjorie cooks these marvellous meals each day and they say they'd rather eat on their own. He won't talk to any of us and yet he'll walk two miles to the pub every day and twice on Sundays to get drunk. Why?'

'He's in despair, I suppose,' said Hamilton. 'And so is she, because she takes her mood from him, having no mind of her own. What we offer is not the cure for his despair, what we offer simply doesn't touch the most peripheral outposts of his despair. I don't know the cause of it, and nor I suspect does he.'

'I asked him about his war experiences. I thought perhaps he might have been shell-shocked.'

'What did he say?'

'Not much, he never does. He said they were a good bunch, the people he was with, that's all. I don't know, we'll have to persevere.'

'Perhaps not for too long. In another week or two could you not put it to him that it hasn't been a success?'

But in another week or two Marcella Maysey-Smith had brought her weekend visitors to lunch.

Marcella, driving over to the Abbey with Raymond Barry the publisher, his wife Pippa and Maurice Makepiece the Communist poet, thought of her mother the famous Kitty Carlington and of her husband the enigmatic Noel; or rather they were both present in her mind, two figures clearly discernible in the swirling mist of general anxiety which otherwise filled her consciousness, a beautiful woman in Edwardian dress, a handsome young man in an aviator's helmet, neither perhaps quite what they seemed. She did suspect sometimes in both of them this equivocality, but she did not wish to speculate as to its nature. 'Funny old Mama,' she preferred to say, 'Funny old Noel'—an adjective in neither case adequate, even as a substitute for speculation.

Raymond Barry drove in silence, absorbing the two large gin slings he had drunk rather quickly before they set out, and Maurice Makepiece in the back quarrelled with Pippa who had also had two large gin slings and was accusing him of being in the pay of the Comintern. Marcella remembered her mother telling her that grown-up life was Hell. They had been playing at being grown-ups, Marcie and her two sisters, at bedtime in their cream flannel nighties before the War, and their mother, who had come to say goodnight to them and was gazing abstractedly at her own sweet face and huge blue eyes and mass of golden hair pinned loosely on top of her head, had said, 'Oh my darlings, grown-up life is *Hell on earth*.' She seldom spoke to them like that, her light rapid voice running rather on everything that was nice and good and pretty. Marcie remembered the voice particularly, and the little curiously frightened laugh along the passage warning them that she was bringing some kindly bearded visitor with her on her goodnight visit, so they must be on their best behaviour.

Marcella had inherited the little laugh, together with its message that everything was lovely, everything was the greatest fun, and any other way of looking at things was simply unthinkable; if the unthinkable did sometimes rear its head it had to be firmly suppressed.

C*

'What fun,' said Marcella accordingly, leading her group upstairs to the library at the Abbey. 'Too sweet of you to have so many of us. We're only the advance party, there's another carload on the way.'

Pippa's eyes lighted first on Fisher, as he rose to greet them. After a cursory glance round the room she focussed intensely on his face again; the rest, she thought, looked a dreary bunch. She lit a cigarette. Pippa lighting a cigarette amounted to some kind of preliminary flourish before battle was joined. Arnold and Marjorie, the Arkwrights, Gerda, Timothy, Gerda's husband Philip, all felt it, all either physically or mentally closed ranks, as the bracelets clashed, the sleek dark hair fell first forward as the scarlet-nailed hands were cupped round the flame and then back as the fierce white face emerged, tilted backwards, and the nostrils flared, exhaling smoke; there was no doubt about it, Pippa was a challenge. Up the stairs came the reinforcements, headed by Cousin Penelope in full flood, finding this Bohemian weekend such a lark, really Marcie was too amusing for words, the people she got hold of. Richard Fuller the journalist was with her, weighed down with inside knowledge, self-esteem and beer (he'd made Penelope stop at the pub for cigarettes and had managed to swallow a pint, but too quickly for comfort). His wife was also there, fair, fat and hopelessly resentful, and two Cambridge undergraduates already exchanging expressions of previous acquaintance and mutual distrust with Timothy.

'Really what the hell is one to do about this bloody country?' said Richard Fuller the journalist, puffing at a short cigar (at the Abbey no one smoked tobacco, though Gerda liked an occasional herbal cigarette). 'Wherever one goes in Europe and meets other intellectuals and tells them about this country they say, My God if there are people like you, people as well-informed and concerned as you are, there must be hope for England, things can't be as bad as you say. How can one explain one's uniqueness, the wall of complacency against which one battles?'

'Which particular wall do you have in mind?' asked Fisher cautiously. 'There are so many. The German situation is your special field, I know.'

'Bloody pacifists, that's what I mean,' said Richard Fuller.

'Peace pledge, and all that crap. We've got to re-arm, we've got to tell people why.'

Marjorie hung her head, gazed at her own tightly clasped hands on her knees. He launched on facts and figures. She knew they were true; she'd seen Gerda's friends, the Jewish or liberal refugees who passed through the Abbey, of course she knew something awful was happening in Germany, but how could the answer to anything be tanks and bombs and death, the killing of people like the dear German teachers in the school in Switzerland, and little children, like Joe? How could it be right glibly to talk of things like that and for such talk to let the lunch go cold? All the children had helped to get it ready, Mrs Trew had done the dumplings; the outside world should stay outside.

It was a day for crossed purposes. The long table in the kitchen seated them all, though rather close together. Dorothy had been asked to stay and help, and was looking after Joe, so that Marjorie could concentrate on serving the food. The trouble was that by the time they sat down Fisher had got into an argument with Richard Fuller and so sat next to him and let other people sit where they liked. Pippa, finding herself too late to sit next to Fisher where she thought she ought to have been, had to sit between Stanley Arkwright and Hamilton, who had slipped in quietly for his lunch and was not introduced to her.

Stanley Arkwright was a thorough though uninspiring teacher, who knew a great deal about the early history of the Industrial Revolution and had an unswerving and, it must be admitted, unsmiling faith in the potentiality for good of Guild Socialism. In no way was he equipped to deal with Pippa. She, soon discerning this, turned her attention to Hamilton, whose appearance she was prepared to consider intriguing. He had seen at once that she was what he called 'a vamp', but he consented to answer her enquiries about the origins and history of the Abbey. When however she showed what he considered an improper interest in the possibility of there once having been monkish orgies in the room where they sat, he murmured something about work to be finished, rose from his chair and quietly left the room.

'Oh but there's Bakewell tart,' said Marjorie, unable to restrain her surprise.

'Bakewell tart, Hamilton!' called Mrs Arkwright cheerfully. But he had gone.

'He often does that,' said Arnold apologetically.

'Not when there's Bakewell tart,' said Mrs Arkwright tactlessly.

'Oh yes,' insisted Arnold, who had seen his face as he left. It had worn the same expression as when they had been taken to the circus in Bath when Hamilton was six or so: when the clowns came on he quietly left with just that look. (He came back later for the lions.) 'He often does it,' Arnold said.

'I expect I frightened him away,' said Pippa, smiling furiously.

She was not enjoying herself.

'Do give me some more wine,' she said to Stanley Arkwright. 'And tell me, don't you find sandals give you blisters, even with socks?'

There was plenty of good claret. After much discussion it had been decided that the occasion warranted its being brought up from the cellar. They did not often drink it, but there was a considerable supply down there. The Reverend Frederick Whitehead had always kept a good cellar and since in his later years he had suffered from duodenal ulcers, there had been dozens of bottles left at his death. Some of it had passed its prime but most of it was excellent. Fisher was faintly irritated to see the speed at which Richard Fuller was drinking it and the number of short fat cigars with which he accompanied it. None of the guests was exactly holding back—it was lucky he had brought up so many bottles. Pippa's husband the publisher at least seemed to appreciate it, guessed the year right, though thought it was a Château Margaux rather than a Latour, interrupting his literary gossip with Gerda, who had managed to extract from him a promise to read some of Timothy's poetry. He looked uneasily towards Pippa. She was his third wife, and though he had always liked women who brought about drama, she did sometimes go a little far, even for him. She now abruptly pushed back her chair and emphasising the phrase embarrassingly said, 'I'm going to sit *below the salt*.' She picked

72

up her wine glass and went towards the end of the table where the Hedges and Trews and the children were sitting. Perching on the edge of the bench near Ivor Hedges, she said, 'Now who are *you?*'

Marjorie, who was near that end of the table, had already realised to her discomfiture that while some of the visitors seemed to be feeling the effects of alcohol there was one of the Abbey residents who far exceeded any of them in that respect; and she had been hoping that the meal could be got through without this becoming evident to everyone. It was Sunday, and on Sundays Mr Hedges went to the pub before lunch as well as in the evening. Possibly the prospect of the large lunch party had encouraged him to fortify himself even more than usual. However it was, he was quite drunk. Turning a thoughtful gaze on Pippa he said indistinctly, 'Ivor Hedges is the name,' and then gave a perfectly enormous belch.

Jane and Caroline giggled, Dorothy turned scarlet in the face, hasty conversation started up all round the table, and Pippa said, 'This is *mar*vellous,' and gave the throaty laugh that her acquaintances knew only too well as a harbinger of trouble.

'*Do* tell me more,' she said, putting one braceletted arm round his considerable shoulders. 'We must have a long talk.'

Most of the Abbey residents scattered after lunch, to work or in some cases to sleep (after all it was Sunday and they were not used to wine at lunch), leaving Fisher and Arnold to conduct some of the visitors on a brief tour, while others, less interested, sat in the library with Gerda, who was talking a great deal and rather enjoying herself. Marjorie and the Arkwrights and the children politely gathered in the hall to say goodbye when they thought the tour must be coming to an end, thus exposing themselves to the awkward scene which arose when the visitors were all gathered together preparing to leave and it became clear that Pippa was not among them.

Fisher, beaming and expounding, happy in the knowledge that he had charmed Marcella and managed to throw off the journalist and the publisher (who had stayed in the library with Gerda) said cheerfully, 'One of the children will find her, if you really must go. Dorothy, run and see if you can find Mrs

—er—Barry, and tell her her party's on the move, would you?'

As far as he was concerned everything had gone very well. Marcella had said to him in her abrupt way as they walked across the garden, 'I'd like to give you something towards the building work. Will you let me do that?'

Of course he said he'd be delighted. He rather liked her when she calmed down, or anyway felt that he would like her if he knew her better, for she still seemed very nervous. He also liked Maurice Makepiece the Communist poet, who was full of good-will and dreadfully short-sighted, and he found the undergraduates an appreciative audience. Cousin Penelope had now decided the whole thing was too boring for words and just like some ghastly boarding school and so had mercifully fallen silent; so all in all he was in a sunny humour and waited without apprehension for Dorothy to return with that obvious hellpiece (for so he considered her), the publisher's wife.

Dorothy, however, was not looking for the publisher's wife. She had gone to the very end of the garden and was planning to stay there quite a long time. She had seen Pippa lingering in the vegetable garden as the rest of the group moved on, she had heard her throaty laugh as she discovered the little stone god which Dorothy thought disgusting, and she had seen the motionless figure of Ivor Hedges over by the far wall. She did not want to know why he was there—usually on Sunday afternoons he disappeared to sleep—nor did she want to know why Pippa lingered and looked at him over the stone god and the cabbages, but she did know that nothing would have induced her to go and look for either of them.

So the guests ready to depart and the hosts ready to say goodbye had quite a long wait in the hall until as conversation was failing and they were beginning to grow restless Pippa burst in from the garden, breathless from running.

'Thank God you're all still here,' she said. 'I thought you might have gone.'

She leant against the wall, lit a cigarette, and surveyed her gratifyingly large and attentive audience.

'I must say,' she said, beginning to smile. 'Your miner. I mean he simply raped me. Among the cabbages. Too extraordinary.'

74

She exhaled smoke, still smiling. There was silence. Her glance, superficially amused, moved from face to face.

Cousin Penelope said, 'Well *really*!'

Maurice Makepiece, true to his name, shuffled towards Pippa in an exaggeratedly short-sighted and fussy manner, saying, 'Come along, come along, we've all been waiting, oh what a naughty girl you are . . .' and everybody else, relieved, began to move and talk and make farewells.

Pippa shook off the gentle Makepiece. She went up to her husband and putting her face very close to his and narrowing her ferocious eyes said, 'You don't believe me, do you? You don't believe I've been raped.'

He returned her gaze, matching her dislike but not her venom, and said, 'I believe you.'

'What are you going to do about it then? Your wife has just been raped by a drunken miner. Are you just going to stand there? Do something.'

'I suggest you don't work yourself up,' he said, but he lowered his gaze, unable to meet those eyes.

'Come along, you two,' said Marcie, asserting herself as pack leader. 'You can do all that in the car. They're famous for their rows, these two. Oh dear, never mind, what fun. Come along now.'

'Come along, come along,' echoed Maurice Makepiece, shooing gently like a well-trained sheepdog.

'Oh leave me *alone*, Maurice,' said Pippa irritably, but she did move towards the door, did shake hands with Fisher—'Thank you for lunch. I apologise for my husband's spinelessness.'— did climb into the back of Marcie's Morris and allow herself to be driven away, breathing, if not fire, at least a cloud of smoke.

'Well well well.' Fisher came back into the hall when both cars had driven away. 'Thank you very much everyone. Quite hard work, I must admit. Never mind, we've been promised a big contribution towards the building fund so it was all worth it.'

Marjorie burst into tears.

'If you take one penny from those wicked, wicked people I'll never have anything to do with this place again.'

She ran noisily up the stairs and along the passage. Her bedroom door banged. Everyone in the hall remained motionless. Marjorie, of all people!

Dorothy's half-brother Rory, the elder of her father's two sons by his first marriage, announced his engagement to the daughter of one of the partners in the firm of stockbrokers for which he worked. The firm was called Morton Charlesworth and Astaire, and Rory's fiancée was Rosemary Astaire. The announcement came as a surprise to his father because Rory and his brother by now led lives of their own in London and came to Winterstoke with increasing infrequency. They were both kind to Dorothy but seemed quite remote and grown-up to her: she hardly ever thought about them when they were not there. The idea of Rory being married was strange; she could not imagine him falling in love. When he arrived for the weekend with his fiancée she saw that the only effect it had had on him was to make him even more remote and grown-up. He talked a lot to his father about the way things were going in the City, and Rosemary Astaire sat looking neat and attentive and as if she had her notebook ready on her knee. She had been a secretary to a merchant banker and seemed to know as much about financial affairs as Rory and his father, if not more. She was sallow-complexioned and not very pretty, but neat and quiet. She and Rory behaved as if they had been married for years, with no fuss. Dorothy approved of that, and thought the whole thing, though perhaps not very romantic, just right for Rory.

She expected her father to feel the same, and had no reason to suppose he did not until after lunch on Sunday when the engaged pair had driven away to return to London. Charles Grant came back into the drawing-room with Dorothy and her mother, sank heavily into an armchair and said in tones of great bitterness, 'So that's what my daughter-in-law's to be.'

'Oh Charles, surely. . . .'

'They won't be your grandchildren, will they?'

'But I'm very fond of Rory, I'm sure I shall regard them as if they were.'

'It won't be your blood which will be tainted.'

76

'Oh Charles.'

'Why tainted?' asked Dorothy, much surprised.

'Your little nephews and nieces, my dear,' he said heavily, 'will be what are sometimes known as hookies.'

'Hookies?'

'Yids.'

'I've never heard those words. I haven't the faintest idea what you mean.' Dorothy was completely bewildered.

'Jews,' he said.

'You mean, Rosemary is Jewish?' she said, still trying to grasp his meaning. 'But you—do you mind that?'

'I'm not exactly delighted.'

Dorothy was beginning to tremble. The only Jews she had ever to her knowledge met were the German refugees who passed through the Abbey from time to time. She had never heard of anyone being anti-semitic except in Germany. She was alarmed by the violence of her own sense of shock.

'I don't—I just don't understand. . . .'

'I've met too many of them in business to want one in my own family.'

'Oh Charles,' said Mrs Grant again. 'I really don't think that sort of thing matters these days.'

'But then . . .' burst out Dorothy in an unfamiliar voice. 'But then, there's no difference between you and Hitler!'

Charles Grant had had to suppress his annoyance and disappointment all weekend. The sight of Dorothy's evident emotion added a touch of sadism to his frustration.

He said provocatively, 'I take it you mean that as a criticism?'

He expected her to burst into tears, which in his present mood would have given him satisfaction. Instead she went rather pale and said quietly, 'Yes, I do.'

'Then in that case,' he said. 'You had better leave the room.'

Without hurrying, she picked up the book she had been reading and did so. There was a short silence after she had gone. It was not quite clear whose was the victory. Then Charles Grant sighed heavily.

'It's the influence of that dreadful place,' he said. 'I knew they'd fill her head with left-wing propaganda.'

It was decided that Nora Grant should look for a suitable boarding school for Dorothy. Dorothy was delighted at the idea because one result of the unsettled feeling which had come over the Abbey, where for the time being nobody seemed able to resolve the difficulty over whether or not to accept Marcella's money, let alone decide what to do about the Hedges, was that Stanley Arkwright applied for a job at a co-educational boarding school in Sussex and was accepted. The family was going to move there in time for the beginning of the next term and Jane and Caroline were to be pupils at the school. There could be no question of Dorothy's going to the same school because her father did not approve of co-education, but at least it was nice to be able to say that she was probably going to boarding school too.

She had apologised to her father, not because she meant it but because she could not bear to see her mother upset. Her father had been very reasonable.

'One doesn't always mean every word of what one says, you know,' he said, smiling at her across his big desk as if the very idea that she could have taken him seriously was amusing. 'And after all one must be allowed to let off steam in the privacy of the family circle. Not being very keen on having a Jewish daughter-in-law is very different from wanting to get rid of all the Jews in the country. I hope you realise that, do you?'

'Yes.'

'Run along then and forget about it.' He turned back to his papers.

She did not quite forget about it. She thought his reasonableness was the result of Nora Grant's having begged him to make up the quarrel (which was only partly true), and the incident was one more stage in her gradual recognition of the distance which separated her from her father.

The search for a school took some time, and ended in failure. Whether or not Dorothy would have been unhappy at the various institutions which her mother inspected, Nora Grant was quite certain that she herself would have been miserable at any of them, and since that was the criterion she was using in order to form her judgement she decided that on no account

78

should Dorothy go away to school at all. The long passages, smelling of cabbage, the unbecoming gym tunics, the enormous senior girls, the terrifying headmistresses with iron-grey hair and dreadful-sounding diplomas—the whole thing seemed to Nora Grant so unfeminine and really quite beastly—and when Dorothy said that Jane and Caroline's school didn't sound in the least like that she said, 'But that's progressive, darling, which means no discipline at all, which means you're simply at the mercy of gangs of bullies!'

Dorothy agreed that that didn't sound at all nice. She also thought that whereas Jane and Caroline would be quite capable of standing up to gangs of bullies she would not. So she agreed with her mother that perhaps it would be better to forget about boarding school.

Charles Grant was pleased by the decision.

'Too much education's no use to a girl anyway,' he said. 'We can use the money we would have spent on it to give her a Season in London when she's old enough. And a dressmaking course or something.'

To Dorothy's surprise, he next allowed himself to be persuaded that she should receive extra tuition in certain subjects from, of all people, Arnold Whitehead. Having dismissed the idea of school, and having agreed as everyone seemed to do that Dorothy had outgrown Miss Gamage, he found it difficult to suggest an alternative. In spite of his suspicions about the Abbey, he had found Arnold reasonable enough when he had met him. Besides, Nora was keen on the idea. In Charles Grant's view children, especially girl children, were chiefly the concern of the mother, with the father in the background as the ultimate authority. If Nora was convinced that a few sessions a week with Arnold Whitehead would solve Dorothy's problems for the time being, he was content to give his blessing. Dorothy's chief function, as he saw it, was to give pleasure and companionship to Nora, especially while he himself was busy in London. Sometimes when he saw this function being fulfilled he found himself irritated. He depended a great deal on his wife's affection—and indeed constant attention—but he would never have said that he was jealous of his daughter, only that he was not very interested in children.

Nora liked Arnold and Marjorie, whom she had met from time to time when she had been to the Abbey to collect Dorothy in the car. She thought they were just what school teachers ought to be like, kind and unassuming and reassuring —if only they had been running a boarding school instead of those dragons of headmistresses she had seen!

'Besides,' she said to Charles, as if that settled everything. 'He is the married brother.'

'You are married,' said Marjorie.

Arnold sat humped miserably in a chair. Marjorie was standing.

'I never thought my love of you and my love of this place could come into conflict,' he said. 'It's the most awful thing that could possibly have happened to me.'

'It's only because your love of the place has made you lose your sense of proportion,' she said remorselessly. 'You can't take money from bad people to do good things. It isn't right.'

'I think you over-simplify.'

'I am a very simple person.'

He was silent.

'Your brothers think I am a very limited person.'

'I don't care what they think.'

'Yes, you do. You care more about what they think than about what I think.'

'No.' He shook his head. 'No, no, no.'

'Or about Joe.' Her eyes filled with tears. 'You want to bring up your child in a place which is based on a lie.'

He stood up and began to walk about the room. He had never known that she could be like this. All the strength and resolve he so much admired, all the simplicity and faith and rock-like obstinacy he so much loved, all turned against *him*: it was unbearable.

'The thing is,' he said, trying to get back to reason, 'Fisher would very much like to accept that money. It will be very hard to persuade him not to.'

'If he does I shall go.'

'But if we go it breaks up the whole community.'

80

'Better that than that it should become a false thing.'

'I'm just in the middle of arranging this conference. . . .' he said weakly.

'Cancel the conference.'

'You don't think you're being a bit uncompromising?'

'There are some things you can't compromise about. Once you start . . . the next thing is I suppose you'll be accepting money from the Oxford Group. Or the British Union of Fascists. That'll be the next thing.'

He sighed.

'Let me have another talk to Fisher,' he said. 'I am trying. Believe me, Marjorie, I am trying.'

Fisher had a letter from Sir Giles Lambert asking if he might call and see him. Fisher agreed, because it was impossible not to, but with some reluctance. He found the man difficult to talk to and did not at all relish the idea of showing him round the Abbey and satisfying his curiosity as to the point of the enterprise—which he imagined must be the object of the visit.

What made it worse was that Sir Giles, when he did come, was obviously embarrassed. It took him a long time to get round to explaining why he was there. He refused Fisher's invitation to sit down but walked up and down the library instead, commenting on the books on the shelves and the trees which he could see out of the window (revealing considerable knowledge in both instances) and talking, though not volubly —indeed, with many pauses for silence—about the weather, the state of the world and other such generalities, before finally saying, 'Look here, I'm beating about the bush most awfully, wasting your time, frightful cheek. . . .'

'Not at all.' Fisher's polite murmur was not convincing.

'The fact is—it's most frightfully interfering of me—Marcella told me she'd been over here. She just happened to mention someone you've got here—I mean it would be the most extraordinary coincidence—I had a chap under me in the War, fellow by the name of Hedges.'

'Hedges?' repeated Fisher, taken by surprise.

'Yeomanry regiment you know. All local people. Splendid

chap, Hedges, fine physique, strong as an ox.' His melancholy face was lit by an affectionate smile. 'One of my sergeants.'

'Ivor Hedges?' asked Fisher cautiously.

'That's it. Ivor Hedges. Splendid chap. Glutton for work.'

'It can't be the same,' said Fisher.

'Well, that's it, you see.' Sir Giles looked embarrassed again. 'Marcella told me you'd been having a bit of trouble with him.'

'He's lazy and drunken and rather violent,' said Fisher.

'You don't say,' said Sir Giles, looking serious. 'What a shame. What a shame.' He seemed to sink into melancholy at the thought.

After some moments of silence Fisher said, 'Would you like to see him?'

'Well, that's it, you see. That's just the thing. We do happen to have a gardener leaving. There is a cottage—of course I couldn't possibly suggest anything without seeing you first.'

'That might be a very good solution,' said Fisher. 'I must say,' he added conscientiously, 'I'm not sure that he's much of a gardener.'

'Never mind about that. It isn't much of a garden, actually. I mean it's mostly grass, don't you know. Shall I just nip along and have a word with him, then, now that I've cleared it with you?'

Evidently relieved to have got off his chest a proposition which he seemed to have expected Fisher to regard as impertinent rather than heaven-sent, Sir Giles became much more decisive. Within an hour, a strangely revivified Hedges presented himself in the library and stood to attention in front of Fisher, asking permission to leave as soon as possible.

Granting it, Fisher said, 'I hope you will be better there than here.'

'Oh, I think so, sir,' said Ivor Hedges confidently. He had never called Fisher 'sir' before. 'I shall know where I am there.'

'I see.'

'I'd do anything for the Colonel, sir. Anything in the world.'

Fisher walked on the Plain in the rough wind and occasional

drizzle of an October day and thought of his vision, and of his brothers.

The vision, he supposed, was a question of mood, which was why it could not be summoned at will. It was a question of tone, of colour, as if a certain filter had to be fitted over the lens he looked through; it was a question of a frame of mind. He had long recognised that more than reason was involved. That was why he had developed his theory about the influence of the liver, but he knew it to be a wholly inadequate theory.

> '. . . that calm existence that is mine
> When I am worthy of myself . . .'

That was what he was always trying to get through to, like Wordsworth.

'Have you got the blues?' his mother would say. (Not until long afterwards did it occur to him that it was an odd expression for her to use in that time and place—when he later came across its American usage it was the latter that struck him as odd—he thought of it as her invention, as indeed it perhaps coincidentally was.) He would be crouching somewhere, probably on the floor, and she would sit beside him and gather him into her arms, his bony muddy knees up against his nose, and squeeze him and kiss the back of his neck and inhale the smell of his skin and say, 'Resignation renunciation reconciliation'—rolling all the rs—'Pain must be gone along with, never resisted, go with the river and let it take you to a calmer place,' and she would rock him gently and then her large cool hand would stroke his forehead and slowly every muscle in his body would seem to relax and calm would succeed the tension. Once she said, 'The Bishop of Bath and Wells said I had healing hands.' (Why? When? On what conceivable occasion? For some reason he did not think to ask.) After the physical calm came the mental clarity, and sometimes they talked and sometimes they didn't. Sometimes they just sat there, and the rocking gradually ceased and it seemed he had no body but only room after room of the mind to wander through, limitless space but within a building, doorways opening onto vaster, emptier, more glorious rooms, a singing silence, an enormous understanding; and then she'd say, 'Ah well, there are the apples to pick,' or something

83

of that sort, but the happiness would stay with him for the rest of the day.

He walked on Salisbury Plain in a flapping overcoat and a wide-brimmed black hat, and waited for his idea of the Abbey to regenerate itself, and in the meantime worried about his brothers.

Arnold's attitude to Marjorie had always irritated him. He thought her a useful woman, pleasant to have about the place, an excellent wife for Arnold; but to take her opinions about anything in the world at all seriously seemed to him mere folly. She hadn't a brain in her head, had never read a book—except possibly some kind of rubbish about reincarnation—she was a kindergarten teacher, that was all. That Arnold should seriously entertain the notion of withdrawing altogether from the Abbey because this naïve creature had had her nose put out of joint by Marcella Maysey-Smith's sophisticated friends was maddening to Fisher. How could Arnold be so *wet*?

He suddenly felt he'd like to see his sister Mary. She was so unemotional, unlike all three brothers, so decisive. She simplified life (though life probably *was* much simpler if you were married to a millionaire). He'd go there. He'd do another lecture tour— why not?—instead of accepting the controversial bequest from Marcella. The Hedges episode had been a setback, and to have been rescued from it by Sir Giles Lambert reasserting the authority of his class was a humiliation he preferred to forget. Lunch with the bank manager to persuade him to hang on a little longer, and off to the land of opportunity, that was the answer.

'Noel thinks life as a sort of test,' said Marcella. 'He told me that. Everything's a test, he said.'

She looked doubtfully across at Ralph Blatchford, as if she thought he might be able to explain.

They were sitting at the table in the Abbey kitchen, with mugs of coffee, the two of them, and Fisher, Arnold and Marjorie. It was raining outside. The kitchen was warm and smelt of baking bread, the scrubbed table was bare except for a bowl of apples and a basket of blackberries. Even Marcella's optimistic account of her last visit to the Abbey had sounded

84

bad to Ralph. He had insisted that they should drive over on the chance of seeing Fisher alone to find out what damage had been done. Fisher had been in the kitchen talking to Arnold about the possibility of his going to America, while Marjorie did the baking. Fisher would have preferred to discuss his plans alone with Arnold, but it was becoming harder than ever to speak to him without Marjorie. Fisher did not understand that his brother's reluctance arose from Marjorie's present mood. She suspected them of plotting to accept Marcella's money without telling her. Rather than meet her suspicious gaze Arnold avoided speaking to Fisher except in her presence.

Ralph smiled. 'Yes, he has that compulsion. A Childe Roland complex, one might almost say. I think there is such a thing, don't you?'

'I don't know,' said Marcella. 'I'm too badly educated to know what you mean exactly. Although I sort of do and it's rather sad, isn't it? I mean, when he got to the dark tower, there wasn't anyone there, was there? In that case I hope he never finds it—Noel I mean—I hope he just goes on looking. I don't feel like that myself at all. I'm not looking for anything. But I feel you people here are. That's what I like about this place. It's quite mysterious to me, the searching and testing thing. I suppose that's what I like about it, in painters, or in Noel or in you. I feel I know how to support it. Do you see what I mean?'

'Yes I do,' said Fisher.

'Noel doesn't need much help or support,' she said, clasping her hands round her mug. 'He's very self-sufficient, isn't he Ralph?'

'Very.'

'I don't want to search or test because I shouldn't know what it was when I found it, and I'd be bound to fail the test. But I like people who can do it, and who aren't, for instance, terrified of change, like I am. Are you terrified of change?' she asked Marjorie.

'I don't believe the important things do change,' said Marjorie.

'Oh I think everything can change, and might at any minute, just suddenly shift, you know, under one's feet.'

'Not some things, surely. Not the really important things,

like human relations. Only customs and attitudes, not the underlying human true things, because if they changed then we shouldn't be human beings.'

'No but . . . oh I don't know. I can see they need you here, they must depend on you. I bet you know all about the human true things. Perhaps that's what the search is for. What is it for, Ralph? What is Noel searching for?'

'I think you were nearer it when you said he saw life as a test. I think he's always testing himself. Perhaps he's preparing himself for some bigger test which he thinks he's going to have to undergo in the future, something quite unspecified, quite vague.'

'Like dying, do you mean?' Marcella asked, intently.

'Perhaps.'

Marjorie went over to open the oven door. A delicious smell of fresh baking filled the kitchen.

'There was a boy at school who used to put peas in his shoes before the long-distance run,' said Fisher. 'He never told anyone. I just happened to see one day. Farquhar, his name was. He became a missionary.'

'Oh I do hope Noel won't become a missionary,' said Marcella dreamily. 'We'd have to go and live somewhere quite awful and certainly be eaten.'

Marjorie came back to the table with a tray of ginger cakes. Her face was flushed from the heat of the oven.

'Try one,' she said to Marcella.

Marjorie's capitulation took place in the big bed, under the duvet, and was the occasion of the conception of Joe's sister Meg. After Marcella and Ralph had left, Arnold had said to Fisher, 'Don't say anything about it for a day or two. Leave it to me.' It was one of the first cold nights of that autumn. A thin mist, smelling faintly of sodden leaves and woodsmoke, crept in at the window which Marjorie had opened a few inches just before getting into bed. It was a wonderful relief to her to feel that Arnold had been right all the time, and that Marcella was a woman of good intent. At the same time he made her feel he loved her all the more for having been so determined that their beautiful idea should not be contaminated: he made

86

it easy for her to climb down. He had been so patient, she had been so conscientious. Meg, like her brother, was a love child.

Miss Gamage, though she had surrendered Dorothy's education in English literature to Arnold, was rather good at French. They read Pierre Loti's *Pêcheurs d'Islande* that autumn. Dorothy skipped ahead to read the last paragraph long before they reached it. It was about the hero's drowning, the celebration of his marriage to the sea, and how all his friends were there, fellow fishermen, '. . . tous, excepté Sylvestre, qui, lui, s'en était allé domir dans des jardins enchantés, très loin, de l'autre côté de la terre.' Every time she read this it made her cry.

With Arnold she read Jane Austen, which she enjoyed very much. (Arnold felt that this bore out his view that Jane Austen was a children's writer, rather like Daisy Ashford.) She also read Shaw and Wells, Arnold Bennett and Ibsen, none of which she enjoyed as much as Jane Austen, but she liked the idea that they were making her think about grown-up subjects. Sometimes she and Arnold, and anyone else who could be persuaded to join them, read plays aloud. Dorothy enjoyed this so much that she decided that when she was grown-up she would like to get a job reading aloud on the wireless. Although she did not mention this to anyone, since her parents would not have liked the idea of her having a job at all, she found it reassuring to feel that she knew what she was going to do and that she would earn money and be independent and not have to get married unless she wanted to. Arnold congratulated her on her reading of Shaw's *Saint Joan*, but his essentially sober temperament did not lend itself to enthusiasm. He encouraged her to read widely, and introduced her to a fairly random selection of books. She learned by heart long passages from Shakespeare, Tennyson and Swinburne, and would declaim them walking on the Plain in the wind.

This susceptibility to literature seemed part of a general increase in her awareness of things. Conscious of it, she connected it with the onset of puberty, another sign of progress. Her mother had, with a good deal of embarrassment, told her more or less what to expect, Miss Gamage had for some time been solicitously on the look-out for headaches, pains or 'moods'. Thus she was surprised to find when one day she noticed a bright red spot on her knickers as she lowered them to sit on the lavatory that neither panic nor horror was among her emotions and that satisfaction was, or perhaps a kind of pride. The thought that her body by obeying its own laws was leading her into her proper destiny as a grown-up person pleased her. Wisdom and understanding no longer seemed unattainable but rather as if they might one day in the nature of things begin quite easily to flow. In this expectation she passed the years from fourteen to eighteen, after which she became less certain.

The play-reading brought her into closer contact than before with Timothy Moore, who joined many of their sessions. He had a light quiet voice and read expressively—he was the Dauphin to her St Joan—and he quite often brought his two friends James and Oliver, who were staying for a few months and who went some way towards filling the gap left at the Abbey by the departure of the Arkwrights. They had both recently left Cambridge and were looking for jobs, at that time hard to come by, and were only helping at the Abbey in the meantime. They were more conventional than Timothy, polite, helpful and with a tendency which they could not quite repress to call the three brothers 'sir'.

Timothy had been at the Abbey for some time now and though his relationship with Fisher had changed, in that the latter had lost interest in him and found Gerda a more efficient secretary, he was generally felt to reflect credit on the community by publishing his poetry in a number of magazines (it remained to be seen whether Gerda's efforts with Raymond Barry would result in a book), and by being known to be engaged on a highly experimental novel. He had also, under Gerda's influence, become more considerate; even Marjorie who had not much liked him at first now found him quite helpful. He went to London a certain amount to see the editors who published his poetry and for whom he wrote occasional reviews, and the fact that he had another life there, and that it was, she suspected, a homosexual one, was beginning to displease

Gerda, whose influence was nevertheless still paramount. He had lost his spots and Dorothy wished he would not so completely ignore her. When she asked him some questions about modern poetry, for instance, he told her she wouldn't understand it, which she considered quite unnecessarily insulting. By that time the Boulders had moved into the cottage next to the Trews, and she could go to them for comfort.

Tom Boulder's letter arrived before Fisher's departure for America. It was written in a fine copperplate hand and said that the writer had been given to understand that there were plots of land available at the Abbey for former miners who were suffering from the present unemployment. Fisher answered cautiously and this time everyone at the Abbey was asked to meet the family and was consulted before the offer to join the community was made to them.

Once they were there, it was as if they had always been there, the coal fire glowing in the little grate which, blacked and shined by Pat Boulder, now revealed to full effect the hearts and flowers embossed in Victorian times upon its cast-iron hood. Tom Boulder sat on one side of the fire in his red plush armchair with tassels round the legs, Pat on the other side with her mending, Griff on the rag carpet playing with his cars, Joan doing her homework at the table. Tom Boulder, though still a young man, had a slow and thoughtful way of speaking which made him seem to Dorothy a figure of total authority, utterly benign and never wrong. Pat his wife was in contrast rather frivolous and liked nothing better than a thoroughly scandalous gossip, a fact she explained to her own satisfaction as being due to their difference in religion.

'I'm only a simple Irish Catholic, you see,' she would say. 'What can you expect?'

Tom Boulder would then put on a sheepish expression which meant that he knew it was good for him to be teased, but he didn't much like it all the same. He was a very strict Wesleyan, and the children were brought up to be the same.

'If the priest at home knew what was going on in this household I'd be excommunicated, that's all. Putting my immortal soul in danger indeed,' Pat would sometimes say after she had seen them off to Gospel on Sunday.

She must have been very pretty, Dorothy thought, in her teens, before she became quite so fat. She found life at the Abbey full of interest, partly as a result of her own tendency to dramatise, and would welcome Dorothy with all sorts of questions and suggestions as to the various relationships which obtained there. She had made up her mind that Timothy Moore was romantically in love with Dorothy and was only waiting for her to be a little older before proposing marriage. Dorothy knew this to be total invention, but found that she did not mind being teased on the subject. She rather enjoyed Pat's irreverent attitude to the Abbey and its inhabitants, and felt no disloyalty because the wildest speculations usually ended with a comfortable, 'Ah well, they're good people after all.'

The Boulders' presence went a little way towards filling the gap in Dorothy's life left by the departure of Jane and Caroline. They did write from their new school, but not as often as Dorothy wrote to them. Dorothy took to dropping in at the cottage after her lessons with Arnold. Sometimes she took Joe with her, if Marjorie was busy. He was more or less the same age as Griff, so they could play with their cars together (Joan was a few years older). If Tom was at home he would sometimes reminisce about his days down the mine. He did not do this often, but once he had somehow started he could be encouraged to go on at length. His recollections seemed extraordinarily vivid; she saw that her easy assumption that being a coal-miner must be awful did not quite cover the case. It was more complicated than that. He was all the same determined that Griff should never do it : he wanted him to work on the land.

'It's not what it was, the mine,' he said. 'They've introduced all this machinery. It's too noisy now.'

'What am I to do?' said Arnold to Hamilton. 'What is anyone to do with someone so totally wrapped up in his own concerns? You ought to have some sort of heating in here by the way.'

Every available surface in Hamilton's little work-room was covered with manuscripts; even the stained glass jigsaw puzzle was completely overlaid, mostly with the correspondence be-

tween Father Augustine and his American benefactress Mrs
Roper Mirrlees during the early days of the Order of the White
Rose in the 1880s when things were going well and letters flew
to and fro across the Atlantic. . . . 'My dearest brother in Christ,
what happiness your letter gave me, bringing as it did con-
firmation that Our Lady herself has given her blessing to our
undertaking. You are too humble. If Our Lady was to show
herself to anyone it would be to you, dearest Father Augustine,
and your sweet little acolyte our beloved Boy David.'

'Just out there it was,' said Hamilton, seeing Arnold's glance
resting on that particular letter. 'It was out of this window that
he saw Her first. She appeared to him three or four times, always
in that field. He wrote a lot of hymns about it. They sang them
in their services.' He ruffled through another pile of papers.
'Beautiful writing he had. He used italic script long before Eric
Gill and those sort of people, you know. Here we are. . . .

> She to our meadow came
> Her feet have touched our grass
> With Majesty, with flame,
> We saw Our Lady pass
>
> The cattle stood amazed
> Their horns with daisies wreathed
> Amid our hearts she blazed
> We saw, we felt, we breathed.'

'How did their horns come to be wreathed with daisies?' said
Arnold suspiciously.

'Who knows?' said Hamilton. 'Perhaps it was one of the boy
David's pretty tricks. The trouble is there are so few first-hand
accounts of the apparitions, apart from his own. It's all hearsay; but there's plenty of that. Everyone who ever met the man
seems to have felt the urge to write a description of him, in a
diary or a newspaper article or a letter to a friend—or even to
Father Augustine himself—there are sheaves of letters from
people trying to describe to him the effect he had had on
them—it all adds up to quite a legend.'

'Did he believe it himself?'

'Oh I think so. The fact that he cashed in on it doesn't mean he didn't believe it. That's what's so interesting. The link between sanctity and fraudulence is a very close one: they belong in some way to the same genus. It doesn't mean all saints are frauds or all frauds saints, but just that in certain cases . . .' he began to nod slowly in a satisfied sort of way. '. . . in certain cases the two qualities can co-exist.'

'I still wish you'd do something about keeping warm in here. Couldn't you have a paraffin stove or something?'

'I should knock it over.'

'I suppose you would. There's certainly not much room for it.'

'I wouldn't mind a brazier, like roadmenders have. Or chestnut sellers in London. I wouldn't mind that. I could even roast chestnuts on it. I am not being whimsical, I really think it is the solution.'

'I suppose it might be possible,' said Arnold doubtfully. 'If you still refuse to work in the house.'

'Oh I couldn't move,' said Hamilton, shocked. 'Here I can look out of the window and see the very field in which the Mother of God manifested Herself.'

Arnold sighed.

'I sometimes think that in our middle age we are all getting much too much like ourselves.'

'About what you were saying earlier, you could say Fisher is being like himself in being selfish, you are being like yourself in fussing. Let him go to America, what does it matter? The conference will go much better without him. They won't be his sort of people, they'll be too earnest, he'll want to be dazzling and paradoxical and they'll want to talk about sewage.'

'Why should they want to talk about sewage?'

'Accounts then. Or crop rotation. Not the wide sweep, the long perspective.'

Arnold smiled. 'They'd enjoy a bit of wide sweep and long perspective. That must be their inspiration after all.'

'Couldn't Fisher be persuaded to delay his departure just long enough to do the opening address? He could give them Whither Man? in the morning and be on a boat to America in the afternoon.'

Arnold laughed. 'I hope you're not getting cynical.'

'Certainly not. But I've heard Fisher on Whither Man? since

he was six and I was three. It's lost its first impact, that's all. But he'd do that, wouldn't he?'

'He might. It would cut into his time with Mary. I don't think he's got any lectures fixed before then. I'll try anyway.'

He stayed perched on the edge of the table, watching Hamilton slowly sorting through the papers before him, dividing them into neat piles according to their categories.

'It's nice in here,' he said. 'We must do something about that heating.'

'Don't worry. Immediate enquiries shall be set afoot among the road-mending fraternity. I shall find myself a brazier.'

Timothy Moore wrote in a notebook: 'I wish I could tell the truth but I don't think I can. I shall look at this in a few days' time and it will embarrass me and I shall burn it. I can only write about myself at at least six removes from reality, six transmutations. But if that's the case, then my poetry is only disguised self-obsession, camouflaged masturbation. Perhaps that's what all poetry is, or has been ever since it ceased to be a craft and became an art. I think I use politics as a way of trying to get away from the self-cannibalising nature of the poetical process, but the fact is I don't really believe in politics, or rather I don't understand politics. I've a feeling it isn't a question of theories but of personalities, or whether or not a particular person in a particular situation understands and has a feeling for the very odd process of getting something done, of action, of the appropriate action for the moment, and all that is an area in which I am absolutely incompetent. Of course to believe that, to doubt the inexorable truth of theory, is heresy for a Party member. I don't want to be a heretic, I want to share in the faith of my comrades, I want to be part of a movement, of a band of brothers, I don't want to think for myself, I don't really want to *be* myself. Maybe I needn't worry, because I don't think I ever am myself. When I'm with Gerda I'm some sort of sexy young Shelley, in London I'm just one of the boys, when I'm being stared at by young Dorothy with her expressionless face I'm a soulful student of literature, to the critics I'm apparently "one of the more promising of the Pylon Poets" (whatever that may mean), when I'm with Fisher I'm an unloved misunderstood son, when I'm alone I'm not there. What divides me from many of my London friends is that I did not even consider going to fight in Spain—but if I believe in anything it's in not killing people. That's the only thing I do believe in. I myself actually truly in relation to no one, in reaction to nothing, but just myself *am* a pacifist. So though I find Philip's dry friendliness embarrassing because of Gerda, and Arnold, though obviously a nice man, the nearest to boring of the brothers, I will help them organise their conference, and fetch and carry, and type and drive for them, because all that must be better than thinking about war. Maybe also it's better than writing poetry.'

Veils of sunlit dust hung in the air as Fisher addressed his audience, forty or fifty faces turned towards him, appearing a little indistinct because of the shafts of sunlight thrown across the dust from the high eighteenth-century windows of the conference room, where the plasterwork was in need of attention, and the cream paint was here and there peeling from the walls. He told them they were the hope of the world and Marcie, sitting modestly in the back row, tried to believe him but thought they were rather few; however certainly they were not like anyone else she knew and that might be a good sign. The progress and survival of the human race, he told them, was not due to individualism but to the subordination of individualistic struggle to species-maintaining ends. Co-operation, he said, was natural, there was an organic sociality in man. And Noel, she thought, would be in some steaming jungle, exposed to pests and hazards, followed by his loyal bearers, or writing his journal in his tent in the black uneasy tropical night, wearing a clean khaki shirt, thin, disciplined, utterly mysterious. Production for use rather than profit, Fisher was saying through the sunlight and the dust and over the heads of the elect. And when Noel came back he would want to be off again as soon as possible, by air this time, Marcie thought, he would wait only to write up his notes: someone had broken the record from London to Khartoum—or was it Khartoum to the Cape?— forced down by thunderstorms in the desert, delayed by a broken tail wheel; Noel had the record from Australia to London to defend (seven days, nineteen hours, fifty minutes). She'd be on the road from London to Croydon with nervous indigestion, or redirected to some other more lonely airfield, smiling at the one cold press photographer, dreading the fog; or saying good-bye briskly beside the hangar, he turning away, buttoning the flaps of his helmet, happy to go.

She must not think of that, must concentrate on the moment, must listen. There was more than one way of living co-oper-atively, Fisher was telling them, they must not be exclusive, identity of aim need not mean identity of method, some would start with help from enlightened capitalists, some would be-lieve in communal farming, some in individual plots, some would be concentrating on help for the unemployed. Fancy the Japs, Marcie thought, for she watched the newspapers and cut out the interesting bits to keep for when Noel came back. Noel had always said the Japanese couldn't fly, they couldn't stand the altitude, it was centuries of fish and rice that did it; but there they were, Masaki Iinuma the pilot and Kenji Tsukagoshi the wireless operator, they had flown from Tokyo to London in less than a hundred hours in an aeroplane called The Divine Wind. Multiplication of groups, Fisher said, links with America. They clapped him loudly. The thought that he was leaving them at once to forge those very links encouraged their optimism and sense of purpose.

'What a wonderful personality he has,' said the middle-aged man sitting next to Marcie, offering her half a stick of barley-sugar. 'I'm trying to give up smoking,' he said. And somebody now was talking about unemployment, and appropriately enough the sun had gone behind a cloud and the light let in by the high windows was only grey and the visionary aspect of the proceedings seemed to have fled. Clogs and shawls, the man said he saw, where once he had seen smart clothes and boots; and what was anybody doing about it? Marcie saw Stanley Arkwright muttering to his wife, looking indignant, and his wife nodding. They had come from their school, where they were obviously happy: the girls were doing well, they said. Why were £1500 millions being spent on armaments, the speaker asked. It did seem a lot, Marcie thought. Mrs Arkwright had tried to talk to her about Abyssinian refugees, but really there was so much to worry about. It seemed there were missionaries being expelled from Addis Ababa. The Italians had accused the children from a Protestant mission of trying to assassinate the Viceroy. It did seem awfully unlikely. But then the young man Timothy had told her that everything was going to be all right because Mr George Lansbury was going to see Herr Hitler, and though that seemed to her awfully unlikely too, she liked him better for saying it because he had always seemed so aloof and cynical before. And then, just as she was thinking about Germany, there suddenly was a German on the platform, and everyone was listening with rapt attention as he said that unity with God must lead to unity among men, and the sun came out again and shone on his smooth yellow hair parted in the middle, and his fine upstanding frame and dark high-collared shirt, while he told them of the sufferings of his community and that they allowed marriage although their ideals were monastic and they did not believe in private property. Herr Hitler disliked them because they were pacifists and his secret police, the Gestapo, had turned them out, and they had come to England, and were running a communal farm; there were not only Germans in their community, but English and Swedes and Swiss. Wonderful, Marcie thought, but perhaps a bit foreign. However he made the speaker who came after him seem a good deal less noble. In her community, she said, which was based on the ideals of Tolstoy, they had had five nervous breakdowns in as many years among people unable to overcome their competitive instincts. Certain people, she said, seemed to have no idea of the rights of others and no feeling for the good of the community. They were allowed in, she said, appearing to be on the verge of nervous breakdown herself, by certain other people who should have known better, and they were threatening to break up the whole community by the use of brute force. Arnold, as chairman of the meeting, here asserted his authority and firmly but kindly bringing her talk to a close, eased the next speaker onto the platform. And then it was economics, and investments and profit-sharing and accounting methods, and Marcie thought it would be all right if she slipped away, especially as she could see the whole thing was going splendidly and it wasn't as if she were needed to show support; so she crept out and down the stairs and into the spring sunshine, feeling that it had been a good morning and that Noel would be pleased that she had made new friends who were so different from the old.

The German's name was Reinhardt, and he came to stay the night at the Abbey because it was a long way back to his communal farm somewhere in the Midlands. Dorothy saw him the next day and fell in love with him. He was so incredibly clean. He told them that his craft was carpentry, and that he had built a canoe. Dorothy could imagine those strong hands with their clean short oval nails smoothing the wood, planing and shaping it, in some immaculate workshop where everything was calm and serene and unhurried. He told them about canoeing down the Rhine, sometimes over rapids; his face shone with enthusiasm. She could see that such a youth, bronzed as he would be from the sun he loved, guiding the boat he had made through the dashing white water, the spray on his smiling face and shining hair, must certainly be, as he said he was, at one with God. In two years' time she would be old enough to marry him. She knew she would see him again then because one of the results of the conference had been the decision that there should be a Summer Meeting every two years and that the first one should be held at the Abbey in the autumn of 1939.

The only person who seemed to be immune to Reinhardt's charm was Gerda.

'You would not understand,' she said to Timothy. 'But in my country I assure you my family would not speak to the family of this young man.'

Timothy found this remark highly amusing. Gerda was annoyed.

'I hope you are not going to become a bore,' she said, looking at him rather as she used to look at Philip in the old days.

Hilda still came to the Abbey for a few days every now and then, whether Fisher was there or not. She had her own room, a sort of attic or former box-room, right at the top of the house, above Fisher's bedroom. She would turn up, white and self-effacing as ever, find Marjorie so as to forewarn her of her presence at the next meal, and then retreat into her little room. Her latest book of stories had been published and well reviewed and then had sold two hundred and seventy-five copies. She felt the anti-climax, as she felt everything, to excess. She seemed to herself to be walking around in her own private vacuum; it made no difference what she said, no one would hear. Accordingly, alone in her room, she said some terrible things. Only hate seemed to reach across the vacuum and send back some faint reverberation from the periphery. She hated the dull public who would not recognise her, thus denying her existence, she hated Fisher for caring for her so little that he could telephone her only the day before his departure to tell her he was going to America, and not even find time to see her before he left; she hated the humdrum goodwill that emanated from Marjorie and Arnold, and the outsize personality of Gerda and the unresponsive coldness of Timothy and the new self-awareness of quiet little Dorothy; and most of all she hated her father because he wasn't there and never had been, and because it was him in her, his nature in hers, that was spoiling everything. She had a black notebook of formidable size which Fisher had given her (he had a big supply of them, renewed from time to time by a friend of his, a rather flamboyant French anarchist who brought them over from a particular stationers in Paris) and in it she began a series of very short and concentrated poems. 'I hate' they said in effect, and 'I am drowning', words on a page made to seem like wordless cries.

She wandered isolated through the soft spring air and Arnold scrubbing potatoes at the sink beneath the kitchen window said, 'It's nice the way Hilda feels she can come here whenever she likes for rest and refreshment and nobody makes any demands on her. I like people to feel like that about this place.'

She stood in the doorway looking in on Hamilton, who did not raise his head from his work.

'I feel sick,' she said quietly.

He only sighed.

'I am going into a downward spiral,' she said. 'I am bath water and I am going down the plug-hole.'

He did look at her then.

98

'Do some research,' he said. 'Looking things up in books is the only cure I know. A history of suicide, for instance. It's a very interesting subject.'

She turned away, back to her room and the notebook. My father said write a history of suicide, I showed him the red blood gushing from my wrists, have you noticed that blood and ink have the same smell?

Gerda told Timothy that she no longer looked up to him.

'A woman must see her man as a hunter. She must be a little afraid of him.'

'I suppose I'm not your man,' said Timothy apologetically. 'Strictly speaking, I mean.'

'Strictly speaking I have Philip,' Gerda acknowledged. 'I am not afraid of Philip. Philip has never understood the essential polarity between the sexes. The primal instincts are not well developed in Philip.'

'Poor Gerda. Men are a feeble lot these days.'

He had once taken all that so seriously, had listened so eagerly to her theories about the relations between the sexes and how he must become her master. He was growing out of it, he supposed.

'You should have a cause,' she said. 'You are not dedicated.'

'What about my writing then?'

'It is not enough, you are not sufficiently dedicated. How many words did you do last week?'

'Last week I was too busy. I had all that correspondence with the peace people which I said I'd deal with while Fisher was away.'

'Well then, if you are not a dedicated artist you should have a cause.'

'I have a cause. I'm a Communist, remember.'

'What do you do about it?'

'I'll tell you, since you ask.' He stretched himself out on the bed, folded his arms comfortably behind his head and said, 'I try to write like a Communist, and I find it very difficult. I think it's quite wrong to write books which will just pass the time for people, or amuse them. The times being as they are, one should write to show people what's happening, and what must happen, and how they should behave when it does happen. That means writing from a Marxist point of view and being absolutely true to life. But how can I? I don't know anything about the class struggle, crime, war—not from the inside, I mean—I can write about it theoretically, factually—because I can find out the facts—philosophically even if you like, but not in fictional form, because fiction is something much deeper than fact, much truer than fact, because it's felt, absorbed, transmogrified, breathed on by the breath of life, in a whole curious process which is quite different from just finding out the facts about something and putting them down on paper in an orderly manner. I think that in former times I might have been quite a good novelist or poet or something of the kind. But not now. The sort of thing I could have done is simply not valid now. It's too individualistic or something, it just isn't relevant, it isn't valid. When I was at Cambridge—now this is a secret—' He propped himself up on one elbow and looked across at her. 'You won't tell anyone?'

'Of course not.'

'When I was at Cambridge I was asked to work for Russia. I was asked by a don—very young and clever, a man I really liked—he taught me all I know about art—which now that I come to think of it is not very much—anyway he asked me to be an undercover agent, to get some job where I might be useful to the cause and just wait, and be ready for the revolution. Sounds rather melodramatic, doesn't it?'

'To me it sounds wonderful,' said Gerda, her eyes bright with interest.

'I turned it down.'

'But why? It is this lack of seriousness again.'

'Not really. I told him I was a sympathiser and all that but you see—now this you really must not tell—promise?'

'I promise.'

'I turned it down because I thought it would kill my father if he ever found out.' He burst out laughing and lay back with his arms behind his head again. 'If you could see my father. . . .' Gerda looked at him fondly. He could look really handsome sometimes these days. 'My father,' he said, 'is the absolute embodiment of the English middle class, the thing itself, the very thing that made us what we are. Thirty years in India, still calls my mother the Memsahib, obsessed by duty, prestige, not letting the side down. They live in a ghastly house near Reigate, he grows chrysanthemums because they remind him of India, he shouts at the servants, goes to the Golf Club—God it's awful— and my brother's going to be just the same, he's in India now, been there two years. I was meant to do it too, can you imagine?'

'But you rebelled,' said Gerda approvingly.

'Yes, but—the trouble is, oh I don't know—he knows an awful lot about butterflies—he's got cases and cases of them, beautiful—he's told me about some valley in Kashmir . . . And then you see he's rather proud of my being a poet. That doesn't fit, does it? I'm sure the only poem he's ever read is Kipling's *If*. He hopes one day I'll have a story in Blackwood's Magazine— you probably haven't heard of that, it has jolly good yarns about tiger shooting and all that sort of thing. I mean, it's only the way he's been brought up. And I bet he always has done his duty, whatever he's conceived it to be. He's got a kind of innocence, I suppose, or simplicity. I don't want anyone to be like that ever again, but at the same time, if you know what I mean, I don't want it to be me who puts a bomb under his favourite armchair.'

'This is sentimental of course,' said Gerda mildly.

'Certainly it is. But also it's that I don't really see why there have to be bombs. I mean it's all so obvious, self-evident. Communism works. Look at the Soviet Union, their economic success, the speed of the change. The rest of the world must follow. The Communists are the ones who are against war and fascism, they must win support, they can't fail to. Anyone can see that it's Soviet Russia that proposes universal disarmament and the capitalist countries that reject it. Communists and socialists are leading all the peace movements all over the world. Ninety-nine out of a hundred people want peace, ninety-nine out of a hundred will soon be Communists.'

'Too simple,' said Gerda, shaking her head.

'Maybe; but the peace movement's the thing. That's what I'm going to work for. I'm just going to try to earn a living by writing—by reviewing and journalism and that kind of thing—nothing more ambitious, and I'm going to give all my spare energy and time to the Peace Pledge Union. So you see I will be dedicated, I will have a cause, only not literature which is bourgeois and not revolution which is bloody, but peace which is neither.'

'But you will come back to literature,' said Gerda, who was disappointed both by the decision and by the fact that it had been made without reference to her.

'You Europeans have such faith in culture,' he said, smiling at her. 'You must remember the English are the most philistine nation in the world.'

Noel was back in time for the annual cricket match against the village. Dorothy went to it with Fisher, who had just come back from his lecture tour.

Noel was tall and had pale blue eyes and fair hair slicked back with hair oil so that it fitted his head closely. The pale-ness of the eyes made them seem always fixed on distant horizons; his face was sunburnt and thin, a young face but not inexperienced—rather it had a sort of remoteness as if what it had looked on was untellable. His speech was clipped and his manner reserved. His left arm was scarred by a sort of ringworm which he had contracted in the jungle. He spent some time in London being treated at the Hospital for Tropical Diseases and visiting the Royal Geographical Society, for which he was preparing a detailed report of his journey. One of the two undergraduates he had taken with him on the expedition had made certain botanical observations whose originality Noel was anxious should be recognised. He spared no pains to achieve this end.

'We had a marvellous team this time,' he said to Marcie. 'The best lot I've ever had.'

'What fun,' said Marcie, wishing that women could under-stand team spirit. She knew what it meant of course, but she had never somehow got the feel of it.

She wanted Noel to meet Fisher; she knew they would get on famously. The cricket match seemed the first available oppor-tunity.

'At least you can set eyes on each other,' she said to Noel.

'Then we can ask him to lunch or something another time. I mean, for a proper talk.'

'I'm not much good with intellectuals, you know,' said Noel.

'Oh he's not like that at all,' said Marcie. 'At least,' she added less confidently, 'not so you'd notice.'

Fisher's reaction had been uncomfortably similar.

'I'm not much good with the upper classes, you know,' he had said.

'Oh but Noel's quite different,' Marcie had said, and that she did believe.

Fisher thought he did not look different at all, seeing him in his white cricketing clothes on his immense green lawn in the sunshine, except, that was, to the extent that he seemed even more so, an absolute apotheosis of the thing. Led towards him by Marcie, Fisher felt glad of the somewhat crumpled cream tussore suit which he had dug out of a drawer in honour of such an exceptionally hot afternoon, and glad of the wide-brimmed gangster type hat he had bought in America, and glad he had let his beard grow while he had been away. He felt he needed all that for protection, so much so in fact that when eventually the godlike figure turned his gaze towards the approaching group (for he had been looking all this time towards the pavilion) and Marcie said breathlessly, 'Oh Noel, this is Fisher Whitehead,' and the figure clasped his hand in a firm grip and said, 'How d'you do? Good of you to come,' Fisher found himself answering with a quite unaccustomed twang in his voice.

'Howdy,' he said more or less. 'Howdy do?'

'And Dorothy,' said Marcie. 'Dorothy Grant, a friend.'

Dorothy blushed, not because of the manly clasp in which her hand was briefly held, but because she was astonished by Fisher's voice, which was unlike anything she had ever heard before, from him or anyone else.

'I think we're just about ready for the off, aren't we?' said Noel, looking towards the pavilion again. 'Are they all there?'

'Oh yes, everyone's ready,' said Marcie.

Noel raised a hand as if in benediction.

'See you later,' he said.

'Sure thing,' said Fisher.

'What fun,' said Marcie, also rather confused by the voice. 'Let's go and sit.' She led them back towards the deck chairs. 'I want to hear lots more about America.'

'It was great,' said Fisher, modifying but not totally abandoning the twang (it came and went with disconcerting inconsistency throughout the afternoon). 'It always is. I adore America. But I became very depressed about Europe while I was there.'

'Oh poor Europe,' said Marcie. 'Too ghastly. But on a day like this in England it's hard to believe anything could ever change, isn't it?' But Fisher was a revolutionary and so she supposed in a way one ought to be a revolutionary too, so she quickly added, 'Unfortunately I mean,' with a nervous laugh, and then again, trying to be truthful, 'I mean, in some ways. What I mean is, I do like some things, don't you?' She looked rather desperately towards Dorothy.

'I like a lot of things,' said Dorothy, smiling.

Dorothy had been leaving the Abbey to walk home when Fisher had offered her a lift, and on the way he had asked her whether she would like to come to the cricket match too.

'I'm rather dreading it. I wish you'd come and give me some moral support.'

Flattered, she'd said she would, if he wouldn't mind stopping on the way so that she could tell her mother; so he had waited outside while she ran in, and in a moment Nora Grant came out saying in her flustered way, 'Is she all right like that? It's only an old dress. I've made her run up to get her hat and gloves. It's so kind of you. Oh, Dorothy, but you must put them on.'

'I will, don't worry. I'll put them on in the car.' She waved and smiled, but didn't, he noticed, put on the hat and gloves. She did carry the hat, and later, sitting in the sun in a deck chair, she put it on over her nose to shade her eyes—quiet sensible Dorothy beginning to acquire style, beauty, confidence —it was wonderful, he thought.

The Dowager Duchess, as gaunt and fearsome as ever, had lowered herself into a chair beside him and said, 'Well, Mr Whitehead, are we in for a war?' to which he had answered, 'I guess so.'

'My sister's niece by marriage married one of these Yanks,

104

she said, as if irrelevantly. 'Overbearing sort of girl she was. He couldn't stand up to her at all.'

'Who's that young man batting?' Fisher asked.

'One of the Lambert boys. Good-looking, isn't he? There are three of them, all good-lookers. Didn't your people come from round here?'

'My father was vicar of Heverington.'

'I thought I remembered something of the kind. Who was your mother then?'

'She was a Miss Wilde before she married.'

'I thought so. Didn't you get on with her?'

'I was devoted to her.'

'This was her world. Why do you want to turn it upside down?'

'Some things look better upside down.'

She gave a short laugh. 'Speak for yourself. I'm sure I don't look better upside down. I think you're a bad man, Mr Whitehead. I think you're a traitor to your class.'

'I don't want to belong to a class, I want to belong to a species.'

'Species man, class upper,' said the Dowager Duchess firmly. 'Well, let's say upper middle, in your case. If you get rid of the property-owning classes, Mr Whitehead, you are going to start something which you will come to regret.'

'I don't know that I want to get rid of them altogether,' he said mildly, hoping to avoid an argument. 'I think some of this lot might possibly share their advantages a bit more widely.'

'Which team are you referring to?' she said, looking at the players.

'The batting side.'

'From here, if you didn't know, could you tell the difference?'

'I suppose not.'

'Exactly.'

He had no idea what she thought she had proved, but it seemed to have concluded the argument to her satisfaction.

'Pity they've no children,' she went on with hardly a pause to mark the change of subject. 'With a lovely place like this.'

'Perhaps they'll have some.'

'I doubt if he could, don't you? With those eyes?'

'Ah,' said Fisher vaguely.

'Oh I doubt it very much. What about that pretty child you brought with you? Where does she come from?'

'That's Dorothy Grant. She lives nearby, at Winterstoke. She started to come to us for a few lessons, and spends quite a bit of time with us now. We're all rather proud of Dorothy.'

'Grant? I've met them. He's a frightful bore. The wife's quite sweet, very nervous.'

Dorothy under her hat heard everything and felt slightly faint. The quick sequence of the mysterious hint about Noel, the wonderfully unexpected compliment from Fisher and the horrid remarks about her parents took her by surprise. Motionless in her chair, she hoped desperately to escape their attention until such time as they might have forgotten what they had said: otherwise the embarrassment would be appalling. At the same time she would have liked to shout something very rude to the Dowager Duchess, arrogant old hag that she was to talk like that about people she hardly knew, who did she think she was anyway? But young Lambert with an elegant right hook had hit the ball so far it was almost out of sight, and Fisher and the Dowager Duchess were both leaning forward to see where it had gone to, and Dorothy quietly took the opportunity to leave her chair without their noticing.

She walked slowly round the edge of the lawn behind the row of chairs, wondering where she was going to go to now that she had escaped. Further embarrassment seemed inevitable— should she pretend she wanted to go to the lavatory?

'Does cricket bore you?' It was Sir Giles Lambert, smiling and introducing her to his son Gerald, who was not playing because he had strained his Achilles tendon playing fives at school but who had the same fine bone structure and the same soft dark hair and eyes as his father; and in a minute, all quite effortlessly, the two of them, she and Gerald, were sitting side by side talking, in the shade of the copper beech. The cricket went on and on. Sometimes there was clapping, and sometimes people wandered slowly past them in pretty dresses and panama hats and smiled towards them; the warm air smelt of new-mown grass and the roses which climbed on the terrace wall. He

106

told her about the Hedges family and how they were more or less all right now that Ivor Hedges was working for Gerald's father, and Dorothy told him how awful it had been when he'd been at the Abbey and how he'd been always drunk and beating his wife and Gerald agreed that it must have been ghastly and how awful it was when a man lost his self-respect, and Dorothy felt perfectly certain (with the utmost admiration) that he must be a prefect at his school, if not Head Boy, but she did not like to ask. Instead she told him about the Boulders and he was very interested, and he asked her what the Abbey was like and what they did there, and she said it was a marvellous place and everyone there was terribly nice, and he said were any of them a bit mad and she said only in the nicest possible way. Later they went together to where the tea was spread out on the long table in the hall. Gerald limped round passing cucumber sandwiches and so Dorothy took a plate too and offered it round, and most people smiled benignly at the two young people, whose good looks and polite manners easily gave rise to pleasant sentimental notions. Dorothy, who in spite of her sheltered upbringing was not shy, found the whole occasion quite delightful, and failed completely to discern those elements of political and social skulduggery which Fisher found on every side and which kept him in a state of sensitivity and intermittent transatlantic manifestation throughout the afternoon.

He knew it all, he felt, the smugness, the incredible patronising ease of manner of the English upper class at work consolidating its position. Those smiling faces, that friendly exchange of comment and banter between the gentry and the village people, were all part of a plot, only half conscious of course, to make the latter believe they had more in common with their landlords than they had with their fellow members of the working class, who were sweating out their lives in the filthy factories on which the whole edifice of swindle and error was based; and what was especially maddening about this particular afternoon was that it was he—the only one who saw what was wrong and cared about it—who was the odd one out, the one with whom neither side had anything in common. Perhaps, though, he might be wrong about that, perhaps he was not the only one, for he did notice that Noel Maysey-Smith was often to be seen simply standing, with that same remote unapproachable look he had worn when Fisher had first seen him, his pale gaze fixed somewhere beyond anyone else's horizon, one foot placed slightly in front of the other as if he were about to begin a fencing match. There, certainly, it looked as if there might be someone else who lacked the common touch.

Fisher approached him, and made some sort of banal remark as to the general pleasantness of the occasion. The gaze returned from the snow-capped mountains and met his own.

'A place needs its festivals,' said Noel.

'I entirely agree. Of course, things which are very familiar are hard to analyse. One can't quite be sure what it is they symbolise or whether one would like it if one did know. It's really easier to be an outsider.'

'It's always easier to be an outsider. I know more about the Amazonian Indians than I do about my fellow countrymen.'

'There again, I wonder if you would like it if you did know more about your fellow countrymen,' said Fisher tentatively.

'I've a feeling I might like the Amazonian Indians better.'

That was all the conversation they had but though it was quite inconclusive, even mysterious, it was enough to achieve Marcie's object. Each was left with the feeling that he would like another opportunity to talk to the other.

His awareness of this fact, and the thought that it would please Marcie, put Fisher in a better humour for the journey home.

'I see you and young master Lambert seemed to click,' he said to Dorothy in the car.

She smiled, not at all embarrassed.

'Thank you for taking me. It was great fun.'

Timothy had hoped that Fisher would be pleased at his conversion to the pacifist cause, and when he found that Fisher's reaction was more equivocal than he had expected, he was surprised by the bitterness of his own disappointment. He had not realised how much he still hoped for Fisher's approval.

'After all, you were a conscientious objector,' he said in a hurt voice.

'That was another war,' said Fisher. 'This one is going to be a war against Fascism and I'm glad I'm too old to have to make the choice about whether or not to fight in it.'

'But it doesn't have to happen," said Timothy indignantly. 'Not if enough people are determined that it shouldn't.'

Fisher shook his head.

'You're being naïve.'

He did not mean to be unkind. He was not really thinking about Timothy at all. He had become obsessed with what he had seemed to see with sudden clarity while he was away, the inevitability of a European war.

'No one cares much about Europe in America,' he said. 'It's all too far away. You look back at it in a different way when you're there, it's easier to see what a goddam mess it's in. There's no way out of a war against Hitler.'

'England doesn't have to join in. We're not part of Europe.'

'We'll join in. Late, unwilling, ignoble, but we'll join in, we'll have to. Of course it will need a revolution to bring it about, because the present lot won't do it. Or if they do, they won't be able to run a war. So either before or immediately after we go into the war, there'll be a revolution of some kind. The war will be run by a revolutionary dictatorship of the Left. After the war, if anything survives the aerial bombardment and the gassing, it won't be England as we know it.'

'I don't believe anything is inevitable.'

'It wasn't once. We could have stopped it once. At the Rhineland, in Spain. We didn't stop it. Now it is inevitable.'

'I don't see how you can just calmly accept something so appalling.'

'It's no use rejecting it. It's going to happen.'

'But personally, I mean, how can you accept it personally?'

'Personally? Oh, it has no particular horror for me from that point of view. I've got to die some day anyway. I've no children, no wife, to worry about.'

Timothy laughed awkwardly. 'I don't know why that shocks me so much. It's not even what you say, it's the way you say it. I mean—children, wife—I suppose I used to think you looked on all this, on what happens here, the people here, like people look on children or wife. I suppose I just am, as you say, naïve.'

This time Fisher did hear the note of hurt, but he was quite mystified by it. He wondered what could be the matter with Timothy. After a pause he said mildly, 'I expect I was sounding harsh because I was hoping that what I said wasn't true. Maybe you're right. Maybe it isn't inevitable.'

Later, alone in her little room with Hilda, he said to her, 'It is inevitable, it is you know.'

In the autumn of 1937 Gerda's husband Philip decided to go to Spain as an ambulance driver for an organisation called Spanish Medical Aid. The decision took everybody at the Abbey by surprise. They all agreed that Philip was not at all a suitable person for such an undertaking, and they all tried to dissuade him from going. He was adamant.

'I can drive and maintain a car,' he said. 'Or an ambulance or a lorry. I can speak a bit of Spanish and I can do First Aid. How can you possibly say I'm not suitable?'

The truth was that with the work of the conference over, and the new building project not scheduled to start until the spring, Philip had not got enough to do. He had started to revise his work on the life of Corelli, and had realised anew how much it bored him. He was afraid he might begin to feel useless again, as he had felt before he and Gerda had come to the Abbey. At the same time Gerda, with whom his relations had been more or less harmonious for some time, was becoming more difficult to live with: it seemed that her relationship with Timothy was no longer so satisfactory. All this had contributed to the decision. So had his meeting at the conference with a man of his own age, a schoolmaster, who was going to do the same thing.

'I'll probably be back in a month or two,' he told Gerda. 'Volunteers come and go on these things. It's not like joining the army or something.'

'You will die,' said Gerda.

He was touched that she should look upon his going as a tragedy. It was the first time for years that it had seemed at all likely that she might be genuinely fond of him. Even then the cynical thought occurred to him that she might be displeased with him for doing something which she would have enjoyed admiring in, say, Timothy, but which was not nearly so interesting when he did it. He tried to repress this thought and to say goodbye to her with appropriate tenderness, but as usual he felt he had failed to come up to the mark, and left with relief.

Everyone else seemed to assume, as Gerda did, that he was going to his death. For some time after his departure a general sadness settled over the Abbey, lightened only by the four children—the two young Boulders and Marjorie and Arnold's children Joe and Meg—whose cheerfulness it seemed nothing could dim.

Hilda saw Philip in London. She was walking from the London Library to Piccadilly tube station and there was Philip striding towards her with a khaki haversack on his back. He was going to Spain, he told her, and what with his haversack and his heavy boots it looked as though he might simply stride on down Piccadilly and on and on until he heard the rumble of the guns on the Catalonian plain. She had never seen him look so purposeful.

'What about the others?' she said. 'Are they going too?'

Fisher might easily have decided to go without telling her; it was just the sort of thing he would have done.

'Oh no, they've all been trying to put me off,' he said, smiling easily. 'Well . . see you when I get back . .' and off he went.

Irritated, she thought that nothing could be more boring than a man whose conscience was clear; weren't guilt and insecurity the only things that made people bearable? She felt as bitter at the idea that Fisher might have gone to Spain without telling her as if he had actually done it. By the time she reached Bayswater she had indigestion. Her legs felt so weak, climbing the stairs to her flat, that she wondered if she might be going to be ill. If only she could be really ill—not miserable, tired, beset by dyspepsia and sinusitis—but ill with a proper illness, an illness with a name, an excuse to relinquish all personal responsibility for anything. Then perhaps he would notice whether she was there or not; even though he was the world's most self-centred man.

The flat was in an old block. It had two quite reasonable front rooms but the kitchen was at the back, along a dark passage, and had one narrow window of frosted glass giving onto a dreary inner courtyard or well, with high dirty white walls randomly scattered with other frosted glass windows and a number of thick black drainpipes. She had left the window open in the hope of improving the atmosphere in the kitchen, but all that had happened was that it had become very cold and the loose sheets of paper with poems on which she had left on the table had blown onto the floor.

She shut the window, picked up the poems, and made herself a cup of tea. The poems were bad, she thought, waiting for the tea to cool. They were bad because she herself had become utterly banal. Her whole life—for she was determined to be harsh with herself—her whole history, and especially her present situation, were of a dreary unoriginality which made it not in the least surprising that her poetry should be pointless. All she had ever had was just a little extra intensity, and that had come, she thought, drinking the tea which was still too hot, from her being really rather an unpleasant person. Perhaps now she was not even particularly nasty any more. She was just ordinarily nasty.

It had been easier when Fisher was away in America. Now that he had come back, and that it was perfectly clear that his relationship with her would never be of central importance in his life—and she could not in fairness pretend he had ever said it would—she could no longer avoid the fact or imagine grounds for hope of change. But she felt such need to be needed by him. It seemed odd that such an ugly grasping thing as her obsession now seemed to her to be should be known by the gentle name of Love. There ought to be another word for it.

She finished her tea, took two cushions, one large and one small, from the corner of the kitchen and put them on the floor by the gas cooker. She went to the door of the flat and put it on the latch, so that anyone who wanted to could push it open and come in. Then she went back to the kitchen, opened the oven door, put the smaller cushion inside the oven and sat down on the larger one with her sheets of looseleaf paper and her blue fountain pen.

This was how she spent most of her evenings. They were not evenings of indecision—some of them were almost happy —it was just that she liked to have the feeling that everything was ready, so that if she did want to turn on the gas, it would be no trouble at all.

Fisher went over to see Marcella about some details to do with her bequest to the Abbey. The problem was one of restraining her generosity in order to avoid putting the community under too crippling a debt of gratitude. They had to safeguard their freedom to develop in ways of which she might not approve. He wanted to explain that to her.

'For instance,' he said. 'Supposing there's a war, and we all decide not to fight in it, to be conscientious objectors.'

It didn't bother her. She was indifferent to public opinion. Also she believed the police to be more or less upper servants and the magistrates' courts to exist for the purpose of fining poachers: she was irredeemably aristocratic in that way.

'Noel's in his training session,' she said. 'But he'd love to see you. Shall we go and see?'

'What is he training for?'

'A long flight.'

He followed her without asking the destination of the flight. The awe with which she spoke of Noel precluded enquiry. It put him beyond question.

He followed her towards the back quarters of the house until she stopped outside a door, listened for a few moments and then quietly opened it and put her head round it to ask in a whisper, 'May we come in?'

There was a longish pause before she signed to Fisher to follow her, and they went into a big dark room which might once have been a gun room but had been converted into a gymnasium. It smelt of leather. There was a leather vaulting horse, a leather handled trapeze hanging from the ceiling, and a set of leather Indian clubs standing like ninepins at one side of the room. One wall was fitted with wooden exercise bars. As well as the trapeze there were two ropes hanging from the

113

ceiling. The floor was entirely covered with pale soft leather—shoe leather, Fisher afterwards learned.

Noel had just emerged from the shower, which was behind a brass-studded green baize door in one corner of the room. He wore a silk dressing-gown and a pair of slippers embroidered with his initials. He smiled diffidently when he saw Fisher.

'Sorry about all this,' he said with a vague gesture towards the gymnastic equipment.

'Very impressive,' said Fisher. He took a handkerchief from his breast pocket and blew his nose.

'Have you got a cold?' asked Noel sharply.

'No, no, it's nothing, a piece of dust,' said Fisher, in whom the gesture had been nervous rather than necessary.

'Oh good,' said Noel, looking at him keenly all the same.

'When do you set off?' asked Fisher, to change the subject.

'At dawn.'

'And it's . . . ?'

'The North.'

Noel led the way back to the drawing-room.

'A drink?' he offered, moving towards the tray.

Fisher accepted a glass of sherry. Noel carefully measured out a small glass of gin and Italian vermouth for Marcella, and crushed an orange for himself in a large fruit-squeezer with a shiny chrome handle.

'Well,' he said. 'How's it all going?'

'Rather well, I think,' said Fisher. 'A lot of people come and see us, to have a look at what we're doing. Some of them are pretty crazy, of course. But let me bore you with these terrible finances for a moment.'

'I don't need to know,' said Marcie. 'I just want to make an unconditional gift and forget about it.'

He insisted on telling her how the Abbey conducted its finances, how everyone who joined it contributed what they felt they could afford, and that if there was a profit it would in theory be shared out according to the investment, but as there never had been a profit because everything had always been ploughed back into new undertakings, Marcie, as the only substantial outside shareholder, would be the only one to gain nothing because the others at least gained their subsistence. He noticed that Noel's question and comments were acute, and rather wished he had brought Arnold with him to answer them.

'Would you like to come and talk to my brother about it some time?'

'No, no, I'm more than satisfied.'

Noel had visited the Abbey only once. Although he had been polite he had not been at ease. Possibly he had found the atmosphere too informal.

'So how long will you be away?' Fisher asked.

'It shouldn't be more than five weeks. I hope nothing blows up while I'm away. No war, I mean.'

They went on to talk about farming. Fisher believed that under his guidance Noel and Marcie were becoming model landowners, and he was proud of his achievements in this respect. Neither had thought of their land as being anything other than an inherited nuisance until he had begun to persuade them otherwise. Most of the consequent re-organisation was being done by Marcie, under Fisher's guidance, because Noel had other preoccupations. Noel's interest and approval seemed genuine, but he still puzzled Fisher. It was as if he were trying to be something that was not natural to him, but what that was, or what indeed would have been more in accordance with his true nature, remained a mystery. Fisher was interested by him, to the extent even of feeling a little guilty at finding these rich neighbours more intriguing than some of his friends at the Abbey. He felt he had better keep his motives under strict surveillance. There must be no question of his being dazzled by the glamour of the privileged classes.

Dorothy was in a dream for most of that year. People came and went and talked of war; she read Proust and walked on the Plain.

She carried on an intermittent and rather formal correspondence with Gerald Lambert. They met in the holidays—his parents asked her to lunch—but the friendship remained tentative. Dorothy did not mind. She almost preferred not to see him: it disturbed the dream. The letters continued at intervals. One day they would progress to the next stage; there did not seem to be any need to hurry.

In the meantime she read. Her reading had the effect of altering her perception of things. She had had very little visual education, but the writers under whose spell she now fell—Proust, Henry James, Virginia Woolf—acted on her consciousness like a mildly hallucinatory drug. Even a page or two sent her out onto the Plain in a state of heightened sensibility. Everything was bathed in a new and extraordinarily beautiful light. Long shadows on the wide grassy expanse of the Plain, or the darkness of wet tree trunks beside a pale road lined with sodden leaves and beech mast, or a stream dashing down a hillside with a yellow wagtail on its bank, were given such sensual power and such definition that everything stood also for something else, in a marvellously easy language of correspondences and significances which were incommunicable but crystal clear. This was reality; everything else was dream.

In the dream Hilda died, and Philip came back from Spain. Dorothy had hardly known Hilda, and what she had known she had not liked. Suicide was so much beyond her imagining that she could not be awed by it: it seemed only senseless. She had never known about Fisher's relationship with Hilda and could not understand why the black mood which overcame him after her death lasted so long. Hilda had been found with her poems beside her. Fisher read them and found in them the message that it was all his fault. It was open to him to reach a different conclusion, because as she had lain there, giving in to the longing for death itself which had become almost independent of her desire to be relieved of the pain of living, and at the same time and on another level certain that she would be found and rescued, she had pencilled on the sheet of paper beside her the scrawled words, 'War war war'. Whether this was a final act of kindness, so as to give Fisher an escape from guilt, or a wish to appease him should she survive (since she knew how much he would disapprove of her action), or the expression of a genuine anxiety, no one ever knew. Those who knew her least assumed it was the latter; others guessed that there might be more to it. Fisher, in spite of the alternative she had left him, chose guilt. He felt at the same time a certain self-pity. He had never pretended not to be a selfish person, had he? And how could he have known she

116

was on the verge of suicide? Hadn't she always talked like that? Grieving and aggrieved, his brooding presence at the Abbey became for a time rather oppressive.

Almost as much of a surprise to the community as Hilda's death was Philip's reappearance. He rang up from Paddington one day and asked Gerda to meet him at Westbury station as if he had been away for a weekend instead of eight months. Even then everyone somehow assumed that he must have been wounded in battle and that that was why he was back. Gerda had been too astonished to ask more than whether he was all right, to which he had just had time to answer 'yes' before the pips went and he shouted, 'I've no more pennies. See you at the station.'

'He sounded utterly exhausted,' she said, ready for drama.

He might have lost a leg, she thought. Certainly his nerves would be shattered; he would need vegetable soup, herb poultices, much patient understanding.

He walked off the train looking sunburnt and well, thin certainly and having lost a good deal more hair, but more like a middle-aged schoolmaster back from a walking tour in the Lake District than a war veteran.

'What was it like?' she asked, awed by his self-contained look.

'Pretty good Hell,' he said rather grandly.

'Oh Philip and you came back,' she said. 'How fine that was.' Her voice trembled.

'You'd have thought it much finer if I'd died you silly old thing,' he said, putting his arm briefly round her shoulders. 'I'd had enough of it though. Besides, it looks as though we've got to get ready for something here now.'

'Oh yes you are right. Certainly you are right.'

She picked up the heavy kitbag he had put down on the platform in order to greet her, shouldered it and followed him out to the car park. He would never have called her a silly old thing before he went to Spain. Something amazing must have happened there.

So Philip was back, Dorothy saw, and less nervous for some reason, and everyone talked about war more than ever. She could not think why they all worried about it so. It seemed to her that there was nothing anyone could do about it, and that if it came it would just be the next thing, which might or might not be interesting, but it couldn't possibly change what was without doubt the really interesting thing, which had very little to do with outside events and a lot to do with just waiting, with just a certain alert expectant state of being, with every now and then the flash of reality, the click of the shutter, the sighting of the true thing.

Since the true thing was incommunicable, it never occurred to Dorothy to talk to anyone about it, although she did occasionally wonder whether other people were on to it in the sense that she was. She thought that perhaps some were and some weren't. Hamilton, for instance, probably was. Once she met him quite unexpectedly, walking on the Plain. She was surprised to see his large figure approaching her along a footpath she often followed between two low hedges with a wide expanse of open country on either side. She knew that Fisher often went for walks, but she had never met Hamilton on the Plain before. As they approached each other, he with his overcoat flapping and his long white hair blowing round his head, he threw out his arms and intoned in a loud voice,

> . . . ere Babylon was dust
> The magus Zoroaster my dead child
> Met his own image walking in the garden.

She stopped, smiling nervously, but then he spoke most rationally about the ancient milestone she had just passed, which showed that they were on the old way between Salisbury and Bath, and they proceeded calmly on their separate ways.

Another time he leant across the table to her at lunchtime and said, 'Only the unicorn can draw the evil out of the water you know. An hour before dawn and an hour after sunset he touches it with his horn. All the other animals wait to drink until then. Conning the waters, it's called.' And yet he was not mad.

The talk of war faded. Apparently it was not coming after all. No one seemed to be as pleased about that as one might have expected. Dorothy's father, however, said that there was no doubt at all that it would have been an act of folly to have gone to war with Hitler over Czechoslovakia, and that

Chamberlain was quite right. At the Abbey most people seemed to think that Chamberlain was quite wrong—including, which seemed odd, Timothy and his pacifist friends. Dorothy was used to this divergence of views between the Abbey and home, and since politics bored her she found no difficulty in refraining from mentioning at home what she heard at the Abbey, or at the Abbey what she heard at home. She had for a long time been convinced that the people at the Abbey—or at any rate Fisher and Arnold—were right in what they believed, but that at the same time her father was often also right in a different and more practical way, which was something to do with knowing a lot of people in his Club who were running things. She liked the Abbey's ideas much better than her father's, but she could not quite believe that the people who were running things were completely wrong because things did not seem to her so very bad. In other words she had had, so far, a happy life.

The summer of 1939, however, was not so happy. She and her parents moved to a small flat in Kensington, returning to the country only at weekends. Dorothy went every day to a finishing school, where she was taught dressmaking, deportment and French, and in the evenings she was introduced to the highly respectable fringe of London Society. It had been decided that in view of the troubled times they could not afford a proper Season, and that they would just have a few little evening parties, and Mrs Grant would renew her acquaintance with such of her friends and relations as might be nice for Dorothy to know now that she was grown up (or, to put it another way, through whom she might hope to meet a suitable husband). Mrs Grant was enormously relieved by this decision. Her husband persisted in his view that her family connections gave her a natural right of entry into the best circles, but the fact was that in so far as she ever had known anyone who moved in those circles, she had certainly lost touch with them since her marriage. There were the Dorset cousins, of course, but she had not seen them since her wedding. She had been presented at Court as a debutante in 1920, but she had not been presented again on her marriage and was therefore not entitled to present her daughter. The problem of who to ask to perform this vital function had been bothering her for some time, and she was thankful to be able to stop worrying about it. Still determined to do her duty, however, she overcame her shyness in order to approach a number of old acquaintances. Thus Dorothy, appropriately dressed, hatted and gloved, was submitted to her first grown-up London social engagements. She did not enjoy them.

'What an odd sort of girl little Nora Grant seems to have produced,' said Mrs Corbett, up from Kent with her daughter Jennifer. 'Such a pity. I wonder what made her so bolshie.'

'She's brainy,' said Jennifer, flatly.

'Oh, is that it? What bad luck. Poor Nora. Men hate brainy girls.'

'Yes,' said Jennifer, with a sigh. She had a nasty feeling they didn't much like plain ones either.

Dorothy did her best, because she wanted to please her mother, but she was disheartened by her lack of success. She had always thought she got on well with people; but now it seemed you weren't meant exactly to get on with them, but rather to join with them in an elaborate game in which all that mattered was that you should show that you knew the rules. For the first time in her life, Dorothy realised that this game, which was accepted without question by her mother and believed in as an article of faith by her father, was a game she did not want to play.

'An amazing thing happened to me when I was in Spain,' Philip said to Arnold soon after his return to the Abbey.

They were in Arnold's office, a little panelled room whose window, which gave onto the courtyard, was infringed upon by a thick mass of honeysuckle. Books, pamphlets and correspondence lay about in more or less orderly piles. Arnold sat at a table in front of his typewriter, Philip on the low window seat. Arnold, who had hoped to get down to some hard work on the organisation of the conference which had been planned to take place at the Abbey in the autumn, merely grunted, sorting through a pile of letters, but Philip was not to be deflected.

'I met a girl,' he said.

'Oh?' said Arnold, concealing his surprise. He was so used to seeing Philip on the run from Gerda that he had taken for granted that any entanglement with any woman would be similarly unwelcome to him.

'Her name is Rosamund Barnes,' said Philip.

He paused, but as Arnold made no comment he went on.

'She's thirty-six. A Quaker schoolteacher living with her mother, who is the widow of a colonial servant. As it happens they live not far from here, in the Mendips. She teaches at a Quaker boarding school there. History is her subject.'

'What was she doing in Spain?'

'She had gone with a group of Quakers to help with the refugees coming over the French border. Beautiful country there. We walked a lot in our spare time.'

Arnold nodded slowly.

'She's not particularly devout or anything,' said Philip. 'It's just that her mother happened to come of a Quaker family. I mean she's the very opposite of a religious fanatic. She's just —extraordinary sensible.'

'Will you see her again?' asked Arnold.

'That's the thing. That's what I want to ask your advice about. I don't know whether it would be right to ask Gerda to divorce me so that I can marry Rosamund. I'd like to, but I don't know whether it's fair on Gerda. Seeing her again, after what's happened, I somehow feel I'd hate to hurt her. I suppose it's because I'm not afaid of her any more.'

'Do you really think you'd be happy?'

'I think so. But of course I was wrong last time, wasn't I? Couldn't you meet her, Arnold, won't you let me arrange it?'

So Arnold went with Philip to the Pump Room in Bath, where between the potted palms a string trio played Offenbach's Barcarolle and where across the ladies in hats taking tea and the elderly waitresses moving slowly between the tables, he saw a hatless brown-haired woman with a pleasant sensible face.

When Philip made an excuse to leave them together she said at once, 'Has he told you?'

'Yes.'

'Should we be very wrong, do you think?'

'I don't know.'

'We get on very well. It would be a wonderful thing for me, but I don't want to do it at someone else's expense.'

She had spent most of her childhood in Africa. Her father had refused to send her back to school in England. Her education at various mission schools, often interrupted, he had supplemented himself, and as a result she had been unusually well-informed about history, which was his favourite subject, so that when he died unexpectedly soon after his retirement to the cottage in the Mendips she had been able to apply for a job as a teacher at the nearby school. She was still there, fifteen years later.

'I couldn't leave my mother, you see,' she explained. 'I'd have liked to travel but she's not very well. I suppose you could say this is my one chance of happiness.'

'But you'd have to leave your mother if you married.'

'Oh no, Philip would come and live with us. We've talked about it. It's a nice cottage, quite big, there'd be enough room. He could teach too—it's a very musical school. And in the holidays, if we wanted to go on a walking tour for instance, there's a neighbour who can move in to look after my mother. We'd both like to go back to the Pyrenees when the war's over.'

She smiled. He could imagine them hiking through the hills, just the right amount of provisions neatly packed in each haversack, never a cross word.

'It's nothing to do with me,' he said. 'But I daresay you'd better do it. We'll look after Gerda.'

Dorothy saw a certain amount of her half-brother Hector during these months in London. The other brother, Rory, had moved to Surrey with his wife and baby daughter. Hector was in his thirties now, not married, working for a firm of solicitors in the City. Dorothy found him a bit pompous, but kind. He sometimes took her to the theatre, making up a foursome with a younger colleague and the colleague's sister who went to an art school. Dorothy enjoyed these evenings very much. Sometimes after the theatre they went to dinner in a restaurant and when the play had been very good—like Hamlet, for instance, with John Gielgud—Dorothy became rather excited and talked too much.

Once Hector spoke to her about this.

'One must be very careful not to show off,' he said.

'That's what Father says,' said Dorothy. 'There are two things he's always convinced I'm going to do—show off and make myself cheap. They're the two unforgivable sins. Nothing else matters.'

'There's something in it. A girl has to be jolly careful. It's different for a man. For a girl, everything depends on who she marries.'

'Oh rubbish, Hector, not nowadays surely?'

'Yes, Dorothy, even nowadays. It's different for people like the sort you always seem to admire in restaurants, who belong to the fast set, or for people like your friends Jane and Caroline Arkwright, who aren't out of the top drawer.'

'You sound like Mummy. You can't mean all that.'

'Your mother's right, you know.'

'Of course she's right, according to her way of looking at things. No one will ever get me to say anything at all against Mummy. But what she thinks isn't right for everybody. It isn't in the least little bit right for me. As for our mutual father, I am sorry to say I think he's mad. I think he lives behind an enormous barricade of perfectly ridiculous opinions because he's terrified someone will come along and expose him for what he is. I don't know what he is, I don't suppose he knows what he is, but I do know that he's absolutely terrified of finding out.'

Hector looked shocked. 'I don't think a girl ought to talk like that about her father.'

'Of course a girl oughtn't to talk like that. A girl oughtn't to do anything, according to you, except echo the opinions of her elders and betters—as long as they're out of the top drawer of course. But you don't really think that, Hector. You only say it because you think that's what you ought to say to me, because you think I'm not old enough to be talked to like a grown-up person. That's true, isn't it?'

He put the tips of his fingers together and looked at her like the middle-aged family solicitor he was becoming.

'Yes,' he said thoughtfully. 'Yes, it is true, to a certain extent. And perhaps it's true that to talk to you like that is an insult to your intelligence. But you should realise that I don't want you to get hurt. I don't want you to do something impetuous which you might regret just because you find certain conventions silly. I suppose also, given that I know what you mean about Father—although of course I think you exaggerate —I dread that you should come into open conflict with him. No good could come of that.'

'No, it couldn't, I do realise that. For a long time, I wouldn't even allow myself to think what I do think about him for just that reason. It's only since I've been in London and seeing more of him with other people that I can't help admitting it to myself. It would upset Mummy terribly if I had a real row with him. But something will have to happen some time. I'm not just going to sit at home and wait to be married. After this summer I'm going to either get a job or go to a University. I don't know which he'd hate most, do you?'

'No,' said Hector. 'University, I should think. But look here, keep in touch with me about this. I may be able to help smooth things over.'

After that there was a certain conspiratorial bond between them, even though they had agreed that nothing should be said to their father about Dorothy's plans until the summer was over. Dorothy now felt able to admit to Hector all sorts of things which loyalty to her parents prevented her from talking about to her friends at the Abbey. Although he in no way encouraged her, she found him surprisingly understanding and felt she had never known him before. They spent more time together now that he knew how deep was her boredom and irritation with the circle to which her parents had introduced her. Sometimes she invented an excuse not to go to her school and they met for lunch, and sometimes afterwards they went to an art gallery before he went back to his office. Once they went down into Charing Cross underground station to see a Spitfire which was on exhibition there, as part of an RAF recruiting campaign. Hector seemed to be fascinated by all the technical details. Dorothy looked at an illuminated map called 'The RAF spans The Empire.' It had little white aeroplanes moving over the routes used by the RAF and the Dominions' Air Forces, and a little red aeroplane showing where the RAF had established the world's long distance record flight. She told

Hector about Noel Maysey-Smith, who had already volunteered for the RAF and was very anxious in case they turned him down for being too old.

'Would you join up if there was a war?' she asked him.

'I've joined the Territorials already.'

'If there was a war, Father wouldn't mind my having a job, would he? Girls do have jobs in wars, don't they?'

'There might be other consequences,' said Hector. 'Possibly less desirable.'

'When a worm meets another worm,' said Gerda, 'there is not an absolute necessity for them to unite.'

She was taking it hard. Marjorie got the worst of it, because she was so often in the kitchen and therefore vulnerable. It was part of the Abbey way of life that when Marjorie was cooking she was available for consultation to anyone who cared to drop in, sit on the edge of the table, pick at whatever she was making and tell her their troubles. During the few days immediately succeeding Philip's announcement of his intentions, Gerda monopolised this time. She did not want to divorce Philip. At the same time she wanted everyone to know that in view of his many tiresome habits, his complete lack of human feeling and his quite extraordinary sexual inadequacy, she had been wonderful to have put up with him for so long. The combination of these complaints with her refusal to let him go irritated Marjorie—it had been her mild suggestion that perhaps his new friend was more his type which had elicited the sweeping generalisation about worms—but at the same time she could see that Gerda was suffering, and that it did not seem to be only her pride which was hurt.

'I believe you are fonder of Philip than you will admit,' she said.

Gerda walked towards the window of the kitchen, her heavy figure coming between Marjorie and the light.

'I am weaker than I seem,' she said. 'I need a companion.'

After a pause she added in a low voice, which trembled slightly, 'There is another thing. I am an alien. If I am married to an Englishman I have some protection. If not, and there is a war, I shall be shot.'

'I can't believe that,' said Marjorie, shocked. 'Not in England. It's impossible. Besides, we'd all protect you. We wouldn't let it happen.'

Gerda shook her head slowly. 'You do not know this war madness. I have asked Philip if they cannot live together, without marriage, but this it seems the mother would not like.'

She sighed, staring out into the courtyard. Then she turned and gave Marjorie a brave smile.

'I am for the firing squad,' she said.

Marcella was having her small sitting-room redecorated.

'If I'm to spend the war in here, it might as well look nice,' she said to Fisher. 'Don't you like that cream for the walls?'

'Very much,' he said. 'But why are you going to spend the war in it?'

'The rest of the house will be full of evacuees. I've put my name down for simply hundreds. Nigger brown carpet, green leather chairs—you don't think it's too masculine, do you?— and the best thing will be these niches, with all my pretty china on glass shelves, lit from inside, you see, isn't that clever? Of course I shall spend all my time dusting because there won't be any servants.'

'How is Noel?'

'He's in the gym. He's always in the gym. He's terrified of not being passed fit to fly. Oh dear it is all rather horrid, isn't it? I don't think it's going to happen, do you?'

'I don't know. Timothy has a very depressing friend staying, one of his pacifists, who says even a German occupation would be better, because otherwise the people in the towns will be killed by bombs and the people in the country will die of starvation. It doesn't sound much fun either way.'

'Your lot won't starve, you can grow food. I shall too. I'm enlarging the kitchen garden already. Noel says we must plough up the lawn but I think we should wait. After all it may not happen. We should look pretty silly with a ploughed-up lawn then, shouldn't we?'

'It may not happen,' said Fisher. 'But I think it will.'

So in due course they listened to Neville Chamberlain on the wireless telling them in a plaintive tone of voice that they were now in a state of war with Germany, and they expected, as most people did, something immediate and horrifying, and were bewildered, as most people were, by the subsequent inaction. There were no bombs, no guns, no evacuees—though a number of the latter did appear at the next village and the rumour was that Winterstoke was on the list for the next batch.

The Autumn Meeting which Arnold had spent so much time organising had to be cancelled. The response had been good. Most of the people who had been at the last conference had been planning to come, as well as almost the same number again of new people. Apart from the proposed discussions, a programme of diversions and festivities had been prepared. Fisher had always felt that the community ought to develop its own festivals, and that they should recur and thus become traditions. He wanted the biennial conference to be the excuse for a week of jollification into which all the local inhabitants should also be drawn. He wanted to attract anyone who could provide music, dancing, drama, or any kind of entertainment. 'But not highbrow,' he had said. 'Nothing rarified. Skittles, beer, bowling for the pig. Flower show. Punch and Judy.'

'You're describing the Church Fête at home,' objected Arnold.

'Why not?' said Fisher, only momentarily checked. 'That's just what we need, with a few extras.'

It was all cancelled, and Fisher was more disappointed than anyone. It had been the first idea for which he had been able to summon up any enthusiasm since Hilda's death, and he knew it would have been a success. Now he was left with time on his hands. He worked in the garden but it bored him and he was not much good at it. He thought of settling down to write the long book about the theory of the perfectibility of man which he had been planning for some time, but the uncertainty in the air made it hard to concentrate. He and his brothers would all be too old for the call-up, but Philip and Trew the cowman would have to go if they put the age limit up to forty. Jim Boulder, who was in his early thirties, had announced his intention of going anyway. Then there was the question of what would be considered reserved occupations, and whether women would be conscripted. Arnold was determined that they should extend their agricultural and market gardening activities as much as possible and man them with conscientious objectors, to whom the Abbey might be a more congenial billet than some others. Gerda would have to be registered, possibly interned. She was rather silent about this time, and sighed a good deal. Philip, his marital problems still unsolved, spent most of his time away from the Abbey, presumably with Rosamund.

Fisher felt a responsibility for them all, which he did not relish. He had a letter from his sister Mary in America, generously offering space for all of them in New Hampshire if they wanted to transfer the whole of their community there. For himself he was tempted. He was too old to be any use in the war. He did not feel himself at one with his living countrymen, only with the dead. In America he would be able to write in peace. His reputation was higher there than in England. He would have more opportunities to talk, make known his views, meet people who were involved in important affairs. Here in England he was out of things. No one paid much attention to what he said or wrote. He had expected that by now, by the time he was over fifty, that would have changed; but he had to admit to himself that it had not. Now presumably the war would put an end to everything that was not a direct contribution to the war effort. Would books continue to be published, for instance? Would there be enough paper?

He could not interest any of the others in going to America. Timothy would have supported him if there had seemed any chance of their getting a majority of votes, but none of the others would hear of it. It was the place, they said, the Abbey itself, to which they felt so much attached. They heard news from Wolfgang Reinhardt, their young German friend, that he and the whole of his co-operative farm community, distressed by anti-German feeling in their part of the country, were moving to South America, where they had made contact with a similar enterprise. When Dorothy heard this she remembered how wonderful Wolfgang had seemed to her two years ago, and felt nostalgic for those happier days. She had just passed her eighteenth birthday and had tried to suggest to her father that she should volunteer for war work. It had led to a scene.

Charles Grant was full of views as to how the war should be organised, though at the same time—and this he concealed from Dorothy though not from his wife—convinced that it would be lost. He told Nora that the population of the towns would panic when the bombing started, and that they would pour out into the surrounding countryside, marauding and looting as they went, and that therefore it was most important that new locks and bolts should be fitted to the outer doors of the house.

'Surely they won't come here,' she said weakly. 'We're such miles from any big town.'

'They'll spread out. As more people pour out behind them, they'll go further and further afield. The population of Bristol is enormous, remember. It's not all that far away. Nor is Southampton for that matter. The ports will be the first to get it. Oh yes, I'm afraid we're going to see some terrible things. They'll have to use troops, of course, to keep the civil population in order. It's not going to be pleasant, I'm afraid.'

When Dorothy told him that she would like to volunteer for one of the women's services, he said that the best possible war service for her would be to stay at home and help her mother.

'But she doesn't need any help. Surely I should be much more useful as a V.A.D.?'

'Certainly not. It's a preposterous suggestion. A young girl like you? You'd have to wash men, do you realise that? Naked men. In bed.'

'Well, but . . . surely I wouldn't have to do that all the time? Besides, it might be useful to know how to give people bed baths.'

'Nonsense. It wouldn't be in the least useful. Unless you are planning to marry a cripple. If you want to be useful you should stay at home. There'll be plenty to do here.'

'It's not just that I want to be useful. I think it would be interesting. I mean, for the experience. . . .'

'Experience? A young girl doesn't need experience—except of a decent home life, of course. Experience of what, may I ask?'

'Well—of life, of people, so that I can . . . expand.'

'Expand! Ha!' He blew out his cheeks, turning quite red in

the face before exploding into a loud coarse laugh. 'Expand! That's just about it I can tell you. I know a thing or two about girls who go into the Services, that's just about what they do, expand. Pregnant within six months, the lot of them. Ha! We don't want any of that, thank you very much. It'll be bad enough if we have to have evacuees here without adding a whole lot of illegitimate brats of our own. No thanks, is all I can say to that. No thank you very much.'

'Don't be ridiculous,' said Dorothy.

'Ridiculous, am I?' he stood up and began to walk up and down behind his desk. Dorothy prepared to sit it out, 'A young girl like you is completely at the mercy of an experienced man. It's no use thinking you can deal with people like that. Servicemen, people from the roughest ranks of society, completely brutalised. Soldiers. To a soldier a young girl means one thing, and one thing only. Sex.'

'Well, but surely not all V.A.D.s get actually raped?'

'Don't they? Do they not? Do you know what the statistics for rape are in this country?'

'No. Please don't tell me.'

'I won't. I will spare you. But life will not spare you. Experience, which you are so keen to enjoy, will not spare you. You don't know how lucky you are to have been born into a sphere of society where you can be protected from experience, from evil. You take it for granted, don't you? Young people these days are spoilt. They take their parents for granted, the protection of a loving home, they take it for granted. . . .'

'I don't take it for granted, Father, I am grateful. It's just that if I volunteer for war service now, I am more likely to be able to choose what I do than if I wait until they bring in conscription for women.'

She knew this was a good point and she had brought it up just as he was beginning to run out of rage. He paused.

'I am very much against nursing,' he said. 'I don't think it would be at all suitable.'

'It doesn't have to be nursing.'

'All I will say is that I am prepared to talk to your mother about it. That is all I will say at the moment. I am prepared to discuss it with your mother.'

130

'Thank you,' said Dorothy crisply.

She went out of the room, unaware that by doing so she left him feeling that he had lost the argument. Obscurely he both knew and resented the fact that she despised him: it was one of the reasons for the rapidity with which in any discussion with her he reached the point of rage.

'I've said nothing, mind,' he said as she went. 'I've only said I'll talk to your mother.'

But she had gone. It could not be good for anyone, she thought, to hate their father. She ought to get away from home as soon as possible.

Marcie had heard that evacuees were covered in lice and liable to defecate on the carpet. Bracing herself conscientiously —'poor things how too utterly ghastly,' she said briskly, tossing back her hair—she went up to the bedrooms which she had in her imagination consigned to the twenty or so children she was expecting, and completely covered the floors with layers of newspaper, making sure that there was a good supply in reserve so that it could be changed every day. She bought two fine tooth-combs for each bedroom and a good supply of disinfectant. One evening she received a telephone call from the local billeting officer and went down to the station to find three pale clean teenage children in spotless school uniform who were given into her charge by an equally correct schoolmaster. They were David, Kevin and Doreen, from St Alphege's School somewhere near Shepherds Bush.

She led them up to their rooms.

'So difficult to get dustsheets these days,' she explained, hurriedly bundling together the sheaves of newspaper and slipping the tooth-combs unobtrusively into her pockets. They gazed at her in silence, their impassive faces concealing completely the active amazement each was experiencing. Infinitely more embarrassed by them than the troupe of wild animals she had been expecting, she bought them bicycles so that they could get to school every day, allotted them a downstairs room as their own sitting room and handed over their care to Mrs Scrimgeour the cook.

Noel was stationed at the nearby flight training camp. Marcie had become a local representative of the Women's Land Army and had given over the big drawing room to piles of green jerseys, brown corduroy breeches, socks, gumboots, and other items of the Land Girls' equipment, and had retreated into the newly decorated smaller sitting room. It was through her that Fisher, appealed to in some desperation, obtained for Dorothy her enlistment in the W.L.A. and her assignment to the Abbey as her place of work. It was not the adventurous solution Dorothy had had in mind, but it was better than nothing and at least her father was prepared to agree to it. She was to help with the cows and the poultry and the vegetable garden, and Timothy was detailed to give her driving lessons so that she could take over the delivery van.

Thus it was in her new green jersey and corduroy breeches, feeding the geese—they were new too—that she was first seen by the three young Guards officers who, stationed on Salisbury Plain and being entertained to lunch one Sunday by Marcie, accompanied her after lunch on some errand to the Abbey before returning to their camp.

'A goose-girl,' said one of them.

'How charming,' said another.

But as she turned and smiled at them it was the third, who had not spoken, whose eyes she met.

Hamilton came into the house more often these days because he liked to listen to the news. Most of all he liked to listen to the news in English from Germany. He happened by chance to hear one of William Joyce's programmes and immediately became an enthusiast, the earliest and most loyal of Lord Haw Haw's English fans. The most easily accessible wireless set being the big one on the kitchen dresser, it was Marjorie who was most often obliged to listen with him. She did not share his enthusiasm.

'You don't believe it, do you?' she asked him.

'No, no. I don't necessarily believe the other version, mind you.'

'But you must, Hamilton. Why would our own people tell us lies?'

'They don't want us to panic.'

'But we won't panic. People are rather brave on the whole.'

'They don't know that.'

'Well I wish you wouldn't listen to it. It frightens me.'

'It's his style I like, that's all.'

'Why does he know so much? It's uncanny.'

'Fifth Column,' said Hamilton, rolling his eyes.

'For goodness sake,' said Marjorie. 'It's not a joke, this war.'

'It has its funny aspects. But I promise you I take it very seriously. I know there may be parachutists in my own field at any moment, and bombs and destruction and a German occupying army. I do recognise all that, Marjorie, I assure you. I mean to defend my homeland to the last gasp. I am making myself a special belt with pouches for food and money, so that I can take to the hills at a moment's notice. Would you like me to make you one too?'

'Do you think that would be the right thing to do? I hadn't thought. But then you would have to make one for Arnold too and for Joe and for Meg. Oh Hamilton, do you really think we will have to do that?'

'It's possible, isn't it?'

'I hadn't thought. I suppose I really thought it was all destiny. You see, supposing most people alive in Europe today are people who have committed a serious crime in another life, then they can atone for it in this one by dying bravely, so it might be all part of the design, don't you see? But you wouldn't see, of course. None of you understand what I mean by all that.'

Hamilton's large face, which had been quite animated at the thought of the belts, fell into folds of comic embarrassment. There was room in his scheme of things for almost every system of beliefs, but there was something about Marjorie's deeply-held though seldom expressed faith which made him uncomfortable. Fortunately Arnold happened at that moment to come into the kitchen to ask Marjorie whether she knew the birth dates of the Trew family.

'All these forms are a nightmare. The war makes bureaucracy run wild. We shall be such a police state at the end of it, I don't see how we shall ever get back to normal. I never have time for anything else. Tomorrow I've got to go and vouch for

Timothy at his tribunal, next week it's Gerda's. How I'm supposed to run a farm as well I don't know.'

'I'll do it,' said Marjorie easily.

'You can't possibly,' said Arnold, so irritably that Marjorie flushed.

'You might at least let people help you,' she said.

But he only said, 'I'd better go and see Mrs Trew then, if you don't know,' and went out again with his uncompleted form.

'He's over-working,' said Hamilton.

'There's no need for him to be bad-tempered about it,' said Marjorie, rolling out the pastry with unnecessary vigour.

'They may be younger, the other fellows,' said Noel. 'But none of them has had anything like my experience.'

'I should think not,' said Marcie.

'Young Bruce is going to be a very good pilot. He asks my advice a good deal. He asked me to show him how I loop the loop today. I was rather pleased, as a matter of fact, because he can do a perfectly adequate loop himself. It's just that I hit my own slip stream when I come out of it. You can feel her shudder as she runs into it, that's how you know you've done it. You ought to do it every time for a perfect loop. He's not bad though. He can't quite master the slow roll, goes into a spin too often.'

'But won't the Germans be awfully surprised if they come over in their bombers and there you all are, looping and spinning and rolling?' said Marcie. 'Or perhaps it will send them away like when the geese do all those funny threatening gestures to keep the hens off their territory.'

Noel did not smile.

'We shall be shooting as well,' he said stiffly.

Timothy did well at his tribunal, Gerda rather less well at hers.

Gerda had been the cause of several visits from the local police, who only too obviously suspected that the Abbey was the sort of place where they might expect to find German spies. There was also the question of Fisher's inability to

134

manipulate the black-out curtains which Marjorie had made for the gothic windows of the library, which was finally resolved only by the nailing of thick cardboard templates into the arched part of each window. This failure of practical efficiency on Fisher's part was associated in the minds of the police and the ARP wardens with Gerda's presence at the Abbey and added to their doubts. After due investigation, however, Gerda was graded as a Class C alien, which meant that she had to report to the police station once a month.

'They wish to be able once a month to humiliate me,' she said. 'One day I shall go there to report and I shall not return. I shall never be seen again. I know how it is, there will be no record, nothing, silence.'

Timothy quoted Tolstoy at his tribunal, and said that he believed in the law of love and not the law of violence, and that he thought it wrong to bear arms. He said this in a modest, rather sad, tone of voice, was asked a few questions about his past life by the chairman of the tribunal, a local business man, and given exemption from military service on condition that he continued to work on the land. The whole thing was over in a few minutes.

Gerda was rather offended that he should have got off so lightly.

'The tribunals in this part of the world are not unsympathetic,' said Philip. 'They are used to the Quaker tradition.'

Gerda gave one of her gigantic sighs: it was obvious to her that this information had come through Rosamund.

After Christmas the snow began. It was the coldest January and February for many years. Dorothy wrapped herself in jerseys, scarves and an overcoat and in her Land Girl's gumboots walked through the village and up towards the Plain to meet Guy, the young Guards officer. Whenever he could he slipped away from the camp in his green two-seater MG, in whose cramped interior, parked up one or other of the quiet little roads which led to the Plain, their love was consummated.

His eyes were grey, like hers; but hers sometimes looked green whereas his were flecked with brown. His eyebrows, which were quite thick, were brown too. So was his hair, which was straight and though cut short and parted at the side tended to fall over his forehead. His face was thin, and wore a habitually mild expression which turned to a pleasant irony when he smiled. He was thin and of medium height. In his uniform he looked smart, but at the same time because his expression was peculiarly unmilitary there was something inappropriate and rather touching in his appearance. In the casual clothes he wore beneath his British warm overcoat when he came to meet Dorothy in the green MG he looked like a handsome student, but on the rare occasions when she saw him in a London suit, with a bowler hat, he looked quite different. This worried her.

'I think what I mean is, you look what my father would call a bounder,' she said, trying to explain her feeling.

'Oh do you really think so?' He looked so pleased she did not say she had not meant it as a compliment.

When there were other people there he talked a good deal in his quiet pleasant voice, and often made them laugh. He seemed to find the world ridiculous, and because she had never before met anybody to whom frivolity seemed more or less an act of faith she found his attitude liberating. When they were alone together he was occasionally a little more serious. He told her a lot about his friends. He had been at Oxford when the war started, and had joined the Army rather than ask for his conscription to be deferred so that he could take his final examinations. His mother had known the Colonel of his regiment. He had never been to any lectures, he said, so he would probably have failed to get a degree. Why hadn't he been to any lectures? No one did, it seemed. Everyone went to parties instead. The parties sounded different from any that Dorothy had ever been to, and a great deal more full of incident. Her mother subscribed to the *Tatler* and the *Sketch*, and quite a few of the people whose photographs Dorothy had seen in these magazines figured in Guy's descriptions, though they apparently behaved with a good deal less dignity there than anyone could have guessed from the photographs.

She listened to the stories as if to fairy tales. In an odd way she felt no curiosity about his life. It was as if it were all in his face, just as she felt that everything about her was in her face; as if their long mutual gaze disclosed each to the other without any need for history. Even their first look, as she stood with her bucket among the geese, had been too long for propriety. She had never set eyes on a face on which her glance could rest so long without a thought of embarrassment, or one on which there seemed to be written so clearly a being in its entirety. It would have been enough for her simply to look— that is to say, for the time being—or perhaps as well just to learn the bony nature of the back of one of his hands, so slow was her notion of progress, or so much did there seem to her to be absorbable from these quite extraordinary activities. However at their third meeting he kissed her.

The second meeting had been when the green MG drew up beside her as she was walking home from the Abbey a day or two after that first Sunday. At the third they went to the cinema in Trowbridge. She had told her parents she was going to the Abbey, to a lecture. No doubt they would have to meet him some time but she hoped to put it off as long as possible. She supposed she would have to meet his parents too: one day she did ask him where he lived. He told her Surrey but did not seem to want to talk about it. Much later he told her he lived in a horrid little house because his father who had been a rich stockbroker had lost all his money a few years ago.

'How awful,' said Dorothy easily.

'It was awful,' he said. 'Really awful. Fortunately some old great-uncle or other paid for the rest of my education. But they never got over it, it ruined their lives.'

'But can't you be just as happy poor? I mean, when you've got used to it.'

'They'll never get used to it. It's horrible, poverty, a horrible, lowering, demeaning thing. And when you combine it with aspirations to gentility it's very bad, very bad indeed.'

'But do you feel that too? That poverty is very bad? For you?'

'Certainly. But I don't mean to be poor. After the war I shall go into the City with a friend of mine and I shall make an incredible amount of money.'

'What will you do with it?'

'I shall live a life of unexampled splendour.'

She wished he would include her in his plans when he talked

of the future. It was so obvious to her that they must be together for the rest of their lives that it seemed odd of him not to admit it more openly, but if for some reason he preferred to pretend it was not so, she had no wish to impose anything on him; nothing could affect the inevitability of it. He would not even say he loved her for some time. This she did regret. For herself the words 'I love you' were always in her head whether she was with him or not, but it did not seem right that she should be the first to say them. This was not so much for reasons of pride as that she wished to take her tone from him. If he did not think the time had yet come for them to say they loved each other, she would wait. So when he took her by the shoulders and said to her with some solemnity, 'Dorothy, you do—do you like me?' she only answered 'Yes I like you.' One evening in the green MG, warm in spite of the draughts let in by the side flaps, he said rather suddenly, 'I think I might be falling in love with you.' She almost laughed, it seemed so late in the day, but instead she said, 'Oh well, in that case I shall fall in love with you.' He seemed moved. He kissed her solemnly and then with increasing passion, saying, 'It's mad, what am I doing?' Once she asked him whether he had ever been fond of a girl who had been unkind to him, but he did not like that question and answered briefly, 'No, never.'

She would have been content with the kisses, as before she would have been content to gaze at him. The kisses, of which she thought constantly when she was not with him and which in her imagination always ended in the avowals of eternal love which he had not yet made, seemed to her sufficient in themselves, but were not so to him; and since their lovemaking had soon progressed beyond that stage it began after a time to seem to her mere coyness on her part not to go further. He said he would see to it that she did not have a baby. She wished he had not said that, but understood that it had to be said. Afterwards she thought that perhaps her reluctance had not been coyness so much as a proper caution about something which although at the time and in view of what had already happened between them seemed nothing much—was at first rather disappointing in fact—did amount to a considerable development.

She felt that the clichés used in romantic novels, such as 'he possessed her' and 'she gave herself to him' had meaning after all. She felt that she had given herself to him and that he possessed her. She was glad that this should be so.

When the cold weather came, meetings became more difficult. Many of the small roads leading to the Plain which had been hospitable to them in the autumn were impassable because of snow. Sometimes they took shelter in pubs or cinemas; often they walked, to keep warm. They must have covered many miles that winter, arm in arm, muffled in coats and scarves, either along the narrow road which links the villages at the foot of the escarpment, or up the tracks and paths which lead to the Plain and which even when they were thick with snow were so familiar to Dorothy that she never lost her sense of direction. There were afternoons on the Plain when the sky was clear blue and the sun on the snow extraordinarily bright. Guy said he would send for his skis and teach her how to ski down Bratton Down over the submerged White Horse beneath, but he never did. Flocks of hungry birds came to feed on the berries of the wild hawthorn; sometimes they found their starved bodies frozen in the snow. One grey cold day a dead bird lay in their path as they climbed up on to the Plain.

'Poor thrush,' said Dorothy, stopping to look down at it.

Guy crouched down to pick it up.

'It's not a thrush,' he said.

He stood up and held out the bird for her to see. He had taken his gloves off and held the bird in his cupped hand, his fingers supporting its head. With a finger of the other hand he gently moved its wing so that she could see the red feathers underneath.

'A redwing,' he said.

He ran his finger along the white line over the eye.

'They tend to die in cold winters. They're smaller than thrushes. Their beaks aren't strong enough to get into the earth for worms when there's heavy frost.'

'I've never seen one.'

'They're quite rare.'

He stood looking at the bird in his hand.

'If we were children we'd bury it, wouldn't we? And put

a cross of sticks at the head of the grave. Did you use to do that?'

'Of course.'

'But we'll leave it here,' he said, bending down to lay the bird in the snow. 'Some animal might need the food.'

They walked on. His arm held hers very close to his side. She felt as though they were walking through the frozen snow in a cloud of incandescence, or a column of flame.

'What are you thinking?' he asked her.

'I was thinking it was a bit like walking with the Holy Ghost.'

'Oh quite. People often feel like that, walking with me.'

She liked the way he never asked her what she meant when she said something odd. It was not so much that he always understood as that he did not seem to think it mattered. She liked that too.

When Fisher heard that Marcie had offered Penelope and her husband the banker a share of her house for the duration of the war he was horrified. He had got into the way of dropping in to see her on this or that small pretext. He found it a relief to be able occasionally to get away from the Abbey, to which he was more confined now than he had been before the war, and he knew that Marcie was pleased to have someone to talk to. Noel was obsessed by his flight training and though his Commanding Officer had given him permission to live at home because the camp was so near, he only returned to sleep, and was obviously looking forward to the coming action which would make it necessary for him to do even that at the camp.

'He's not shooting a line,' said Marcie. 'He really does think that RAF life is absolutely wizard.'

Her adoption of the slang which was just becoming current and which Noel used rather self-consciously as a symbol of his oneness with his squadron had been immediate and uncritical. As a result her usage was at first occasionally eccentric. When Fisher said, 'Don't you think you might find that Penelope and her husband would get under your feet?' she replied, 'Not if I keep them browned off,' which left him no clearer.

'You might be sent more evacuees surely?' he persevered.

'There's lots of room,' she said. 'Besides if they're like the three little mice I've got already one would hardly notice. Anyway I haven't said anything definite. They don't even know if their house is going to be requisitioned or not, it's all just an idea.'

It was through Penelope that Marcie had been asked to be kind to Guy when his regiment came to Salisbury Plain. She often asked him to lunch on Sundays, and because she thought it would be nicer for him if there were a young girl to talk to and because Dorothy was about the only young girl she knew locally, she often asked Dorothy too. She usually asked several other people because of her long-held faith in the safety of numbers and because Penelope had told her that Guy liked social life. Dorothy enjoyed these lunches. They were the only occasions on which she and Guy met as it were officially, and though she was careful to behave with discretion she liked to be near him, to feel that he had noticed that she was looking nice (having taken quite a lot of trouble), and herself to notice that people liked him, which made her proud. Only Lucy Lambert, two of whose sons were already in the Army, the third being only a year too young, and whose perceptions were sharpened by her painful anxiety on their account, noticed that the girl she had thought might do for one of them one day evidently now had other ideas; but Lucy Lambert was a woman who kept her own counsel.

One morning Marjorie went out in the snow to get some eggs to poach for breakfast and when she tried to break them on the side of the saucepan she could not do it; they were frozen solid. It seemed the last straw: she was hating this winter. Everyone was in a bad temper. The war did not seem to have begun and yet it hung over them as a perpetual menace which prevented anyone from doing anything which was not conducive to their survival in extreme conditions which had not yet arrived. Arnold was busy and anxious. He had already lost two good men to the Army, and Dorothy who did her best was too frail physically to be worth even half a man. The incredible freeze-up made matters worse. He had increased the herd of cattle and it was impossible to bring them all in for

141

shelter. It was as much as Dorothy could do to get a sufficient supply of hay round the fields. Only the children enjoyed the weather. Joe and the two Boulder children spent all their time skating or tobogganing; Meg was too young and got cold and cried. Joe and Griff Boulder took their bicycles onto the canal until Arnold told them it was too dangerous. Then they went to Trowbridge with their skates and skated all the way to Bath and back on the canal. Huge icicles hung everywhere for days on end, telegraph wires were down, roads impassable. The Army, still waiting for the war to begin, helped to clear the roads and re-erect the telegraph poles. Noel, flying every day in clear skies over the snow-covered country, was promoted from Flight Lieutenant to Squadron Leader and because of the weather now lived all the time at the camp. Philip was prevented by the snow from visiting Rosamund, isolated in the Mendips. Without her calm optimism to encourage him he began to see his case as hopeless: he could not foresee their ever being able to marry. His misery made him absent-minded: he forgot to order the extra supply of hay which was needed for the animals, with the result that on the coldest day of all when the road was blocked by snow drifts, and even to walk across the yard was hazardous because of the ice, they ran out completely. For the first time he and Arnold, those two models of reason and sobriety, had an actual quarrel.

'The one thing that matters,' Arnold said. 'The only point of this whole place, is that everybody is responsible, nobody has to be supervised, everybody is a principal, nobody is an employee. . . .'

'I can't spend my whole life on nothing but pettifogging detail like some wretched clerk. I thought Gerda had ordered the hay. She does the typing, doesn't she?'

'You're supposed to be in charge of foodstuffs.'

'I've been fully occupied with the pigsty. Suddenly we decide to have pigs—why didn't we think about who was going to build the pigsty before we went to the market?'

'We argued all that out at the farm meeting. We agreed that we could do it. We all have to do some of the pettifogging detail as you call it. I'm absolutely overwhelmed with it. There's an impossible amount of paperwork, forms for the War Agri-

142

cultural Committee, God knows what. I really do think I might be able to leave you to order a few bales of hay so the animals don't actually die on us.'

'Well you can't, that's all,' Philip's voice rose. 'You can't leave anything to me. I'm incapacitated by private anxiety, that's all.'

'Oh for God's sake, Philip, what are these bloody animals going to eat?'

Philip snatched up a pile of papers from Arnold's desk, violently dashed them down again, shouted, 'Let them eat straw!' and rushed from the room.

Arnold reached for the telephone and then remembered that the lines were down. He went to look for Dorothy to tell her to take the tractor and a cheque and drive about until she found a farmer who would sell her some hay. On the way back he met Marjorie, who said, 'It's just absolutely mad, Arnold, to accept COs unconditionally like you're doing. The new one has sat in the kitchen all morning lecturing me about the evils of capitalism, and when I suggested he went and chopped some wood, he said he couldn't until his mother sent him his dungarees. You must say you'll only take them on a month's trial.'

'*You* say we'll only take them on a month's trial,' said Arnold. 'You do it. Work out a letter with Timothy and send it off. I'll sign it.'

He went back into his office, leaving Marjorie with tears in her eyes: she did not think a man should talk to his wife as if she were just one more person bothering him. Arnold, shutting the door firmly, thought a wife ought to support her husband, and not criticise just when everyone else was criticising. He could not understand why she took so long getting into bed at night. All that washing and hair-brushing and looking at the children and opening the window—he could not help suspecting that she did it on purpose, knowing he'd be asleep by the time she got into bed. Of course he was older than she was and often tired through over-work. Perhaps she didn't want to go to bed with him any more. But if they didn't have that, it would be perfectly terrible, that was where all difficulties were dissolved in the milk and honey of love; if she wouldn't

143

do it any more everything was utterly dreary and depressing. He had tried going upstairs later than she did but then she would be asleep—or pretending to be asleep—and would be cross if woken and say, 'I'm asleep. I'll be here in the morning,' but then in the morning she was not there, she was already up and in the kitchen, talking to the children, to whoever it was who was doing the milking that week, absorbed and busy, putting his breakfast in front of him as if he were nobody special, the same 'good morning' for him as for the others. No wonder he was getting irritable, that was what he thought, no wonder.

When the spring eventually came it was a particularly vigorous one, as springs that follow hard winters often are. Dorothy lingered over her work, so as to feel the first warmth of the sun and smell the growing grass. She particularly lingered with the geese, of whom she had become fond. She had started by being nervous of them because she knew they could nip one quite hard on the thigh, but as she got to know them better she began to see them as virtuous and gentle birds. They fed from her hand without undue greed and looked at her with small bright trustful eyes: their limited mental capacity and touching obedience to the instincts which impelled them to preserve their species made her feel protective towards them. Every day she checked their fences, she was determined that the fox who had twice made havoc among the hens should never get his murderer's teeth into her geese.

She was tired after the winter: the work on the farm was hard and though she was healthy she was not exactly robust. Also she was often short of sleep because of staying out too late with Guy and having to get up early for work the next morning. Even loving itself tired her sometimes. She thought of Guy so continuously, so repetitively, all the time she was not with him that sometimes when practical necessity forced her to give full attention to her work it was a relief. It did not happen often, most of the time she could fulfill her obligations as a not very efficient Land Girl by giving the job only half her attention. Only his presence eased her mind. Her hope that they might soon marry was in some ways a hope that she might thus be made free to think about something else.

She bicycled to lunch with Marcie one Sunday. He was not there when she arrived. Marcie was in her sitting-room with Penelope and another girl.

'This is Daphne Maudling,' said Marcie. 'It's only us four. Guy was coming with a chum but they rang up to chuck. Too boring.'

'He's hopelessly vague,' said Daphne. 'It was only when I rang him up to remind him I was coming that he remembered that he couldn't. We've got to meet in a tea-room, can you imagine? He can't even get away long enough to come here for tea.'

'Funny old Guy,' said Marcie.

Dorothy knew that something terrible was happening and that she was without any defences at all. She accepted a glass of sherry and sat down.

'He's a monster,' said Daphne, indulgently.

She had shoulder-length fair hair, well cut and shining. She was thin and fairly tall and wore the sort of coat and skirt which could only have been very expensive. The skirt was short and the shoulders of the jacket square and padded. She wore the jacket unbuttoned, showing a cream shirt and a number of pearl necklaces. The effect was careless as well as smart, perhaps because she sat back among the cushions, smoking, with her silk-stockinged legs curled underneath her. She had very white hands with red nails and wore quite a lot of make-up. She looked to Dorothy quite extraordinarily elegant. She had a deep rather grating voice and a drawling manner of speech which emphasised a number of words as if they had capital letters.

'Have you come fresh from the Farm?' she said to Dorothy, in this exaggerated sort of way. At the same time she smiled. Without the smile almost everything she said might have seemed calculated to give offence, but the smile had a kind of rueful, almost conspiratorial, air which seemed to invite her interlocutor to join in the game which she was playing and which was not really, she seemed to be admitting, all that much fun. The smile took away the sting.

Dorothy smiled back.

'I'm allowed to wash the mud off on Sundays.'

But she could not smile for long because of the awful thing that was happening, even though she was not yet quite sure what the awful thing was.

'I've said I'll go into the WRNS when they get to my age group,' said Daphne. 'Can you imagine? I faint with seasickness every time I see a pond. Do you think I ought to tell them?'

'They won't send you to sea, you'll be driving an Admiral about or something,' said Marcie. 'Let's go and eat our disgusting rabbit pie.'

'Why don't you join the ATS?' said Penelope. 'Then you might be with Guy.'

'The uniform, my dear,' said Daphne. 'That horrid khaki.'

Following them into the dining room Dorothy thought if only it needn't happen now, just not this minute, not at lunch, not when I'm in my old tweed skirt and that shirt I thought was so nice but now isn't and my hair needs cutting and I'm fat, let it wait until I'm outside somewhere, until he can tell me himself and make it all right.

'Come along,' Marcie said, putting her arm briefly round Dorothy's shoulders as they went into the dining room.

Forgetting Marcie's obtuseness where human emotions were concerned, Dorothy thought for a moment that she might have understood, might be going to shield her.

'It's what Mrs Hancock would call a hen party,' said Marcie. 'What fun.'

'Who on earth is Mrs Hancock?' asked Penelope.

'She lives in Bradford-on-Avon,' said Marcie. 'She used to have a bull-terrier called Musso, but now she's changed his name to Winston. It doesn't make any difference to him because he's deaf as a post anyway.'

'My sister's got a dachshund called Fritzy,' said Penelope. 'She's changed his name to Tutankamen because she says dachshunds are Egyptian really and not German at all. I never knew that, did you?'

But it was not to be averted.

'So when's the wedding anyway?' Penelope asked briskly.

'God knows,' said Daphne. 'That's what we've got to talk about. It was supposed to be this summer. A June Wedding,

146

my dear. St Margaret's Westminster. Everyone asked. Can you imagine? At least in wartime one can get out of that I suppose.'

'I don't see why,' said Penelope.

'We might all be bombed or something,' said Daphne. 'Anyway he's been so shifty lately. I haven't heard from him properly for ages. I should think he's having a wild affair with an At, wouldn't you?'

'I haven't heard anything about an At,' said Marcie. 'Have you, Dorothy? Dorothy often comes to lunch when Guy's here. We haven't heard anything of an At, have we Dorothy?'

'No, not a thing.'

'Or a Land Girl,' said Daphne. 'Tumbling a buxom Land Girl in the hay.'

'We're terribly short of hay,' said Marcie. 'And we haven't heard anything of a Land Girl either.'

'Oh you wouldn't have heard,' said Daphne. 'He's far too shifty for that. Never mind, I'll be terribly bossy at tea-time. A Crack of the Whip, my dear, to Bring him to Heel.'

'Are you sure you want to?' said Penelope sharply. 'I didn't realise he was unreliable.'

Daphne answered rather dreamily, scraping her fork round her empty plate, 'I've always had a weakness for a shit. So has he. For the female equivalent I mean. Which I suppose is a bitch. We're a pair of terrible . . . adventurers I suppose. Can I have some more of that lovely pie?'

She was not hungry, but unlike Marcie neither was she obtuse: she was beginning to wonder if she had been quite tactful in her remarks about Land Girls.

'There's a lot more,' she said, sitting down again with her replenished plate. 'We must eat while we can. When the invasion comes it'll be nothing but acorns.'

Dorothy went over to the sideboard in order to hide her face, and for the rest of the meal it was Daphne who, having delivered the blow, administered the First Aid, talking determinedly about farming while both of them consumed with some difficulty the peculiarly dry rabbit pie. Dorothy was concentrating so hard on sitting upright and not allowing herself to be overcome by what seemed purely physical weakness, that she had no time to notice that Daphne's thin face seemed to have become more finely drawn, as if she too were feeling the strain. Anyway it would have seemed to Dorothy that Daphne was about as likely to suffer from strain as a high tension steel wire.

'I'm afraid I can't stay for coffee,' said Dorothy. 'I'm so sorry but I promised to go over to the Abbey to feed the geese. They're all so busy there at the moment.'

As soon as she got on her bicycle she began to cry. There was no one to see. From time to time as she rode home along the lane, the pain was so bad that she bent over the handlebars, swerving from one side of the road to the other, and let out a sound somewhere between a bellow and a groan, the sort of sound which might have made anyone who had happened to hear it across the muddy fields think a cow must have lost a calf.

When she got home she went up to her room without seeing either of her parents. If she could somehow survive the next few hours he must then telephone, must arrange to see her. There was still the slim hope to cling to that the unbearable truth could be annihilated, and the original meaning restored to all those events of the last few months which had become retrospectively unrecognisable in the new light so coldly and so quickly cast on them. In the meantime if nothing were what it seemed, or what it had once seemed, there was nothing to be done but to crouch on her bed, trembling and stiff, like a rabbit caught in the glare of headlights on a country road at night.

'What did you think was happening?'
'I didn't think.'

She understood at once that the only thing he could have done would have been not to think. The effort she was making to force her imagination to grasp the thing from the aspect in which it must have appeared to him was so absorbing as to make her for the moment calmer than she would have thought possible an hour or two ago. This was a relief to Guy, but at the same time it added to his pain that she should be behaving so well. It would have been easier for him if he had been able in some way to fault her.

148

'Couldn't you have told me?'

'I thought I had in a way. I mean once when you were looking at a magazine . . . Don't you remember?'

'When I asked who she was?'

'There was a photograph, yes.'

'But you only said, a girl I know called Daphne.'

'You didn't ask any more. I thought that was because you'd guessed.'

'But how could I have guessed?'

'I don't know. But you often do guess things.'

'Not things like that. That would have seemed impossible.'

They were in the MG, parked under the beech trees whose leaves were just opening, on the lane that led up to the Plain. Their bodies, as if unaware of the vagaries of the minds which inhabited them, were full of the familiar excitement and tenderness; this made their conversation doubly difficult. Dorothy suggested that they should get out and walk towards the higher ground. They did so, but the difficulty in which they were embroiled seemed to overwhelm them and they sat down on the steep grassy bank which bordered the lane and which was scattered with wood anemones and blue and white violets.

'Are you in love with her?' asked Dorothy.

'I don't know.' He sighed. They were both feeling rather sick. 'I suppose I fell in love with you without meaning to. I suppose I was behaving badly. I am very fond of Daphne, but it is quite different. We have known each other a long time. We have a kind of alliance, I don't quite know what to call it. We are the same sort of people.'

'And I'm not?'

'Not at all.'

'Perhaps the same sort of people shouldn't—are not necessarily—good together.'

'We both want the same things—mostly materialistic sort of things—we're both tough and not very nice and enjoy being not very nice—we're like a couple of pirates—we're dishonest, we cheat.'

'Why?'

'I don't know. It's just the kind of people we are.'

'I could be like that too, perhaps.'

'We even cheat each other. That's part of it, we like cheating each other. I should cheat you, I should have to, that's how I am.'

'I can't understand that. I am trying to but I can't.'

'What you are is something quite different. You don't know that, you don't know how different you are. I'd have to have been someone else, someone I'm not, I'd have to have started earlier. I'm not sure whether I'd have wanted to be like that anyway, but what I do know is that I can't, do you see, I simply can't.'

'I don't understand. Don't two people just love each other and then manage as best they can?'

'People love in different ways, it means different things to them. I am different from you. I should make you very unhappy.'

'But did you always know that?'

'No. I didn't know what was happening. I'd never met anyone like you.'

'Do you mean I take it all too seriously?'

'I mean you're too good for me.'

'Oh!' Furious, she hit him as hard as she could on the shoulder with both clenched fists. 'How can you say anything so awful? Why is everything a cliché? How can we ever have got involved in something so boring? Having a last fling with a silly Land Girl before marrying an heiress. How can any of us be so unoriginal?'

'She's not an heiress.'

'I thought you said she was rich.'

'But not an heiress.'

'But that's part of it all, isn't it?'

'Yes. She knows that. That's another thing, you see. You don't care about money. Daphne's father's the head of a big merchant bank. He'll give me a job. That's the kind of person I am. You don't recognise that, you don't see that I want all sorts of things that you'd hate, without them I should turn nasty, I'm not—just not capable of being nice without all that.'

'I'm too unsophisticated you mean. I see that. I see I am what you say. I just wish you'd told me before, that's all.'

'I didn't know. I mean I didn't know that I would . . . that we would be so fond of each other.'

'I was so pleased with myself. I thought it would be so nice for you to have all this horrible burden of love hanging round your neck, to have me like a millstone, a horrible heavy disgusting fleshy millstone, round your neck.'

'Don't. Please don't.'

He put his arms tightly round her shoulders. There seemed nothing they could do except sit weeping on the flowery bank in the evening sunshine. Eventually he had to go back to camp. He left her at the end of the drive to walk home without anything being resolved. The night passed in retrospective and repetitive pain: when she thought rationally, she was forced either to believe that his grief was less genuine or at any rate less isolated from his other emotions than it seemed, or else that when he came to think it over he must realise that it was mad that they should part when parting made them so unhappy.

The night seemed very long, but for most of the time she did at least assume that the end had not yet been reached, that there would be further conversations whether more or less painful than the last; but in the morning a boy on a bicycle arrived with a letter which he said a soldier had given him. The letter said, 'The regiment is being moved tomorrow so I shan't be around any more. I am sorry I made you unhappy. I made myself unhappy too. I never have thought much of myself (you may be surprised to hear) and I think even less of myself now. As I said I wish we had known each other when we were children, then perhaps we could have stayed together always. Forget me, won't you?' Before she had fully absorbed it—in the interval between the impact and the effect—she thought, as long as I live I shall never understand it.

Noel sat by the telephone, turning over the pages of *Picture Post* and experiencing a succession of mild stomach cramps. The other pilots of the squadron were already in their cockpits. The weather was clear and sunny, perfect for flying.

Noel lifted the receiver.

'Hello, Ops. Squadron Leader Maysey-Smith here. B Flight at super readiness. How are the plots?'

'Coming in now. You'll be off shortly.'

'How many? Jesus Christ. O.K. Thanks.'

He replaced the receiver.

'Hell's bells. A hundred and twenty plus of the bastards.' This was the voice he used in the mess, not the one Marcie knew. 'Let's get cracking then, let's not hang about.' There was no one to hear him; it was just that the voice reminded him who he was, Squadron Leader Maysey-Smith, still one of the boys, to all of whom the fear which he was now experiencing was as familiar as it was to him: he was that Maysey-Smith, none of the others.

The telephone rang.

'Hallo.'

'Start up.'

'Start up.'

He ran towards his plane as the engine started. The fitter was out of the cockpit and holding his parachute ready for him to slip into.

'Good lad.'

'Good hunting, sir.'

'Thanks.'

The fitter jumped off the wing. Noel opened the throttle and taxied forward, buckling the chinstrap of his helmet as he did so. He swung the machine into the wind, pushed the throttle wide open and eased the stick forward. Once off the ground he glanced round to see the others taking off in quick succession behind him. He throttled back a bit to give them a chance to get into position.

'Alligator calling Daisy leader. Are you receiving me?'

'Daisy leader answering. Loud and clear.'

Everything was normal. They were climbing hard. He slid open his cockpit roof. The sun was hot on his face. He felt better, except for the dryness of his mouth. 20,000 feet. He shut the hood. 25,000. Throttle back, close formation. He could see his wing men, Dicky Markham and Tiny van Hughes, leaning forward in their cockpits. The sun was shining from the direction of the sea, the direction from which the Germans would be coming. Avoiding the dazzle he looked round the bright blue sky. There were no enemy planes in sight. Below

152

him, weaving, he could see another squadron waiting to intercept the bombers: his own squadron was to deal with the escort fighters. Blast the sun. Christ, there they are.

'Hallo Daisy leader. Tally-ho. Bandits just to our left. Line astern, line astern, go.'

He saw Tiny and Dicky drop behind him. The German bombers were in close formation about 10,000 feet below. The squadron of fighters below him dived, heading for the bombers. The German fighters were approaching, Messerschmitt 110s, circling, making no attempt to dive. Above them were the supporting 109s, lines of black dots receding into the distance.

'Here goes.'

He dived at the nearest circle of 110s. The white crosses on their wings came into focus as he kicked the rudder and set his sights just in front of one of them. He pressed the firing button. The sky seemed momentarily full of flame. It died, and was followed by puffs of white smoke as the 110's rear-gunner fired back. The 109s were diving on him out of the open sky. He turned steeply, a stream of tracer bullets just missing one wing. Another 110 in the sights, thumb on the firing button, a rush of smoke from the 110's engine, then the glint of the wings as it rolled on its back. Thumb on the button again. A flash of fire from the 110's engine, then a puff of white as the pilot's parachute opened. Stick hard over, turn and keep turning. Three 110s just behind and below. Hold the stick in the bottom right hand corner. Down, flashing past the 110s, towards the bright sea, which rushed to meet him. Not this time, God, not today. He pulled out, screamed towards the beach. The sea was full of wreckage, the sky mercifully clearing. The Germans had turned for home.

He climbed to 5,000 feet.

'All aircraft return to base and land.'

He pushed back the hood to get some air. A group of people on the beach below looked up and waved. He waved back, realising that he was dripping with sweat, looked at the instruments—temperatures were high, not surprisingly—and made for home.

Two fitters ran out to meet him, climbed on the wing.

'How many sir?'

'Two.'

'Good show sir.

'How many of the boys are back?'

'All except Mr Rogers and Sergeant Cameron.'

'Hallo Noel. What luck?'

'Hallo Tiny. Two 110s. What about you?'

'Good show. I got one and a probable, a 109, couldn't see what happened to the bastard because I was trying to get my sights on another. Pretty hot wasn't it?'

'You can say that again. Good show, though, getting two. Seen Dicky?'

'I don't think he's back yet. Hope he's O.K. I saw someone in the drink, waiting to be picked up.'

'I'll see if Ops have got any gen.'

'Wonder why Jerry turned back so soon this time.'

They walked over to the dispersal hut together.

'You're on forty-eighters tomorrow aren't you, Noel? Lucky sod.'

'If it doesn't get stopped. Ops say they're expecting a flap.'

'You're due for it. We'll look after Jerry while you're away.'

'Some of the farmers really are too naughty,' said Marcie. 'They seem to think they have a sort of *droit de seigneur* over these girls. I had to speak very sharply to Campion this morning—Campion of all people with that nice Mrs Campion—I mean I do think our own tenant farmers ought to behave themselves, don't you?'

'Certainly,' said Noel.

They were in the small sitting room. Noel was sitting in an armchair with a glass of beer in his hand. Beside him, on a stool, was a tray on which stood more beer in bottles. Marcie seemed to find it necessary to bring him things on trays at frequent intervals throughout his leaves. Marcie was sitting at her desk, filling in progress reports about her Land Girls. The thick black-out curtains were drawn and the lights were turned on in the alcoves where the Dresden figures stood on their glass shelves.

'I never really liked the drawing room you know,' said Noel. 'Too formal.'

154

'This is much cosier, isn't it?' said Marcie. 'But I thought you liked formality.'

'In its place it's all right I suppose,' said Noel.

He was feeling pleasantly relaxed.

'I never made the Rugger team at school. I was too small.'

'Too small?' said Marcie indignantly. 'At six foot two?'

'I was thin, though, not strong. I could run quite fast but I hadn't the strength. Maybe I wasn't bold enough about tackling. I think perhaps I wasn't. I think perhaps I was rather cowardly about it.'

Marcie looked at him in surprise.

'You've certainly made up for it since.'

'Yes,' he said speculatively. 'Perhaps I have. Of course flying is more like cricket really, it's the team game and the star solo in one. I say, Marcie, I'm awfully glad you've stopped filling the house up with people all the time.'

She looked rather confused.

'Well, you did say you wanted quiet leaves. I had thought, I mean, it must be so boring just with me.'

'No, I like it, really. It gives us a chance to talk. We never talk, you know. There are always too many people here. I've noticed, these chaps in the Squadron, a lot of them have got girl friends—most of them are too young to be married though some of them are—but it's the same sort of thing, whether they're married or not. They seem to get on awfully well with them—the girl friends or the wives I mean—do things together, if you know what I mean. Rather jolly.'

Marcie was so completely astonished by the course the conversation was taking that she could only stare at him.

'Have you ever played golf?' he asked her.

She shook her head.

'Some women are quite good at it. Especially if they're stockily built.'

'How wonderful,' said Marcie humbly. 'I'll learn then.'

'Why not? Then we might have a round or two sometimes when I get leave.'

'Yes,' said Marcie, tossing back her hair. 'What fun.'

'You know,' he said, leaning further back in his chair and stretching out his legs in front of him, 'I really think our life before the war was too complicated. I thought perhaps afterwards we might sell the house and get something more convenient.'

'Well, it's quite convenient this house really, I mean one can put up twenty people quite comfortably.'

'Life's not going to be like that after the war. It won't be so easy to get servants for one thing. I thought something quite small and modern. Just room for you and me and perhaps a couple of kids. Near a decent golf course.'

'You can't mean it. I mean, I think it's an absolutely wizard idea but it does sound so terribly unlike you.'

He looked pleased. 'I know. I've been thinking a bit, you see.'

'I'm absolutely with you,' said Marcie earnestly. 'I mean I really am. I'll find out about the golf lessons tomorrow.'

'Fair enough,' said Noel, getting to his feet and stretching. 'Anyway I think I'll push off to bed now.'

Marcie carried the tray through into the kitchen. She found the evacuees sitting at the table doing their homework.

'Oh my darlings, how can you possibly do your prep with the wireless full on like that? Anyway you ought to be in bed.' She beamed at them warmly. 'Kevin, you're looking tired, you really are. Up you all go, go on.'

'What's up with her then?' said David after she had gone.

'He's home on leave,' said Doreen, knowingly. She was thirteen, and quite often took the boys' margarine rations to make hard dry cakes, after which she sulked if she considered their praise insufficiently extravagant.

Kevin, who was fourteen, picked up his books and went out of the room. He did not want the mystery of Marcie's smile explained by the presence of the immaculate Air Force officer who occasionally passed them in the drive. He had his own relationship with Marcie, and he believed that though she pretended to be unaware of it she was not. How could anyone remain unaware of feelings as strong as his, or fail to respond to them? When she said 'Kevin, you're looking tired,' she must mean something else, something which could not be put into words but of which the message in effect was, 'I am aware of and acknowledge what exists between us.'

156

There was an exceptional crop of hay at the Abbey that summer. They harvested it early. Marcie took all three evacuees over to help at the weekend. They worked until the late evening. Marjorie, helped by Mrs Trew and Mrs Boulder, prepared baskets full of food and carried them out to the hayfield. In the middle of the day Dorothy was overcome by the heat and fell on her face into the pile of hay she had been about to pitchfork up onto the trailer. Arnold told Timothy to drive her home. She sat in silence looking out of the car window.

'Are you feeling sick?' he asked.

'Not really.'

'Have a good sleep. I would.'

'I do nothing but sleep,' she said angrily.

They drew up at her house.

'Are you all right?' he asked.

'Yes, of course. Thank you for bringing me back.'

She went into the house without looking back. Timothy drove away, wondering why no one had noticed before that there was something the matter with Dorothy.

Dorothy stood at the bottom of the stairs, listening. No one seemed to be about. Her father was probably in his study, sleeping in his armchair as he often did after lunch. Her mother and Nanny might be picking peas in the garden. Miss Gamage had long ago gone to live with her sister in Dorking, where she took on relief teaching jobs between increasingly crippling attacks of migraine. Nanny had shown a stronger instinct for survival. She had become what she herself called a general dogsbody. Old, slow, cross, but always there, she cleaned sketchily, cooked vilely, sewed and ironed beautifully and irritated, but at the same time reassured, Nora Grant by her companionship and unvarying pessimism.

Dorothy went upstairs quietly and lay on her bed, exhausted by her struggle with unhappiness. She wondered whether it had been more than unhappiness which had made her collapse onto the pile of hay. Perhaps she was really ill, and could be taken into hospital and purged of pain, by drugs, or bleeding, or death. Perhaps a real illness would distract the attention of her flesh from its continuous mourning for its loss. It was as

F

if it were a separate part of her, her fleshly self, some gentle animal she had been given care of and had betrayed. How could you explain to a hairy female baboon that the bond which it had welcomed with such an upsurge of confidence in its own instinctual processes was only a temporary pairing and was now broken? How could the poor creature be expected to understand? The language of reason and of philosophy was meaningless: the baboon had lost its mate and pined.

No one had known of Dorothy's love affair. There was no one to whom she could talk of it now that it was over. If her mother noticed anything it was only that the process of abstraction from home interests which had been going on for some time in Dorothy seem to have accelerated: one often had to say the same thing twice before she seemed to hear. As for her work at the Abbey she went on with it as usual, and until the day of her collapse into the pile of hay no one had noticed anything out of the ordinary about her. This was a result not so much of obtuseness on other people's part as of effort on hers: she did not want them to notice, whether through secretiveness or for reasons of pride, she would have been unable to say. It was just that there seemed to her no alternative to concealment of what had always been a secret—concealment and endurance and in the end, she hoped, resignation. All the time the gentle baboon mourned; she had done it such an injury.

Timothy raised the question of Dorothy one evening after supper at the Abbey. The four registered conscientious objectors who now worked on the farm lived separately in the guest house, and in the evenings there were usually only the three brothers and Marjorie, Philip and Gerda, and Timothy, sitting round the kitchen table.

Nobody could think of any particular reason why Dorothy should be unhappy. Hamilton, who had not been looking very well himself lately, suggested that it might be love.

'If so it is not serious,' said Gerda authoritatively. 'Dorothy is not sexually awakened. I can tell.'

Fisher frowned, helping himself to some of the dandelion

and chickweed salad which was generally considered to be one of Gerda's better contributions to the Abbey diet.

'Talking about that sort of thing . . .' he began.

'Yes?' said Gerda as he did not continue.

'I was wondering if I should go on,' said Fisher. 'But I think I should. Marcella told me the other day, in the most round-about sort of way as you can imagine, that she and Noel have certain difficulties. I'm not telling you this in a gossipy spirit, but because I wonder what I could possibly say to her.'

'Ah,' said Gerda interested. 'You mean they cannot achieve a climax?'

'Nothing approaching it, I understand.'

'Nothing at all?'

He shook his head.

'I always imagined they didn't have any sex life,' said Marjorie. 'I don't know quite why I assumed that.'

'I think they would now like to,' said Fisher.

'This is good,' said Gerda, nodding. 'They need help. Someone to free them from their inhibitions. I am prepared to put myself forward. With music.'

'Music?'

'She likes jazz. The two of them alone with me, jazz on the radiogram, one thing leads naturally to another, we shall cast our inhibitions to the wind.'

'I have a feeling that even with your dedication, Gerda,' said Fisher cautiously, 'you might find it more difficult than you think.'

'Why do they suddenly want to do it now, after all these years?' asked Philip.

'I expect it's something to do with the war,' said Marjorie.

'You're quite right,' said Fisher. 'He wants to be more like the other pilots.'

'I suppose he's really queer, is he?' said Timothy.

'I imagine so,' said Fisher.

'He must pleasure her with his boots on,' said Hamilton.

The others looked at him in surprise. No one had expected him to contribute to this particular conversation. Sex was not thought to be one of his subjects.

'Like the Duke of Marlborough,' he said. 'If he wants to feel like a dashing pilot officer, she must be in bed when he arrives, in a seductive pose, and he must pleasure her three times with his boots on like the Great Duke after a battle. It's well known.'

'This is right,' said Gerda, generously acknowledging the superiority of this solution over her own. 'This is true psychology. This will work.'

'How am I supposed to tell her that, for Heaven's sake,' said Fisher.

'In the same way as she told you,' said Timothy. 'Roundabout.'

Hamilton, having thus initiated the happiest year of Marcella's life (though it remained the unhappiest of Dorothy's), himself became slowly less and less well. All that hot summer he sat in his cell and groaned and belched (he suffered from frightful flatulence), and fidgeted with the little pieces of stained glass and sorted aimlessly through Father Augustine's letters. Only Lord Haw Haw brought him shambling into the kitchen, and even Lord Haw Haw did not invariably draw him. Marjorie fed him and tried to talk to him, but she had never felt that Hamilton considered her as anything more than a useful housekeeper; they had never been exactly friends.

Arnold was too busy to spend much time with him. When he did, and when he asked Hamilton if he were depressed, Hamilton answered that he was, but that he was all right. No, he said, there was no reason for it. Arnold felt that it was impossible to ask him why he never talked of unicorns any more or of Father Augustine's visions of the Mother of God among the buttercups outside the window of his cell. When Hamilton went through a period of more than his usual disassociation from real life, there was not much anyone could do: there never had been. The groans and belches and sighs reverberated from Father Augustine's cell all through that summer, while Noel took his aeroplane up to fight day after day and on his leaves enjoyed with his wife a honeymoon the innocence of which would have astonished most of their friends and relations (Timothy had been wrong—in so far as Noel was homosexual in his inclinations, a kind of fastidiousness so acute as to be more or less neurasthenic had prevented him from ever doing anything about it), a honeymoon made possible

160

by the fantasy in which they both believed and which indeed contained an element of truth, the fantasy of the simple manly pilot and his girl, the round of golf, the drink at the pub, the jolly nice little house they were going to look for when the war was over. They almost persuaded themselves they were saving up for it, as if the generations of banking and landowning forbears had not resulted in a really quite massive amount being saved up already.

In the intervals between the leaves Marcie sang happily about her work, sorting green jerseys and gumboots in the big drawing room, the blinds drawn against the sun, the radiogram as she would have phrased it 'full on', playing either her favourite 'hot jazz' or the popular tunes of the moment. Kevin came to ask if he and David could use the tennis court and found her waltzing slowly across the room with a huge pile of green jerseys in her arms to the sound of Vera Lynn singing 'We'll meet again . . .' There were so many green jerseys that she did not see him standing quietly by the door with his St Alphege's Shepherds Bush blazer and his intense unsmiling gaze. She waltzed on, singing loudly and not specially tuneful. 'Don't know where, don't know when, But I know we'll meet again Some sunny day . . . Oh Kevin I didn't see you.' She blushed and laughed, putting down the jerseys. 'You must think I'm quite dotty.' She laughed again, tossing back her hair.

'I wondered if we could use the tennis court,' he said.

'Of course, do, it's good for you to be outside, you're getting quite brown.'

This time he smiled back, a shy rather charming little smile which could have given not the slightest indication even to someone a great deal more acute than Marcie of the state of his feelings, which were passionate. He had lived all his life in a respectable street on the borders between Shepherds Bush and Brook Green. His father had a greengrocer's shop and his mother took in dressmaking. He was the only child. Both parents believed in hard work and 'getting on'. Indeed it some- times seemed to him that they never talked of anything else— 'You won't get on if you don't work hard at school' seemed to be the burden of all they ever said to him—otherwise they talked (though not very much since the philosophy of getting

161

on precluded unnecessary conversation) to each other about their neighbours, all of whom seemed to be getting on either so well as to arouse suspicions as to their business ethics, or so badly as to attract derision and the immediate withholding of their credit at the shop. The haphazard character and quite extraordinary spaciousness of the life now more or less organised for him by Marcie amounted to a liberation such as he could never have envisaged. David and Doreen, neither of whom had been particular friends of his at school, found their new life boring, the big house spooky, and Marcie barmy. They wrote frequently to their parents begging to be allowed to come home. Kevin wrote short neat letters home in which he said, not quite truthfully, that the school he was now attending was much better than St Alphege's and that he thought he had more chance of getting on if he stayed there as long as possible. In the meantime he developed an intensely romantic feeling for Marcie, the casual giver of all this bounty—'Do borrow any books you want, won't you, as long as you put them back when you've read them—Noel hates gaps in the shelves—Just tell Mrs Scrimgeour if you want sandwiches to take to school won't you?' (Of course he didn't because Mrs Scrimgeour, though kind enough, made it quite clear that evacuees were in no sense to be considered as guests). 'Go any-where you like in the garden, it's so good for you—eat the peas if you like, they're so much better like that, raw from the pod, I always think—oh are you interested in pictures? Come with me and I'll tell you all about them. . . .'

The fact that all this warmth and interest was intermittent and that often she seemed almost to have forgotten who he was (or at least whether he was Kevin or David) only added to the fascination, even in large part accounted for it, since he sensed in her a vulnerability which he found extraordinarily moving. The breathlessness, the apparent physical unsteadiness, the con-stant nervous tossing back of the hair, the uncertain focus of her attention, all conveyed to him a mysterious spiritual unease which was strangely attractive. He was adept at concealing his feelings, since feelings were considered by his parents likely to be inimical to the process of getting on, and in this regard he underestimated his own skill: contrary to his view of the

162

situation, Marcie at no stage during all of the three years that he lived in her house had any idea of the state of his emotions.

It was agreed at the Abbey, where concern was still felt about Dorothy's evident unhappiness, that Fisher should ask Marcie to arrange for Dorothy to be transferred by the Land Army to some other part of the country. This proving difficult for various administrative reasons, Marcie instead arranged through friends for her to be transferred from the Land Army to the FANYs and to be attached as a driver to a unit at the moment stationed at Pirbright. Dorothy, who felt that she hardly cared where she went anyway, set off obediently for Surrey.

Her father scarcely had time to protest. He was by now so much involved in controversy with his neighbours over the organisation of the local Home Guard that such protest as he did make was only a token. Fisher, who was working on his book on the theory of the perfectibility of man, with Gerda and Timothy both spending such of their time as could be spared from agricultural activity helping him, was one of Charles Grant's chief sources of irritation. Fisher had joined the Home Guard because he felt that the Abbey should contribute towards the defence of the local community in case of invasion, but he had had every intention of playing a silent and subservient role. Unfortunately every utterance of Charles Grant's seemed to him so patently foolish that he was unable to prevent himself from voicing the contrary opinion. The Winterstoke unit of the Home Guard was not therefore a harmonious one. Fisher occasionally toyed with the idea of confirming Charles Grant's worst suspicions of the Whitehead brothers by taking him over to the Abbey at a time when he knew Hamilton would be listening to the wireless, and either nodding or smiling appreciatively at the sound of Lord Haw Haw's harsh tones or frowning and muttering as Churchill's eloquence unfolded. Hamilton had a low opinion of Churchill.

'The man's drunk. Any fool can tell that. Bloodthirsty mouthings, crazy grandiose outpourings—he's in an alcoholic stupor when he makes them. The nation is led by a power-crazed alcoholic. It's obvious.'

These views were considered by everyone else at the Abbey

163

to be eccentric, even, as far as Marjorie was concerned, unacceptable. Eventually she banned him from the kitchen whenever Churchill was broadcasting. Arnold bought him a wireless of his own which he could have in his workshop. This meant that he very seldom came into the house at all, even for meals. When he missed a meal, in spite of having been reminded that it was ready, someone would eventually take it out to him.

'I'm very worried about him,' said Arnold. 'What can we do? He can't go on like this.'

He did go on for many months; but in the spring of 1942 he had a heart attack and had to be taken to hospital in Bath.

'Everything that I read only reinforces my conviction that if one hopes for the amelioration of the human condition, but without the loss of choice inherent in communism or State socialism, one is bound to pin one's hopes on the proliferation of co-operative associations,' said Fisher. 'What concerns me is how best to link these associations into a larger network. Also of course, one can't help becoming depressed from time to time by the slow pace of progress.'

'One of the great illusions, progress,' murmured Hamilton from his pillow.

'A lifetime is so short,' said Fisher, pacing up and down on the worn green linoleum of the hospital room.

Hamilton groaned.

'A publicist, a polemicist, has often so little to show for all his work, all his words,' said Fisher. 'Who cares about being read after one's death? This blasted war makes it so difficult to get about, to circulate—and yet do you know people are reading more than ever before? And they're already thinking seriously about what should happen after the war is over. If only I could get the book finished. No one ever understands how much time one needs for a book, how many uninterrupted hours. People think they can come in and ask you some idiotic question, and then you'll just go straight back to work as if nothing had happened. They don't understand it may take as long as half an hour or more to get your concentration back—that's if they haven't ruined it for the whole day by obtruding their jarring little concerns.'

Hamilton groaned again, louder this time.

'How are you feeling?' said Fisher, interrupting his pacing for a moment to stare down at the large exhausted face of his brother.

'Ghastly,' said Hamilton, closing his eyes.

'You should get out of this place,' said Fisher. 'It's depressing. You should come home. Marjorie's a better nurse than anyone here.'

Hamilton opened his eyes. 'Marjorie's busy. She doesn't want to look after a dying man.'

'It's better to die at home than in hospital,' said Fisher. 'I'll speak to the doctor.'

'I might not die,' said Hamilton irritably.

'Of course you won't die,' said Fisher. 'You always look on the dark side.'

'And you never do,' said Hamilton, closing his eyes again. 'That's just the trouble.'

'Nonsense,' said Fisher. 'If you're going to start telling me not to be an idealist I shall have to leave. Dorothy will come and see you tomorrow. She turned up this morning on a few day's leave, looking much better. She's got a bit thinner. It suits her.'

Bath was bombed that night, in the first of what were called the Baedeker raids. In the morning when the news was broadcast, it was impossible to get through to the hospital on the telephone. Arnold decided to go with Dorothy to find out what had happened.

As they drove towards the middle of Bath they began to smell the charred and sodden plaster of the bombed buildings. ARP Wardens in tin hats were among the men clearing away rubble near the station. In other parts of the town life in the streets seemed normal. Arnold was moved and shocked, Dorothy less so because she had by now been through several air raids near London.

They found Hamilton sitting up in bed, bright-eyed. The nurse who was with him had eyes swollen with crying. It had been terrible, she said, a woman doctor whom she had known well had been killed on her way to tend the wounded; no one had expected the bombs to fall on Bath—they were used to hearing the planes going towards Bristol and South Wales. No one had thought that Hitler would bother with Bath. Arnold went with her to find the doctor who was looking after Hamilton in the hope of getting his consent to Hamilton's leaving hospital.

Hamilton sat very straight against his pillows, washed and brushed and wearing clean striped pyjamas, and talked to Dorothy. It was evident that he was in a high state of excitement.

'Fire dries the air,' he said. 'The atmosphere in Bath is so damp and soft, that's why everyone who lives here is sunk in melancholy and somnolence. This morning is quite different. One might be in New York.'

'Have you been to New York?' asked Dorothy, surprised.

'No but I've heard about it. It's wonderful how the atmosphere's changed. You should have seen them, these little girls, while it was going on, running to and fro, reassuring everybody, dealing with the casualties, bringing us cups of tea and the latest news, you'd have been proud of them, you really would.'

'That one looked tired, I thought.'

'They love it, my dear. They're having the time of their lives. People love to be called upon to exert themselves. It narrows the choice, leaves no time for doubt. I can't tell you how splendid it was last night. The noise was terrific. Fires all over the place. People love to be frightened too, you see.'

'All the same I do think you may be rather unusual. I mean, in positively enjoying being bombed.'

'I don't mean that one should have too much of it. Don't misunderstand me. I don't mean that I think it's a positively good thing. But it does relieve inner tension.'

'Some people would say it induced it.'

'Depends how much you've got already, doesn't it? I can tell you, the noise, the fires, the destruction—all that is nothing, nothing, compared to the sound of battle in my own soul.'

Dorothy looked at him questioningly.

'Oh, yes,' he nodded emphatically. 'I'm not exaggerating. You know, you have a very nice expression on your face, a frank and thoughtful look—I've often noticed it. You are a good girl I'm sure. And yet I feel with you that the other side is not unknown to you, the side Fisher will persist in ignoring, the dark side he called it yesterday. You always look on the dark side, he said to me. He ignores it, you know. He always has. Although it is rampant in him, rampant.' He nodded again, apparently as pleased by that thought as by every other this morning.

Dorothy looked worried.

'I know he gets depressed sometimes,' she said.

'And he is such a raging egotist. It is bound to lead him into various forms of self-deception. Not but what he is one of the best men in the world for all that. But I can tell you— the noise of battle, oh yes—it nearly deafens me some days.' He smiled in a reflective sort of way. 'If I were to relax my vigilance for a moment, I could be as mad as my father. I feel the drag of it so often, the awful downward drag of it. You may not believe me—I don't really want you to believe me—but I fought it in my father, with my father, and I fight it in myself, and it is the dark, it is isolation and it is evil. Don't ever let anyone tell you that evil doesn't exist. I see its face every day, its dark slothful sly lustful filthy face. And I am not alone in this, indeed I am not. Fisher thinks you can fiddle about with Man as if he were a bicycle, tighten a screw here, a touch of oil, adjust the chain, and you'll have him running smoothly in no time. He doesn't understand that what's wrong with the thing is the design; it's the design that's no good.'

'I don't understand that either,' said Dorothy. 'At least I don't want to understand it because I shouldn't like it to be true.'

'That's as it should be,' said Hamilton. 'Because you are a nice young girl. But I am a nasty old man and I know better. The externalisation of the struggle, the embodiment of evil in the persons of the warmongers Hitler and Churchill, is only the momentary acting out of our common preoccupation. We dream, they strut and shout and threaten, not knowing they are only figments of the imagination of sleeping Europe. This is a dream we happen to remember, that's all. But every day it's the same, the same battle rages. All over the darkling plain the lights flicker as in one or other of us the glory defeats the horror. And at the back of each of our minds must be the thought, on what level shall I be when I die?'

'On what level?' repeated Dorothy, held by the intensity of his dark shining eyes.

'Will it be the glory or the horror? On what level shall I be when I die?'

Dorothy walked over to the window to escape his gaze. She saw mown grass and clumps of trees, a few nurses hurrying along tarmac footpaths, nothing to show the devastation of the night before.

'I don't see things in the same way as you do,' she said. 'Although I can imagine how a person could see things in that way. But if any of it is true, even if it is only true for you, I am quite sure that you will be on the level of glory when you die.'

'I knew you would say that. What a good girl you are. But when it goes, you see, each time it feels as though it's gone for ever. Never mind, we must do what we can while the going's good, mustn't we? Where has Arnold got to? I must get home, I must get back to work. There's the Father Augustine book and the letters and the windows. I must get going. Shall I start getting dressed do you think?'

'No, no.' Dorothy turned round quickly to see that he had already swung his large white feet out of bed. 'For goodness sake, you must wait.'

'What can they do to me?' he said, amused by her alarm. 'I can walk out. They can't stop me.'

Fortunately Arnold reappeared with the doctor. It was decided that Hamilton could return to the Abbey as long as he remembered his pills and undertook no manual labour. He talked most of the way home, and recited a long passage from the Anglo-Saxon Chronicle about the destruction of Bath at the hands of the Saxons, Cuthwine and Caewlin, destroyers. ' "Wondrous is this masonry, shattered by the fates. The city has been broken, and the fortifications raised by giants are crumbling. The roofs have fallen and the towers are in ruins," ' he quoted. 'And yet it rose again,' he said. 'It rose again.'

Noel's two most constant companions, Dicky Markham and

Tiny Van Hughes, were both killed on the same operation, a night fight with German bombers over the Channel. Fourteen members of the squadron had died before them, but these two had been Noel's particular friends for over two years and their deaths distressed him more than any of the others. He had some days' leave after the two funerals. The Germans seemed for the moment virtually to have given up daylight attacks. The squadron was under orders to have one flight always on night-flying. This meant in effect that Noel was flying at night every other week and that his day-flying week was comparatively inactive. Even so he told Marcie that he was afraid he was losing his nerve.

Marcie, who a few months ago would certainly have suggested that he had a word with his nice Commanding Officer who always seemed so understanding, now realised that such frankness could have no place in the code of behaviour by which he was living, offered instead a more carefully judged solicitude and concealed her fears. On his return to camp, Noel suspected that his CO had already noticed something. They had an embarrassing conversation in which Noel did not answer the questions the CO half asked and ignored the suggestions the CO half made; but he could not hope to avoid the issue much longer. Thus when he took off for the next operation which was one of the by now rare daylight sorties, he was worried. Whether he was also determined to do what he subsequently did he himself would hardly have been able to say. There was nothing unusual about the take-off. The German fighters which the squadron had been sent to intercept spread out and dived. Noel twisted and turned and sweated and swore as usual until—perhaps in desperation—he closed in on a climbing Messerschmidt and followed it, shooting, as it climbed towards the sun. Black smoke poured from the German plane but Noel, blinded by now by sweat and sun, still followed, was hit, was aware of the cockpit being full of flames, of struggling to open the hood, of brief unbearable heat and pain, and had then just time to think of Dicky and Tiny and to be if not exactly glad and relieved then to experience some complex emotions in which gladness and relief were present at the thought that he would die as they had died,

169

before, tearing in flames through the sky, he lost consciousness, and shortly afterwards fell into the sea.

So Marcie received the message she had been dreading—'picked up at sea after some hours—in hospital—very badly burned—you'd better come at once . . .' When she saw him he was still unconscious and almost completely concealed by bandages. She talked to the doctor and understood that if he survived he would have to suffer months of terrible pain and that the physical appearance by which he had set such store was certainly gone for ever. A nurse with eyes which belied her optimistic words said, 'They can do wonders these days.' Marcie held his bandaged hand to her cheek and prayed that he might die.

The immediate danger of a German invasion having receded with the entry of America into the war, Fisher decided it was no longer his patriotic duty to remain a member of the Home Guard: his resignation was accepted with unconcealed relief by Charles Grant. Fisher's excuse, had one been needed, had been that he was going to devote all his time to his book, but the fact was that he was bored with his book. It irritated him to notice that no one else at the Abbey seemed to be bored by their work, or to feel constrained by the atmosphere. The Abbey at this time seemed to him more and more like a boarding school, with Arnold as Headmaster and Marjorie as Matron —and hadn't he always hated boarding school? He wasn't of course in the position of pupil—he was rather a sort of visiting professor, not expected quite to conform—but it was the atmosphere which he was beginning to find uncongenial. There were not enough girls, for one thing. No Hilda now, no Dorothy. Gerda, hardly a girl anyway, was only able to spare him one day's secretarial help a week. The rest of the time she was working in the vegetable garden. She had become very fit and muscular as a result, her rather heavy features weathered and lined—physically more repulsive than ever, Fisher unkindly considered. She had decided after all to give Philip a divorce so that he could marry Rosamund. This meant that Philip had left the Abbey and gone to live with Rosamund and her mother. He was teaching at the same school as Rosamund, and though he still helped Arnold by keeping up the correspondence with other communal projects which they had been determined to maintain in spite of the difficulties brought about by wartime conditions, his absence was a loss to Arnold and left him with even more paperwork to do himself.

Fisher carried on a mild flirtation with Pat Boulder, whose pretty complexion and shining dark hair he admired, while regretting her plumpness. She missed her husband, who was stationed at an army camp in the North of England, and appreciated Fisher's attentions. Marjorie disapproved. Fisher enjoyed teasing her. Besides, when he went over to Pat Boulder's cottage he often found the children there as well and that cheered him: he was fond of them all except his nephew Joe.

Joe was no longer a little boy, but a youth with ungainly sudden movements and a loud laugh which he repeated nervously and often. Fisher found him graceless and unresponsive and wished his parents would teach him some manners. If ever there was a boy who would have benefited from a traditional boarding school, Fisher thought, it was Joe. He would have been exercised there—he tended to be too fat—and toughened up mentally and physically, like a young hound pup in need of constant whipping in. This was the unfairness of life: it would never allow you quite to stick to your principles. Some awkward observation always came up to put them in question: you had to keep shifting your ground. If there was one thing on which all three brothers were agreed, it was that the public school through which they themselves had passed represented everything most regrettable about English life, everything most retrograde, philistine, snobbish and cold-hearted—and yet here was Fisher wishing to goodness Arnold would send Joe to just such an establishment. How, if one was to be honest, was one to deal with such self-contradiction? By falling back, he supposed, on irony rather than passionate conviction. But he did not want to be ironical. He preferred passion; which was one of the reasons why he disliked growing older.

'He's young,' was all Arnold would say in answer to Fisher's tentative criticisms of Joe. 'He'll be all right.'

Arnold always had something else more pressing to deal with. He loved Joe, but his sense of responsibility towards everyone else led him sometimes to neglect him. As for Marjorie, Joe felt he had outgrown her and at this time of his life was hardly polite to her.

Gerda suddenly gave expression to an outburst of feeling, quite unexpectedly, at lunch. Philip had come over to see her about some unimportant details connected with their already agreed upon and impending divorce, he had stayed to discuss various practical matters with Arnold, had been offered lunch, and was still pursuing his discussion with Arnold when Gerda from the other end of the table, where she was sitting next to Fisher, said in her heaviest and flattest tones, 'Life is impenetrably, ineluctably sad, is it not?' She rested her elbows on the table and her chin on her clasped hands. 'The hopes of youth inevitably are dashed.'

'Certainly, Gerda, certainly,' Fisher agreed, passing salad and not offering discussion.

'I mean,' she continued loudly, gazing ahead of her as if addressing herself to no one in particular, her chin still resting on her hands and her mouth in consequence shutting itself rather firmly between sentences, 'I married not exactly for love but in the expectation of a certain kind of partnership, a certain kind of shared participation in the cultural life of my time. I expected to be in the thick of the intellectual maelstrom. That was what I expected. So the first shocks, the first disenchantments, were nothing to me. What did it matter that he never cut his toenails? That every time he turned over in bed he farted? He was an intellectual, that was how it seemed to me.'

But at the mention of farting young Joe had given out an insufficiently muffled guffaw, an uncontrolled calf-like sound too loud to be ignored. Both his parents became stiff with anger and disappointment, in Arnold's case not altogether repressed, for he said, though very quietly, 'Leave the room, Joe.'

Taken by surprise—for his father had never before told him to leave the room, nor indeed to do anything else as far as he could remember—Joe pushed back his chair and went, but as he reached the back door the shock of his father's having spoken to him in such an unexpected manner, together with a renewed appreciation of the utter absurdity of the thought

172

of Gerda's married life, brought on another attack of awkward spluttering. He fumbled his way out of the door, banged it behind him and was to be heard running heavily across the yard giving voice now to loud and unrestrained 'Ha-ha's'.

Arnold and Marjorie both stared at their plates. In their different degrees, it seemed to them just for the moment as if there was no point in anything they had tried to do in their lives, if the effect of the upbringing they had given their son had not been exactly that he should be able to hear people talking about farting without bursting into giggles.

Gerda, however, was checked only for as long as it took her to lean back in her chair and fold her arms.

'I am too old for pretence,' she said. 'I am without pride.'

'Oh so am I,' murmured Philip from the other end of the table. 'So am I.'

But his sour little smile infuriated her.

'Evidently,' she said, her deep voice beginning to vibrate. 'Evidently. One is not proud if one lives on the charity of one's mistress's mother. Ca se voit.'

'Gerda dear,' said Timothy patiently.

But the patience was infuriating too.

'My intellectual capacity is of the highest. I have sacrificed it to nonentities. I was to have been the handmaid of genius. I have been the scullion of the second-rate.'

'I always thought a scullion was a man,' said one of the conscientious objectors, whose name was Arthur. He said it in rather a silly voice, too evidently preparing to enjoy a scene.

'Scullery maid then,' said Gerda dismissively. 'Laundry maid, scrubber, slave. If I had been a man I should by now have been in an exalted position in the profession of letters.'

'But you are, my dear,' said Fisher. 'Your translation of Kafka. . . .'

'There is another better one.'

At this there was a general silence. It was true, though no one had ever said so in Gerda's hearing. There was another better one.

Fisher broke the silence.

'It's true of anything any of us do,' he said. 'There's always another better one. Almost always, anyway. But one had better not think about it, because if one thought about it one wouldn't do anything, and if one didn't do anything one would in the first place be unhappy and therefore a nuisance, and in the second place the communal pool of thought might begin to sink a little lower than is desirable. There has to be the pool. All of us here are after roughly the same sort of thing and what we do or leave, written work or cultivated ground or building or just some kind of hearsay, adds to the common pool from which those who seek to make a better world draw their sustenance. That must be so, mustn't it?'

'It must be what we believe anyway,' said Timothy.

He liked what Fisher had said. It took some of the tension away from his feelings about his own work, for one thing. He had written very little in the last year or two—he lacked a subject, doubted as to form, fussed about being forgotten— but if you were contributing to a necessary pool, that took away both your isolation and your individuality. You could think of yourself as an anonymous craftsman working on a Gothic cathedral rather than a twentieth-century artist with a name to make. He found that even after all these years and a certain amount of disenchantment, Fisher could still appeal to his imagination. Hearsay, he had said. He liked the idea of that, of people saying in distant parts or years to come, oh yes there's a place, you know, somewhere in the South West of England, they live in harmony there, cultivate the ground, write books, weave cloth, discuss ideas, it really works, they say. . . .

Not long after Noel's crash, and supported by Cousin Penelope, Marcella went to Buckingham Palace to receive a medal on his behalf. She told Dorothy afterwards that the funny old King had been too sweet and had looked too sad for words when he heard how Noel had pranged.

Dorothy was at home on one of her now less frequent leaves. She had been sent to France after the Allied landings as driver to an American colonel. Marcie was still dividing her time between her Land Army work at home and her visits to a succession of hospitals and convalescent homes where Noel's burns were being treated and where he was submitted to a series of complicated skin-grafting operations. She told Dorothy in passing that Guy and Daphne had been married on one of Guy's leaves, and that he had gone to North Africa with his regiment, while Daphne had joined the WRNS and was doing something secret in the Home Counties.

Dorothy came to look on her affair with Guy as an unmitigated mistake. She could not allow herself to see it as having been in any sense for the best. She hoped it had widened her sympathies; she knew it had curtailed her future choices. Looking back, none of that time seemed to her to have been happy. Even at the height of the enchantment, she seemed to herself now to have suffered from a sense of loss of control over events and loss of contact with the real world. Love might be divine but it was also mad: she preferred to stay sane in future. Her struggle with depression and her recurrent and agonised longing for lost love led her to think of herself as particularly vulnerable to the madness, in the same way as some people reacted more violently than others to germs or poisons, and that therefore she ought to be particularly careful not to expose herself to it in future. In order to cauterise the wound she undertook a brief loveless union with the American colonel.

She felt she was being unscrupulous, but this too contributed to her renewed sense of being in control of her own life. It was as if she needed the colonel as a defence against ever suffering in that way again, as if supposing somewhere in Europe in the aftermath of some battle or other she should happen to see Guy among all those uniformed men, defeated or victorious (although now it was becoming increasingly likely that he would be among the latter), and he should happen to hold out his arms to her—as how could he fail to do, taken by surprise—she would be able to avert all the otherwise inevitable pain and bewilderment by quickly interposing either literally or metaphorically the substantial, well-washed and lightly cologned body of Colonel Thaddeus Brewster from Denver, Colorado.

He was a kind, long-winded and extraordinarily hygienic man whose chief virtue in Dorothy's eyes lay in his absolute, but at the same time absolutely uninteresting, strangeness. The fact that they had nothing at all in common, and that though they used the same language they were almost always at cross-purposes because the same word meant something different to each of them, was pleasing to Dorothy. It made her feel anaesthetised against the particularly sharp pain which she had found to result from thinking that she did understand someone and finding that she didn't. He was generous and grateful, but at the same time businesslike, about their relationship. He had a wife and two children back in Denver. He showed Dorothy a photograph of the wife. She looked rather fat and pasty-faced but he made no complaints. For more than a year their relationship continued on a level as close to the impersonal as such a relationship could be. Then he changed; it turned out that after all he had feelings as well as clean habits. He declared that he had fallen in love with her, sought reassurance as to his physical prowess as a lover, told her that he had never been able to satisfy his wife and that his first sexual experience in the fifth grade at Denver High had been humiliating, and begged her to marry him when the war was over.

She had herself transferred to another unit. She told him that she had used him as a means to cure herself of an unhappy obsession, and suggested that the best thing was a clean break with no hard feelings on either side. He was shocked by her ruthlessness as well as by her refusal to accept any parting gifts, and afterwards wrote her many letters analysing her character and suggesting various ways of improving it: she did not answer them. She did not feel she had known him well enough to feel guilty about the way she had treated him. After quite a short time she would probably not have recognised him if she had passed him in the street, and yet when she did occasionally think of him it was on the whole with gratitude. He had made it possible for her to feel that she had chosen the rest of her life rather than having had it thrust upon her.

Towards the end of the war Arnold and Marjorie decided to send Joe to the boarding school in Sussex at which Mr and Mrs Arkwright were both teaching. It was a co-educational school with progressive ideas about education and both Arnold and Marjorie liked the headmaster and his wife. Letters from Joe, though infrequent, indicated that he was happy: he was building a canoe, he wrote, and had a friend called Mark.

Hamilton's book on Father Augustine was finally published. There had been considerable delay because the publishers thought that parts of it might be libellous, but a surviving relative of the subject having been traced—a retired Colonial Servant living in Malvern—he was exposed to Hamilton at his most euphoric and bewildering, and agreed to sign a document undertaking not to initiate any legal proceedings. The book was sparingly, though well, reviewed, and sold only a few hundred copies. It aroused interest here and there, however, and set in motion several correspondences which Hamilton enjoyed, including a highly acrimonious one with the local vicar, who took the strongest possible exception to Hamilton's interpretation of the history of the original community at the Abbey as well as to his tolerant view of the unorthodox Father Augustine. There was also a series of immensely learned letters in perfect English from a French lady professor who had been lent the book by an English colonel and sent her letters by Forces Mail. She was an expert on the history of the Cathar faith, and announced her intention of coming over to meet Hamilton in person as soon as wartime travel restrictions were lifted. She sounded so alarming that Hamilton finally wrote to tell her that the present community at the Abbey consisted entirely of male celibates all of whom had taken a vow never to set eyes on a woman. Undeterred, she suggested that they should meet on neutral ground and that she herself should be veiled 'albeit,' she wrote, 'many years have passed since beauty and I shook hands.' To this letter Hamilton was too cowardly to reply at all.

It was the book too which introduced Peter and Jane Ridley to the Abbey. They were archaeologists, experts on Early Britain, and having met Hamilton to discuss an archaeological point he had raised in his book, asked if they could come and live at the Abbey while they finished their book on the Ridgeway, the ancient highway which crosses part of Salisbury Plain. They were young—twenty-two and nineteen—he had had one leg shorter than the other since birth: they had met as students, she also having been exempted from war service as a consequence of having once been very ill with rheumatic fever. They were curiously alike physically, fair and good-looking in the same fragile sort of way. They were obviously very fond of each other and as a result self-contained, but Fisher enjoyed having someone new and intelligent to talk to at the main meal of the day, and Arnold soon found that Peter could take over all the paper work which Philip used to do. They were both too frail to be much help over the manual labour, but the conscientious objectors had now been supplemented by a couple of hard-working Tuscans from the nearby camp for Italian prisoners of war, who were experienced in agriculture and apart from occasional bouts of home-sickness a cheerful presence at the Abbey. They had certain ways of using tools and binding up young plants which Fisher remembered as having been described in Virgil's Georgics. He found the relevant passages and translated them for the Italians. They were unimpressed. Since the methods they used were obviously the best adapted to the task they found nothing surprising in the fact that they had been used for hundreds of years. The needs of the land do not change, they pointed out; but they were pleased by his appreciation.

'Swine!' shouted Charles Grant. 'Low-down, unscrupulous, treacherous swine, that's what they are!'

He was pacing up and down his study, red in the face and evidently distraught.

'Another cup of tea, dear?' suggested his wife, hopefully.

She and Dorothy and Nanny were sitting by the wireless which was giving out the final results of the General Election. It was already clear that Labour had won.

'Infiltrators, that's what they are,' said Charles, waving aside the suggestion of tea. 'Snakes in the grass. Creeping round the troops pushing their filthy propaganda while our side were concentrating on winning the war. It's the postal vote that's done it, the troops are rotten with socialism, their minds have been poisoned with it.'

'To think they could turn out Mr Churchill,' said Nanny. 'After all he's done for us. It doesn't seem possible.'

'Ingratitude, base ingratitude. Imagine his feelings today. The country he saved from destruction. He'll emigrate I should

178

think. He'll go and live in America where they do recognise great men. He'll abandon us to our fate. Who can blame him?'

'Disgusting, I call it. Driving him out of his own country like that.'

'Well, Nanny, they haven't driven him out of the country exactly,' said Dorothy, anxious only to prevent Nanny from encouraging her father in further excesses of rage.

'You agree with them I suppose,' he said. 'You and your red friends up the road. Which way did you vote, I wonder? It's people like you who do the damage. So-called intellectuals. The intelligent man is to the intellectual what the gentleman is to the gent, that's what Baldwin said. Knew what he was talking about. Intellectuals! Too clever by half, that's what I say.'

'I don't know anything about politics,' said Dorothy. 'I voted Liberal because I thought Sir Archibald Sinclair looked so handsome. I wish Labour hadn't won because it makes you so upset, that's all.'

'Archie Sinclair!' he snorted. 'Wet as a dishcloth. So wet you could wring him out.' He sat down in an armchair at last. 'No, it's the end of England. The end of England as we've known it. Thank God I haven't got long to go, that's all. Thank God I shan't see it.'

'Oh dear, I'm sure you will, Charles,' said his wife. 'I mean, I'm sure you've got much longer to live. I do hope it won't be quite as bad as you think.'

'I hope so too,' said Dorothy. 'I really do hope so.'

Home on leave, not yet demobilised, she wanted sleep rather than scenes. The scenes were by no means over, though their nature changed. Nobody ever knew whether England under a Labour Government would have seemed to Charles Grant to have fulfilled his worst expectations or not. That night he suffered a massive heart attack and was found dead in bed in the morning.

After the immediate consequences of the death had been dealt with, after the doctors, the coroner, the funeral, the solicitor, Dorothy returned to her unit, now among the wreckage of defeated Germany, in the knowledge that her post-war future, which she had thought about only vaguely but always as a time of increased independence and variety, must now be

179

curtailed by an obligation, which she did not grudge, to look after her mother.

Fisher was delighted by the Election result. For one thing, for the first time in his life, he had a number of contacts with members of Parliament and even with members of the Government. People whom he had known or worked with at some time or other in his life had suddenly become insiders: he hurried up to London—a London in which even to walk was exhilarating, especially at night now that the blackout was over—to give them the benefit of his advice. He also produced at great speed a number of articles for weekly journals on topical subjects—alternative methods for the reconstruction of Britain, the ways in which the necessary organisation could be combined with an equally necessary restoration of individual liberty, the folly of seeking revenge against Nazi war criminals, the need to face the facts about the nature of Russian tyranny. He was so busy that he found it necessary to rent a small flat in London and to spend most of his time there. He acquired a new secretary and mistress, a girl as physically like Hilda as it was possible to be. Her name was Laura Pinkus and apart from her tendency to knock things over—she was small and apparently neat in her movements and Fisher was convinced that her clumsiness had a psychological explanation—she fulfilled his needs adequately and caused him no irritation.

He was relieved to have an excuse to spend less time at the Abbey. Although he went back there most weekends, it still depressed him. Arnold and Marjorie bickered, Gerda was boring, Timothy seemed perpetually in low spirits and Marcie, Fisher's usual refuge, was preoccupied by Noel, who was now at home, restored to health though not in looks. His eyes were the only familiar part of his face. They said the skin would look more natural with time. At the moment it looked like patches of pale stretched scar tissue with an occasional reddish mark like a birth mark: there was not much nose. Fisher found it very difficult to talk to him naturally, and when he did he was distressed though not surprised to find an irritability and bitterness which was very different from the mood of the early war years.

Arnold and Marjorie did not bicker as much as Fisher thought they did. He brought it out in them. They both knew that his opinion of Marjorie was not as high as his recognition of her worth might have been expected to make it, and this awareness made Arnold defensive and Marjorie argumentative, and the effect of that was that they quarrelled with each other, though the differences between them were only minor ones.

Marjorie in her mid-forties was as healthy and energetic as she had ever been. Her face had weathered but was not much wrinkled, her figure was more solid than it had been but still pleasing. Arnold, twelve years older, looked his age.

'None of you wash enough,' Marjorie said to him. 'I don't think your mother can have washed. She has a lot to answer for.'

'I don't remember,' said Arnold. 'She always smelt nice, I remember that. My hands are quite clean, look.' He held them out to be inspected, like a child.

'It's your face,' she said. 'When you cut wood you always get your face so dirty, I can't think why, and then the dirt gets in the wrinkles and it'll never come out. Look at all those blackheads on your chin for instance. And you never wash before meals, you sit down just like that.'

'But I always get up again and wash because you tell me to,' he said smiling.

'It's such a bad example to the children.'

'I'll see to it.'

'You never comb your hair either. It's like an old dog mat.'

'I'll see to that too.'

'You shouldn't laugh. It's not funny.'

'Listen, Marjorie, I've had an idea. Why don't you and I go away for a holiday? I mean a really long holiday, six months or something. We could take a cottage somewhere.'

'But what would happen here?'

'It would be all right. Gerda and the Ridleys can look after things. Meg can stay here in the term time and come to us in the holidays. Joe will be away doing his National Service. Think about it, Marjorie. We easily could. We don't have to do it immediately. We could wait until Dorothy's demobbed. I'm sure she'd help. Meg likes her, too.'

'I suppose if Dorothy were here to look after Meg we could go. We've never had a holiday, have we?'

Joe had not grown so large as it had once seemed that he would. He was solid, tending to fat, and had a round pink-cheeked face and bright eyes rather like Marjorie's. His healthy looks seemed unaffected by his liking for late nights. His infrequent letters mentioned visits to London to go to night clubs—he was stationed at Caterham—'Last week had a good trip to London to do the clubs and pubs,' he wrote. His parents were mystified. Arnold wrote to him suggesting that the time was getting near when he ought to think of entering himself for the agricultural college which it had been agreed he should go to when he was released from the Army. Weeks later, a letter came saying 'Don't bother about the agricultural place. After National Service I'm going into property with a man I know called Major Thornton and a friend of his who's an estate agent. They're counting on making a killing.'

'Making a killing? Going into property?' Marjorie repeated. 'What does he mean?'

'I suppose he wants to work for some sort of house agent,' said Arnold.

When Dorothy was demobilised from the FANYs, she went back to help at the Abbey while Arnold and Marjorie took a cottage in Cornwall. It seemed a reasonable temporary solution to the problem of what she was to do while her mother adjusted to widowhood. Nora Grant feared change above everything: it made it very difficult for her to make decisions of any kind except purely negative ones. Dorothy thought her mother ought to sell the house, which was too large for just the two of them and Nanny, or if she would not sell it she ought to divide it into two parts and let half of it. Nora was shocked.

'Charles would have hated the idea,' she said.

Charles would have hated their going to London too, it appeared. Dorothy had suggested it because unlike her mother she thought a change might be good for both of them. Nora was still only in her fifties and her stepson Hector, who was living a comfortable and well regulated life as a prosperous bachelor in St John's Wood, would certainly have helped her to meet people and make friends, but she would not hear of it.

'I can't leave poor Lucy Lambert,' was her excuse. But Lucy Lambert, though indeed in need of comfort—two of her sons had been killed in the war—had never been a particular friend of Nora's.

Dorothy gave in and went back to her work at the Abbey. Tom Boulder was out of the Army and Pat was pregnant. She complained a certain amount—'another baby at my age, it's ridiculous'—but hardly pretended to mean it. Tom began to make a floor for one of the disused outbuildings which it had been decided to make into an extension of the guest house. He was a good carpenter and his son Griff, who was waiting for his call-up papers, worked with him. Griff was good at maths and was going to learn to be an accountant after his National Service. After a few weeks of restlessness Dorothy settled into a routine. Her mother talked of taking her abroad sometime soon, to Italy perhaps, for a holiday.

'Look,' said Marcie to Noel. 'Can you believe it? Kevin's written a book. You know, the evacuee. It's had fantastic reviews. I got it today in Bath. You must read it.'

'Is it a children's book?'

'No of course not, he's grown-up now. It's a novel. Hot stuff, the reviewers say, all about the working-classes and premarital sex and all that.'

'How perfectly appalling.'

'No but Kevin, you know, the quiet one who was so sweet. Do read it Noel.'

He held out his hand.

'I don't remember him. I was away for much of that time, you may remember.'

She put the book into his hand.

'He was the one we liked,' she said. 'I bet it's jolly good, funny old Kevin.'

Noel opened the book at random.

' "Her breasts were bigger and softer than he had expected," '
he read out coldly. ' "Bigger and softer than he would have
thought possible. He tried not to think of Nigel, up there in
the dark in his Spitfire. 'My darling . . ." ' Have I really got
to read this rubbish?'

Marcie was blushing.

'You can skip those bits,' she said. 'All novels have to have
those bits nowadays. You know, ever since D. H. Lawrence
and everything, you have to put them in. I mean, he couldn't
have got it published without, probably.'

' "Peas are much better like that, straight from the pod,"
she said" ' read Noel, turning to another page. ' " No one need
ever know". Her smile, conspiratorial but at the same time nervous, asking to be liked, her way of tossing back the straight
brown hair that kept falling forward over her face, her slight
unsteadiness, so that she had to put one hand on the trunk of
an apple tree as she looked across the bed of peas at him, all
seemed quite wonderfully familiar to him, as if he had known
her as a child. "I love you Martha," he said. She pushed herself
abruptly away from the apple tree and turned back towards
the house. "That's ridiculous. You're fifteen." ' Noel stopped
reading. 'Was he fifteen?'

Marcie had sat down slowly on one of the big chintz armchairs—they were using the drawing room again now. 'No,'
she said, looking anxious. 'I think he was younger than that.'

'Even younger. Well, well. I look forward to reading the
rest of it.'

'Well but Noel, I don't think you ought to read it if you're
going to think it's based on, I mean, fact or anything, if you
know what I mean?'

'I'm looking forward to it.'

She sighed. 'Oh dear, I do wish you wouldn't use that voice.'

'The voice of the cuckold, do you mean?'

'Oh Noel, no.' Her eyes filled with tears. He had been saying
unkind things to her for some time now, but that did not mean
she minded any less.

He threw the book at her feet.

'You read it then. I've better things to do.'

She read it all, that night in bed. It was about a shy boy from a conventional and unloving lower middle-class home, who was sent as an evacuee to the house of an upper-class woman in her late thirties whose husband was in the Air Force. It described the huge house, which seemed to be a mixture between the Abbey and Marcie's own house, and the unfamiliar people he met, and the extraordinary vastness of the countryside, but most of all it described the overmastering passion which the boy conceived for his benefactress and which eventually she returned. Marcie read the passages about their love-making with astonishment. What most amazed her was their verisimilitude.

'How could he have known?' she said aloud more than once, sitting up in bed in her pink satin nightdress in the middle of the night—Noel had slept in the dressing-room since his return —for he described details which she recognised to be true of herself. She did like being kissed on her breasts and in the nape of her neck, she did find it difficult to say 'I love you,' or use endearments, she did often feel shy immediately after love-making and like to be reassured by conversation about some-thing impersonal like the progress of the war before being able to relax. How could he have known? Could he have spied on her when Noel was at home? Because of course it was just at that time that she and Noel had been so happy together. But it was impossible that Kevin could have seen them making love —or even heard them—her bedroom had double doors, like all the rooms which opened off the first-floor landing. She could not understand it, not realising that with the intuition with which his obsession had endowed him he had simply guessed.

When she had finished the book, she turned back to re-read the description of the first declaration of love. They had been picking blackberries—she remembered that—on the way up to the Plain. It was a mild autumn day. The sun was shining after rain, the bushes were covered with a network of cobwebs on which the raindrops glistened, the air smelt of damp earth and woodsmoke, there was no wind. Their baskets almost full, their fingers and lips stained with juice, they walked slowly on up the hill, finding a few mushrooms in the short grass of a field where cattle stared at them and a hare ran. They helped each other through the barbed wire fence and on to the open plain. Walking towards the clump of beech trees which grew on a

185

grassy mound which concealed the remains of an ancient burial place, they fell silent under the weight of their mutual longing. They sat under the trees and the boy said 'Oh Martha my love,' and they kissed for the first time. Marcie remembered it all, except for the longing, of which she had been unaware, and the kiss, which had not happened. When she read it for the second time, she wept.

Dorothy's captivity, though ill-defined, nevertheless seemed to her to be absolute. She could go to London for a few days at a time, stay with Hector, see a few friends from the war years, have lunch with Caroline Arkwright, who had finished her course at the L.S.E. and was working for the Fabian Research Group (Jane was teaching games at a girls' school in Yorkshire), or go to the theatre or the cinema with Hector; but she could not ignore the fact that her mother was lonely without her and in her helplessness quite incapable of imagining that she might be being selfish. The ideas Dorothy had had about travelling, about jobs abroad or living in London, had to be abandoned. In spite of that, she liked working at the Abbey and enjoyed the companionship of her mother, of whom she was fond and with whom she never quarrelled. When Timothy said, 'You know, you aren't really the sort of girl I'd expect to be living with your mother in the country,' she could answer quite cheerfully, 'There's no alternative.'

'Everyone has a duty to save their own soul,' he said.

'I'm not losing my soul. I'm lucky, I have all of you. I'm rather happy most of the time.'

'I know. I like that. But I've a feeling you may be wasted on us.'

'I don't think so. I'm quite useful sometimes, aren't I?'

'Yes, but. . . .'

'You mean I should have a husband and children.'

'I suppose so.'

'I think I may have got too independent. I believe I might find a husband awfully irritating, and I don't really like babies. I mean, the Boulder's baby seems rather revolting to me. I quite like older children. I could marry a nice widower with six children when I'm thirty-five, what about that?'

186

Joe had a twenty-first birthday party at the Abbey to which
he asked all his London friends. None of them had been to
the Abbey before. Joe himself appeared there only rarely and
when he did he left his parents baffled. They could not understand why he seemed to be making so much money. He said
he was working for an estate agent. They imagined him sitting
behind a desk, receiving enquiries, showing people round flats,
being paid a modest wage at the end of the week. Why then
the extraordinary air of prosperity? The new Vauxhall, the
dark overcoat with the fur collar? The expensive shoes, brief
case, bowler hat, umbrella? The number of telephone calls and
the mysterious air of urgency and importance? When they
questioned him his answers were so vague as to be in no sense
reassuring. Meg, whom they did understand and who was
training to be a physiotherapist in Bath, said, 'You're a crook,
that's all, aren't you, Joe? I bet you're a jolly good one.'

Joe looked modest and said in his new sophisticated voice,
'You're too kind.'

Arnold and Marjorie knew that this must be a joke, but they
were left feeling uneasy. Gradually, as he came to see them
less and less, they worried about him less and less.

'Young men should leave the nest,' Marjorie said. 'It's only
natural.'

When he announced that he wanted to return to the nest
to celebrate his coming of age, she was at first rather annoyed.

'We don't know any of his friends. They won't want to
come here, it's a most unsuitable place for a party.'

Even she had to admit quite soon that she was wrong. It
was a marvellous place for a party, as long as it was a big
enough party and it seemed that there need be no anxiety
about that. Joe had hired a band—'the best in town,' he said—
and arranged for champagne and supper—'I could have done
some food for you,' said Marjorie, rather hurt. 'No, no, Mum,
not that sort of food.' He arranged for people coming from
London to be put up with neighbours or at the Abbey—'Everyone's coming,' he announced, mentioning names which meant
nothing to his parents but evidently a great deal to him. There
was floodlighting and flowers and it was a beautiful night in

187

June. Dorothy came early to look at it all before the guests arrived.

'It is the apotheosis,' Gerda declared, swathed in yards of dark red brocade furnishing material. 'It is the great apotheosis of the Abbey.'

Meg and her friend Joan Boulder wandered into the courtyard from the ruins by the tower where they had been looking at the effect of the floodlighting on the roses which climbed all over the walls.

'It's so romantic, you must look,' they said.

They had found Hamilton reading in his workroom wearing a silk lined cloak and had brought him back with them, telling him the party was about to start. No one had ever seen Hamilton so well-groomed.

'We should always dress up like this,' said Dorothy.

Fisher had found a dinner jacket of Edwardian and now once more fashionable cut. He had tucked Laura Pinkus' arm under his and was leading her around to admire the well-set scene. Other people emerged one by one from their own doorways—Marjorie nervous, the Ridleys pale and pretty, Pat Boulder fat and smiling in a dress that Gerda had made for her, Timothy a middle-aged literary figure in a velvet jacket and a floppy bow tie.

'We must have a photograph,' said Meg, and Griff who was a good photographer went to get his camera.

They were all there, in a group in the courtyard among the roses and the lights and the soft, sweet-smelling night air, with Joe the initiator of all this excitement smiling and sweating slightly in the middle and the band beginning to tune up, having their photograph taken as the guests began to arrive.

'How does Joe know all these people?' Marjorie kept saying as they poured in.

'Thank goodness it's a fine night,' said Arnold, looking almost as distinguished as his brothers but a great deal more anxious.

'They're awfully good-looking aren't they?' said Dorothy to Timothy, with whom she was walking round looking at the guests. 'Or if they're not good-looking they're Red Indian, like that one.'

188

'Or very small, like that one.'

'Ah but he's very important, you can see that.'

'This is my boss,' Joe said, introducing them.

'Fabulous,' the man said. 'Simply fabulous.'

It was not somehow what Dorothy would have expected him to say. He was very small and dark, with bright lively eyes, a clean, soft-skinned, talkative, restless man. Girls kept coming up and kissing him and he said 'Fabulous,' but looked restless. A large expressionless man stood beside him without speaking.

'That's his bodyguard,' said Dorothy. 'He's the head of the Mafia, I expect.'

Suddenly she took Timothy's arm and said, 'Let's go this way.'

'Why?'

It had been the back of someone's head, but someone else was standing in the way now and so she said, 'Oh nothing,' and walked on. But she had been right. It was Guy, looking confusingly unchanged.

'I hoped I'd see you,' he was saying, but he did not meet her eyes.

It had crossed her mind that the Major Thornton for whom Joe had said he was going to work might have been Guy, but that had been some time ago and she had put it out of her thoughts. He was talking to Timothy. Dorothy wondered if she could move away, but then Timothy took her glass and carrying Guy's and his own as well went off to get more champagne. Guy did look at her then.

'I'm so glad I've seen you. I hoped I would. Tell me what you've been doing.'

'I'm here at the Abbey as much as anywhere now. I didn't go on with the Land Army. I went to France, driving people about.' Once they had looked at each other it was easy to talk. 'And you?'

'We're living in London. It's all right. It's fine in fact.'

'And you're making a fortune in the City.'

'It's not quite a fortune and it's not quite the City,' he said with his gentle smile. 'But that's the general idea. Who did you drive? In France, I mean.'

'An American Colonel.'

G

'And he fell in love with you.'

'Of course.'

'And you with him?'

'In a way.'

'And now—married?'

She shook her head. 'I'm going to marry a widower with six children when I'm thirty-five.'

He nodded.

'It *is* nice to see you,' he said.

Marcie appeared, in a Balenciaga tulip line dress, and then Timothy came back with the champagne. The conversation became general. Timothy asked Dorothy to dance and as they walked away she saw Daphne clinging to the arm of the small man, Joe's boss.

'My dear,' she said. 'The Land Girl. How are you? Have you seen Guy?'

'Who was that friendly lady?' Timothy asked when they had passed her.

'Just one of my smart friends.'

She had never danced with Timothy before. There was not much dancing at the Abbey. Marjorie used to do eurhythmics on the lawn with the children but had given it up as they grew older, and Gerda occasionally expressed herself in movement while listening to music on the gramophone, but this she usually did in solitude. Timothy danced well. He said he used to foxtrot with young men in night clubs before the war.

The slight extra impetus to show that she was having a lovely time which Guy's presence provided made Dorothy dance with more energy than she might otherwise have shown. The appearance brought into being the reality, and she began genuinely to enjoy herself. Later she danced with a tall man who said he kept two lemurs in his flat in Chelsea and was engaged to be married. 'There she is,' he said, waving to a red-haired girl on the other side of the room. 'No, wait a minute,' he said. 'It's that one,' indicating another girl who bore no resemblance to the first. 'Anyway,' he said, 'it's one of them.' He said he made furniture but mostly walked up and down the King's Road because he did not like to feel confined having been a prisoner of war for two years. 'Besides,' he said. 'You meet a lot of people that way.' He said Dorothy was the most beautiful girl he had ever met and suggested that they got married. 'The lemurs do smell rather,' he said. 'But I suppose I could get rid of them.'

Seeing Joe at some point, Dorothy said, 'I didn't realise you knew the Thorntons.'

'I work with him. He's fantastically amusing, isn't he? Do you know Daphne too? She's fabulous. They're terribly social. I never thought they'd come. They're meant to be at a party in Sussex.'

Perhaps that was why they left early. Dorothy was dancing with Peter Ridley when Guy came up behind her, gripped her elbow and said quietly, 'What a wonderful person you are. I knew you would be.' He patted her on the shoulder and disappeared through the dancers.

The party went on and on. The band stopped playing but were persuaded to start again. When dawn came people danced in the courtyard. Dorothy danced with the man with the lemurs in the early morning sunlight. There seemed to be quite a lot of broken glass around. Two or three people were asleep on the grass: one of them held a bottle firmly grasped in his hand.

'We are the survivors,' said the man with the lemurs. 'Others fell, some never to rise again. We few won through.'

Indeed some such sense of shared glory made the five or six dancing couples smile at each other in tired and solemn exaltation as the sun continued to rise. When at last Dorothy went to her mother's car to drive home she could not find the key. She could not be bothered to make the effort to remember in what safe place she must have put it, but instead walked the familiar road home between the hedges piled with honeysuckle and the grass verges thick with cow parsley. An early farm worker on his bicycle was surprised by her ecstatic 'good morning'. She felt extraordinarily happy.

Marcie sat in one of the many drawing room armchairs. She had recently had them re-covered in the same pink and green chintz as before. 'It will look better when it's faded,' she had said, forgetting how long the last lot had taken over that process. The same early morning sunlight through which Dorothy was striding so light-heartedly shone through the gaps in the still closed curtains, making the electric light look inappropriate and dreary.

Noel walked up and down.

'They'd all read it,' he said. 'Complete strangers came up to me and said they'd read it. How can they have known it was anything to do with us unless they'd already been told it was true?'

'But it isn't true.'

'Why go on saying that? What's the point? Why would he write it if it wasn't true?'

'I don't know. Why don't you ask him?'

'You should ask him. You should have written to him. You would have if you hadn't known it was true. You'd have sued him for libel. It's libellous, that's what it is if it isn't true. Why haven't you sued him for libel?'

'I couldn't, Noel, it would be so embarrassing. Besides it's a good book, it's been a great success. No one thinks it's true. It's just a story.'

'A story based on fact. That's not my idea of a good book. He hasn't made anything up. He hasn't had to use his imagination. Anyone could write a book like that.'

'He has used his imagination. It isn't true. Anyway most people have forgotten it by now. They're talking about some other book. You only think of it yourself when you've had a few drinks.'

'It's going to be made into a film. Someone told me tonight.'

'Is it?'

'I'm surprised you haven't been offered the starring role. You'd hardly need to act, would you?'

'Oh Noel, please. It's all so awful, this. I mean we're both quite old and I've never been very pretty. It seems so pathetic somehow.'

'He didn't seem to mind your not being very pretty. I didn't mind it once myself, I seem to remember.'

'Let's go to bed.' She stood up and took his arm.

'I'm impotent. Do you need reminding? That's what I was doing while you were committing adultery with this youth.'

192

Remember? I was castrating myself for the sake of what I thought was going to be our future together.'

She was propelling him slowly towards the door.

Putting her cheek against his upper arm she said, 'I didn't mean that sort of bed. I meant the sort of bed in which we could sleep, that's all.'

Fisher had approved of the party although he had gone to bed quite early himself. He absented himself from the aftermath saying that he and Laura had work to do in London.

Dorothy came back to fetch her car and saw Joe.

'What a lovely party,' she said. 'It was a great success, didn't you think?'

'I wish you'd tell my mother that. She thinks it was an orgy of vice.'

'I didn't see much vice, I don't think.'

He groaned.

'She found people in her bed. Also some teddy boys from Trowbridge gatecrashed and Fisher gave them a lecture on the meaning of manners while my father tried to get them to leave, so then they got incredibly drunk and Joan Boulder burst into tears and Tom Boulder and Ben Trew threw them out, and then someone knocked over a table covered with glasses and people stubbed their cigarettes out on the carpet and someone stole Hamilton's favourite bit of stained glass from his workshop, and Gerda got locked in the lavatory and someone was sick in a flower pot. And so on.'

'I don't think most people had any idea all that was going on. I think most people had a simply lovely time.'

'Well I thought it was all right too,' Joe began to look more cheerful. 'The trouble is my parents are so hopelessly conventional. They just don't understand.'

Thinking how much Arnold and Marjorie would dislike that description, Dorothy went through to the kitchen and found Marjorie washing up glasses.

'How can it have happened, Dorothy? How can he have acquired such wrong values.'

She would not be comforted. In fact it was days before Marjorie recovered from the party.

Dorothy walked on the Plain. She had two young sheepdog bitches, bought from a nearby farmer. Nothing could tire them. The plain stretched on either side of her into clear distance, the paths that crossed it went on for miles and were because of their great age irrefutable. She needed this high clear region to appease her restlessness.

She was pleased to have seen Guy again, to feel she had made peace with him, pleased too to find how easily she could forgive herself for having fallen in love with him. He had a lovely smile. What other reason was needed?

On the Plain her mind worked smoothly. When she came home she re-organised the furniture in her father's study and decided to ask the Ridleys if she could help them with the research on their next book, a study of Stonehenge.

The child Mary Boulder grew fast.

'It will be so lovely to have a baby around the place again,' Marjorie had said, but the fact was that Mary was one of those babies for whom being a baby seems to be quite intolerable. She suffered from frustration and complained vociferously. She wanted to feed herself and was furious when the spoon would keep turning upside down before it got to her mouth, she wanted to walk and could not understand why her legs would not support her, she wanted to talk and could not bear the stupidity of the grown-ups who would not understand what she was saying. Her mother found her exhausting and could not always be patient, although she did try.

'Tom says it's because she's intelligent,' she said. 'There's a lot to be said for stupidity, it seems to me.'

'I'm sure he's right,' said Marjorie. 'She'll be much better when she can do more.'

More patient than Pat, Marjorie tried to interest the child in making things with plasticine or wooden bricks, but it was not until she was old enough to push a toy wheelbarrow round after her father as he worked at his carpentry or in the vegetable garden that Mary showed more than very meagre signs of content.

194

Fisher's high hopes of the Labour Party did not last.

'It's because they don't pay enough attention to him,' said Marjorie unkindly.

But it was not only that. He remained a supporter for several years and he went on defending the Attlee Government's legislative record even after he ceased to believe in its sense of direction; but after a time he began to complain that this was the wrong sort of socialism—it was going to lead to a combination of state socialism and syndicalism—the right sort of socialism, the radical, anarchist, diffused sort of socialism was being ignored. He found no one—at that time literally no one —to agree with him.

'They don't listen to me,' he said to Gerda, who was trying to persuade him to do some work on his book on the perfectibility of man, which was by now about two-thirds finished. 'They don't listen to me because I don't matter. It's impossible to do anything in this country from the outside. You've got to be a member of the Establishment. I'm not. I'm an outsider. I'm a freak.'

'But you have written so much,' said Gerda.

'Not really. I haven't really got a decent body of work to show. I've talked too much.'

'But in this way you influence.'

'Rubbish. I've never influenced anyone or anything in my life.'

'But you are anyway so well-connected.'

'I'm not. I'm an utterly undistinguished member of the lower upper middle class.'

'Lower upper middle, what is this?'

'A perfectly well-defined category. I needn't have been, of course. I could have edged up a bit. There was no reason why I shouldn't. I could have become a member of the Establishment. Even with my bloody awkward character I could have done it. If I'd got into something early, if I'd known enough people. My mother was quite unworldly. Why didn't my parents make more effort for their sons?'

'I don't know. But I think you are blaming them because you are disappointed.'

'Yes I am. I am a disappointed man. A disappointed old man.'

'Then come. Let us finish this perfectibility and make some reputation while there is still time.'

Fisher groaned. 'I'm so bored with it.'

'We must soldier on. We are now linking Kropotkin with Saint Benedict. To me it is interesting. You talk, I make notes.'

Fisher sighed. He lay back in his chair, his long legs stretched out in front of him, his eyes closed, and began to speak rapidly.

'The concept of the "natural system", variously as it has been interpreted through the ages, nevertheless underlies the whole stream of thought which runs from St Benedict to Peter Kropotkin. One finds adumbrated in the works of the pre-Socratic philosophers that notion of the "web of life" so dear to Darwin. Aristotle was not a bad naturalist. . . .'

Joe came to see his parents once or twice a year, that was all: it was obvious that his interests were elsewhere. Marjorie no longer worried about him; there seemed no point. She had Meg who, when she had qualified as a physiotherapist, became attached to the neighbouring group of hospitals and most of the time was able to live at home. Marjorie liked small children better than older ones anyway. She was fond of Mary Boulder and delighted when Peter and Jane Ridley announced that they were going to have a baby too. She fussed round the delicate Jane all summer until with considerable difficulty she gave birth to a boy, Francis. Unlike Mary Boulder, Francis showed from the very first every possible sign of being quite extraordinarily satisfied with his lot.

Marcie slipped away with Dorothy to see the film of Kevin's book when it came to Bath.

'Noel doesn't really approve of it,' she explained. 'So I thought we'd just go on our own and not mention it to him.'

She was disappointed. The heroine had been changed into a long-haired French girl and the boy could not have been more than a year or two younger than she was. Marcie thought the treatment of the story sentimental and the musical score over-obtrusive. The theme song became very popular and as the film had been well-reviewed she supposed Kevin must have made a lot of money. She read an interview with him in a newspaper in which he said his own experience as an evacuee had been quite different; the book was not in the least autobiographical: he had lost touch with the people to whom he had been sent. They had been very kind to him, and he had nothing but happy memories of that time. There was a photograph of him looking confident in horn-rimmed glasses and rather a smart hair-cut. She was glad he had had such a success.

After a time Noel stopped referring to the book. He was persuaded to stand for election to the Rural District Council, and local politics gradually took up more and more of his time. Marcie, richer than ever because her last surviving aunt had died, went back to the picture collecting which the war had interrupted. With Ralph Blatchford again at her side, she began to buy work by Dubuffet and Francis Bacon as well as some of the American abstract expressionist school of which Ralph was an early admirer. Her pre-war acquisitions had already enormously increased in value. Ralph Blatchford began the series of delicate negotiations at the end of which, some years later, she agreed to leave the whole collection to the Tate Gallery on her death.

The brothers maintained their vigour into their old age. Hamilton, who had been told by his doctor to follow a strict routine of abstinence and exercise, had no recurrence of his heart trouble, and though Fisher's optimism declined and he complained increasingly of dyspepsia and sleeplessness, he was in fact remarkably healthy for his age. It was Arnold who because he worried the most looked the oldest. He became very lined and grizzled. His face habitually wore an expression of strain even when he was feeling none. During the time of Joe's troubles the strain was genuine.

Arnold and Marjorie had heard nothing of Joe for some months when a man whose name they had never heard rang up one evening and told them that he was a solicitor, and that Joe had been arrested and taken to Fulham Police Station on a charge of bribery and intimidation. He said he had every hope that the courts would be lenient; it was a first offence, he could produce character witnesses, it ought to be possible to imply that he had been led astray. All the same it would be wise if Arnold were to come to London straight away.

'I can't understand why this man Norman can't do anything for you.'

'Morgan,' said Joe patiently (the mistake occurred nearly every time the bewildered Arnold referred to the man who seemed now to be Joe's ex-employer). 'It's nothing to do with him.'

'But he seems to be paying for the defence. Or is it not really him? It's all so mysterious.'

Joe looked embarrassed.

'It's a bit complicated.'

They were in Joe's flat, which consisted mainly of an enormous room looking out over a quiet square just off the Kings Road. Outside there was fog, not impenetrable—white rather than the grey-green of the real pea-souper—and revealing a few bare colourless trees through its whiteness. Inside, the room too was mainly white, though the three tall windows were hung with blue curtains.

'What a beautiful room,' Fisher had said on first coming in. He had come too. They had persuaded Marjorie to stay at home, promising her to bring Joe back as soon as they had arranged bail. The three of them sat in comfortable chairs. Guy Thornton, also on bail, stood by the window.

'The actual firm,' said Joe, making an effort, 'was me and Guy and Lewis Miles, the man you saw at the police station.'

'He looked the part,' said Fisher. 'Better than you two anyway. Who is he?'

'An accountant, who used to work for Morgan too. I suppose he is a bit . . . I suppose Guy and I should have been more careful.'

'He only did more or less what Morgan did,' said Guy from the window. 'Only he wasn't half so clever.'

'And what did Morgan do?' asked Fisher.

Guy sighed. 'Morgan . . . well, Morgan is the Welsh Wizard, you see. Morgan is above and beyond. The Lloyd George of the property world.'

'Is he dishonest?'

'Flexible. Just flexible. He's a great man.'

'Is it he that's got you into this mess?'

'Only by charming us into thinking we were as clever as he is.'

'Well,' said Joe. 'He did directly tell Lewis how to deal with the man from the planning committee.'

'We've no real proof of that.'

'But Lewis said. . . .'

'Morgan's a great man,' Guy repeated dreamily.

'But not a good one,' said Fisher.

'Not a good one, no.'

'But what does he actually do?' asked Arnold.

'He deals. He's a dealer. It could have been sheep. Or bags of grain. But he happened to have an uncle with a small estate agency in Cardiff. He started by buying bomb-damaged houses in Fulham in about 1944, when he decided we were going to win the war. After the war it was office property. There was tremendous demand and at the same time there was inflation —everything he bought went up in value immediately. So of course he could borrow money for the next deal. His own expenses were nothing much. He always got the building licences and the planning permissions. Then when you didn't have to have building licences any more he went in for office building—there's been the most fantastic boom, you see, he's not the only one who's done this sort of thing. It's just that he's one of the most spectacular. Now he's going public. The actual floatation's in a week or two. The stock exchange is mad about him. He'll be a multi-millionaire without any doubt at all.'

'And so of course any possible connection he might ever have had with this little situation has to be kept quiet?' said Fisher.

Guy nodded.

'Naturally.'

'But doesn't that make you angry?' said Arnold.

'It's a hazard. He lost interest in the Fulham property. He hived it off into a separate company which we three were meant to run. He'd started negotiations for pulling down some houses and putting up a block of flats with shops at street level. It meant planning permissions and it meant getting rid of the tenants. We mucked up both.'

'Lewis didn't tell us everything,' said Joe. 'He didn't tell us about the tenant who was causing all the trouble. At least he said something about a loony nig-nog barrack-room lawyer.'

'He's a Pakistani law graduate,' said Guy. 'Delightful man, as a matter of fact.'

'Yes, you see,' said Joe. 'If you'd met him earlier it would have been all right.'

'I'd have given in completely, that's all. I don't know whether that's all right exactly.'

'It seems to me,' said Arnold, 'that you two have a perfectly good defence in saying that the whole thing was Norman's idea carried out by Lewis Miles and neither of you knew anything about it.'

'Morgan,' said Joe. 'And we can't bring Morgan into it.'

'We've no right to bring Morgan into it,' said Guy. 'We really haven't. And as to not knowing, we either did know and didn't take it seriously or should have known. I'm a director and Joe's company secretary.'

'Company secretary?' said Arnold. 'How could he have been company secretary? He's no qualifications.'

'You don't have to have any,' said Guy. 'Joe, be an angel, go and get us some food. I'm starving. Go to that good delicatessen.' He brought two five pound notes out of his pocket. 'Get us something decent—and a couple of bottles of that Côte du Rhône they have there.'

Joe went out of the room obediently. Guy looked out of the window into the white fog. Fisher looked at Arnold.

'I am trying to understand,' said Arnold eventually. 'But I can't. Why should it happen? If ever there was a . . . if ever there were parents . . . I mean, we tried to teach him to be honest. . . .'

'I will of course say that Joe didn't know,' said Guy, still looking out of the window. 'That he was foolish, that he never went near the house, never saw any of the tenants, didn't know what was going on. I'll say all that of course.'

Arnold nodded.

'Thank you.'

Guy shook his head.

'It doesn't matter to me, going to prison. Supposing I do get sent down for a few months. It simply doesn't matter. I haven't got a reputation to lose. My friends are such a rackety lot they won't care. My wife's a survivor in any circumstances. We've just got a house in the south of France. I can go there afterwards, until everyone's forgotten. I can think of some way or other of making a living. I'm all right, d'you see. I shall probably enjoy it—well, anyway, it's a new experience. It's not the same for Joe. Don't think I don't see that.'

Arnold nodded again.

'I see that you do.'

But he was still preoccupied with causes.

'What did we do wrong?' he said. 'What do people want?'

Fisher would have liked to calm him but did not know how to. He said, speaking rather pedantically, 'Perhaps one doesn't always make allowances for the craving for excitement.'

As neither of the others spoke, he had time to notice his own tiredness. He had not slept much the previous night. There seemed to be a slight singing in his ears. He felt that the inside of his head was white too, like the room and the fog. His tiredness seemed to lift him out of his chair to float in the white air. He was suddenly struck by how intensely blue the curtains were. Staring at one of the tall windows which gave from whiteness onto whiteness framed by this extraordinary blue, it seemed to him that he and the slight figure with the dandyish attitudes who stood by the window were united in their concern for the erring boy and the desolated father and both of them, he then felt—he and this other—both of them knew that the truth was that no other craving, nothing, was as imperative or as profound as the white on white with blue of man's passionate impulse towards harmony.

Joe came back with the provisions, and as they began to eat and drink they became more optimistic.

Later, when the trial came, the optimism turned out to have been misplaced. Lewis Miles—who, it appeared, had a previous conviction—was sentenced to a year's imprisonment, Guy to six months, Joe to three.

When Peter and Jane Ridley heard of a printing press which was for sale, they became very enthusiastic about the idea of a private press for the Abbey. They worked out that if they only printed a small number of books a year and were discriminating in their acceptance of orders from outsiders, they could run it at a small profit. Their enthusiasm, together with the fact that one of the people who had been working at the printing firm which was selling the press was willing to come and work for them for at least six months to teach them all he knew, persuaded everyone else at the Abbey that the proposition was a sound one.

'We always meant to have a press,' said Arnold. 'It was one of the many things we didn't do.'

'Well we can do it now, can't we?' said Fisher, who was beginning to find his brother's continuing depression irritating. 'We'll start by printing Hamilton's history of the Abbey.'

'I haven't written a history of the Abbey.'

'Write one, man, write one.'

It was decided to start with the Ridleys' book about Stonehenge. Dorothy, having done a good deal of the research for the book, became involved with the process of production. At just this moment her mother summoned up enough resolution to decide to take Dorothy for a holiday in Italy. Neither of them had ever been there before. They took a car and a great many guide books and duly marvelled. In Florence they watched some people binding books with beautiful traditional papers.

'You should learn all this, darling, for the Abbey Press,' said Nora Grant.

They found somewhere where Dorothy could take a course and they found a charming surgeon's widow who took students on mezzo-pension terms. Nora Grant went home alone, leaving her daughter hardly able to believe her luck.

In the end Dorothy stayed for a year—with one brief return home for Christmas—learning Italian as well as book binding, and living, rather belatedly, the life of a student in a town which in spite of its residents' frequent complaints as to noise, traffic, tourists and general deterioration she found entirely satisfying.

Her mother wrote to say that she was well, and doing work for the Red Cross with Lucy Lambert. News from the Abbey come from Timothy, who wrote frequently in a fine italic script.

'The Press is a success, though hard work,' he wrote. 'It's a pity it wasn't going in time to do my poems (they're a Poetry Society choice, by the way). I shan't have enough for another book for at least five years unless my output increases which is unlikely. They're doing a book of Wessex legends by an old looney who's been collecting them for years—rather well-written. The Press is the best thing at the moment. The brothers are getting old, you know. I've been thinking how much this place depends on them. I believe in spite of all the things that are going on here and all the other people involved, the whole place will simply collapse when they go. Fisher in his optimistic days used to tell us that this place proved all sorts of things about society, but I think it only proves something about personality, and only the Whitehead personality at that.

'The Ridleys are a good thing of course, but they and the Press are somehow separate from the rest of the Abbey because they are so self-contained. They are so deeply concerned with each other and with the child on whom they both dote that in some funny way they don't quite work *with* the Abbey. They aren't much interested in things outside it either—most of the rest of us at least go off to an Aldermaston march every now and then (though Fisher's becoming rather disenchanted with all that because of the internal strife). Marcie's friend, the art expert Ralph Blatchford, spends a certain amount of time here now. He's a very keen Ban the Bomb man. He's nice, but the more one knows him the less impressive—though no less nice—he becomes. He's so much in favour of everything that you long to find something he disapproves of (apart from the Bomb of course). Besides he's getting old, like the brothers, and we're going to need younger people here some time. I don't know whether we'll ever find them. Fisher's a little embittered because no one in the outside world pays any attention to him any more. His books are out of print and no one asks him to lecture. Arnold is aged by Joe's disgrace. He and Marjorie potter round the garden together supporting each other like very old people. Marjorie still murmurs "He had such a happy home,"—it makes one weep—silly boy. He's out of prison and gone to France with the Thorntons. He only came down here once. He looked awful I must say—couldn't meet anyone's eyes and jumped when spoken to—oh dear.

'The person I myself am most interested in here—now this will surprise you—is young Mary Boulder. I know I've never particularly liked children, but she's not like a child—nor an adult—nor a girl—nor a boy—although she's a very good carpenter. Better than her father. I don't know what it is about her that's so original. There's that extraordinary hair, now longer thicker darker curlier than ever—the surprising and in no way unhealthy pallor of the face, the pronounced features which might become heavy with age, the way of looking straight at you, appearing to consider, then giving a quick nod and a businesslike little smile which is at the same time start-lingly—well what?—you can't exactly say beautiful, it's more —unusual—original, as I said before. Then she brushes her arm over her forehead to wipe off the sweat, just as her father does, and bends over her saw again with all that hair falling right over her face so that you think it must get tangled up. An amazing creature.'

When Dorothy came back from Florence she found that the friendship with Lucy Lambert which her mother had sur-prised her by claiming as an excuse for not moving to London had now become a reality. Nora Grant was constantly at the Lambert house on one pretext or another. She and Lucy worked together on a number of local activities—the Red Cross, the Conservative Party, the Church Fête—and Nora was busier than she had ever been during her husband's lifetime.

Dorothy was never quite at ease with the Lamberts. They were always so friendly and she seemed to have so little to talk to them about. Their one surviving son, John, lived not far away, working as a land agent on a big estate. Lucy very much wanted him to marry: the trouble was, he had always been the dull one. Dorothy sometimes felt she could hardly meet Lucy's gentle hopeful gaze. At least when she was with Sir Giles there was no question of meeting his gaze—it was always bent on his embroidery. He had had to sell most of his land soon after the end of the war, before the value of land went up. Most of his time was spent in producing exquisite needlework, sitting by the window in a small oak-panelled room full of examples of his art and giving onto a small herb garden which was surrounded by box hedges and might have been another piece of embroidery. Dorothy sometimes sat with him while he talked about gardening, or mediaeval Latin poetry, about both of which he knew a great deal. She often noticed how extraordinarily clean and shiny his shoes were.

She had come back with every intention of staying, and working at the Abbey Press, but when after a few months she had a letter from a friend in Florence offering her a job cataloguing an English library there, she felt there was no longer any need to feel obliged to stay with her mother, and accepted.

Timothy wrote: 'I see her on the bus on Tuesdays and Thursdays (did I tell you I was teaching Eng. Lit. at the Grammar School twice a week—pecuniary necessity?). All our village girls seem to go overboard for the external signs of femininity about the age of puberty—the morning bus is a riot of mini-skirts and fancy hair-slides. There are endless battles with the schools about earrings and skirt-lengths. On the bus I think they probably all talk filth—fortunately there's so much whispering and giggling among the girls and scuffling and animal noises (like a truck-load of bullocks) among the boys that I don't hear much of it. Anyway I sit right up in the front and read my paper. Mary sits with her friend Margaret, talking about Margaret's pony. They are different from the others. Pat Boulder says Mary takes no interest in her appearance, but I don't think that can be true, her hair always looks so clean and well-brushed though it's true she doesn't (I'm glad to say) restrain its exuberance. Margaret comes from Town Farm. Her way to the bus joins ours a hundred yards or so down the road. If she's not there we wait for her, and then she and Mary talk all the way to the bus about Smokey, the pony. They don't go to the same school any more because Margaret passed the 11+ and goes to the High School, but they still spend most of their free time together, with the pony. Mary's good with animals, as you probably know.'

Joe came home for Christmas for the first time since his misfortunes. He seemed to be recovering his confidence. He said he was working in the car trade, restoring vintage cars. He assured his parents that the man he was working for was highly respectable and that it was a good business. He was thinking of getting married and would bring his girlfriend down next time he came. She was a French girl he'd met when he'd been staying with the Thorntons. Fisher asked what had become of Guy.

'I think he's travelling in the East. Daphne's still in France, or she may be in England now. They might have had to sell the house in France. They were getting very short of money. Daphne's a great friend of Montague Morgan's. She spends quite a bit of time with him in fact.'

'While Guy is travelling in the East,' said Fisher.

'I think Guy likes being on his own quite a lot. I mean, they never seem to quarrel or anything, and Daphne has rather expensive tastes, you see.'

'Are you earning enough to think of marrying?' asked Arnold. 'Are you sure you're being wise?'

'I think so. Jeanie's a dress designer. She wants to have her own boutique. Anyway I'm only thinking of it, I won't do anything rash. I'll bring her down some time. You'll like her.'

Marjorie and Arnold were more cheerful after this visit.

'He's more mature,' they said. 'Less likely to do something foolish. She must be a sensible girl.'

Philip, married now to Rosamund but still living with her and her mother in their cottage on the Mendips, wrote to Arnold. 'Some young friends of ours are coming in your direction—one of them's an ex-pupil of Rosamund's and mine, a boy called Steve—could they camp in your field for a night or two do you suppose? They don't need anything except water.'

Days later, when Arnold had forgotten all about them, they arrived—Steve, Milt, Johnny and Mush—in an old wooden
206

caravan pulled by a stolid brown horse and followed by two thin greyhounds and another horse of nondescript appearance. They settled themselves in the field behind Hamilton's workshop, made a camp fire and stayed two nights. They were going on to Wales they said—they had a friend there with plenty of grass. They asked if they could come back later on some time. 'The vibes are good here,' Steve said.

Steve was rather handsome and more talkative than the others. Milt was an American boy who had run away from the most expensive boarding school in England. He was pale and spotty, with a tendency to tremble. He seldom spoke, except for the occasional 'Yeah man' or 'Just wild'. Johnny was rather older, dark and taciturn. Mush, his Canadian girlfriend, did most of the cooking. She was quiet too, but in the evenings she got out her guitar and sang folk songs, rather well.

Timothy was glad that Mary had her friend Margaret to talk to. It seemed to him that her mother was out of sympathy with her. Pat was so frivolous and talkative, Mary so quiet. Pat got on well with her older daughter Joan who had a job on the local newspaper and was engaged to a young man who worked in a bank. Joan was pretty and lively and flirtatious like her mother: Mary was more like her father.

Tom Boulder's slowness and certainty had settled now into a benign but usually impenetrable taciturnity. Everyone liked Tom but his few needs did not seem to include human intercourse. He and Mary often worked together for hours on end with hardly a word passing between them. Perhaps they did not need words. Later on, though, when they did, they could not find them. That was Timothy's conclusion anyway.

Timothy had been pleased to find in himself a feeling for Mary. That was what he called it—'I have a feeling for her', he wrote to Dorothy. Once he had recognised it he did not particularly want to analyse it. What mattered was that it was a feeling. He had been afraid that middle age had robbed him of feelings, leaving only the dry pleasure to be derived from the exercise of his intellectual faculty, the cold consolations of criticism. The discovery that in his fifties he still could wait with inexplicable eagerness and anxiety for the sight of a white face and a cloud of dark hair, and that one of those sudden smiles could lighten his heart for the rest of the day, was a welcome one: he was inclined to congratulate himself. He expected nothing, except the strange and occasionally painful pleasure of concern: but their twice weekly walk to the bus, however brief the minutes before Margaret joined them, was already a small step towards some kind of friendship. He began to think that she liked him.

Through the imaginative initiative of her Primary School headmaster Mary was able to go to the Technical Secondary School (later abolished) and to specialise in woodwork. When she came home she often worked with her father, who now did more carpentry than agriculture, leaving most of the work on his own piece of land to Pat. Timothy used to walk over and watch them. He liked to see Mary's strong well-shaped hands smoothing the wood, and her intense and silent concentration. She was an artist in a medium which was quite mysterious to him. She did not use words but shaped wood instead. When she did speak, it was with a more pronounced West Country accent than either of her parents, who spoke standard English with only a touch in his case of something from Radstock and in hers of County Cork. Mary's school companions were country boys and girls—on the work-bench they were all boys, and it was possibly in order to be more like them and so break down their suspicion of a girl carpenter, that she exaggerated rather than otherwise her local accent. Every vowel, particularly when it came at the end of a word, had a shadow of an 'r'—or was it an 'l'?—after it. Verbs sometimes had 'do' in front of them. 'I do think . . .'—but the 'o' was hardly sounded—'I d'think'—'she d'go'. Slight though it was and variable, it yet was noticeable enough to be part of something which with the striking appearance and the height —she was a tall girl, well-built though slender—and later the clothes she favoured—added up to a personality which seemed to Timothy unlike anyone else's.

He wrote some poems about her. Once on an autumn day he watched some rooks swooping from a group of high elms down onto a field of stubble. There was sunlight through faint mist, casting long shadows. The birds swooped, tumbled, soared, then tumbled again, with the sun gleaming on their black wings, aerial acrobatics only to be explained by pure joy in flight—and from prosaic rooks. The way the unexpectedness was part of the beauty made him think of Mary; but that was after he had seen her dancing.

The hippies came often after that first visit, and usually stayed for several days at a time. The thin dogs would first announce their coming, running ahead into the courtyard and in if they could through the kitchen door. If the door was shut they began at once to rummage through the dustbins. Then there would be the sound of horses' hooves and rumbling wheels and there they would be, on their way to or from Glastonbury, sometimes with others in caravans of their own, and sometimes just the original four.

There was a girl called Elsa who often came with them. She was a big girl with long fair hair and slightly sticking-out teeth, and the guilty smile of a child caught stealing sweets by someone she knows is going to forgive her. She was a marvellous cook. She never came for more than three or four days at a time, but when she did the standard of food—and indeed of conversation—improved. She wore long trailing skirts and beads and was often wrapped in a huge evil-smelling Afghan coat, but she was not a full-time hippy and went back to a life in London which sounded a good deal more conventional. Timothy suspected that it was an interest in Johnny rather than anything else which accounted for her visits. Marjorie took to her at once. Indeed everyone liked her—it was hard not to, though Steve did once surprise Timothy by telling him she was the most selfish person he'd ever met. She was extraordinarily friendly; unlike the others who were characterised rather by their complete lack of any sort of unfriendliness than by anything more definite. It was she who brought the music.

'You see we all dance now,' Timothy wrote to Dorothy. 'Fisher has been persuaded to exchange his good Pye Black Box—on which he used to listen to classical music alone in the library—for something more up to date (and much louder)

209

which is kept in the downstairs room of the new bit of the
guest house. When the hippies aren't there, there's the occasional Mozart or Beethoven—actually the thing's rather a
snare because the sound is so wonderful it spoils you for ever
having anything less well performed, and also it's fatally easy
to over-play something you like very much and suddenly it
goes over the top into surfeit and you can't listen to it again
for years, if ever, because it no longer works. Anyway, when
they come this is what they bring, along with the mangy
dogs and the bored horses and the vague dissociated smiles
and the sweet pervasive smell of marijuana, they bring the
music. We haven't yet dared to put it on when we're by ourselves, even the time when Elsa left her records behind—but
that was only for one night, they came back for them the
next day. We may have let our hair grow a little longer, we
may have allowed one or two new words to creep into our
vocabulary (well, some of us have anyway—you should hear
Gerda wrapped in a huge Indian tablecloth pronouncing that
"Love"—or really even after all these years still more or
less "loff"—"is where it's at"—she'll be taking to the road
soon—the oldest drop-out in the business—I wish you were
here, I really do)—but you see we haven't yet quite liked,
even Gerda, to listen to the Rolling Stones without *them*. But
when they come—it's Elsa chiefly—Elsa loves to dance. Earth
tremors from the pop explosion, my dear, have hit West Wilts.
It's so lovely, this music, and so loud. One resisted it at first
—I mean it's a bit violent—and then this delicious weakness
began to creep to one's extremities, a softness spreading along
the limbs, an abandonment of thought, a surrender of the will
—and then perhaps Elsa holds out her hand—they're all on
their feet, all moving—and one finds oneself up there with
them, absorbed—one can't feel a fool because they're simply
not looking, their eyes are unseeing, such is their rapture—
and one progresses in a minute from the first self-conscious
little bit of running on the spot to jerking and gyrating and
waving one's arms about and waggling one's hips and rolling
one's head—oh the liberation. . . !'

In his diary he wrote less flippantly. 'I wish I could describe
the utter unexpected glory of Mary dancing. She's taken to

wearing a big Paisley shawl. It's something of her grand-
mother's: they used to have it on the table in the front
parlour in Radstock, Pat said. She holds back at first, just
swaying a little, the shawl tightly drawn round her shoulders
by her folded arms, and then the music takes her and she
begins to move; and then she's swooping and turning, straight-
backed, arms outstretched, the Paisley shawl and the abundance of hair flying behind her, across the room from side to
side in huge skips and jumps, but always controlled, sometimes turning elaborately like a Spanish dancer, her chin
above her shoulder and her hair covering her face, then the
hair tossed back as the arms fly out with the shawl swirling,
and off she sweeps again. You have the feeling it's something
incredibly rare, something you might travel miles to see, the
legendary ritual dance of the black swan of Mauritania, one
of the wonders of the world.'

'Of course they're hopelessly romantic,' said Fisher. 'I mean,
I'm absolutely in favour of them—I'm in favour of anything
which questions the current orthodoxy—but I can't quite take
them seriously.'

'People have always done it,' said Hamilton. 'In times of
social uncertainty the disaffected have always taken to wandering. These ones wait for King Arthur or Jesus or a space-
man on a flying saucer—in mediaeval Europe they expected
Charlemagne or the future Frederick. It's the same thing,
looking back to some notion of an earlier authority.'

'It's all right as long as no one turns up,' said Arnold. 'On
a flying saucer or anything else. I mean, since they don't trust
reason they're easy meat for extremists. If they ever start
getting interested in politics I hate to think what might
happen.'

'They never would,' said Timothy. 'Not here anyway.
There's nothing mad enough in English politics. You can see
they might do it in America, with Vietnam and all that.'

'Anybody who says love is more important than war and
inner enlightenment than success must be right,' said Gerda
firmly.

'One would think so, wouldn't one?' said Fisher. 'One

shouldn't expect them to make sense probably—it's a fashion not a philosophy. As a fashion I absolutely approve. Much more attractive than mini-skirts.'

They were having supper in the kitchen, and afterwards some of them walked out in the dusk to the field behind Hamilton's workshop where a fire was burning by the caravan. Mary was already there, sitting beside Steve. They were passing round a cigarette. Hamilton murmured something and disappeared. He had smoked pot once and it had made him depressed. Fisher liked it; he said it was good for his digestion. Gerda approved of it in theory, but in practice a few puffs sent her off into a heavy silence, and she secretly thought that an evening spent in silence was an evening wasted. Timothy smoked cautiously. Sometimes it made him giggle and he liked to be sure that everyone else was going to be giggling too. As often as not he passed the joint on without taking any and looked across at Mary, who sat beside Steve in silence but as far as he could tell happy. Some time ago Steve had asked Mary's advice about one of the horses; then he had taken her with him one day to see a horse he was thinking of buying. They had had to go to a farm somewhere near Frome: it had taken them all day. Timothy had said to Tom, 'Does it worry Pat, Mary seeing so much of the hippies?' and Tom had said easily, 'You can't do anything with them these days. She's beyond her mother. Been so a long while now.'

'I see now what Steve meant about Elsa,' Timothy wrote later on to Dorothy. 'She's not exactly scrupulous. We have witnessed a little drama here over the last few weeks. We were not required to participate. We could only watch as it unfolded. I have to admit I was on the side of the victor—victrix, rather.

'Elsa decided she wanted Johnny. They all went to some kind of Gathering at Glastonbury. I don't quite know what it was. I asked Steve but they're so vague—they murmur about people coming together and grooving. I'm getting slightly irritated by Steve. I'm afraid Mary may be falling for him and of course he's no sense of responsibility or anything like that. He's good-looking, but anyone can see he's weak. I can't

212

decide whether I ought to talk to her mother about it. I mean, would she have taught her about birth control do you suppose? I feel I'm being absurd in fussing so, but I can't help it. She went with them to Glastonbury—they were away four days. Fancy her mother letting her go like that! I wish her friend Margaret hadn't gone to London to learn to be a nurse. Anyway, when they came back it appeared that fires of feeling, hitherto dormant, between Johnny and Elsa had sparked into a blaze. And over the next few days she simply took him from the helpless Mush. She was quite ruthless, but without showing a trace of ill-feeling. Smiling guiltily, cooking superbly, she wove such a web of luxury—emotional and physical—round the vain and flattered Johnny that he hadn't a chance. She was just so incredibly nice to him. And when she had secured him she took him away. They went to London on some pretext or other, then he came back alone to tell Mush it was the final break, and to cap it all they actually got married, with a dawn freak-out at Stonehenge to celebrate it. Of course Mary went, with Steve.

'What Elsa has is some kind of absolute assurance which is just what Mary lacks. I don't know what it is, it's not just selfishness as Steve says, and it's not just knowing what she wants. I don't know anything about Elsa—her parents may be loving or rich or both or neither—but something has given her this absolute confidence in her social and sexual status—of which, incidentally, every meal she makes is a celebration. Now why hasn't Mary got that? It's the one thing a parent ought to try to give a child.

'Look at young Francis Ridley, for instance. Pat Boulder says Peter and Jane spoil him, but it's not true. They give him a lot of attention, which is quite boring for everyone else, but they don't spoil him. He can't be in any doubt that they adore him, but all that gives him is a kind of munificence in his dealings with the rest of the world. It's as if a child who has once been a king has royalty in the blood for the rest of his life. Everyone agrees he's what Pat calls a lovely fellow. I believe that nothing can change that now.

'But Mary, you see, Mary can be shaken. That's why I worry about her. That's why I'm afraid she may take Steve too seriously—she hasn't got balance, based on assurance. I think she confides in me as much as in anyone, but we've never talked about Steve. I can't raise the subject unless she does. She might suspect my motives.

'When they came back from Stonehenge they brought an American with them, a man called Ergo. I don't like him. He comes from North Carolina, and has been persecuted for his beliefs. This gives him an advantage over the others, who immediately appear lightweights beside him. Where he comes from it is not acceptable to be a hippy. Also he is a draft dodger and takes heroin. Since he's been here the tone of things has changed, become more serious. Less dancing, more brown rice.

'He talks about ecosystems and says the world is poisoning itself to death. He has a mass of appalling statistics at his fingertips. Thirty-four tons of dirt a month fall on every square metre of Tokyo—did you know that? There's going to be a world population of eight billion by the year 2,000 and the earth's resources are running out. If one ventures to suggest that technology may be able to cure some of the evils it's brought about, he breaks into the most violent abuse. Mostly no one dares to question his facts. We just listen and feel more and more depressed. Except Hamilton. He's looking forward to the end of the world.'

'It's the final separation of light from darkness, that's what it is,' said Hamilton. 'That's what's coming, the final separation. You and I will witness it, I'm convinced we shall. I never thought it would happen in my lifetime.'

He was pacing up and down in the kitchen. He had come in from his workshop, his fingers blue in his mittens (it was not yet cold but his circulation was bad) to make himself a cup of Nescafe, and had found Timothy and Dorothy about to do the same. Dorothy had come back to spend a few days with her mother, but was still living in Florence.

'Astrology has always said it, science has been pointing to it. That is, if only the scientists had had the wit to interpret the evidence correctly. Matter is evil, don't you see, its doom is coming, the light will go back to the light.'

214

'What light?' said Dorothy.

'The spirit, so called. After the destruction of matter.'

'Do you mean, by an earthquake or something?'

'It might be an earthquake, yes,' he said, as if pleasantly struck by the notion. 'There are bound to be more of them. Underground nuclear explosions, for instance. It only needs a minor miscalculation to set off an earthquake. Look at that one in India, only the other day. An earthquake killed two hundred people, and they'd never had one there before. There's no doubt at all that it was caused by a dam.'

'You seem pleased.'

Hamilton's eyes glittered. 'Shouldn't one be pleased? If an evil thing comes to an end, shouldn't one be pleased?'

'It may seem evil to you,' said Dorothy in a governessy tone of voice. 'But I don't think you ought to go around saying so. What about young people, children? It isn't fair on them.'

'There shouldn't be any children,' said Hamilton heavily.

'You're getting all that from that man Ergo. I don't approve of him. He smells, for one thing. And what about the glimmering lights all over the dark plain that you told me about once? Who's going to provide them if there's nobody young? Old people lose hope, they can't possibly glimmer.'

'What glimmering lights?' said Hamilton looking displeased.

'You told me about them when you were in hospital in Bath, after the bombing. I thought that was a black enough view of the world, but your present one's even worse.'

'The world's worse,' said Hamilton crossly.

He clasped his mittened hands round his mug of Nescafe and shuffled out of the kitchen, muttering, 'Glimmering lights indeed.'

Timothy was smiling.

'No really,' said Dorothy. 'He shouldn't be allowed to carry on like that. It isn't good for him. He gets too wild, you know, he really does.'

'Ergo approves of wildness. They all do I suppose. Not being wild is a sign that you're suffering from Freudian middle-class hang-ups. You should aim to achieve a permanent high, a constant state of ecstasy. You should hear Thornton on the subject.'

215

'Who's Thornton?'

'He's a sort of guru. He takes them on wonderful drug trips. He lives in Wales most of the time, I think.'

'Nothing to do with Guy Thornton?'

'That's it. I'd forgotten you knew him.'

'You mean it's him? Guy Thornton? Don't be silly.'

'I never really knew him before so it doesn't seem silly to me. He's a mystic. I don't know whether that's a recent thing. He lived in Morocco for some time I think. He had a house there but some people took it over to run an ashram in—or maybe he started the ashram himself. I don't know. I think anyway he somehow got done out of his house, or can't go back there or something. And then he must have gone to Ibiza because I know that's where he got so keen on LSD. But he's frightfully learned, you know. Hermes Trismegistus and the Rosicrucians and all that sort of thing. He and Hamilton ramble on for hours.'

'How utterly extraordinary.'

Dorothy went to see Marcie and found that she had grown quite fat. She said that she saw no one from the Abbey except Fisher nowadays.

'Fisher is one of my mainstays,' she said. 'Fisher and Ralph Blatchford. I don't know what I should do without them. Ralph has put me onto a whole lot of committees, my dear, in London, too funny.'

'What sort of committees?'

'To do with supporting the arts and that sort of thing. I've no idea what I'm meant to do but at least I can pay for the drinks. I simply love it.'

'How's Noel?'

'In marvellous form,' said Marcie, tossing back her hair. 'Quite marvellous, incredibly busy with all sorts of local things—the Council, the Conservative Party—he's frightfully good at it and no one seems to mind him being a raging Fascist.'

'And he's more cheerful?'

'Not exactly cheerful,' said Marcie, tossing back her hair again. 'One couldn't say that exactly. He watches a lot of

216

television. He likes that because he can get cross about the vulgarity of mass culture. And he's suing someone who's writing a book about my mother. That's giving him a lot of enjoyment.'

'I believe I read something about that book. Didn't it have rather good reviews?'

'It's very well-written. He's supposed to be a brilliant historian, the young man who wrote it. But I think it's awfully difficult to tell the truth in a work of non-fiction, don't you? He says my mother went to bed with all those Prime Ministers and people who used to write her such passionate love letters, and Noel says that's libellous and distressing to her family and people of that period wrote to each other like that the whole time, it was part of the idolisation of women which they had instead of sex, and it's only because this young man is so lower-class and modern that he can't understand that.'

'What do you think?'

'My dear, I haven't the faintest notion. I find I have no idea what anyone is doing at any time unless I actually see them doing it. Even then I'm often not too sure. Whatever she did I hope she enjoyed it. I used to think that as well as being perfect in every other way she was also perfectly happy but now I'm often rather haunted by the idea that she wasn't at all. Poor old Mummy.'

A few days before Dorothy was to return to Florence, she went up to the Abbey in the evening and was told that the hippies, who had been away to Glastonbury for several days, had come back, bringing with them, among others, the man they seemed for some reason to call only by his surname, Thornton.

'We'll go out there after supper,' said Timothy. 'And you can see how much he's changed.'

'He hasn't changed at all,' said Fisher.

Timothy was obviously relieved to see the group again. Mary had been to Glastonbury with them—she spent most of her time with Steve now—and it was the transformation of Timothy at just the thought that she was safely back which made Dorothy realise how much he must care for her. He was unusually lively at supper, teasing Gerda more kindly than he sometimes did, stimulating Fisher to talk, tactfully diverting Hamilton when it looked as if his random ferocity might be going to focus itself on some too sensible remark of Arnold's.

Aware of having given himself away to the observant Dorothy, he said to her at a moment when no one else was listening, 'Are you wondering how a middle-aged homosexual can make such a fool of himself? There's no fool like an old fool, you know.'

'You mean, Mary.'

'I mean Mary.'

'I suppose I was wondering. Does she know?'

'I think so. I think she's glad of it. I think she'd turn to me for help if she needed it.'

'Will she need it?'

'I think so. I think that ass Steve is taking heroin.'

'Is Mary?'

He shook his head. 'It doesn't interest her. She told me that. But the thing is, when he feels bad he turns to Mush the Canadian girl, not Mary, because Mush has more experience with drugs. I think Mary is going to feel that he rejects her when he needs help and that will hurt her. There's nothing anyone can do. But I shall be there, that's all.'

'That's all anyone can do for anyone.'

Dorothy had been to the Abbey once or twice while the hippies were away—she had spent a whole day in fact helping the Ridleys to bind a rush order of books—and had been up to see Hamilton in his workshop. It had become more than ever like a badger's den, in which the creature itself coughed and rustled and grumbled and tried to keep itself warm. No one knew what he did in there all the time. The stained glass jigsaw puzzle was still unfinished. He was supposed to be preparing a revised edition of his book on Father Augustine, but it did not seem particularly likely that any publisher would want to produce it. He had discovered another figure in the course of his investigations, a nineteenth-century vicar of a small village in the Mendips who had experienced hallucinations and kept a rather incoherent diary, in which minute archaeological observations were interspersed with encounters

218

with beings from other worlds. Hamilton was editing the diary. It was not an easy task because it was written in a number of small notebooks in handwriting so small that Hamilton, whose sight was anyway failing, could only make it out with the help of a magnifying glass.

The little cell was untidy, warm and fusty, Hamilton himself alarming, as she had found him as a child. He was too strong. She looked out of his window onto the field sloping up to the belt of beeches before the Plain, the field where Father Augustine claimed to have seen visions, and tried to talk to him about Florence, but he was not responsive. His eyes still seemed to her too bright.

At supper he talked of the Holy Grail.

'Thornton will have it that it was at Montségur, but it won't do I'm afraid. Sometimes I think they might have brought it with them when they first came here in 1280, those slightly mysterious French monks. What about that, Fisher? The Holy Grail here all the time, buried under the tower.'

'For goodness sake keep quiet about it if it is. We don't want hoards of lunatics swarming all over the place trying to dig it up. They'd have the tower down, I shouldn't wonder. I'd rather have the tower than some old pot.'

'But it is a symbol,' said Gerda. 'An object of quest.'

'The whole point of a quest is that you don't find the thing.'

'But you've got to think you're going to find it,' said Timothy. 'So that to have the Holy Grail here and deliberately conceal it would be a terrible thing to do.'

'Rubbish. It would be an act of kindness. Besides this is a silly conversation. Hamilton's being frivolous as usual. He knows perfectly well there's no possible indication of anything of the kind. Let's go out and see our friends. I want to get to bed.'

'I am not being frivolous,' said Hamilton, following him out into the moonlight. 'Frivolity and free-ranging speculation are two quite different things.'

'Pooh,' said Fisher.

There was a full moon and a faint ground mist. It was late October. They passed the ruins and walked towards the light of the fire. Most of the hippies were sitting round it, except

Ergo the American who was walking about apparently aimlessly outside the circle. Mary's head was on Steve's shoulder and she was gazing into the fire. Her face was thinner than it had been when Dorothy last saw her. The intense pre-Raphaelite looks, pale and melancholy but at the time passionate, were so extraordinarily of the moment that Dorothy found herself wondering how it could have happened that Tom and Pat Boulder should have produced this embodiment of the spirit of the age. Mary raised her head momentarily from Steve's shoulder, smoothing with her large competent hands the abundance of hair which fell on either side of her face and passing it back over her shoulders before greeting their arrival with her quick smile. By the time they had found somewhere to sit by the fire her head was back on Steve's shoulder and the mass of hair had fallen forward, half concealing her face.

They sat in silence until Gerda began a conversation with the Canadian girl Mush about root vegetables which was obviously a continuation of an earlier discussion, and Hamilton who was wrapped in an overcoat, two scarves and an old felt hat, said to the robed figure Dorothy had recognised with some difficulty as Guy Thornton, 'I looked up that reference. You were quite right. I was thinking of the earlier outbreak, the one in 1418.'

Guy was wearing a saffron coloured kaftan. His hair came down to his shoulders. His face, always thin, was a little thinner, otherwise unchanged. Later, breaking off his conversation with Hamilton, he came over to sit beside Dorothy and said, 'Good to see you.'

'I like your new clothes,' she said rather drily.

'Nice, aren't they?' he answered easily. 'Comfortable too.'

'I hear you've been all over the place.'

'I lived in Morocco for a bit. But I like moving around.'

'Where else did you go?'

'I went to Goa. Goa was a good place. Then I came back to Morocco but I found too many people in the house, so I went to Ibiza. Ibiza's crazy. They're all out of their minds on acid. I had a great time there. But you're living in Italy I heard.'

220

'Yes, I love it.'

'What about the widower with six children?'

'I think it's too late. I've got too selfish to share.'

'I don't believe that.'

'What about Daphne?'

'She's married to Montague Morgan. I see a lot of them. She's very happy with him. We're all happy. It's good. He's enormously rich and influential and everything she likes.'

'Everything you used to like too.'

'That was before I found acid. I still quite like it every now and then, but when I feel in that mood I can go and stay with them—so it all works out very well.'

'You make everything sound so easy. I won't ask any more questions. Although there are one or two that come to mind.'

'You mustn't tease me. I have only tried to escape the tyranny of the ego. Perhaps you have done that too.'

'I am not ambitious, if that's what you mean. And my needs are few. Like you, I like travelling.'

'Lovers?'

'I had a nice Italian friend. I'm awfully fond of him. But he's quite silly really. I don't see so much of him now as I used to. I'm sometimes afraid I'm getting hard-hearted.'

'It might not be a bad thing. Everyone's so soft-hearted these days. Besides, the truth is whenever one begins to think like that, something happens to make one realise it isn't true. And wish it was.'

She said nothing, thinking that perhaps he had suffered more than he would admit.

'I'm glad you've travelled,' he said. 'Where have you been except for Italy?'

'Greece and Turkey mainly.'

'One's at peace moving—I mean slowly of course—wandering. A sort of primaeval peace. We should never have stopped wandering. We should be hunter-gatherers still. If Cain hadn't killed Abel. . . .'

'But no, it is because we reared up on our hind legs,' interrupted Gerda loudly. 'The mistake was there. On all fours there was a greater volume of blood in the brain.'

'I'm going to bed.' Fisher stood up slowly. 'If you wish

to go around on your hands and knees tomorrow, Gerda, I shall have no objection. I can't promise not to fall over you.'

Ergo moved over to take Fisher's place beside Gerda. 'I'd like to turn you on,' he said looking at her fixedly.

Guy accepted some green tea from Mush—offered on her knees, Dorothy could not help noticing, and with an expression of breathless if slightly stoned admiration—and looked if anything more detached.

'Is that all true?' Dorothy asked him, nodding her head towards Ergo, who was expatiating on the wonders of mind-expanding drugs.

'Oh yes. But evangelism is not my scene.'

Gerda was nodding attentively but looking faintly embarrassed. Hamilton, who had got up as if to leave with Fisher but had lingered behind him, was walking up and down with his overcoat clutched tightly round him and his long scarf trailing down his back. He walked faster and faster, muttering to himself. The muttering became gradually louder.

'The Last Days, that's what it is, the Last Days. The last of the world empires. Now it's the devil's empire and the coming of the millenium. He considered himself one of the elect. You do, don't you?' He gesticulated towards Ergo. 'You think you're the Elect, you think you've received the Holy Spirit, become God. That's why you say the printed word is finished, books are anathema to you. That is how it is written that it should be. You think you will sweep everything away, that everything rightly belongs to you, the Elect. Isn't that true, that you think you have become God?'

'Right,' said Ergo, looking at him without expression.

'This mind at large you talk of,' said Hamilton, beginning to walk up and down again. 'This seeking of frenzy, this mental space walk—you are using all this aren't you? You are using it as a means to make men mad because then you can control them. Do you know what you are unleashing? You are unleashing the untamed evil in man's minds. Strip your minds down, you say, free them from restraint. But freed from restraint what is the human mind? How is the good, deprived of its army, of its weapons of reason, of discipline, of the trained affections of a civilised heart, how is it to triumph over the brute force of the other thing? Tell me that, how is it to triumph? How can it save itself from death by strangulation, from murder?'

'Wow,' said Steve, who was gazing at him in admiration. 'Too much, man.'

Ergo was still looking at Hamilton with an expressionless face, his immobile bulk vaguely threatening. 'Cool it oldie,' he said quietly.

'It's not a joke,' said Hamilton. 'Look at yourself. Free your mind. Blow your mind, if that's the expression you use. And what happens, what do you do? Murder. Rape.'

'This is not necessary,' Guy said to Dorothy. 'Where's Fisher gone?'

'Kill. Rape. Be killed,' said Hamilton.

Timothy laughed nervously. 'Speak for yourself,' he said, with a weak attempt at a joke.

'I do,' said Hamilton. 'I do. That is what I am, what we all are. To kill, to rape, to be killed, all at once, all three at once. To kill, to rape, to be killed.'

Dorothy stood up and walked slowly towards him as if he were a wild animal she was hoping to catch.

'Oh yes it is,' he said, shaking his finger at her. 'That is what the human mind is.' He spoke in the same thick voice and with the same dreadful emphasis with which he had frightened her when as a child she had watched him talking to himself in his workshop. 'Don't you try and tell me otherwise. I know, I tell you. I know.'

Still walking towards him she held out a hand as if to take his arm. He turned and ran, stumbling across the field towards the ruins where his workshop was, his coat and his scarves flapping round him.

Dorothy ran to the house, and upstairs to the room where Marjorie and Arnold slept. She banged on the door, calling for Arnold. Hearing an answer, she went in and saw their two anxious faces turned towards her, side by side on their pillows, the duvet massive over the rest of the bed and the moonlight pouring in through the wide open window. She spoke hurriedly, partly because of what she considered to be the urgency of the situation, and partly because she was embarrassed by a feeling of intimacy with the essence of their joint private life.

'It's Hamilton. He's in a state. He's gone to his workshop but he's over-excited. I think you ought to come.'

Arnold was already out of bed, pulling on his trousers over his pyjamas.

'Wretched people. How dare they upset him?'

Marjorie in her flowered flannel nightdress swung her legs over the side of the bed and reached for her dressing-gown.

'Bring him into the kitchen. I'll put a kettle on.'

Dorothy followed Arnold, running through the ruins to the workshop. Hamilton was sitting in his chair, slanting sideways, and facing the window which looked out onto the moonlit field. He was still wearing his hat and coat. Arnold gently removed the hat and kneeling beside him with one arm round his shoulders stroked his forehead.

'Should I get a doctor?' whispered Dorothy.

She thought he might have had a stroke because his face was distorted and he seemed to be struggling to speak.

Before Arnold could answer, Hamilton said, 'I saw her.' His speech was slurred but his voice more or less normal. 'I saw her,' he said again and the tone of his voice was mild and conversational, amused, a little surprised and, in a certain half-teasing way which was absolutely peculiar to him, childish. The awful urgency and heaviness which had so frightened Dorothy was gone. She realised too that although one side of his face was expressionless the other side, and the eyes, were smiling.

'He wasn't such a fool you see, old Father Augustine,' he said in the same tone of voice.

They only looked at him and at his one-sided smile.

'Not in person,' he said. 'I didn't see her in person exactly. But all her attributes were there. All her glorious attributes were there.'

'Hamilton,' said Arnold quietly. 'Come indoors now.'

But Hamilton's gaze was fixed on Dorothy.

'Tell my mother,' he said, but not as if it was of great

importance, 'that I held him down until they came for him and that it was all right.'

'I'll tell her.'

Dorothy went out of the workshop and across to the house to telephone for a doctor.

'Wasn't that nice, Arnold?' said Hamilton. 'Seeing her like that.'

After that he was quiet and seemed ready to sleep. Later they carried him back to the house and put him to bed. He died without waking, of a second stroke.

It was the dark time of the year, a good time to die, Fisher thought. Now that Hamilton had done it, it seemed easy. In those dark weeks before the winter solstice, when the days were brief and grey between darkness and darkness, when there were mild damp silent afternoons on which the occasional sudden sunlight on the wet slopes of the Plain was like a revelation, or when the grey of the sky was so steely it was almost green and the distant bare-branched woods almost brown, the colour of a mouse; in that sodden and regenerative season it seemed easy for an old man to die. He still walked, most afternoons, with the three dogs—the same collie-Labrador strain they had always had at the Abbey—restless brutes, Fisher called them, selfish too, they took his chair and ate food from the kitchen table with shameless over-confidence— nevertheless he took them for a walk most afternoons and they came when he called them even when they were on the track of a rabbit, though in the latter case less immediately, and it was nobody's fault so much as his own that they were spoilt.

Being old, he thought often of the earlier part of his life. The stories which he and Hamilton and their mother had invented years ago and which she had illustrated were by his bed in the edition which the Abbey Press had produced as one of its first enterprises and which had been reprinted many times since. He sometimes thought of doing some more and finding an illustrator to do some drawings for them. For some reason this idea interested him more than the forthcoming publication of his book on the theory of the perfectibility of

225

man, finally finished, revised and corrected in proof—perhaps because there was no one left among possible reviewers whose opinion he cared to know.

'The best time of the day for me is bed-time,' he said to Timothy. 'I like the whole business of it, filling my hot-water bottle, getting everything I need beside me, winding my watch, setting the alarm, settling the pillows, the book I'm reading, the wireless, clean sheets—that's what's important when you're an old man.'

'I wish I were older in that case,' said Timothy. 'I hate going to bed. It's the time I really start to worry.'

'You worry too much. The teaching's going all right, isn't it, and the book?'

'The book's awful. I've never written a novel before and I don't think I'm any good at it. I don't like the people enough. I can put them in their places and assign them their roles—I know what they're meant to prove—but when they begin to do anything it shows too much that I don't really care for them. Except for the girl and I care for her too much.'

'Perhaps you should forget what they're meant to prove.'

'Then there's no point in it. I don't want to write stories.'

'I thought that's what novels were.'

'Not ordinary stories. Fairy stories, dreams, the other language of one's deepest preoccupations. And not, oh not, self-expression. I hate that word. That's what those students I went to lecture thought they were doing, expressing themselves. They think they've nothing to learn from outside and it's all in themselves. They won't read, they've never heard of any writers, except a few nonsense poets who read aloud to them. Their imaginations are totally impoverished, starving, because they won't feed them. It's almost as if they daren't feed them, they're such conformists, such intellectual cowards. I hated that experience. But the teaching, no, that's all right. I like my schoolboys, the rot hasn't set in with them yet. I'm even beginning to teach them quite well I believe. I never thought I'd be a good teacher. It's talking to Mary that's helped, I think. I never liked young people before.'

'Don't worry about her. She'll come back.'

'Why should she? Why should she ever come back?'

226

'She hasn't quarrelled with her parents?'

'But they mean nothing to her now. And the hippies will never come back. They think we blame them for Hamilton's death.'

'I should be sorry if I thought that was true. I didn't care for the fat American I admit. But I shall be surprised if we never see Guy Thornton again. He has a way of reappearing.'

'I don't understand Guy Thornton. Is he a fraud really?'

'A bit of a fraud, I'd say,' said Fisher. 'But mostly, you know, he's just a pleasant friendly fellow. I find him most understanding and humorous, there's no one I'd rather talk to. He loves ideas but he can't really take them seriously. As far as he's concerned, almost everything's a little bit true— it's the corollary, to his way of thinking, of the fact that nothing's absolutely true. He wanted to be a dashing young Guards officer, a bit of a cad—that was what he was trying to be when he first came here, in the war. He'd picked up a good deal of phoney snobbery somewhere in his youth. He wanted to make money and cut a dash in London Society—he didn't mind being a minor criminal on the way—even now I'd say he'd think of moral values as being pretty relative. Yet no one could have been nicer or more helpful than he was to young Joe over that whole episode.'

'I remember that.'

'Then he was ditched by his wife for that millionaire fellow. Does he bear a grudge? Not a bit of it. They're all on the best of terms. The millionaire lets him have a cheque when things are bad. He's no pride you see.'

'But what about this mystic bit?'

'Oh he's got a touch of that. It's just there, in spite of himself. It's to do with that detached way he has of looking at things, which you might expect to be cold but is somehow the opposite, all bright awareness and sympathy—he can't help that, he just has it. It doesn't stop him being a fool, picking up notions in a superficial sort of way until the fashion changes, being hopeless over money. . . .'

'I know he was completely cheated over the house in Morocco. Elsa told me that.'

'Of course he was. And wandered off round the world with-

out a penny, always friendly, always interested, always expecting the big deal that's going to make his fortune and really
set him up for life. He's had some bad moments, I daresay.
And now he's there in Wales for a bit in his footloose sort
of way—it suits him well enough, he's a gregarious fellow,
people come and go a lot up there. I like him. There's no one
I'd rather see walking through the door.'

'Well all right then, he may come back. But Mary's with
Steve. Wretched boy. I think they're wretched people, all of
them. Why did we welcome them so in the first place?'

'Because they seemed happy, I suppose.' Fisher smiled. 'I
remember you dancing about like a young lamb.'

Timothy groaned. 'Old mutton.'

'No really,' said Fisher. 'I still think it was good, that first
hippy impulse. Funny and mad. It wasn't their fault that
it all turned out to be much more difficult than they thought,
and that it wasn't part of the mystique to say no to looney
bedfellows. I really believe it's had an effect, all that, it's
made a point. Our children don't want to live by bread alone
and take it as an insult when cynical politicians assume they
do. This will make its mark, of course it will.'

'You're always optimistic,' said Timothy.

It was not Fisher who was the next to die. Jane Ridley had
dropped the eleven-year-old Francis at school, done some shopping and was driving back to the Abbey when a long distance
lorry driver who had, it was later proved, far exceeded the
number of hours he was legally allowed to travel without
rest, failed to react quickly enough—or possibly failed to
react at all—as she turned out of a side road in front of him.
Her small car was wrecked and she herself killed instantly.
The unexpectedness of the tragedy and the existence of the
one so much loved child made it particularly distressing.

'We've felt so inadequate,' Timothy wrote to Dorothy, back
in Florence. 'We tried to close round Peter and the boy like
a sort of poultice to stop the blood running to the wound
but of course we couldn't. I think we helped, by being there
—as you said once, all anyone can do for anyone—and of
course they were marvellous, as people usually are in these

228

circumstances—the boy so brave and understanding and so eager to co-operate in his cure, like a good little creature with the measles—it is perfectly heart-rending. Peter, apart from looking after Francis, buries himself in work. There's a lot to be done at the Press. Jane did a great deal of it. She was so quiet, so extraordinarily private, I don't think anyone except Peter realised how much she did do. He's going to need more help. When are you coming back?'

But Dorothy was deferring coming back. Her mother had mentioned in a letter that she was having some trouble with arthritis in her hip. Nanny was very old by now, and unlikely to be much help if the condition worsened. The Lamberts were still constant companions and there were other neighbouring friends; nevertheless Dorothy felt that the next time she came to England she might have to stay. She put off her return as long as possible. Sometimes this made her feel ashamed, not because she might have been neglecting her mother, but because she had a suspicion that the life she was living was for the time being so satisfactory partly because it was not quite real. She had in Florence by now a certain character which, though she was quite pleased with it, was an artificial one, corresponding not quite exactly with her true character. In some moods it seemed to her a good thing that her self should be thus self-created, chosen; but at other times there seemed an element of pretence which did not please her. This cultured English lady, well-read, widely travelled, a little mysterious, a little reserved, yet capable of being a stimulating companion—she quite charmed the French ambassador at the Maggio Musicale—always in demand when the British Consul gave a dinner or the expatriate smart set a lunch in one of their beautiful villas on the way to Fiesole; known too in her own little piece of the Oltr-Arno—she had a flat at the top of a neglected palazzo near Santo Spirito—known as a discerning customer when she went to do her marketing and a lover of Florence who had worked hard to bring relief to the flood victims in the winter of 1967 (and rescue to the sodden books floating outside the Biblioteca Nazionale)—but all this, and the good shoes and the shiny little Fiat, while it was amusing, felt still at times like a game. One day she would have to go

H*

back, and put on her gumboots and her old coat and walk through the rain to the Abbey, or up on to the Plain with the dogs. It did not horrify her, this prospect, but at the same time she could not blame herself for deferring its actualisation.

Timothy wrote to her, 'There is a man here doing a television interview with Fisher. It's to be one of a series on unfashionable thinkers. It's taking days. The interviewer is a terribly intelligent young man, a serious Marxist and a great believer in the importance of the media. He is also quite vain, being handsome and a good television performer. He exists on a different plane from his producer, an earthier creature altogether, and despises the camera crew whom he bewilders with his technical expertise, which far exceeds their own. He in his turn is equally bewildered by Fisher, who is hamming it up disgracefully, alternately whimsical and contentious, retreating when threatened into a maze of irrelevant but impressive learning, and when questioned going into an outrageous caricature of senility. It is perfectly clear that the interview will in the end consist of Fisher saying exactly what he wants to say, and no more or less.

'Mary has reappeared. She came alone and stayed two days with her parents. She didn't say much, but seemed all right. She said she wanted to bring some friends to stay in the guest house. Pat was delighted that she had come, Tom a little sore after she had gone because he was afraid that she had only come in order to make the arrangement about the friends and not in order to see her parents. I don't know. I had a long conversation with her about Steve. I said perhaps they'd get married one day. She looked shocked. "What's the point of marrying unless you want children?" "Don't you?" Even more shocked. "Never. There's too many people in the world as it is." I tried to say that I didn't think he was worthy of her, at least I said none of them was, I said they weren't serious people in the sense that she was. But she wouldn't have that. Then I got her to admit that Steve was still taking heroin and I went so far as to beg her to leave him—rather melodramatically I said she could only watch him die, etc. But only that straight look—"He do need me"—like someone out of Thomas Hardy. Really I do get cross with her.

'Anyway she brought him back with her later. He looks pretty ill. I can't make out who the others are. "They're into politics," she said when I asked her. But when I asked her what politics she said "International politics," which didn't get one much further. Anyway there's a perfectly marvellous woman with them, about eight feet high with vast bosoms in an incredibly tight Che Guevara tee shirt. She has a bottom like a man's—in jeans, also incredibly tight—and cowboy boots. She pays more attention to Mary than the hippies ever did and I think is a good influence on her—she makes her talk more—I think she used to be a friend of Ergo's but he seems mercifully to have disappeared these days. She's unbelievably friendly and we all rather like her although she's quite alarming and terribly frank.'

Dorothy came back in the summer of 1970. Her mother had had an arthritic hip for some time now and it had been decided that she should have an operation to give her an artificial hip-joint, after which it might take her a little time to learn to walk again. Dorothy gave up her job in Florence, but not her flat. She let that to an American for six months, hoping to be able to come back.

All that summer she worked at the Abbey Press. When there was not much to do there and when her mother did not need her she walked on the Plain, often with the boy Francis.

The Abbey was very peaceful that summer. The tempo of its life seemed to have slowed down to keep pace with that of its founders, the two surviving brothers. Fisher was in a benign frame of mind. The publication of his book and the subsequent television interview had brought about a mild revival of interest in his ideas, and he was at work on a series of articles to follow it up. Arnold had been slowed down by a persistent troublesome cough, and he and Marjorie often sat side by side in deck chairs in the sun, with rugs over their knees, she knitting, he dozing, like passengers on a cruise. Timothy was working on his novel and would emerge for meals, rumpling his hair and saying, 'I don't know, I don't know.' Mary had gone abroad with Steve and the huge woman, whose name was Marilyn Skinner.

'They're going all over the place, North Africa mainly I think,' said Timothy. 'That must be good for her, mustn't it?'

'What does she do, Marilyn Skinner?' Dorothy asked. 'Is she a student?'

'No, she's older than that. She teaches teachers at a polytechnic. Although she doesn't approve of teachers, so I'm not quite sure what she teaches them.'

Guy Thornton came to spend a couple of nights on his way somewhere, his movements as ever mysterious. His appearance had changed slightly since Dorothy had last seen him, the hair a little shorter, the robes abandoned for more ordinary jeans, sometimes a conventional tweed jacket and a knitted pullover or even a grey flannel suit, slightly short in the trouser as if he were growing out of something he had worn as a schoolboy. The effect was mildly donnish, symbolising perhaps a change of emphasis from hippy to scholarly recluse, for he claimed to see no one in his remote Welsh farmhouse and to spend most of his time reading. Dorothy asked him whether he still took LSD, but he said he had more or less given it up; it was hard to get and anyway he thought it was impairing his memory. He wanted to get more land and farm properly, and wondered if anyone at the Abbey could think of a partner for him with some capital. He said that his neighbours in Wales were mostly lotus eaters who smoked and gazed at the beautiful scenery and did not mend their roofs—he wanted sheep, he said. 'I'm taking it all very seriously. It's time I settled down. I'm sure I can make it pay.'

Arnold, delighted, loaded him with books and pamphlets and the benefit of years of experience: he promised that he and Marjorie would go up there one day to discuss the project in detail.

Fisher was bored by all this practical conversation. He wanted to talk to Guy about less mundane matters. Dorothy was amused to notice how good with them both Guy was: she recognised that he was also good with her, knowing what it would interest her to talk about, flattering her by the amount of attention he gave to her opinion, flattering her too by occasionally paying her some rather old-fashioned compliment, about her looks or her clothes, an echo of a much earlier Guy, assorting oddly with the present one, and for that reason, because of the incongruity, rather endearing. She was reconciled to being never quite sure about him, never knowing whether he meant what he said, or thought he meant what he said, or neither; whether his detachment was real or assumed, his irony genuine or defensive, his apparent insights his own or borrowed from his interlocutor by some sleight of hand resulting from a rare sensitivity guided by an equally refined cunning. It no longer seemed to matter. This left her free to recognise in him something, some vein of fantasy perhaps, which made her feel extraordinarily at ease with him, and at the same time extraordinarily alert. She noticed that his presence seemed to have the same effect on Fisher.

She walked by the river with the boy Francis. Hearing two short whistling calls he said, 'There's the kingfisher.'

They waited. The bird skimmed low over the water, a flash of blue.

'Sometimes his mate comes now,' said Francis.

After a minute or two another flash sped past them.

Francis smiled. 'Like to see the nest?'

He knew it all, the round hole in the bank with the droppings and fish bones below it, and the water vole's hole opposite and the moorhen's nest further along the river. He knew the country for miles around in this way. Walking with him was an introduction to the familiar spirits of the place who might or might not manifest themselves on any particular occasion. When they did it seemed like a sign. The best sightings came only with him; he was the mediator.

He would not subscribe to her fanciful way of looking at things. He was a serious naturalist and kept notebooks in which everything was methodically written down, with date, time, weather and place. He had kept these books for years and when he showed her the earlier ones he apologised for the spelling—'I was rather young,' he said—in fact the spelling in the later ones was not very good either.

He knew where the grey wagtails were and the dipper. She

233

had taken him to a reservoir to see the wildfowl and they had checked their observations with his reference books. On the way back to the car they heard a high squeaking in the long grass. A family of young weasels was hurrying from a fallen branch into the hedge, sleek little brown animals with white fronts. One of them stayed by the branch, his front paws resting on it, staring at them, his curiosity overcoming his insufficiently developed fear. A tremendous scolding came from the hedge behind him until he turned and ran towards it.

Francis fished in the reservoir sometimes, standing on the bank, casting with what looked to Dorothy like professional expertise.

'Isn't it boring if you don't catch anything?' she asked him.

'Oh no, that isn't the point at all. Of course you've got to think you're going to.'

'Have you ever caught anything?'

'Nothing big enough to keep.'

He laughed, showing his white teeth. It was extraordinary that two such frail beings as his parents should have produced a boy whose health was so remarkable as to constitute almost an extra attribute, a sort of faint refulgence surrounding him. She supposed his health might account for his serenity of temperament. She knew no other children of that age, and could only compare him with what she remembered of herself. She had been less competent and less confident, a more complex child perhaps; but the interesting thing about Francis's simplicity was that he gave the impression of having chosen it rather than having been born with it. His inclination seemed always in the direction of reconciliation, of everything being only another way of saying the same thing. It was only as she came to know him better that she began to see how much of this came from his mother.

'My mother told me,' was nearly always the answer to her surprised query as to how he knew something he had just told her. It applied to much of the natural history and to many of the odd pieces of general knowledge as well as to the occasional moral pronouncement. It seemed that Jane Ridley, who had appeared so nebulous and pale—though always pleasant, never foolish—had been much more than that. Sometimes it even seemed to Dorothy that she must have known she was going to die young, so determined did she appear to have been to tell her son everything she knew before she died.

Dorothy tried to talk about Francis to Peter, but he only said, 'It's nice that you've made friends.' Dorothy liked Peter but found him rather unimaginative. He fussed about getting orders out on time and about his health. She supposed Jane had looked after that as well. When she tried to say to him that she thought his son was really rather remarkable he only said, 'Yes, he's nice, isn't he? Nice and normal.' Marjorie said that too. 'Such a nice boy, so normal.' Perhaps that was what normality was.

He told her he had had his appendix out. They had been to Bath, doing some shopping for the Abbey, and had stopped to take the dogs for a walk on a hill overlooking the town and the valley of the Avon.

'It must have been so beautiful a hundred and fifty years ago, before the development,' said Dorothy.

'I'd be dead if it was then,' he said. 'Before anaesthetics.' And he told her about his appendix. It had been three days before Christmas, he said, but they'd let him out of hospital for Christmas Day.

'I must do something, mustn't I?' he said, 'I mean, for the good of the world.'

'I'm sure you will.'

But he was crouching down to pick up a hairy caterpillar.

'Beautiful?'

'No,' she said.

'Haven't you got a matchbox?'

She found him an old envelope. She could at no stage have thus avowed it but she had been ambitious once too, for nothing specific, just some sort of glory. She had been aware of this in him before, though it had shown itself only in a certain responsive gleam. It was as if there were stored right at the back of his mind something which occasionally flashed across his consciousness like a memory, a clash of lances, shouts, a little hill, a tattered flag.

Mary came back after the summer. With her were Marilyn

Skinner, Marilyn's bearded lover Gardner Leach, and two fair girls with stringy hair from Northern Ireland, Cilla and Nina, Marilyn's acolytes. Steve was not with them. He had left them halfway through the summer and gone back to Wales and Mush.

'It seems he missed her more than he thought he would,' Mary told Timothy. That was all she said about it.

'I don't know how you can go on,' said Marilyn, clattering saucepans about in the sink. 'I mean, everyone knows the realistic novel is dead.'

She seemed to enjoy cleaning saucepans, scrubbing away with a Brillo pad so that the muscles showed in her strong arms, still brown from the North African sun.

'Of course it is,' said Timothy, picking up one of the saucepans from the draining board and flapping at it feebly with a cloth.

He was so much in awe of Marilyn's physique that he tended to agree at once with whatever she said, though as often as not on second thoughts he cautiously questioned it, as now.

'Why is it dead?'

'Well, reality's dead isn't it?'

'Of course it is.'

He put the saucepan into the cupboard in a semi-dry condition and said, 'You mean, because of relativity and so on?'

'Right.'

'No independent world of facts?'

'Right. Only interpretations. Determined or preconceptions.'

'You see what you expect to see. That's how our eyes work, they have to. If you didn't expect something you would see chaos.'

'Who's afraid of chaos?'

'I am. Anyway, why can't we work to hypotheses, like scientists?'

'What scientists?'

'You mean there aren't any scientists either?'

'Of course there are scientists. But independent science is a myth. It's all political.'

'Oh yes.' Timothy bent down to put another saucepan into the cupboard. 'So it is.' He fitted the saucepan carefully into the one he had previously put there. Since both were still damp somebody was going to have a bad time later trying to separate them. 'The trouble is, it's the only thing I know how to do, write. I don't really know how to do that as a matter of fact. And since I know that what you say about the novel is true— more or less true anyway—I find it very difficult. I can't write the thing straight. I haven't the confidence. I have to keep stopping and starting and jumping about and putting in defensive little clever bits so that an ordinary reader can't tell what's going on most of the time. I sometimes wonder whether there might be someone tucked away somewhere very remote who hasn't heard about reality being dead and truth being a lie. They might be quietly writing big fat old-fashioned novels about character and morals and so on without knowing that that's all over.'

'But why should anyone ever want to read them?'

'To find a humanity that speaks to theirs.'

'Cosy reassurance maybe. What's this? Sentimentality Sunday?'

'I admire your confidence more than anything, I really do. Where did you learn it?'

'In the front line of the battle between the sexes, boyo.'

'You can't call me boyo, that's ridiculous. Even if all your best friends are in the IRA. Thank goodness there weren't any girls like you at Cambridge when I was there. I bet you frightened all the men out of their wits.'

Marilyn frowned, squeezing out a dishcloth. 'I don't know what you mean,' she said, obviously offended.

'Being so much cleverer than them,' he said quickly. 'Firsts and things, that's all I meant.'

'Some of the boys took firsts too,' she said, not yet mollified.

'I think you're wasting your talents, you know,' said Timothy. 'I mean the sort of students you're teaching aren't good enough for you.' He said this because he was trying to please her, but when he had said it he realised that he meant it. He also realised that if she knew that he was trying to make up for having hurt her feelings by flattering her, she would despise him, and that he might therefore just as well give up the attempt and follow his own train of thought.

237

'The people who go to teacher training colleges are usually the ones who were too stupid to get into universities. Unless they're post-graduates, and yours aren't, are they? So you see you're really wasted on them. Also they aren't clever enough to see you don't mean half of what you say, so it probably worries them to death when you tell them schools ought to be abolished because they're only propping up the capitalist system and they ought to go in there and teach the children revolution rather than the alphabet. I mean you ought to be teaching this to clever people who'd enjoy it rather than stupid people who might take it literally.'

Marilyn had stopped wiping round the sink and was staring at him, the dishcloth in her hand.

'Are you out of your mind?' she said slowly.

'Yes,' said Timothy at once.

'Do you know what you're saying?'

'No. I didn't mean it.'

'My students are not stupid,' said Marilyn, speaking very quietly. 'They may be educationally underprivileged, but they have a valid knowledge of real life which means that they are ready to identify with the oppressed and exploited everywhere. These are the people I want to reach. As for not being serious, do you know where we spent this summer?'

She walked slowly towards him.

'I didn't mean you weren't serious, I really didn't,' said Timothy, backing. 'I just meant that your approach obviously, being an intellectual one, was not exactly meant to be taken in every respect as an absolutely literal guide to practical action. Do stop looking so fierce.'

'Do you know where we spent last summer?'

'No. I mean, yes. North Africa.'

'Right. Libya. And what happens in Libya?'

'I don't know.'

'We spent the summer training with the Palestinian guerillas. Is that, or is that not, serious?'

'But training for what?'

'Direct action. We were with the Irish freedom fighters.'

'You took Mary?'

'Of course we took Mary.'

238

'But why? You're not going to Ireland or something are you?'

'We can't just stand aside. We must be politically involved. We must identify ourselves with the struggle against British imperialism in Ireland, against the attack on tenants by landlords, against the assault on the working class by capitalism, we must provoke the violence inherent in democratic institutions in order to expose it. Otherwise how can we call ourselves radicals?'

'Yes but listen, Marilyn. You don't really mean this. How can you? There's no need to behave like that, there are perfectly possible channels by which one can get change in a society like ours without having to resort to violence. You know there are. I mean if you're patient and determined and so on. You aren't serious, Marilyn, you can't be. You're much too nice.'

She suddenly yelled, 'Will you stop being so fucking patronising?' She seized a plate rack on which a dozen or so plates were drying. Holding it high above her head she said, 'Will you get it into your head that I am not nice?'

With a tremendous crash she smashed the plate rack with its contents onto the floor, rushed from the room and banged the door behind her. He heard her running across the courtyard. Trembling slightly, he began to search through the kitchen cupboards for a dustpan and brush.

There was still a meeting every month at the Abbey, theoretically to decide on farm policy but in fact to raise any subject which anyone felt should be generally discussed. Often it consisted only of Arnold and Marjorie and Tom and Pat Boulder. The younger couple had more or less taken over from the older as farm managers, an arrangement which was so successful that there was rarely any need for anyone else to enter into the discussions, though Gerda would sometimes attend the meetings to watch over the interests of the vegetable garden, which had become her special province. When there was a particular matter which someone wanted to raise, advance warning was usually circulated.

After Timothy's stormy conversation with Marilyn Skinner, he had told everyone that he wanted to discuss the matter of

239

her and her friends' continued presence at the Abbey, and by common consent he had also asked Marcie and Dorothy, who had through long association both become unofficial external members of the community, to come to the meeting. Marcie was still financially involved and she also had various agricultural connections, in that certain machines were shared and the work force pooled at times of extra pressure. She brought Ralph Blatchford with her to the meeting, because he happened to be staying with her and was an old friend to the community. Noel never came to the Abbey now. He referred to it as 'one of Marcie's artistic charities' which was a convenient though hardly accurate description: as it happened the Abbey had never had much connection with the visual arts.

Timothy told the meeting about his conversation with Marilyn, and said that he thought she and her friends should be asked to leave. In fact, since he had thought of nothing else during the few days which had passed since the conversation, he had already told everyone about it separately—apart from Marcie and Ralph Blatchford whom he had not happened to see—and he hoped that he had persuaded most of them that he was right. Peter Ridley indeed had been so shocked that he had suggested that they should inform the police. Fisher, on the other hand, to Timothy's disappointment, seemed almost indifferent, certainly far from shocked.

'I suppose they should go,' he said. 'I suppose so. If everyone feels so strongly about it.'

He settled back into his chair and reached out for his book, as if to imply that the days when he could feel strongly about anything were long over, that he was an old man who ought not to be bothered about unpleasant matters. Yet Timothy knew that although he had acquired a useful little trick of affecting senility at convenient times—a trick Timothy had often enjoyed seeing brought into play—he was as capable as ever of the firmest of convictions, the most lapidary of summings-up.

'It does matter,' said Timothy. 'You do see that, don't you?'

Fisher mumbled vaguely, turning over a page of the book he held.

'You do see it's important not to let people like that take
240

over? They would, you see. They're so determined, and so sure they're right. They'd take over the whole Abbey if we'd let them.'

Fisher shifted slightly in his chair.

'People talk,' he said. 'They don't always mean it.'

Timothy had tried to persuade him that in this case they did mean it, but he was not sure how well he had succeeded. At the meeting, however, it emerged that both Gerda and Pat Boulder thought that Marilyn and her group should be allowed to stay. Pat was afraid that if they went Mary would go with them and be led into further dangers; Gerda thought they might be right in what they were doing.

'How do we know?' she said. 'We are old now and out of touch. Perhaps the necessities have changed. The younger ones among us are Dorothy and Peter. Neither is interested in politics. Dorothy has been living out of England. Peter has a conservative temperament.'

'But none of us has ever been in favour of violent politics, Gerda,' said Arnold. 'Some of us were pacifists in the last war, Fisher and I were pacifists in the First War, and as for terrorism. . . .'

'We fought in Spain,' said Gerda, identifying herself for the first time in years with her ex-husband.

'Those were wars,' said Timothy. 'This is different.'

'We don't know enough about it,' said Gerda obstinately. 'For instance, I asked Marilyn why she was no longer a friend of the American Ergo, and do you know what she said? She said he had given himself entirely to the Ecology Movement and this had led them to quarrel because she knew that the Ecology Movement was being subsidised by the C.I.A. to divert young people from radical international politics. And just as I was thinking how far-fetched, what a joke, I thought, no, how do I know this is not true?'

'I think it's very likely to be true,' said Ralph Blatchford in his soft earnest voice. White-haired now, but still with bright dark eyes, his lean face reflected a lifetime's unfaltering sincerity. 'I agree with Gerda. I think it would be a tragedy if they were asked to leave. I think it would be the end of the Abbey in fact. Nobody who wanted to change the world has ever been asked

241

to leave the Abbey. Such a thing would be false to everything it stands for.'

'But they're would-be murderers,' said Timothy. 'Pat, Mary will stay with us. She must. Now that there's no Steve to hold her there, why should she choose to stay with them? We'll show her how much we need her here. We'll make her feel that, I know we can.'

They voted, with some solemnity. Pat gave in and voted with the majority. Only Gerda and Ralph Blatchford voted against.

Peter Ridley volunteered to fetch Marilyn. She came in at the head of her group, the two pale girls, Gardner Leach and Mary.

Fisher said, 'My dear, I am so sorry but I am afraid we are going to ask you and your friends to leave. We like you but we do not like your views.'

'Why?' said Marilyn. She did not look surprised. Having known of the meeting, she had probably guessed as to its outcome.

'We find you a bit too intolerant for us,' said Fisher in the same benign tone of voice, very slightly exaggerating in it a faint old man's tremor. 'And we can't help thinking that you are teaching the young to despair. These are things which we don't like very much, and so we feel our community cannot embrace people who practise them.'

'The politics of despair is a very different thing from the personal despair of an oppressed being without hope.'

Fisher sighed. 'But you hold out no hope,' he said sadly. 'You say that everything that exists in the present scheme of things is wrong, disordered, evil, but you can't point to any system which is different. You only say destroy and then let's see what happens. But this is a doctrine which can only be tenable in a state of affairs far more desperate than anything we have here.' His voice strengthened, as if the sound of it had started the flow of thought. 'You call yourself radical, but you have no roots in any actual conflict, you know. In fact, I rather suspect that you envy those who do have such roots in conflict—your Palestinians or whoever it may be—just as in our youth some of us used to envy the genuine unemployed working classes.'

242

He smiled at her. 'You must remember that we are old, most of us. I was deciding that I didn't care for the "propaganda of the deed" before the First World War. Even Timothy, who seems young to me, was a member of the Communist Party in the 1930s. He believed he had found an alternative worth working for, he believed Russian Communism was working. But you don't believe that any more, you believe only in destruction. You may think of something, some new development of Communism perhaps. But I think we're too old to see it. It doesn't mean we don't like you—we do. You may go on, with all your energy and intelligence and ferocity, and lead your generation somewhere. We may all be proud to have known you. But we can't join you, and we don't want you to join us. You may even find that our particular notions may be the next to come into fashion—it may well be—it's about the only thing left that hasn't been tried. You may get a disillusionment with political systems, a turning away from the vaster ideologies, an attempt at particular solutions to particular problems, new autonomies, decentralisation—but if it happens I'll tell you something, in fact I'll tell you two things—one, we'll never say it's the one and only orthodoxy and all else is heresy and must be persecuted, and two, we ourselves, we here, as like as not, we shan't even like it.' He laughed, as if the prospect pleased him. 'We'll complain like anything. We won't like our new friends, we won't think they've got the message right, none of it will be really what we meant. But then you see there'll be somebody somewhere who goes on trying to get what we did want, knowing what we did mean. You have to believe in the possibility of human goodness. It does exist and it is the light by which we live. It's that possibility which we believe that you exclude.'

Marilyn had listened attentively, her head bent. The two girls behind her looked blank, Mary embarrassed, Gardner Leach angry.

'You have become reactionary,' said Marilyn, raising her head and looking at Fisher. 'We are your heirs and you don't recognise us.'

He shook his head.

'We believe we have other heirs.'

Timothy was staring at his feet. His sandals and socks suddenly blurred—he had been in an emotional state for days. Fisher had done it, he thought, his heart already expanding at the idea of those other heirs, though goodness only knew where they were. Fisher had come through.

Marilyn and her followers were moving towards the door.

'If we leave,' she said, 'the house we're living in now will become wasted living space. Wasted living space is a crime. We won't submit to landlordism. We shan't leave.'

She spoke without defiance, even rather sadly; and led her followers from the room.

Dorothy and Francis walked on the Plain.

'Everyone at the Abbey is in a filthy mood,' he said.

'It is horrid for them. No one thought of the possibility that they might not go when they were asked to.'

'Daddy thinks we should send for the police, but no one agrees with him. Fisher says lawyers cost too much and you have to do all the work yourself anyway. And anyway he says it's all right to ask them to leave but not to force them to leave. But he's terribly depressed. He's started making those awful groaning noises like Hamilton used to make. What do you think ought to be done?'

'I don't know. It's different for me because I never got to know any of them. Most people seem to like Marilyn—or did before this happened. I never got to know her, but I don't think I would have liked her as much as they did. They all said she was so friendly, but I thought it was just that she was completely insensitive to any notion of privacy which is not the same thing at all. Perhaps they'll just go. It can't be very nice for them.'

'I expect they will. What I thought was, in the meantime'— he looked at her questioningly—'the geese should have arrived, don't you think?'

'Oh the reservoir, yes, let's go.'

'That would be lovely,' he said politely. 'There should be lots of ducks there.'

'You didn't mean that I suppose. I suppose you meant Slimbridge. It's miles.'

'Yes it is, it's much too far isn't it?'

'Much too far. I mean it. Why don't you believe me?'

'I do believe you. I believe you utterly. It's just that I had thought that if you had wanted to we could have gone on Saturday. My father's got a lot of binding to do and he'd be awfully glad to have me out of the way.'

Mary was in her parents' cottage, collecting her few remaining belongings from the bedroom which used to be hers but which she had used very little over the last five years. Timothy watched her from the doorway.

'It's embarrassing,' she said. 'I can't stay while it's going on. I'm going up to Wales. I can stay with Steve for a bit.'

'Is Mush still there?'

'Yes,' she said indifferently.

'Is he all right?'

'I think so.'

'You're too loyal. I think that's what it is. You've transferred your loyalty from Steve to Marilyn. You have to have someone to be loyal to.'

She looked at him directly.

'I haven't transferred anything from Steve. And Marilyn's right, that's all.'

'You ought to have had a husband and children to be loyal to.'

Mary giggled.

'Don't let them hear you say that. I don't know what they'd do to you.'

'I don't care. Isn't there some man you'd marry, Mary?'

'Course not. I told you that.'

'I'd marry you myself if you would. I would, Mary, I mean it. I've always loved you. Odder marriages do happen. We could live anywhere you like. I'd leave here. I know I'm much too old for you but perhaps you'd see that marriage wasn't so bad after all and then you could marry someone more suitable after I died.'

'Hey, come on.' She put her hands on his shoulders and looked into his face with her dark uncompromising eyes. 'I appreciate your saying that, I do really. I've given everything

245

to the fight for freedom now. I'm under orders, see, to Marilyn. But I really like you, Timothy, you know that.'

'It might work, Mary,' he said, beginning to tremble.

She shook her head, smiling. 'You wouldn't like it. You'd find it ever so hard.'

She turned to pick up her bundle from the chest of drawers and then passed him in the doorway and began to go downstairs. Halfway down she turned back and putting her hands on his shoulders again kissed him warmly on both cheeks.

He followed her downstairs. She went out into the courtyard. He turned into the kitchen where Pat was stirring something on the stove, with the wireless on rather loud.

'You haven't a cup of tea, I suppose, have you?' he asked her.

He sat down at the table and put his head in his hands.

A week later Guy Thornton rang up from Wales. Arnold answered the telephone, and Guy told him that Mary had spent a few days with Steve and Mush in their house not far from his own and that she had found Steve in a very bad way again. Possibly she had taken some drugs too. Steve and Mush were not clear on this point. They said that towards the end of her stay she had become very upset, had talked incoherently about over-population and revolution and had walked out one evening saying that she must go back to Marilyn but leaving her few belongings behind her. Twenty-four hours later she had stolen a can of petrol from a farm two miles away, walked a little distance up the hill, poured petrol over herself, and lit a match. No one knew where she had been during the twenty-four hours between leaving Steve's house and burning herself to death.

'Ralph was right when he said it would be the end of the Abbey if they were asked to leave,' said Dorothy. 'It was.'

She was sitting with Guy Thornton in front of the fire in the library. Fisher's desk was untidily covered with his papers and notebooks, but he himself was in bed with bronchitis in the next room.

'Was it because of that that Mary killed herself?'

'No one knows. But I don't suppose it helped. Marjorie thinks it was entirely because she was in love with Steve and couldn't bear to be rejected by him and then to see him killing himself with drugs. Her father thinks it was because she really believed the world was too bad to live in and she's heard too much about people killing themselves in that way as a protest. He says she was a very matter-of-fact person who always thought you should do what seemed logical however inconvenient. He also says she had no physical fear. Poor Pat won't even guess as to why. She's just horrified. I think she has an awful feeling that Mary might go to Hell. Everyone else is just mystified.'

'Even Timothy?'

'He asked her to marry him, did you know? Before she left. He told me that if he hadn't done that, he'd never have been able to forgive himself. He's going to leave. He's going to live in London and teach at an enormous comprehensive school.'

'Good Heavens. He won't like that, will he?'

'He's a good teacher, you know. He thinks they're going to be tremendously violent and wave knives at him in the classroom and so on because he's read about that sort of thing in the papers. He rather wants that because he wants to sacrifice himself for Mary's sake by trying to give young people hope and enthusiasm and develop their critical faculties, but the fact is that if anyone has any sense he'll be teaching the older children who want to learn, like the A-Level classes he's done so well with down here, and then he might be very happy.'

'But he's been here all his life hasn't he?'

'Most of it. Now he's going out into the world for the first time, in his late-ish fifties, for love of Mary. And if you dare laugh. . . .'

'Of course I won't laugh.'

Marilyn and her friends left the Abbey as soon as they heard the news about Mary. Marilyn left a letter for Pat Boulder which Pat refused to read. It said that they were all sorry about Mary's death and that they were leaving because they did not want to add to the sadness which they knew everybody at the Abbey would be feeling. Tom Boulder felt bitter because she had made no reference to her own possible part in Mary's death, but as Fisher said no one really knew what had been in Mary's mind in those last twenty-four hours before she died.

Fisher and Arnold made their wills that winter. Most of the Abbey property still in effect belonged to them. There was a trust, but they had the controlling interest. They left the Boulders, Peter Ridley and Gerda each their own cottages. They left the Boulders about half the farm land, and they left their share in the printing press to Gerda so that she and Peter more or less shared it. This was so that Gerda should have something to live on for her remaining years. The rest of the property they left to Arnold's son Joe and his wife Jeanine.

In earlier days they had assumed, on the rare occasions they thought about it, that when they died the community would have enough life of its own to continue as a community without them. In its most flourishing days they had hoped that it would by then have close links with other communities and would not have to stand on its own. Joe had little sympathy with their ideas and Jeanine less: her one concern was to make a success of her own clothes business, which she appeared to be doing with remarkable shrewdness. Their two daughters, according to Fisher who did not care for Jeanine, were being brought up as 'hard-headed little French bourgeoises'.

The dispositions which Fisher and Arnold made that winter could be taken as a sign that in their old age they had lost heart. That was what Dorothy had meant by saying that Marilyn's refusal to leave had brought about the end of the Abbey.

In the winter Francis did not get back from school until it was nearly dark. The responsibility for exercising the three dogs had devolved in the main upon Dorothy. She took them up onto the Plain in mild damp weather when mist obscured the distance and the Plain was for once almost windless and infinitely silent.

'I thought it was a ruin when I first saw it.'

She was speaking to Guy Thornton, who was walking with her.

'I've only known it as a place where for some reason I always felt happy,' he said. 'It was just them, really, wasn't it? The Whitehead brothers.'

'Yes, it was just them. But they thought it was more, they meant it to be more, at times I think it was more. They meant it to set the pattern for Utopia. It didn't exactly work.'

'Or exactly fail.'

'No, but you see they never found any heirs. That was what they wanted, people to carry it on.'

'It needed their personalities I suppose. It was a more personal thing than they thought. What about Peter Ridley? He's nice, isn't he? But not a strong personality.'

'Not at all. And he's not really interested in the idea of the Abbey going on as a community. He'd prefer it split up, I think. It doesn't appeal to him, the other thing. It never did.'

'The boy's nice.'

'The boy's a marvel, I think. Though everyone keeps telling me how ordinary he is. As a matter of fact I thought I might marry Peter. Then I could help bring up Francis.'

'Ah.'

'I thought it would be rather sensible.'

'Yes. Have you discussed it with him at all?'

'Not exactly. But I've more or less sounded him out. I think it would probably be all right. I'd be very nice to him and he does miss his wife.'

'The only thing is, Francis will be grown up in a few years' time, and there you'll be with Peter for the rest of your life.'

'I expect I'd get quite fond of him.'

'I'm sure you would.'

They walked on in silence. Dorothy, who had not mentioned this idea to anyone else, felt that by speaking of it, even in so apparently casual a manner, she had brought it much nearer to actuality. She was pleased at the thought, and allowed her mind to run ahead, to her mother's pleasure at the news, the quiet wedding in Winterstoke church, being Francis' step-mother.

'Steve's selling his house,' said Guy. 'Mary's death gave him a fright and his family have managed to persuade him to go into a clinic. They've got some plan for what he's to do afterwards—I've forgotten what it is—but anyway he's agreed to put the house up for sale.'

'And Mush?'

'I suppose she's up for sale too. Anyway she doesn't go with the house. It's a very old farmhouse in a marvellous position, small but it could be very nice.'

'Will you buy it?'

'No, I like my own. It's nearly as nice, in fact, though it's a bit of a mess still. I had been thinking it might have interested you. Before you told me about this other plan, of course.'

'But I don't want a house in Wales.'

'No. But I think you'd like it if you saw it.'

'But what would I do there?'

'You could live there with your mother if she wanted to move. Or if she didn't want to move, it's really very easy to get from there to here, only a couple of hours' drive. And we could extend the farm, you see. There's this very nice couple who've come in with me—their house is very close to Steve's— he's made a bit of money doing television programmes. He's a naturalist—they both are—and they want to farm. And with a third partner it really would begin to look good.'

'That's the community business again. I'm not particularly keen on that. I'm much too fond of privacy to want to live in any kind of community. The Abbey's different because it's almost my home. But even there I was only ever quite peripheral to it, you know.'

'Oh you could be as peripheral as you like to this. I'm pretty peripheral myself. Just because there would be several people involved in the same project we wouldn't have to have country dancing and evenings of folk song.'

'I should think not.'

'Or even poetry readings. And it's a lovely place for a boy to spend quite a lot of time in the holidays if a kind friend were to ask him to stay.'

'I still think the other idea's much more sensible.'

'Yes, I expect it is.'

They walked on. Dorothy thought about what he had said. She realised that she had no idea why he should have made such a suggestion, or whether he had really been thinking about it earlier or had mentioned it on the spur of the moment as a reaction to the suggestion, which might have struck him as too prosaic, that she should marry Peter. And if indeed he were opposed to the latter course, was that because he had her best interests at heart or for some more obscure reason? And in suggesting that she should join him in his farming projects, how much was he depending upon his intuition that her father had left her a certain amount of money, and how reliable was he likely to be, in view of her knowledge of how unreliable he used to be, over money matters? Or was there, in spite of his denial and however vaguely, a faint notion at the back of his mind that something of the old spirit of the Abbey ought to be salvaged? These questions co-existed in her mind with the thought that any project undertaken with Guy would be likely to be at the very least entertaining. Feeling safe in thinking about all this because of her virtual certainty that she would not waver from her previous resolution, she smiled at the variety of the considerations.

Seeing her smile he said, 'The other possibility—I mean the less sensible one—does exist, though, doesn't it?'

'Oh yes,' she said, committing herself to nothing by admitting it. 'Certainly the possibility exists.'